PITCAIRN'S

The concluding volume of the great trilogy of sea adventure begun with MUTINY ON THE BOUNTY and continued in MEN AGAINST THE SEA, PITCAIRN'S ISLAND completes, in a full-length novel, the tale of the *Bounty*'s mutineers. In it you will read how Fletcher Christian and the ringleaders of the famous mutiny fled from Tahiti with their native wives and servants and established a tiny kingdom on an island completely cut off from the world.

In 1808 the American ship *Topaz* sent a landing party to find water on this tiny shark's-tooth of rock that rises out of the sea a thousand miles from Tahiti. The landing party scaled the rocky heights and discovered, on a fertile plateau, a small Presbyterian community of middle-aged women, many children and youths, and *one* venerable, white-haired man, Alexander Smith, sole survivor of the nine mutineers who had taken refuge on Pitcairn's Island eighteen years before.

The idyllic landing of the refugees, the planting of the new community, the shortage of wives, the hatred which arose between white men and natives, and the death struggle that brought disaster to the tiny kingdom are the elements in this extraordinary island chronicle.

PITCAIRN'S ISLAND

Books by Charles Nordhoff (1887–1947)

THE FLEDGLING, 1919

THE PEARL LAGOON, 1924

PICARO, 1924

THE DERELICT, 1928

Books by James Norman Hall (1887–1951)

KITCHENER'S MOB, 1916

HIGH ADVENTURE, 1918

ON THE STREAM OF TRAVEL, 1926

MID-PACIFIC, 1928

MOTHER GOOSE LAND, 1930

FLYING WITH CHAUCER, 1930

TALE OF A SHIPWRECK, 1934

THE FRIENDS, 1939

DOCTOR DOGBODY'S LEG, 1940

O, MILLERSVILLE!, 1940

UNDER A THATCHED ROOF, 1942

LOST ISLAND, 1944

A WORD FOR HIS SPONSOR, 1949

THE FAR LANDS, 1950

THE FORGOTTEN ONE
AND OTHER TRUE TALES OF THE SOUTH SEAS, 1952

MY ISLAND HOME, 1952

Books by Charles Nordhoff and James Norman Hall

HISTORY OF THE LAFAYETTE FLYING CORPS, 1920

FAERY LANDS OF THE SOUTH SEAS, 1921

FALCONS OF FRANCE, 1929

MUTINY ON THE BOUNTY, 1932

MEN AGAINST THE SEA, 1934

PITCAIRN'S ISLAND, 1934

THE HURRICANE, 1936

THE DARK RIVER, 1938

NO MORE GAS, 1940

BOTANY BAY, 1941

MEN WITHOUT COUNTRY, 1942

THE HIGH BARBAREE, 1945

PITCAIRN'S ISLAND

By
CHARLES NORDHOFF
and
JAMES NORMAN HALL

BOSTON

LITTLE, BROWN AND COMPANY

To
ELLERY SEDGWICK

AUTHORS' NOTE

THE *Bounty* mutineers settled on Pitcairn Island in the year 1790. In 1808, their refuge was discovered and made known to the world by Captain Mayhew Folger, of the American sealing vessel *Topaz.*

Various and discrepant accounts have been preserved concerning the events of the eighteen years between these dates. The source of them all, direct or indirect, was Alexander Smith (or John Adams, as he later called himself), the only surviving mutineer at the time of Folger's visit. He told the story first to Folger, then to Captains Staines and Pipon, in 1814, then to Captain Beechey, in 1825, and finally, in 1829, to J. A. Moerenhout, author of *Voyages aux Îles du Grand Océan.* Later accounts were recorded by Walter Brodie, who set down, in 1850, a narrative obtained from Arthur, Matthew Quintal's son; and by Rosalind Young, in her *Story of Pitcairn Island,* which gives certain gruesome details retained in the memory of Eliza, daughter of John Mills, who reached the advanced age of ninety-three.

Each of these accounts is remarkable for its differences from the others, if for nothing else, and all contain discrepancies and improbabilities of human behaviour which can scarcely be in accordance with the facts. The authors, therefore, after a careful study of every existing account, have adopted a chronology and selected a sequence of events which seem to them to render more plausible the play of cause and effect. Certain details which would add nothing to the narrative and are too revolting for the printed page have been omitted.

The history of those early years on Pitcairn was tragic, perhaps inevitably so. Fifteen men and twelve women, of two widely different races, were set down on a small island, one of the loneliest in the world. At the end of a decade, although there were many children, only one man and ten women were left; of the sixteen dead, fifteen had come to violent ends. These are the facts upon which all the accounts agree. If at times, in the following narrative, blood flows overfreely, and horror seems to pile on horror, it is not because the authors would have it so: it *was* so, in Pitcairn history.

But the outcome of those early turbulent years was no less extraordinary than the threads of chance which led to the settlement of the island. All who were fortunate enough to visit the Pitcairn colony during the first quarter of the nineteenth century agree that it presented a veritable picture of the Golden Age.

PITCAIRN'S ISLAND

THE PITCAIRN COMMUNITY

The "Bounty" Men						*Their Women*
Fletcher Christian	.	.	.	.	.	Maimiti
Edward Young	.	.	.	.	.	Taurua
Alexander Smith	.	.	.	.	.	Balhadi
John Mills	.	.	.	.	.	Prudence
William McCoy	.	.	.	.	.	Mary
Matthew Quintal	.	.	.	.	.	Sarah
John Williams	.	.	.	.	.	Fasto (later Hutia)
Isaac Martin	.	.	.	.	.	Susannah
William Brown	.	.	.	.		Jenny

The Indian Men							*Their Women*
Minarii	.	.	.	.	.	.	Moetua
Tetahiti	.	.	.	.	.	.	Nanai
Tararu	.	.	.	.	.	.	Hutia
Te Moa							
Nihau							
Hu							

The vowels in the Polynesian language are pronounced approximately as in Italian; generally speaking, syllables are given an equal stress. The native names in this book should be pronounced roughly as follows: —

Hu	.	.	.	.	Hoo
Hutia	.	.	.	.	Hoo-tee-ah
Maimiti	.	.	.	.	My-mee-tee
Minarii	.	.	.	.	Mee-nah-ree
Moetua	.	.	.	.	Mo-ay-too-ah
Nanai	.	.	.	.	Nah-nigh
Nihau	.	.	.	.	Nee-how
Tararu	.	.	.	.	Tah-rah-roo
Taurua	.	.	.	.	Ta-oo-roo-ah
Te Moa	.	.	.	.	Tay-moa
Tetahiti	.	.	.	.	Tay-tah-hee-tee

CHAPTER I

On a day late in December, in the year of 1789, while the earth turned steadily on its course, a moment came when the sunlight illuminated San Roque, easternmost cape of the three Americas. Moving swiftly westward, a thousand miles each hour, the light swept over the jungle of the Amazons, and glittered along the icy summits of the Andes. Presently the level rays brought day to the Peruvian coast and moved on, across a vast stretch of lonely sea.

In all that desert of wrinkled blue there was no sail, nor any land till the light touched the windy downs of Easter Island, where the statues of Rapa Nui's old kings kept watch along the cliffs. An hour passed as the dawn sped westward another thousand miles, to a lone rock rising from the sea, tall, ridged, foam-fringed at its base, with innumerable sea fowl hovering along the cliffs. A boat's crew might have pulled around this fragment of land in two hours or less, but the fronds of scattered coconut palms rose above rich vegetation in the valleys and on the upper slopes, and at one place a slender cascade fell into the sea. Peace, beauty, and utter loneliness were here, in a little world set in the midst of the widest of oceans — the peace of the deep sea, and of nature hidden from the world of men. The brown people who had once lived here were long since gone. Moss covered the rude paving of their temples, and the images of their gods, on the cliffs above, were roosting places for gannet and frigate bird.

The horizon to the east was cloudless, and, as the sun rose, flock after flock of birds swung away toward their fishing grounds offshore. The fledglings, in the dizzy nests where they had been hatched, settled themselves for the long hours of waiting, to doze, and twitch, and sprawl in the sun. The new day was like a million other mornings in the past, but away to the east and still below the horizon a vessel — the only ship in all that vast region — was approaching the land.

His Majesty's armed transport *Bounty* had set sail from Spithead, two years before, bound for Tahiti in the South Sea. Her errand was an unusual one: to procure on that remote island a thousand or more young plants of the breadfruit tree, and to convey them to the British plantations in the West Indies, where it was hoped that they might provide a supply of cheap food for the slaves. When her mission on Tahiti had been accomplished and she was westward bound, among the islands of the Tongan Group, Fletcher Christian, second-in-command of the vessel, raised the men in revolt against Captain William Bligh, whose conduct he considered cruel and insupportable. The mutiny was suddenly planned and carried swiftly into execution, on the morning of April 28, 1789. Captain Bligh was set adrift in the ship's launch, with eighteen loyal men, and the mutineers saw them no more. After a disastrous attempt to settle on the island of Tupuai, the *Bounty* returned to Tahiti, where some of the mutineers, as well as a number of innocent men who had been compelled to remain with the ship, were allowed to establish themselves on shore.

The *Bounty* was a little ship, of about two hundred tons burthen, stoutly rigged and built strongly of English oak. Her sails were patched and weather-beaten, her copper sheathing grown over with trailing weed, and the paint on her sides, once a smart black, was now a scaling, rusty brown. She was on the starboard tack, with the light southwesterly wind abaft the beam. Only nine mutineers were now on board, including Fletcher Christian and Midshipman Edward

Young. With the six Polynesian men and twelve women whom they had persuaded to accompany them, they were searching for a permanent refuge: an island so little known, so remote, that even the long arm of the Admiralty would never reach them.

Goats were tethered to the swivel stocks; hogs grunted disconsolately in their pens; cocks crowed and hens clucked in the crates where several score of fowls were confined. The two cutters, chocked and lashed down by the bulwarks, were filled to the gunwales with yams, some of them of fifty pounds weight. A group of comely girls sat on the main hatch, gossiping in their musical tongue and bursting into soft laughter now and then.

Matthew Quintal, the man at the wheel, was tall and immensely strong, with sloping shoulders and long arms covered with tattooing and reddish hair. He was naked to the waist, and his tanned neck was so thick that a single unbroken line seemed to curve up from his shoulder to the top of his small head. His light blue eyes were set close together, and his great, square, unshaven chin jutted out below a slit of a mouth.

The light southwesterly air was dying; presently the ship lost way and began to roll gently in the calm, her sails hanging slack from the yards. Clouds were gathering on the horizon to the north. Quintal straightened his back and turned to glance at the distant wall of darkness, rising and widening as it advanced upon the ship.

Christian came up the ladderway. He was freshly shaven and wore a plain blue coat. The tropical sun had burned his face to a shade darker than those of the girls on the hatch. The poise of his strong figure and the moulding of his mouth and jaw were the outward signs of a character instant in decision, resolute, and quick to act. His black eyes, deep-set and brilliant, were fixed on the approaching squall.

"Smith!" he called.

A brawny young seaman, who had been standing by the mainmast, hastened aft, touching his turban of bark cloth.

"Clew up the courses, and make ready to catch what water you can."

"Aye, aye, sir!"

Smith went forward, shouting: "All hands, here!   Shorten sail!"

A group of white seamen appeared from the forecastle. The brown men turned quickly from the rail, and several of the girls stood up.

"To your stations!" Smith ordered.   "Fore and main courses — let go sheets and tacks!   Clew lines — up with the clews!"

The lower extremities of the two large sails rose to the quarters of the yards, the native men and half a dozen lusty girls shouting and laughing as they put their backs into the work.   Smith turned to the seaman nearest him.

"McCoy! Take Martin and rig the awning to catch water. Look alive!"

Christian had been pacing the quarter-deck, with an eye on the blackening sky to the north.   "To the braces, Smith!" he now ordered.   "Put her on the larboard tack."

"Braces it is, sir."

Edward Young, the second-in-command, was standing in the ladderway — a man of twenty-four, with a clear, ruddy complexion and a sensitive face, marred by the loss of several front teeth.   He had gone off watch only two hours before and his eyes were still heavy with sleep.

"It has a dirty look," he remarked.

"Only a squall; I'm leaving the topsails on her.   By God! It will ease my mind to fill our casks!   I can't believe that Carteret was mistaken in his latitude, but it is well known that his timekeeper was unreliable.   We're a hundred miles east of his longitude now."

Young smiled faintly.   "I'm beginning to doubt the existence of his Pitcairn's Island," he remarked. "When was it discovered?"

"In 1767, when he was in command of the *Swallow,* under Commodore Byron. He sighted the island at a distance of fifteen leagues, and described it as having the appearance of a great rock, no more than five miles in circumference. It is densely wooded, he says in his account of the voyage, and a stream of fresh water was observed, coursing down the cliffs."

"Did he land?"

"No. There was a great surf running. They got soundings on the west side, in twenty-five fathoms, something less than a mile from the shore. . . . The island must be somewhere hereabout. I mean to search until we find it." He was silent for a moment before he added: "Are the people complaining?"

"Some of them are growing more than restless."

Christian's face darkened. "Let them murmur," he said. "They shall do as I say, nevertheless."

The squall was now close, concealing the horizon from west to north. The air began to move uneasily; next moment the *Bounty* lurched and staggered as the first puff struck her. The topsails filled with sounds like the reports of cannon: the sun was blotted out and the wind screamed through the rigging in gusts that were half air, half stinging, horizontal rain.

"Hard a-starboard!" Christian ordered the helmsman quietly. "Ease her!"

Quintal's great hairy hands turned the spokes rapidly. In the sudden darkness and above the tumult of the wind, the voices of the native women rose faint and thin, like the cries of sea fowl. The ship was righting herself as she began to forge ahead and the force of the wind diminished. In ten minutes the worst was over, and presently the *Bounty* lay becalmed once more, this time in a deluge of vertical rain. It fell in blinding, suffocating streams, and the sound of it,

PITCAIRN'S ISLAND

plashing and murmuring on the sea, was enough to drown a man's voice. Fresh water spouted from the awnings, and as fast as one cask was filled another was trundled into its place. Men and women alike, stripped to their kilts of tapa, were scrubbing one another's backs with bits of porous, volcanic stone.

Within an hour the clouds had dispersed, and the sun, now well above the horizon, was drying the *Bounty*'s decks. A line of rippling dark blue appeared to the southwest. The yards were braced on the other tack, and the ship was soon moving on her course once more.

Young had gone below. Christian was standing at the weather rail, gazing out over the empty sea with an expression sombre and stern beyond his years. In the presence of others, his features were composed, but oftentimes when alone he sank into involuntary reflections on what was past and what might lie ahead.

A tall young girl came up the ladderway, walked lightly to his side, and laid a hand on his shoulder. Maimiti was not past eighteen at this time. Of high lineage on Tahiti, she had left lands, retainers, and relatives to share the dubious fortunes of her English lover. The delicacy of her hands and small bare feet, the lightness of her complexion, and the contours of her high-bred face set her apart from the other women on the ship. As she touched his shoulder, Christian's face softened.

"Shall we find the land to-day?" she asked.

"I hope so; it cannot be far off."

Leaning on the bulwarks at Christian's side, Maimiti made no reply. Her mood at the moment was one of eager anticipation. The blood of seafaring ancestors was in her veins, and this voyage of discovery, into distant seas of which her people preserved only legendary accounts, was an adventure to her taste.

Forward, in the shadow of the windlass, where they could

converse unobserved, two white men sat in earnest talk. McCoy was a Scot who bore an Irish name — a thin, bony man with thick reddish hair and a long neck on which the Adam's apple stood out prominently. His companion was Isaac Martin, an American. Finding himself in London when the *Bounty* was fitting out, Martin had managed to speak with her sailing master in a public house, and had deserted his own ship for the prospect of a cruise in the South Sea. He was a dark brutish man of thirty or thereabouts, with a weak face and black brows that met over his nose.

"We've give him time enough, Will," he said sourly. "There's no such bloody island, if ye ask me! And if there is, it's nowheres hereabout."

"Aye, we're on a wild-goose chase, and no mistake."

"Well, then, it's time we let him know we're sick o' drifting about the like o' this! Mills says so, and Matt Quintal's with us. Brown'll do as we tell him. Ye'll never talk Alex over; Christian's God Almighty to him! I reckon Jack Williams has had enough, like the rest. That'll make six of us to the three o' them. What's the name o' that island we raised, out to the west?"

"Rarotonga, the Indians said."

"Aye. That's the place! And many a fine lass ashore, I'll warrant. If we do find this Pitcairn's Island, it'll be nothing but a bloody rock, with no women but them we've fetched with us. Twelve for fifteen men!"

McCoy nodded. "We've no lasses enough. There'll be trouble afore we're through if we hae no more."

"In Rarotonga we could have the pick o' the place. It's time we made him take us there, whether he likes it or not!"

"Make him! God's truth! Ye're a brave-spoken fellow, Isaac, when there's none to hear ye!"

Martin broke off abruptly as he perceived that Smith had come up behind him unaware. He was a powerfully made man in his early twenties, under the middle stature, and with a face slightly pitted with smallpox. His countenance was, nevertheless, a pleasing one, open and frank, with an aquiline nose, a firm mouth, and blue eyes set widely apart, expressing at the same time good humour and self-confident strength. He stood with brawny tattooed arms folded across his chest, gazing at his two shipmates with an ironic smile. Martin gave him a wry look.

"Aye, Alex," he grumbled, "it 's yourself and Jack Williams has kept us drifting about the empty sea this fortnight past. If ye 'd backed us up, we 'd ha' forced Christian to take us out o' this long since."

Smith turned to McCoy. "Hearken to him, Will! Isaac 's the man to tell Mr. Christian his business. *He* knows where we 'd best go! What d' ye say, shall we make him captain?"

"There 's this must be said, Alex," remarked McCoy apologetically, "we 're three months from Tahiti, and it 's nigh three weeks we 've spent looking for this Pitcairn's Island! How does he know there 's such a place?"

"Damn your eyes! D' ye think Mr. Christian 'd be such a fool as to search for a place that was n't there? I 'll warrant he 'll find it before the week 's out."

"And if he don't, what then?" Martin asked.

"Ask him yourself, Isaac. I reckon he 'll tell 'ee fast enough."

The conversation was interrupted by a hail from aloft, where the lookout stood on the fore-topmast crosstrees.

"Aye, man, what d' ye see?" roared Smith.

"Birds. A cloud of 'em, dead ahead."

Pacing the after deck with Maimiti, Christian halted at the words.

"Run down and fetch my spyglass," he said to the girl.

A moment later he was climbing the ratlines, telescope in hand. One of the native men had preceded him aloft. His trained eyes made out the distant birds at a glance and then swept the horizon north and south. "Terns," he said, as

Christian lowered his glass. "There are albacore yonder. The land will be close."

Christian nodded. "The ship sails slowly," he remarked. "Launch a canoe and try to catch some fish. You and two others."

The native climbed down swiftly to the deck, calling to his companions: "Fetch our rods, and the sinnet for the outrigger!"

The people off watch gathered while the Polynesian men fetched from the forecastle their stout rods of bamboo, equipped with handmade lines and curious lures of mother-of-pearl. The cross-booms were already fast to the outrigger float; they laid them on the gunwales of the long, sharp dugout canoe, and made them fast with a few quick turns of cord. They lowered her over the side, and a moment later she glided swiftly ahead of the ship.

The *Bounty* held her course, moving languidly over the calm sea. The canoe drew ahead fast, but at the end of an hour the ship was again abreast. One man was angling while the two paddlers drove the light vessel back and forth in the midst of a vast shoal of albacore. A cloud of sea birds hovered overhead, the gannets diving with folded wings, while the black noddy-terns fluttered down in companies each time the fish drove the small fry to the surface. Schools of tiny mullet and squid skipped this way and that in frenzied fear, snapped at by the fierce albacore below and the eager beaks of the birds. The angler stood in the stern of the canoe, trailing his lure of pearl shell far aft in the wake. Time after time the watchers on the ship saw the stiff rod bend suddenly as he braced himself to heave a struggling albacore of thirty or forty pounds into the canoe.

While the people of the *Bounty* gazed eagerly on this spectacle, one of the native men began to kindle a fire for cooking the fish. It was plain that there would be enough and to spare for all hands. Presently the canoe came alongside and two or three dozen large albacore were tossed on deck. Alexander Smith had relieved the man at the masthead, and now, while all hands were making ready for a meal, he hailed the deck exultantly: "Land ho-o-o!"

Men and women sprang into the rigging to stare ahead. Christian again went aloft, to settle himself beside Smith and focus his telescope on the horizon before the ship. The southerly swell caused an undulation along the line where sea met sky, but at one point, directly ahead, the moving line was interrupted. A triangle, dark and so infinitely small that none but the keenest of eyes could have made it out, rose above the sea. With an arm about the mast and his glass well braced, Christian gazed ahead for some time.

"By God, Smith!" he remarked. "You 've a pair of eyes!"

The young seaman smiled. "Will it be Pitcairn's Island, sir?" he asked.

"I believe so," replied Christian absently.

The land was still far distant. The wind freshened toward midday, and after their dinner of fish all hands gazed ahead at the rugged island mounting steadily above the horizon. The natives, incapable of concern over the future, regarded the spectacle with pleased interest, but among the white men there was more than one sullen and gloomy face.

While the island changed form as it rose higher and higher before the ship, Christian sat in his cabin on the lower deck. With him were two of the Polynesian men, leaders of the others, whom he had asked to meet him there.

Minarii, a native of Tahiti, was a man of huge frame, with a bold, stern countenance and the assured, easy bearing of a man of rank. His voice was deep and powerful, his body covered with tattooing in curious and intricate designs, and his thick, iron-grey hair confined by a turban of white bark cloth. His companion, Tetahiti, was a young chief from Tupuai, who had left his island because of the friendship he felt for Christian, and because he knew that this same friend-

ship would have cost him his life had he remained behind
when the ship set sail.   The people of Tupuai were bitterly
hostile to the whites; good fortune alone had enabled the
mutineers to leave the island without loss of life.   Tetahiti
was a powerfully made man, though of slighter build than
Minarii; his features were more gently moulded, and his expression less severe.   Both had been told that the *Bounty* was
seeking an island where a settlement might be formed; now
Christian was explaining to them the true state of affairs.
They waited for him to speak.

"Minarii, Tetahiti," he said at last, "there is something I
want you two and the other Maoris to know.   We have been
shipmates; if the land ahead of us proves hospitable, we shall
soon be close neighbours ashore.   For reasons of policy, I have
not felt free to tell you the whole truth till now.   Too much
talk is not good on shipboard.   You understand?"

They nodded, waiting for him to proceed.

"Bligh, who told the people of Tahiti that he was Captain
Cook's son, lied to them.   He was not a chief in his own land,
nor had he the fairness and dignity of a chief.   Raised to a
position of authority, he became haughty, tyrannical, and
cruel.   You must have heard tales in Tahiti of how he punished his men by whipping them till the blood ran down their
backs.   His conduct to all grew unbearable.   As captain, he
drew his authority direct from King George, and used it to
starve his crew in the midst of plenty, and to abuse his officers
while the men under them stood close by."

Minarii smiled grimly.   "I understand," he said.   "You
killed him and took the ship."

"No.   I resolved to seize the ship, put him in irons, and let
our King judge between us.   But the men had suffered too
much at Bligh's hands.   For sixteen moons they had been
treated as no Maori would treat his dog, and their blood was
hot.   To save Bligh's life, I put the large boat overboard and
sent him into her, with certain men who wished to go with

him. We gave them food and water, and I hope for the sake of the others that they may reach England. As for us, our action has made us outlaws to be hunted down, and when our King learns of it he will send a ship to search this sea. You and the others knew that we were looking for an island, remote and little known, on which to settle; now you know the reason. We have found the island. Minarii, shall you be content to remain there? If the place is suitable, we go no further."

The chief nodded slightly. "I shall be content," he said.

"And you, Tetahiti?"

"I can never return to my own land," the other replied. "Where you lead, I shall follow."

Four bells had sounded when Christian came on deck, and the *Bounty* was drawing near the land. At a distance of about a league, it bore from east-by-north to east-by-south, and presented the appearance of a tall ridge, with a small peak at either end. The southern peak rose to a height of not less than a thousand feet and sloped more gently to the sea; its northern neighbour was flanked by dizzy precipices, against which the waves broke and spouted high. Two watercourses, smothered in rich vegetation, made their way down to the sea, and midway between the peaks a slender thread of white marked where a cascade plunged over a cliff. The coast was studded with forbidding rocks, those to the north and south rising high above the spray of breaking seas. Clouds of sea fowl passed this way and that above the ship, regarding the intruders on their solitude with incurious eyes. Everywhere, save on the precipices where the birds reared their young, the island was of the richest green, for vegetation flourished luxuriantly on its volcanic soil, watered by abundant rains. No feature of the place escaped the native passengers, and exclamations of surprise and pleasure came from where they were grouped at the rail.

The leadsman began to call off the depths as the water shoaled. They had thirty fathoms when the northern extremity of the island was still half a mile distant, and Christian ordered the sails trimmed so that the ship might steer southeast along the coast. The wind was cut off as she drew abreast of the northern peak; the *Bounty* moved slowly on, propelled by the cat's-paws that came down off the land. The shore, about four cables distant, rose steeply to a height of two hundred feet or more, and there was scarcely a man on board who did not exclaim at the prospect now revealed. Between the westerly mountains and others perceived to the east lay a broad, gently sloping hollow, broken by small valleys and framed on three sides by ridges and peaks. Here were many hundreds of acres of rich wooded land, sheltered on all sides but the northern one.

The sea was calm. Before an hour had passed, the sails were clewed up and the *Bounty* dropped anchor in twenty fathoms, off a cove where it seemed that a boat might land and the steep green bluffs be scaled.

Standing on the quarter-deck, Christian turned to Young. "I fancy we shall find no better landing place, though we have not seen the southern coast. I shall take three of the Indians and explore it now. Stand offshore if the wind shifts; we can fend for ourselves."

The smaller canoe was soon over the side, with Tetahiti and two other men as paddlers. Christian seated himself in the bow, and the natives sent the little vessel gliding swiftly away from the ship. Passing between an isolated rock and the cape at the eastern extremity of the cove, the canoe skirted the foot of a small wooded valley, where huge old trees rose above an undergrowth of ferns and flowering shrubs. The pandanus, or screw pine, grew everywhere above the water's edge, its thorny leaves drenched in salt spray and its blossoms imparting a delicious fragrance to the air. Presently they rounded the easternmost cape of the island which fell precipitously into the sea, here studded with great rocks about which the surges broke.

As the canoe turned westward, a shallow, half-moon bay revealed itself to Christian's eyes. The southerly swell broke with great violence here, on a narrow beach of sand at the foot of perpendicular cliffs, unscalable without the aid of ropes let down from above. A cloud of sea fowl hovered along the face of the cliffs, so high overhead that their cries were inaudible in the lulls of the breakers.

"An ill place!" said Tetahiti, as the canoe rose high on a swell and the beach was seen, half-veiled by smoking seas. "No man could climb out, though a lizard might."

"Keep on," ordered Christian. "Let us see what is beyond."

The southern coast of the island was iron-bound everywhere, set with jagged rocks offshore and rising in precipices scarcely less stupendous than those flanking the half-moon bay. On the western side there was a small indentation where a boat might have effected a landing in calm weather, but when they had completed the circuit of the island Christian knew that the cove off which the ship lay at anchor offered the only feasible landing place.

The sun was setting as he came on board the *Bounty;* he ordered the anchor up and the sails loosed to stand off to windward for the night.

CHAPTER II

AT dawn the following morning the island bore north, distant about three leagues. Close-hauled, on the larboard tack, the ship slid smoothly through the calm sea, and toward seven o'clock she passed the southeastern extremity of the island. About half a mile to the northwest, after rounding this point, was the shallow indentation where the *Bounty* had been anchored the previous day. Sounding continuously, with lookouts aloft and in the bows, she approached the land and again came to anchor half a mile from the beach, in seventeen fathoms.

Christian and Young stood together on the quarter-deck while the sails were clewed up and furled. With his spyglass Christian examined the foreshore carefully. Presently he turned to his companion.

"I shall be on shore the greater part of the day," he said. "In case of any change in the weather, heave short and be ready to stand off."

"Yes, sir."

"We are fortunate in having this southwesterly breeze; I only pray that it may hold."

"It will, never doubt it," Young replied. "The sky promises that."

"Be good enough to have one of the Indian canoes put into the water."

This order was quickly complied with, and a few minutes later Christian, taking with him Minarii, Alexander Smith, Brown, the gardener, and two of the women, Maimiti and

Moetua, set off for the beach. Minarii sat at the steering paddle.   The bay was strewn with huge boulders against which
the sea broke violently.   To the right and left, walls of rock
fell all but sheer to the cove, but midway along it they discovered a ribbon of shingly beach, the only spot where a
boat might be landed in safety.   Steering with great skill, di-
recting the movements of the paddlers and watching the
following seas, Minarii guided the canoe toward this spot.
They waited for some time just beyond the break of the surf,
then, seizing a favourable opportunity, they came in on
the crest of a long wave, and, immediately the canoe had
grounded, they sprang out and drew it up beyond reach of
the surf.

Directly before them rose a steep, heavily wooded slope,
the broken-down remnant of what must once have been a
wall of rock.   Casuarina trees, some of them of immense size,
grew here and there, the lacy foliage continually wet with
spray.   Coconut palms and the screw pine raised their tufted
tops above the tangle of vegetation, and ferns of many varieties grew in the dense shade.   For a moment the members of
the party gazed about them without speaking; then Maimiti,
with an exclamation of pleasure, made her way quickly to a
bush that grew in a cleft among the rocks.   She returned with
a branch covered with glossy leaves and small white blossoms
of a waxlike texture. She held them against her face, breathing in their delicate fragrance.

"It is the *tefano*," she said, turning to Christian.   Moetua
was equally delighted, and the two women immediately gathered an armful of the blossoms and sat down to make wreaths
for their hair.

"We shall be happy in this place," said Moetua.   "See!
There are pandanus trees and the *aito* and *purau* everywhere.
Almost it might be Tahiti itself."

"But when you look seaward it is not like Tahiti," Maimiti
added wistfully.   "There is no reef.   We shall miss our still

lagoons. And where are the rivers? There can be none, surely, on so small an island that falls so steeply to the sea."

"No," said Christian. "We shall find no rivers like those of Tahiti; but there will be brooks in some of these ravines. What do you think, Minarii?"

The Tahitian nodded. "We shall not lack for water," he said. "It is a good land; the thick bush growing even here among the rocks proves that. Our taro and yams and sweet potatoes will do well in this soil. We may even find them growing here in a wild state; and there are sure to be plantains in the ravines."

Christian threw back his head, gazing at the green wall of vegetation rising so steeply above them. "We shall have work and to spare in clearing the land for our plantations," he said.

"I'll take to it kindly, for one," Smith replied warmly. "It does my heart good to smell the land again. Brown and me is a pair will be pleased to quit ship here, if that's your mind, sir. Eh, Will?"

The gardener nodded. "Shall we stop, sir?" he asked. "Is this Pitcairn's Island, do ye think?"

"I'm convinced of it," Christian replied. "It is far off the position marked for it on Captain Carteret's chart, but it must be the island he sighted. Whether we shall stay remains to be seen."

The women had now finished making their wreaths. They pressed them down over their thick black hair, which hung loosely over their shoulders. Christian gazed at them admiringly, thinking he had never seen a more beautiful sight than those two made in their kirtles of tapa cloth, with flecks of sunlight and shadows of leaves moving as the wind would have it across their faces and their slim brown bodies. Maimiti rose quickly. "Let us go on," she said. "I am eager to see what lies beyond."

The party, led by Minarii, was soon toiling up the ridge, the natives, Smith among them, far in advance. Christian and Brown followed at a more leisurely pace, stopping now and then to examine the trees and plants around them. The ascent was steep indeed, and in places they found it necessary to pull themselves up by the roots of trees and bushes. Two hundred feet of steady climbing brought them to a gentler slope. Here the others were awaiting them.

Before them stretched a densely wooded country that seemed all but level, at first, after the steep climb to reach it. Far below was the sea, its colour of the deepest blue under the cloudless sky. In a southerly direction the land rose gently for a considerable distance, then with a steeper ascent as it approached the ridge which bounded their view on that side. To the northwest another ridge could be seen, culminating at either end in a mountain peak green to the summit, but the one to the north showed sections of bare perpendicular wall on the seaward side. The land before them was like a great plateau rather than a valley, traversed by half a dozen ravines, and lying at an angle, its high side resting upon the main southern ridge of the island, its lower side upon the cliffs that fronted the sea. The ridges to the west and south rose, as nearly as they could judge, five or six hundred feet above the place where they stood.

"That peak to the southwest must be all of a thousand feet above the sea," said Christian.

"Aye, sir," Smith replied. "We'll be high and safe here, that's sure. Ye'd little think, from below, there's such good land."

At a little distance before them the ground fell away to a small watercourse so heavily shaded by great trees that scarcely a ray of sunlight penetrated. Here they found a tiny stream of clear water and gladly halted to refresh themselves. Christian now divided his party.

"Minarii, do you and Moetua bear off to the left and climb the main ridge yonder. Smith, you and Brown follow the rise of the land to the westward; we must know what lies beyond.

I will proceed along this northern rim of the island. Let us meet toward midday, farther along, somewhere below the peak you see before us. The island is so small that we can hardly go astray."

They then separated. Keeping the sea within view on the right, Christian proceeded with Maimiti in a northwesterly direction. Now and then they caught glimpses through the foliage of the mountain that rose before them, heavily wooded to the topmost pinnacle, but descending in sheer walls of rock on the seaward side. Save for the heavy booming of the surf, far below, the silence of the place seemed never to have been broken since the beginning of time; but a few moments later, as they were resting, seated on the trunk of a fallen tree, they heard a faint bird-call, often repeated, that seemed to come from far away. They were surprised to discover the bird itself, a small dust-coloured creature with a whitish breast, quite near at hand, darting among the undergrowth as it uttered its lonely monotonous cry. They saw no other land birds, no living creatures, in fact, save for a small brown rat, and a tiny iridescent lizard scurrying over the dead leaves or peering at them with bright eyes from the limbs of trees. Of a sudden Maimiti halted.

"There have been people here before us," she said.

"Here? Nonsense, Maimiti! What makes you think so?"

"I know it," she replied gravely. "It must have been long ago, but there was once a path where we are now walking."

Christian smiled incredulously. "I can't believe it," he said.

"Because you are not of our blood," the girl replied. "But Moetua would know, or Minarii. I felt this as we were climbing up from the landing place. Now I am sure of it. People of my own race have lived here at some time."

"Why have they gone, then?"

"Who knows?" she replied. "Perhaps it is not a happy place."

"Not happy? An island so rich and beautiful?"

"The people may have brought some old unhappiness with them. It is not often the land that is to blame; it is those who come."

"You can't be right, Maimiti," Christian said, after a moment of silence. "What could have brought them so far from any other land?"

"It is not only you white men with your great ships who make long voyages," she replied. "There is no land in all this great ocean that people of my blood have not found before you. Even here they have come."

"Perhaps. . . . Don't you think we shall be happy here?" he asked presently. "You 're not sorry we came?"

"No . . ." She hesitated. "But it is so far away. . . . Shall we never go back to Tahiti?"

Christian shook his head. "Never. I told you that before we came," he added gently.

"I know. . . ." She glanced up with a wistful smile, her eyes misted with tears. "You must not mind if I think of Tahiti sometimes."

"Mind? Of course I shall not mind! . . . But we shall be happy here, Maimiti. I am sure of it. The land is strange to us now; but soon we shall have our houses built, and when our children come it will be home to us. You will never be sad, then."

The relationship between Christian and this daughter of Polynesian aristocrats was no casual or superficial one. It was an attachment that had its beginning shortly after the *Bounty's* first arrival at Tahiti, and which had deepened day by day during the months the vessel remained there, assembling her cargo of young breadfruit trees. During the long sojourn on the island, Christian had made a serious effort to learn the native speech, with such success that he was now able to converse in it with considerable fluency. The language difficulty overcome, he had discovered that Maimiti was far more than the simple, unreflecting child of nature that he had, at first, supposed; but it was not until the time came when it was necessary for her to choose between him and giving up, forever, family and friends and all that had hitherto made life dear to her that he realized the depth of her loyalty and affection. There had been no hesitation on her part in deciding which it should be.

Presently she turned toward him again, making an attempt to smile. "Let us go on," she said. She took Christian's hand, as though for protection against the strangeness and silence of the place, and they proceeded slowly, peering into the thickets on either side, stopping frequently to explore some small glade where the dense foliage of the trees had prevented the undergrowth from thriving. Of a sudden Maimiti halted and gazed overhead. "Look!" she exclaimed. "*Itatae!*"

Coming from seaward, outlined in exquisite purity against the blue sky, were two snow-white terns. They watched them in silence for a moment.

"These are the birds I love most of all," said Maimiti. "Do you remember them at Tahiti? Always you see two together."

Christian nodded. "How close they come!" he said. "They seem to know you."

"Of course they know me! Have I never told you how I chose the *itatae* for my own birds when I was a little girl? Oh, the beautiful things! You will see: within a week I shall have them eating out of my hand."

She now looked about her with increasing interest and pleasure, pointing out to Christian various plants and trees and flowers familiar to her. Presently a parklike expanse, shaded by trees immemorially old, opened before them. On their right hand stood a gigantic banyan tree whose roots covered a great area of ground. Passing beyond this and descending the slope for a little way, they came to a knoll only a short distance above the place where the land fell steeply to the sea. It was an enchanting spot, fragrant with the odours of growing, blossoming things, and cooled by the breeze that rustled through the foliage of great trees that hemmed it in on the seaward side. Beyond, to the north, they looked across a narrow valley to the mountain which cut off the view in that direction. Christian turned to his companion.

"Maimiti, this is the spot I would choose for our home."

She nodded. "I wished you to say that! It is the very place!"

"All of our houses can be scattered along this northern slope," he added, "and we are certain to find water in one of these small valleys."

Maimiti was now as light-hearted as she had been sad a little time before. They sat down on a grassy knoll and talked eagerly of plans for the future, of the precise spot where their house should stand; of the paths to be made through the forests, of the gardens to be planted, and the like. At length they rose, and, crossing the deeply shaded expanse above, they came to a breadfruit tree which towered above the surrounding forest. It was the first they had seen. Another smaller tree had sprung from one of its roots, and by means of this Maimiti climbed quickly to the lower branches of the great one, which was loaded with fruit. She twisted off a dozen or more of the large green globes, tossing them down to Christian.

"We shall have a feast to-day," she called down. "Did you bring your fire-maker?"

Christian brought forth his flint and steel; they gathered twigs and leaves and dry sticks, and when the fire was burning briskly they placed the fruit in the midst of it to roast. When the rough green rinds had been blackened all round, they left the breadfruit among the hot ashes and again set out to explore further. Upon returning, an hour later,

they found Minarii and Moetua squatting by the fire roasting
sea birds' eggs which they had collected along the tops of the
cliffs beyond the southern ridge.   And Minarii had brought
a cluster of green drinking coconuts and a bunch of fine
plantains he had found in the depths of the valley.

"We shall eat well to-day," he said.   "It is a rich land we
have found.   We have no need to seek further."

"So I think," Christian replied.   "Did you climb the ridge
to the south'ard?"

"Yes.   There is good land beyond, better even than that in
this valley.   I was surprised to find it so; but on this side is
where we should live."

"That is good news, Minarii," Christian replied.   "I, too,
supposed that the sea lay directly below the southern ridge.
How wide are the lands beyond?"

"In some places they extend for all of five or six hundred
paces, sloping gently down from the ridge to the high cliffs
that front the sea."

"Have you found any streams?"

"One.   It is small, but the water is good."

"We shall not lack for sea fowls' eggs," said Moetua.
"All the cliffs on that southern side are filled with crannies
where they nest.   I collected these in little time, but there
is danger in gathering them; it made my eyes swim to look
below."

It was now getting on toward midday, but the lofty trees
spread for them their grateful shade, and the breeze, though
light, was refreshingly cool.   While preparations for the meal
went forward, Christian again strolled to the seaward side
of the plateau, where he had a view of the full half-circle
of the horizon.   Far below, to the east, he could see the
Bounty, looking small indeed under the cliffs, against the wide
background of empty sea.   Her anchors were holding well.
Having satisfied himself that the ship had maintained her position, he seated himself with his back to a tree, hands clasped

around his knees, and remained thus until he heard Maimiti's voice calling him from above. He rose and went slowly back to the others.

Their meal was under way before Smith and Brown appeared. Both were enthusiastic over what they had found. "It's as fine a little place as ever I see, Mr. Christian," Smith said, warmly. "We climbed to the top of that peak, yonder."

"How much land is there beyond the western ridge?"

"Little enough, sir, and what there is, is all rocks and gullies."

Christian turned to Brown. "What have you found in the way of useful plants and trees?"

"I need n't speak of the coconut palms and the pandanus, sir. Ye 've seen for yourself that there 's more than enough for our needs. Then there 's *miro* and sandalwood, and the *tutui* . . ."

"The candlenut? There is a useful find indeed!"

"There's a good few scattered about; and the *miro,* as ye know, is a fine wood for house-building. As for food plants, it 's as well we 've a stock on board. We 've found wild yams and a kind of taro, but little else."

"You could overlook the whole of the island from the peak?"

"Aye, sir," Smith replied.

"What would you say of its extent, judging roughly?"

"It can't be much over two miles long, sir, if that; and about half as wide. What do ye think, Will?"

"Aye, it 's about that," the gardener replied. "There 's a fine grove of breadfruit on the shelf of land ye can see from here, sir, but I 'm as glad we brought some young trees with us. We 've varieties I did n't see, here, in looking about this morning."

"Have you found any evidence that people have been here before us?"

"To say the truth, sir, I never even thought of that," Brown replied.

"Ye don't mean white men, Mr. Christian?" Smith asked.

"No. We are the first, I am sure, who have ever landed here; but Maimiti thinks Indians have once inhabited the place."

"If they did, it must have been long ago. Never a trace did we see of anything of the kind."

Christian now turned to Minarii, addressing him in the native tongue. "Minarii, is it possible, do you think, that Maoris have ever visited this land?"

"*É*," he remarked, quietly. "There has been a settlement here, where we now are. It is the place that would have been chosen for a village, and that great banyan tree has been planted. The breadfruit as well."

Maimiti turned to Christian. "You see?" she said. "Did I not tell you so?"

Christian smiled, incredulously. "I have great respect for your judgment, Minarii," he said, "but in this case I am sure you are wrong. Before us sea birds alone have inhabited this land."

Minarii inserted his hand into the twist of tapa at his waist and drew forth a small stone adze, beautifully made and ground to perfect smoothness. "Then the sea fowl brought that?" he asked.

It was late afternoon when the party returned to the ship. Smith and Brown went forward, where they were surrounded at once by the other seamen, eager for a report of conditions ashore. Christian retired to his cabin and supped there, alone. Toward sunset he joined Young on deck. For some time he paced up and down, then halted by his companion, who stood at the rail gazing at the high slopes before them, all golden now in the light of the sinking sun.

"We will call this 'Bounty Bay,' Mr. Young, unless you have a better suggestion?"

"I was thinking that 'Christian's Landing' would be a suitable name, sir."

Christian shook his head. "I wish my name to be attached to nothing here," he said, "not even to one of those rocks offshore. Tell me," he added, "now that we have found the place, how do you feel about it?"

"That we might have searched the Pacific over without having discovered a more suitable one."

"There is no real anchorage here," Christian went on. "The place where we lie is the best the island affords. You can imagine what this cove will be in a northerly blow. No ship would be safe for ten minutes in such an exposed position. You realize what a decision to remain here means? Our voyages are over until our last day."

"That is of course, sir," Young replied, quietly.

"And you are content that it shall be so?"

"Quite."

Christian turned his head and gave him a swift, scrutinizing glance. When he spoke again it was not as the *Bounty's* captain addressing an inferior officer. There was a friendly gleam in his eyes, and a note of appeal in his voice.

"Old friend," he said, "from this time on, let there be no more ship's formality between us. The success or failure of the little colony we shall plant here depends largely upon us. I shall need your help badly, and it may be that you will need mine. Whatever happens, let us stand by each other."

"That we shall," Young replied warmly, "and there is my hand upon it."

Christian seized and pressed it cordially. "We have rough men to handle," he continued. "It was to be expected that the more unruly ones should have come here with me. . . . Tell me frankly, why did you come? There was no need. You took no part in the mutiny; you might have remained on Tahiti with the other innocent men to wait for a ship to take you home. Once there, a court-martial would certainly have vindicated you."

"Let me assure you of this," Young replied, "I have never regretted my decision."

Christian turned again to look at him. "You mean that," he said, "I can see that you do. And yet, when I think what you have given up to throw in your lot with me . . ."

"Do you remember Van Diemen's Land," Young asked, "where Bligh had me seized up at one of the guns and flogged?"

"I am not likely to forget that," Christian replied, grimly.

"I was a mutineer at heart from that day," Young went on. "I have never told you of this, but, had there been an opportunity, I would have deserted the ship before we sailed from Tahiti — for home, as we then thought. As you know, I slept through the whole of the mutiny. When I was awakened and ordered on deck, the thing was done. Bligh and those who went with him had been cast adrift, and the launch was far astern. Had I known in advance what you meant to do . . ." He paused. "I will not say, Christian, that I would have given you my active support. I think I should have lacked the courage . . ."

"Let us speak no more of that," Christian interrupted. "You are here. You little know what comfort that thought brings me. . . . I was thinking," he added presently, "what a paradise Pitcairn's Island might prove, could we have chosen our companions here. We have an opportunity such as chance rarely grants to men — to form a little world cut off from the rest of mankind, and to rear our children in complete ignorance of any life save what they will find on this small island."

Young nodded. "Whom would you have chosen, could you have had your wish, from the *Bounty's* original company?"

"I prefer not to think of the matter," Christian replied, gloomily. "We must do what we can with those we have. The Indians are fine fellows, with one or, perhaps, two exceptions. I have few regrets concerning them. As for the men of our own blood . . ." He broke off, leaving the sentence unfinished.

"Brown and Alex Smith might have been chosen in any event," Young remarked.

"I should have excepted them. They are good men, both."

"And their respect and admiration for you are very near idolatry," Young added, with a faint smile. "That of Smith in particular; you 've a loyal henchman there."

"I 'm glad you think so. I 've a great liking for Smith. What do you know of him? Where does he come from?"

"I 've learned more about him these past three months than I did during the whole of the voyage out from England. He was a lighterman on the Thames at the time Bligh was signing on the *Bounty* men, but he hated the business and was only waiting for a suitable opportunity to go to sea again. He has told me that his true name is Adams, John Adams, and that he was born and reared in a foundling home near London."

"Adams, you say? That 's curious! Why did he change his name?"

"He volunteered no information on that score, and I did n't feel free to question him."

"No, naturally not. Well, whatever scrape he may have been in, I 'll warrant there was nothing mean or underhanded in his share of it."

"I 'd be willing to take my oath on that," Young replied, heartily. "He 's rough and uncouth, but you can depend upon him. He has n't a tricky or a dishonest bone in his body."

"There is a decision we must make soon," Christian said, after a moment of silence. "It concerns the vessel."

"You mean to destroy her?"

"Yes. Do you agree to the plan?"

"Heartily."

"There is nothing else we can do, the island being what it is; but I want the suggestion to come from the men themselves. They must soon see the necessity, if they have not already."

"Supposing there were a safe anchorage?"

'Not even then should I have wanted to keep her. No, we must burn all bridges behind us. I fancy there is not a lonelier island in the Pacific, and yet the place is known, and there is always the possibility of its being visited. A ship can't be concealed, but once we are rid of the *Bounty* we can so place our settlement that no evidence of it will appear from the sea. The landing is a dangerous one and not likely to be attempted by any vessel that may pass this way; certainly not if the place is thought to be uninhabited. We shall have little to fear, once we are rid of the vessel."

"May I make a suggestion?"

"Please do. Speak your mind to me at all times."

"The men are impatient, I know, to learn of your plans. Would it not be well to tell them, to-night, how the island impresses you?"

Christian reflected for a moment. "Good. I agree," he said. "Call them aft, will you?"

He paced the quarter-deck while Young was carrying out this order. The men, both white and brown, gathered in a half-circle by the mizzenmast to await Christian's pleasure. The women assembled behind them, peering over their shoulders and talking in subdued voices. It was a strange ship's company that gathered on the *Bounty's* deck to listen to the words of their leader.

"Before anything more is done," he began, "I wish to be sure that you are satisfied with this island as a home for us. You were all agreed that we should search for the place, and that, if we found it suitable, we should settle here. You will have learned from your shipmates who went ashore with me what the island has to offer us. Remember, if we go ashore, we go to stay. If any object, now is the time to speak."

There was an immediate response from several of the men.

"I 'm for stopping, Mr. Christian."

"It 's a snug little place. We could n't wish for better, sir."

Mills was the first of the dissenting party to speak.

"It 's not my notion of a snug little place."

"Why not?" Christian asked.

Addressed thus directly by his commanding officer, Mills shifted from one foot to the other, scowling uneasily at his companions.

"I 've spoke my mind, Mr. Christian; it ain't my notion of a place, and I 'll stand by that."

"But that 's no reason, man! You must know why you 're not satisfied. What is it that you object to?"

"He 'd be satisfied with no place, Mr. Christian; that 's the truth of it," Williams, the blacksmith, put in.

"You prefer Tahiti. Is that it?" Christian asked.

"I 'm not sayin' I 'd not go back if the chance was offered."

Christian regarded him in silence for a moment.

"Listen to me, Mills," he proceeded. "And the rest of you as well. I have spoken of this matter before. I will repeat what I 've said, and for the last time. We are not English seamen in good standing, in our own ship, free to do as we choose and to go where we choose. We are fugitives from justice, guilty of the double crime of mutiny and piracy. That we will be searched for, as soon as the fact of the mutiny is known, is beyond question."

"Ye don't think old Bligh 'll ever reach England, sir?" Martin interrupted.

Christian paused and glanced darkly at him.

"I could wish that he might," he said, "for the sake of the

innocent men who went with him. As matters stand, it is not likely that any of them will ever again be heard of. Nevertheless, His Majesty will not suffer one of his vessels to disappear without ordering a wide and careful search to be made, to learn, if possible, her fate. A ship-of-war will be sent out for that purpose, and Tahiti will be her destination. There she will learn of the mutiny from those of our company who remained on that island. The Pacific will then be combed for our hiding place; every island considered at all likely as our refuge will be visited. Should we be discovered and taken, death will be the portion of every man of us. For my own part, I mean never to be taken."

"Nor I, sir!" Smith put in. Others of the mutineers added their voices to his. There was no doubt as to the general feeling concerning the necessity for a safe hiding place.

"Very well," Christian continued. "It is agreed, apparently, by all, or most of you, that you have no wish to swing at a yardarm from one of His Majesty's ships-of-war. What, then, is best to be done? Surely it is to seek out some island unlikely to be visited for as long as we may live. We have found such an island; it lies before us. We are distant, here, more than a thousand miles from Tahiti, and far from the tracks of any vessel likely to cross the Pacific in whatever direction. It is a fertile and pleasant place; that you can see for yourselves. Our Indian friends, whose judgment I trust more than my own in such matters, say that it is capable of supplying all our needs. There are no inhabitants to molest us; our experiences at Tupuai will not be repeated here. To me it seems an ideal spot, and Mr. Young agrees that we might have searched the Pacific over without having found one better suited to men in our position. Now, then, reflect carefully. Shall we make our home here or shall we not? And those who are opposed must give better reasons than that of Mills."

"Is this to be for good, Mr. Christian?" McCoy asked.

"Yes. Let there be no mistake about that. I have already said that if we go ashore we go to stay."

"Then I don't favour it."

"For what reason?"

"The place is too sma'. We'd do better for ourselves on that island we raised after the mutiny, on our way to Tupuai."

"Rarotonga, you mean."

"Aye. It's a likelier place."

Christian reflected for a moment.

"I will say this, McCoy. I seriously considered taking the vessel to Rarotonga, but there are the best of reasons why I decided against the plan. The place is known to those of the *Bounty's* company who remained on Tahiti, and amongst them are men who will be sure to speak of it to the officers of whatever vessel may be sent in search of us. Furthermore, it is but little more than a hundred leagues from Tahiti. We could never feel safe there. . . . Have you anything further to say?"

He waited, glancing from one to another of the mutineers. Mills avoided his gaze and stood with his arms folded, scowling at vacancy. Martin looked at Quintal and kicked him with his bare foot as though urging him to speak, but no further objections were offered.

"Very well, then. Those who favour choosing Pitcairn's Island as our home, show hands."

Five hands were lifted at once. McCoy, after a moment of hesitation, joined the affirmative vote. Martin followed.

"Well, Mills?" said Christian, sharply.

The old seaman raised his hand with an effort. "I can see it's best, Mr. Christian, but I deem it hard to be cut off for life on a rock the like o' this."

"You would find it harder still to be cut off at a rope's end," Christian replied, grimly.

"What's to be done with the ship, sir?" Martin asked.

"Burn her, I say." It was Smith who spoke.

"Aye, burn and scuttle her, Mr. Christian," said Williams. "There's no other way."

There was immediate dissent to this proposal on the part of both Martin and Mills, and for a moment all the seamen were shouting at once. Christian waited, then gave an order for silence.

"Not a man of you but is seaman enough to know that we can't keep the ship here," he said, quietly. "She must be dismantled and burned. What else could we do with her?"

The matter was discussed at some length, but it was plain to all that no other possibility offered itself, and when the question was put to a vote the show of hands was again unanimous.

"I have only one other thing to add," Christian said. "In matters of importance that concern us as a community, every man, from this day on, shall have his vote. All questions shall be decided by the will of the majority. Are you agreed to this?"

All were in favour of the proposal, and Christian, having admonished them to remember this in the future, dismissed them. When they had gone, Young turned to his commander.

"For their own good, Christian, you have been too generous."

"In granting them a voice in our affairs?"

"Yes. I think ultimate decisions should rest with you."

"I well realize the danger," Christian replied; "but there is no alternative. I alone am the cause of their being here. Had I not incited them to mutiny, the *Bounty* would now be nearing England — home." He broke off, staring gloomily at the land. "That thought must be often in their minds."

"They were your eager assistants," Young replied. "Not one of them joined you against his will."

"I know. Nevertheless, I swept them into action on the spur of the moment. They had no time to reflect upon the consequences. No, Edward, I owe the meanest man among them whatever compensation is now possible. Justice demands that I give each of them a voice in our affairs; yes, even though I know it to be to their own hurt. But you and I, together, can, I hope, direct them to wise decisions."

The sun had now set and the silence of the land seemed to flow outward to meet the silence of the sea. High overhead, sea birds in countless numbers floated to and fro with lonely cries in the still air, their wings catching the light streaming up from beyond the horizon. The *Bounty* rocked gently over the long smooth undulations sweeping in from the open sea.

At length Christian turned from the rail. "It is a peaceful spot, Edward," he said. "God grant that we may keep it so!"

CHAPTER III

THE *Bounty's* people were astir with the first light of day, and preparations for disembarking supplies went rapidly forward. The mutineers, with the exception of Brown, the gardener, were to remain on board under Young's charge, sending the supplies ashore. This done, they were to proceed with the dismantling of the vessel. The native men and most of the women were to constitute the beach party, transporting cargo to the landing place by means of the ship's cutters and two canoes brought from Tahiti. As soon as a path had been made, they were to carry the stores on to the site above the cove selected for the temporary settlement. Williams, the blacksmith, had converted some cutlasses into bush knives by filing off the upper part of the long blades. Provided with these, and with axes, mattocks, and spades, Minarii and two of his native companions were soon hard at work on shore, hacking through the dense thickets and digging out a zigzag trail to the level ground above.

Although the *Bounty's* stores had been shared with the mutineers who remained on Tahiti, there was still a generous amount on board: casks of spirits, salt beef and pork, dried peas and beans, an abundant supply of clothing, kegs of powder and nails, iron for blacksmith work, lead for musket balls, and the like. There were also fourteen muskets and a number of pistols. The livestock consisted of half a dozen large crates of fowls, twenty sows, two of which had farrowed during the voyage, five boars, and three goats. The island being small, it was decided to free both the fowls and the animals and let them fend for themselves until the work of house-building was under way.

The weather was all that could be desired; the sky cloudless, the breeze light and from the southwest. So it remained for five days. By the end of that time the precious stock of plants and animals had been carried ashore as well as most of the ship's provisions, and shelters made of the *Bounty's* spare sails had been erected on a spot overlooking the cove.

An incident occurred at this time which aroused intense excitement among the Maori members of the company. It was an immemorial custom, among the Polynesians, when migrating from one land to another, to carry with them several sacred stones from their ancestral *maraes*, or temples, to be used to consecrate their temples in a new land. The Tahitians had brought with them two such stones from the *marae* of Fareroi, on the northern coast of their homeland. Minarii, the chief in whose charge they were, had brought them on deck to be taken ashore, and Martin, seeing them at the gangway and knowing little and caring less of their significance to the natives, had thrown them overboard. The native men were all ashore at the time, but Martin's act had been witnessed by some of the women, who were horrified at what he had done. One of them leaped overboard and swam to the beach, informing the men of what had happened. They returned in all haste, and the white seamen, forward, resolved to brazen out the sacrilegious act performed by Martin. A pitched battle was averted only by the quick-wittedness of Maimiti and the tactfulness of Young, who had the liking and respect of the native men. Fortunately, the stones could still be dimly seen lying on the white sand below the vessel, and it was the work of only a few minutes to dive, secure them with lines, and draw them up. This done, peace was restored and the natives returned to their work ashore.

On the morning of the fifth day the wind shifted to the northeast and blew freshly into the cove. All had agreed that the vessel was to be beached as soon as the wind favoured, and Young now put everything in readiness for the *Bounty's* last brief voyage. Christian, who had spent the night ashore, returned at once. Most of the native women were aboard at this time and the mutineers were at their stations, waiting, talking in low voices among themselves. Christian clambered over the rail, glanced briefly around, and went to the wheel.

"It could not have happened better for us, Ned," he said quietly. "There's been no trouble aboard?"

"Thus far, no," Young replied. "We'll have her ashore before Mills gathers his wits together. I've kept Martin working aft with me until a moment ago."

Christian called to the men forward. "Stand by to back the fore-topmast staysail!"

"Aye, aye, sir!"

"Break out the anchors!"

The men at the windlass heaved lustily, their sunburned backs gleaming with sweat. The stronger of the women assisted at this task, while others ran aloft to loose the fore-topsail. With her staysail backed, the vessel swung slowly around, the topsail filled, and, while the anchors were catted, the ship gathered way and drove quietly on toward the beach.

The spot selected for running the vessel ashore lay under the lofty crag, later called Ship-Landing Point, on the left side of the cove. Yielding the wheel to Young, Christian now went forward to direct the vessel's course. It was a tense moment for all the *Bounty's* company; men and women alike lined the bulwarks, gazing ahead across the narrowing strip of water. Martin, McCoy, and Quintal stood together on the larboard side.

Martin shook his head, gloomily. "Mark my word, mates! Many's the time we'll rue this day afore we're done!"

Quintal thumped him on the back. "Over the side with 'ee, Isaac, and swim back to Tahiti if ye've a mind that way. I'm for stoppin'."

"Aye, ye was easy won over, Matt Quintal," Martin replied. "It's all for the best, is it? We'll see afore the year's out. . . . God a mercy! There's bottom!"

The vessel, still a quarter of a mile from shore, struck lightly. The rock could be seen, but it was at such a depth that it no more than scraped the hull gently; in a few seconds she was clear of it, but her end was near. Riding more and more violently to the onshore swell, she approached two rocks, barely awash and about four fathoms apart. A moment later the ground swell carried her swiftly forward, lifting her bow high, and she struck heavily.

The impact was both downward and forward; with her own movement and the sea to help her, she slid on until her bow was lifted two or three feet. There, by a lucky chance, she stuck, so firmly wedged that the sea could drive her no further. The broken water foamed around her, and now and then a heavier swell, breaking under her counter, showered her decks with spray.

No time was lost in making the vessel as secure as possible. The rocks where she struck lay at about thirty yards from the beach, and were protected in a southeasterly direction by the cliff that formed that side of the cove. Two hawsers were now carried from the bow to the shore and made fast to trees. The vessel remained in the position in which she had struck, canted at a slight angle to starboard. Christian, having satisfied himself that she was as secure as he could make her, set the men to work at once at the task of dismantling.

There was no respite for anyone during the following week. The topgallant masts were sent down as soon as the ship was beached. The topmasts now followed, whereupon the fore, main, and mizzenmasts were cut into suitable lengths for handling and for use as lumber ashore. Most of the men were employed on board, and the women, excellent swimmers, helped to raft the timbers through the surf. So steep was the

slope above the landing beach that it was necessary to dig
out the hillside and bank up the earth so that the timbers and
planking might be stacked beyond reach of the sea until such
time as they could be carried on to the settlement. Realizing
the need for haste, all worked with a will. Fortunately, the
shift in wind had been no forerunner of heavy weather. The
breeze remained light and the sea fairly calm.

At length the vessel had been gutted of cabins, lockers, and
storerooms, the deck planking had been removed, and the
men were ripping off the heavy oaken strakes. Their task
being so nearly finished, a day of rest was granted, and for
the first time since the *Bounty* had left England, no one was
aboard the vessel. An abundance of fish was caught during
the morning, and with these, fresh breadfruit, plantains, and
wild yams the native men had found, the *Bounty's* people
made the most satisfying meal they had enjoyed since leaving Tahiti. Never before had they eaten together, and the
feeling of constraint was apparent to all. Christian and
Young tried to put the men at ease, but the meal passed in
silence for the most part. The women, according to Polynesian custom, waited until the men had finished before partak-
ing of the food. Their hunger satisfied, the men drew apart
and lay in the shade, some sleeping, some talking in desultory
fashion. Early in the afternoon, Martin, Mills, and McCoy,
who had seen little of the island thus far, set out to explore
it with Alexander Smith as their guide.

They toiled slowly on into the depths of the valley, making
their way with difficulty through the dense forests and vine-
entangled thickets. An hour had passed before they reached
the ridge overlooking the western side of the island. The
breeze was refreshingly cool at that height, and they seated
themselves in a shady spot overlooking the wild green lands
below. No sound was heard save their own laboured breathing and the gentle rustling of the wind through the trees
that shaded them. Mills sat with his arms crossed on his

knees, gazing morosely into the depths of the thickets beneath them.

"And this is what Christian's brought us to!" he said. "There's what we can see from here, and no more."

"There's room enough," said McCoy.

"Room? Ye're easy pleased," Martin put in, gloomily. "A bloody rock, I call it!"

"Aye, Tahiti's the place," said Smith, scornfully. "Ye'd have us all go back there to be took by the first ship that comes out from England. Ye're perishin' to be choked off at a rope's end, Isaac. None o' that for me!"

McCoy nodded. "It's no such a grand place for size, this Pitcairn's Island; but Christian's right — it's safe. We'll never be found."

"And here we'll bide to our last day!" said Mills. "Have 'ee thought o' that, shipmates?" He smote his horny palms together. "God's curse on the pack of us! What fools we've been to break up the ship!"

McCoy sat up abruptly. "Hearken to me, John. Ye and Isaac had your chance to stay at Tahiti, but I mind me weel ye was all for comin' awa' with the rest of us to a safer place. And now we've found it, ye'll nae hae it. And what would ye hae done with the ship? Hoist her three hunnerd feet up the rocks? Where could we keep her?"

"It's as Christian says," Smith added. "We're not free to go where we like."

"And whose fault is that?" Mills replied. "If he'd minded his own bloody business . . ."

"Aye," said Martin, "we'd ha' been home by now, or near it. We've a deal to be thankful for to Mr. Fletcher Christian!"

"I'd like well to hear ye tell him that," said Smith. "Ye'll be sayin' next he drove us into the mutiny. There was no man more willin' than yerself, Isaac Martin, to seize the ship."

"That's truth," said McCoy. "Give Christian his due. We was all of a mind, there."

"The man's clean daft. Is there one of ye can't see it?"

"Daft! . . ."

"Sit ye quiet, Alex. So he is, and we've all been daft with him. He's queer by nature, that's my belief, and since we took the ship he thinks the world ain't big enough to hide him and us in. He's a master talker when he's a mind to talk; that I'll say, else he'd never coaxed a man of us off Tahiti. What if a ship did come there? Couldn't we ha' hid in the mountains? There's places a plenty where God himself couldn't ha' found us. Or if we was afeared o' that, we'd only to take a big Indian canoe and sail to Eimeo or one of them islands to leeward, a good hundred miles from Tahiti. We could ha' played hide-and-seek with a dozen King's ships till they got sick o' the chase and went off home. Then we'd live easy for ten or fifteen years till the next one came. Ain't that common sense? Speak up, Will!"

"Aye," McCoy replied, uneasily. "Like enough we might hae done it."

"Might! Damn my eyes! I've spoke o' ships because Christian's got ships on the brain, but I'll warrant them as stayed on Tahiti is as safe as we'll be here. Bligh'll never get home; Christian himself knows that. Does anyone but him think they'll send a ship out from England, halfway round the world, to see what's become of a little transport? Bloody likely! They'll mark her down as lost by the act o' God, and that'll be the end of it."

"Damn your blood!" said Mills, scowling at him. "Why couldn't ye ha' spoke like this to Christian? What's the good o' talkin' of it now?"

"Didn't I say we was daft, the lot of us? He's made us believe what he told us, and now we're done for."

"I'd like to see ye with a rope around your neck, waitin'

to be hoisted aloft," said Smith. "It's not Christian ye'd be callin' daft then."

"Leave all that, lads," said McCoy. "We're to stop here now, and there's an end of it."

"And Christian's always to have his way, is he, whatever's done?" Martin asked.

"No, damn my eyes if he is!" Mills exclaimed. "We're jack-tars no longer, mates! Don't forget it! We're to have a say here as good as his own. He's promised it."

"There's no need to fash yersel'," said McCoy. "Was n't it Christian that made the offer? And he'll bide by it; that we know."

"Who's sayin' he won't? But I want us to mind what he's said. . . . There's the rum, now. He's promised us our grog as long as it lasts, and we've had none these two days."

"Curse ye, John, for mindin' us o' that," said McCoy with a wry smile.

"And how would we have it with us workin' aboard and the spirits ashore?" said Smith.

"Aye, we're no settled yet," said McCoy. "Gie him time. We'll have our tot afore the evening."

"There's Alex would a had us go without altogether," said Mills.

"Ye've a thick skull, John. I was for makin' it last a good few years, and, as Christian says, ye can't do that and claim seamen's rations now. How much do we have? Ye know as well as myself, there's but the two puncheons — that's 164 gallons — and the three five-gallon cags."

"There's but eight of us to drink it, Alex. Brown's an abstainer."

"Aye," said McCoy, fervently. "God be thanked for Brown and the Indians! If they was fond o' grog . . ."

"Like it or not, none the Indians would have. We could see to that," said Mills.

"What I say is this," Smith continued. "Christian's give ye yer choice with the rum, and ye was all for yer half-pint a day. With eight of us to drink it, there's three and a half gallons a week. Afore the year's out, where'll we be for grog? And mind ye, there's no Deptford stores here. When it's gone, it's gone, and we'll do without for the rest of our lives."

"We'll no think of that, Alex," said McCoy. "We'll just relish what we've got and thank God it's no less. Mon, but I'd like my dram this minute!"

"What would ye say, messmates, to better than a dram for the four of us within the half-hour?" Martin asked. McCoy turned his head quickly.

"What's that ye say, Issac? How should we hae it, and the rum stored in Christian's tent?"

"Oh, it's rum ye must have, is it?" Martin replied, with a sly smile. "Ye would n't look at brandy, I doubt? And fine old brandy, too?"

"What are ye drivin' at, man?" asked Mills, harshly. "Can't ye speak out plain? There's no brandy in the stores."

"Have I said it was in the stores?"

"Hark 'ee, Isaac! If ye've been thievin' from the medicine chest . . ."

"I've done no such thing. I'll tell 'ee, mates," he proceeded, leaning forward with his elbows on his knees. "A few days back while we was rippin' out the cabin partitions, I found eight quarts o' brandy under what was Old Sawbones's bed-place. I reckon he'd hid it away for his own use on a thirsty day. Anyway, there it was, packed careful in a canvas bag. Sez I when I found it: 'This'll belong to nobody but Isaac Martin. It's not ship's stores, it's finder's luck'; so I hid it away, and last night, after we'd come ashore, I found a safe place to stow it. But I'd no mind to be greedy with it. Ye'll allow that, for I've told what there was no need to tell if I'd meant to keep it."

"That's plain truth, God bless ye!" said McCoy.   "If I'd
found it I doubt but I'd been hog enough to drink the lot
of it on the sly."

"Ye would so, Will," said Mills.   "Ye've your good points,
but sharin' anything in the way o' grog's not one of 'em.
Where's this brandy now, Isaac?"

"We passed where I hid it on the way up here.   It's a good
piece from the camp.   We can drink it somewheres thereabout and the rest none the wiser.   What do ye say, Alex?
Must I give it up as ship's stores?"

"That's no called for," McCoy put in earnestly.

"To my thinkin' it belongs to the ship and calls to be shared
by all."

"There's three of us to say no to that," said Mills.

Smith rose.   "Do as ye please," he said, "but it's a bad
beginning ye're makin'.   I'll go along and leave ye to it."

For a moment his companions looked after him in silence;
then Martin called out, "If we're asked for, Alex, tell 'em
we're walkin' the island and will sleep the night out."

Smith turned and waved his hand.   A moment later he was
lost to view in the forest, below.

McCoy shook his head admiringly.   "He's a grand stubborn character.   And there's no man fonder of his grog;
there's the wonder of it."

"If we'd the brandy with us we could ha' won him over
for all his fine notions o' what's fair to the rest," Martin replied.   He rose to his feet.   "Well, shipmates?"

"Aye, lead on, Isaac," said McCoy, eagerly.   "We'll no be
laggin' far behind."

Once below the ridge they lost the breeze and sweat
streamed from their half-naked bodies as they pushed their
way through the tall fern into the thickets below.   At length
they reached the depths of the valley, where the air was
moist and cool.   Martin led the way, walking in the bed of
a small stream.   Presently he stopped and looked about him

uncertainly. McCoy gave him an anxious glance. "Ye 've not lost yer bearin's, Isaac?"

"It 's somewhere hereabout," said Martin.

"Curdle ye, Isaac! Don't ye *know*? What like was the place where ye hid it?" said Mills.

"It was by just such a tree as this. There was a hollow by the roots and I put it there. . . . No, it 'll be a step farther down."

They proceeded slowly, Martin glancing from side to side. Presently his face lighted up. "Yon 's the one," he said, hurrying forward. A wide-spreading hibiscus tree that looked as ancient as the land itself overhung the stream, its branches filled with lemon-coloured blossoms. Martin knelt by the trunk and reached to his arm's length among the gnarled and twisted roots. The eyes of his companions glistened as he drew out, one by one, eight bottles. He sat back on his heels, glancing triumphantly up at them.

"God love ye, Isaac!" McCoy exclaimed, in an awed voice.

"And it 's old Sawbones's best brandy, mind ye that! Whereabout shall we go to drink it? We can't sit comfort-able-like here."

McCoy and Martin carrying three bottles each, and Mills with two, they proceeded down the valley for another fifty yards until they came to a little glade carpeted with fern and mottled with sunlight and shadow. At this point the tiny stream made a bend, and in the hollow against the further bank was a pool of still water, two or three yards wide. Here they seated themselves with grunts of satisfaction. Martin, taking a heavy clasp knife which he carried at his belt, knocked off the neck of a bottle with one clean even blow.

"Ye needna be so impatient as all that," said McCoy. "Bottles 'll be handy things here."

Martin took a long pull before replying. "If there was one, there was fifteen dozen empties took ashore from the spirit room," he said. His companions were not far behind him in enjoying their first drink. McCoy, replacing the cork in his bottle, leaned it carefully against the tree beside him.

"Isaac, I 'll never forget ye for this," he said. "It fair sickens me to think I could nae hae done the same if I 'd found the brandy."

"Enjoy yourself hearty, Will. There 's a plenty for all. I 'll be blind drunk afore I 've finished my second."

"We needna be hasty, there 's a blessing," McCoy replied. "We 've the night before us, and there 's water close by to sober us up now and again."

"I 'm as willin' Matt Quintal 's not with us," said Mills.

"Aye," Martin replied. "There 's a good shipmate when he 's sober, but God spare me when he 's had a drop too much!"

McCoy nodded. "There 's no demon worse. D 'ye mind his wreckin' the taproom at the Three Blackamoors the week we left Portsmouth? When it took five of us to get him down?"

"Mind! I 've the marks on me yet," said Mills. . . . "God strike me! What 's this?"

A tiny bouquet of flowers and fern, attached to a slender ribbon of bark, came dropping down through the foliage of the tree that shaded them. After dangling in front of Mills's nose for a moment, it was jerked up again. A ripple of laughter was heard, and, looking up quickly, they could see an elfin-like face peeping down from among the green leaves.

"It 's your own wench, Mills! Damme if it 's not!" said Martin.

Mills's rugged face softened. "So it is! Come out o' that, ye little witch! What are ye doin' here?" he called.

The girl descended to the lowest branch and perched there, out of reach, smiling down at them.

"She 's a rare lass for roamin' the woods and mountains," said Mills, fondly. He held out his arms. "Jump, ye little mischty!" The girl leaped and he caught her in his arms. She was dressed in a kirtle of bark cloth reaching to her knees, and her thick hair fell in a rippling mass over her bare breasts and shoulders. Mills held her off at arm's length, gazing at her admiringly.

"Ye 've spoke truth, John," said Martin. "She 's a proper little witch."

"Aye," said McCoy, "ye 've the prettiest lass o' the lot. I wonder she 'd come awa' from her kinfolks and a' with a dour old stick the like o' yersel'."

Mills stroked her hair with his great rough hand. "Ye 'll allow this, Will: ye 've not seen her weepin' her eyes out for Tahiti like some o' the women."

"Nay, I 'll grant that," said McCoy. "She seems a contented little body."

"I 'd be pleased to say the like o' my wench, Susannah," said Martin, glumly. "She was willin' enough to come away with us, but now we 're here she 's fair sick to be home again. I 've had no good of her since we beached the ship."

"It 's in reason she should be, Isaac," McCoy replied. "My woman 's the same way. Gie 'em time; they 'll joggle down well enough. Mills's lass here 'll learn 'em how to make the best of things, won't 'ee, Prudence?"

The girl's lips parted in a ready smile, revealing her small white teeth.

"How d 'ye manage with her, John?" Martin asked. "Ye 're the dumbest o' the lot for speakin' the Indian lingo. Is it sign talk ye use with her?"

"Never ye mind about that," Mills replied gruffly. "I 've no call to learn their heathen jabber. Prudence takes to English like a pigeon picks up corn."

"They 're a queer lot, all these Indian wenches," said Martin. "Why is it, now, they make such a fuss about cookin' the food?"

"It 's against their heathen notions," said McCoy.

"Young's told me how it is. Indian men won't have their womenfolks fussin' with their vittles. It's contrary to their religion, he says."

"I'll learn mine better'n that, once we're settled," Martin replied. "She'll bloody well do as I tell her."

"There's no need to beat it out of 'em, Isaac. They'll come around well enough, once they see how it is with us."

"Aye, give 'em time; they'll follow our ways," said Mills. "It ain't in reason to expect it at the start."

"And the men with 'em, if they know what's good for 'em."

"Ye'll go easy there, Isaac," said McCoy, "else we'll have a fine row on our hands one o' these days. Minarii and Tetahiti's a pair not to be trifled with."

"Say ye so, Will?" Mills replied grimly. "They'd best learn at the start who's masters here."

"Christian and Young treat 'em like they was as good as ourselves," said Martin.

"There's three we can do as we like with, but mind the others!" said McCoy. "Will the lass ken what we say, John?"

"She's not that far along. Will 'ee sing 'em a song, Prudence?" he asked.

The girl laughed and shook her head.

"It strikes me she knows more 'n she lets on," said Martin.

"I've been learnin' her one," Mills went on proudly. "Come, now, lass: —

> We hove our ship to when the wind was sou'west, boys,
> We hove our ship to for to strike soundings clear . . .

Ye mind how it goes? Come, there's a good wench."

After considerable urging the girl began singing in a soft, clear voice and a quaint pronunciation of the English words that delighted her listeners. She broke off and they cheered her heartily.

"Damme if that ain't pretty, now!" said Martin. "Give her a sup o' brandy; there 's nothin' better to wet the whistle."

"Will 'ee have a taste, sweetheart?" said Mills, holding out the bottle. Prudence shook her head. "She don't fancy the stuff," he said, "and I ain't coaxed her to relish it."

"And it 's right ye are," said McCoy, "seeing there 's none too much for oursel's. If the women learned to booze we 'd be bad off in no time for grog."

"What! A wench not drink with her fancy-man?" said Martin. "That 's not jack-tar's fashion. Give her a sup."

"Aye, ye 're right, Isaac," Mills replied. "It ain't natural on a spree. Come, lass, just a drop now."

He put his arm around her shoulders and drew her to him, holding the bottle to her lips. Thus urged, the girl closed her eyes and took two or three resolute swallows. Choking and sputtering, she pushed the bottle away and ran to the near-by stream. The three men laughed heartily.

"Fancy a dolly-mop at home makin' such a face as that over good brandy," said Martin.

"My old woman could drink her half-pint in two ticks, not winkin' an eye," said McCoy. . . . "There 's an odd thing," he added; "I doubt I 've thought of her twice this past twelve-month."

"Was ye wedded to her, Will?"

"Aye; all shipshape and Bristol-fashion. I liked her well enough, too."

"If I know women she 'll not be sleepin' cold the nights ye 've been away," said Mills.

"Aye, she 'll hae dragged her anchor long afore this," McCoy replied. He raised his bottle. "Well, here 's luck to her wherever she is."

Prudence returned from the brook and seated herself again at Mills's side.

"How is it with ye, lass?"

She laughed and pointed to the bottle. "More," she replied.

"There's a proper wench, John," said Martin, admiringly. "Damn my eyes if she won't make a proper boozer, give her time. All she needs is a sup o' water to follow."

Mills smiled down at her, proudly. "She'll do," he said. "Here, darlin', drink hearty."

"Ahoy there, mates!"

The three men looked up quickly to find Quintal standing behind them.

"God love us! It's Matt himself," said McCoy, uneasily.

"Come aboard, Matt; we was wishin' for ye," Martin put in with an attempt at heartiness.

Quintal squatted on the balls of his feet, his brawny hands on his knees, and grinned at them accusingly. "I've no doubt o' that," he said, "and searchin' for me far and wide. And where did ye find all this?"

"Never ye mind, Matt. We ain't thieved it. It's private stock. Would ye relish a taste?"

Quintal looked longingly at the bottle. "Ye know damned well I would. No, don't coax me, Isaac. I'd best leave it alone."

"That's common sense, lad," said McCoy. "Ye ken yer weakness. We'll no think the less o' ye for standin' out against it."

Quintal seated himself in the fern with his back to a tree. "Go on with your boozin'," he said. "What's this, Mills? The little wench ain't shakin' a cloth?"

"She's havin' her first spree," said Mills. "She's took to brandy that easy. Where's Jack Williams?"

"I've not seen him these two hours."

"Not alone, I'll warrant, wherever he is. And it won't be Fasto that's with him."

"Aye, he's fair crazed over that — what's her name? Hutia?"

"Why can't he keep to his own?" Mills growled.

"Where's the need, John?" Martin asked. "I mean to take a walk with Hutia myself, once we're well ashore."

"Aye, ye'll be a proper trouble-maker, Isaac, give ye half a chance," said Quintal. "The Indians can play that game as well as ourselves. I'm with John. Let each man keep to his own."

"Aye, aye, to that!" said McCoy. "Once there was trouble started 'twixt us and the Indians, there'd be the deil and a' to pay. We've the chance, here, to live quiet and peaceful as ever we like. I say, let's take it and hold fast by it."

"And how long will the Indians hold by it, think ye?" asked Martin. "There's three without women. They'll be snoopin' after ours, fast enough."

"They'll leave mine alone," said Mills. "That I'll promise!"

"Say ye so, John? She'll be amongst the first. I'll warrant some of 'em's had her before now."

Mills sprang to his knees and grasped Martin by the shoulders, shaking him violently.

"What d' ye say, ye devil? Speak up if ye've seen it! Tell me who, or I'll throttle ye!"

"Let me go, John! God's name! I've seen naught! I was only havin' a game wi' ye."

Mills glared at him suspiciously, but upon being reassured by the others he released him and resumed his place.

"Christian's gone aboard again," said Quintal; "him and Young."

"There, lads, we can take it easy," said McCoy in a relieved tone. "Prudence, will 'ee gie us a dance?" He turned to Mills: "Ye don't mind, John? It's a joy to see her."

"Mind? Why should he?" said Martin. "Come, Prudence, up wi' ye, wench!"

The fumes of the brandy had already mounted to the girl's brain and she was ready enough to comply. The men well understood the quick rhythmic slapping of hands upon knees that marked the time for the dances of the Maori women. Prudence danced proudly, with the natural abandon of the young savage, pausing before each of the men in turn, her slim bare arms akimbo, gazing tauntingly into their eyes as she went through the provocative movements of the dance. Of a sudden she broke off with a peal of laughter and ran lightly away into the thickets.

The men cheered heartily. "Come back, ye little imp," Martin called. "We 'll have more o' the same."

"That we will," said McCoy. "John, I 'll trade wenches wi' ye any day ye like."

"Keep your own," said Mills, with a harsh laugh. "I 'm well pleased with what I got. Come back, ye little mischty! We 've not done wi' ye yet."

The girl feigned reluctance for a moment; then, running back to Mills, she seized the bottle from his hands and drank again. Quintal watched her with fascinated eyes, nervously clasping and unclasping his great hairy hands. By this time the others were in the mellow state of the first stages of a spree.

"Matt Quintal," Martin exclaimed, "I'll see no man sit by with a dry gullet! Ye 're perished for a drink, that's plain. Come, have a sup."

He passed over a bottle which Quintal accepted, hesitatingly. "Thank 'ee, Isaac. I 'll have a taste and no more."

It was a generous taste that called for another, and yet another, freely offered by Mills and Martin. A few moments later Quintal reached across and seized the partly emptied bottle at McCoy's side.

"Damn yer blood, Matt!" McCoy exclaimed anxiously. "Easy, now! There 's but eight quarts for the lot of us!" Quintal held him off with one hand while he drank. "D' ye grudge me a drink, ye hog?" he said, grinning. "Ye 've another full bottle beside ye. I'll take that if ye'll like it better."

"It's nae that I grudge ye a drink, Matt, but there's enough in the bottle wi' what ye've had to make ye mad drunk, and well ye know it."

"Aye," said Mills. "Drink slow, Matt, and water it aplenty. It'll last the night if ye do that."

The afternoon was now well advanced, and the shadow of the high ridge to the westward had already crept beyond the little glade where the men were seated. They drank and lolled at their ease. There was no need, now, to urge Prudence to dance. Martin, Quintal, and McCoy slapped their knees and cheered her on as her gestures and postures became more and more wanton and provocative, but the expression on Mills's face was increasingly sullen. "That'll do, lass," he said, at length. "Off wi' ye, now. Go back wi' the others." But the girl laughed without heeding and, as though with intent to enrage him, passed him by without a glance, dancing before Quintal, gazing into his eyes with a sultry smile. Of a sudden Quintal seized her by the arm, pulling her into his lap, and gave her a bearlike hug, kissing her heartily. Mills sprang to his feet.

"Let her go, damn yer blood! Let her go, I say!"

The girl, sobered a little, began to struggle, but Quintal held her fast. He turned to Mills with a drunken leer. "She knows who's the best man, don't 'ee, wench?" Pinioning her arms, he kissed her again and again, but as Mills strode forward he got to his feet just in time to receive a blow in the face, delivered with all the strength of Mills's arm. The blood streamed from his nose and he staggered back, but recovered himself. An insane light came into his closely set blue eyes. He tossed the girl aside and clenched his enormous fists.

"Ye bloody bastard! I'll kill ye for that!" He gave Mills a blow on the chest that knocked him full length, but

he was up again in a second.   Rushing forward, he grappled
Quintal around the waist.   McCoy and Martin were both
on their feet by this time, looking anxiously on.

"Stop it, lads!" McCoy called, earnestly.   "Matt, think
what ye do."

Glaring wildly, Quintal turned his head and gave McCoy
a backhanded blow that sent him sprawling.   Mills, for all
his strength, was no match for the younger man, and in a
moment Quintal had him down, with a knee on his chest and
his fingers around his throat.   Mills's eyes started from their
sockets and his tongue protruded from his mouth.

"He 'll kill him, Isaac!   Pitch in!" McCoy shouted.   The
two men sprang upon his back, tugging and straining with
all their strength.   Quintal loosed one hand to seize Martin's arm, giving it such a wrench that he cried out with pain.
Meanwhile, with the pressure partly relieved from his throat,
Mills gave a desperate heave and, with the others to help him,
managed to topple Quintal over.   The three men were upon
him at once, but their combined strength was not sufficient
to keep him down.   Breaking Mills's hold on his legs, he
struggled to his feet, the others clinging to him desperately.

"God be praised!   Here 's Alex," McCoy panted.   "Quick,
mon!"

Before Quintal had time to turn his head, Smith's burly
form was upon him with the others.   He fought like a demon,
but the odds were now too great.   Presently he lay helpless,
breathing heavily, his face streaming with sweat and blood,
his eyes glaring insanely.   "Will ye give in, ye devil?" said
Smith.   With a bellow of rage Quintal resumed the struggle,
and his four antagonists needed all their strength to hold him.
"Is there a bit o' line amongst ye?" Smith panted.   "We
must seize him up."   "Prudence!" Mills called; "fetch some
purau bark!"   The girl, who had been looking on in terror,
understood at once.   Running to a near-by hibiscus tree, she

bit through the tough smooth bark of some of the low-hanging branches and quickly ripped it down, in long strips. After a prolonged struggle the four men had Quintal bound, hand and foot. Presently his eyes closed and he fell into a heavy sleep.

"Ye was needed, Alex," said McCoy, in a weak voice. "He 'd ha' done for the three of us. . . . Ye 'll not let on ye 've seen us?" he added. "We can booze quiet now Matt 's asleep."

"I was sent to look for ye," said Smith. "Mr. Christian 's decided to burn the ship. Ye can stay, or go to see her fired, as ye 've a mind; but he wanted ye to know."

"Burn and be damned to her, now," said Mills.

"He reckons what timbers there is left in her will be more trouble to get out than they 're worth."

"I could ha' told him that three days back," said Martin. "See here, Alex! We 've a good sup o' brandy left. Ye 'd best stay and have a share."

He held out a bottle while Smith stood irresolutely, looking from one to another of them. Of a sudden he threw himself on the ground beside them. "So I will, Isaac!" he said, as he seized the bottle. "We 're hogs for drinkin' it on the sly, but away with that!"

Dusk deepened into night. Quintal was snoring loudly, and Martin had now reached the maudlin stage of drunkenness. His thoughts had turned to home and he blubbered half to himself, half to his companions, cursing Christian the while, and the hard fate that had left them stranded forever on a rock in mid-ocean. Smith and McCoy, having vainly tried to quiet him, at length gave it up and paid no further heed to him. Mills drank in silence; when deep in his cups he became more and more dour and taciturn. Prudence was asleep with her head in his lap.

"Ye 're a marvel for drink, Will," Smith was saying. "I 'll

warrant ye 've had twice as much as Martin, but there 's none would know it from yer speech."

"I 've a good Scotch stomach and a hard Scotch head," McCoy replied. "Ye maun go north o' the Tweed, mon, if ye 'd see an honest toper. We 've bairns amangst us could drink the best o' ye English under a table, and gang hame to their mithers after, and think nae mair aboot it."

Smith grinned. "Aye, ye 're grand folk," he replied, "and well ye know it."

"We 've reason to, Alex; but aboot this burnin' o' the ship . . ."

"Christian's aboard of her now, with Young and Jack Williams. They 'll be firin' her directly."

Presently a faint reddish glow streamed up from behind the seaward cliffs to the east. It increased from moment to moment until the light penetrated even to where they sat.

Smith got to his feet. "We 'd best go and see the last of her, Will. I 'll cut Matt loose; there 's no harm in him now. What 'll ye do, John, stay or come with us?"

Mills rose and took the native girl up in his arms. "Go past the tents," he said. "I 'll leave her there."

Martin was asleep. McCoy took up the bottle beside him and held it up to the light. "Isaac 's a good sup left here, lads."

"Leave that," Mills growled. "It 's his, ain't it?"

"Will it be safe, think ye? Matt might wake . . ."

"So he might; there 's a good Scotch reason," said Smith. "Pass it round, Will."

Having emptied the bottle, they left it at Martin's side, and the men proceeded slowly down the valley, Smith leading the way. They found no one at the tents; Mills left Prudence there and they went along the roughly cleared path to the lookout point above the cove. The ship was burning fiercely, flames and sparks streaming high in the air. In the red glare they could plainly see the other members of the

Bounty's company seated among the rocks on the narrow foreshore.

"She makes a grand light," McCoy, glumly.

"Aye," said Smith.

They were silent after that.

CHAPTER IV

A DEEPER awareness of their isolation from the world of men now came home to them. The empty sea walled them round, and the ship, burned to the water's edge but still lying where she had been driven upon the rocks, was an eloquent reminder to all of the irrevocable nature of their fate. For some of the white men, in particular, the sight of the blackened hulk, washed over by the sea, had a gloomy fascination not to be resisted. In the evening when work for the day was over, they would come singly, or in groups of two or three, to the lookout point above the cove and sit there until the last light had left the sky, gazing down upon all that remained of the vessel as though they could not yet realize that she was lost to them forever.

Among the mutineers, Brown was the one most deeply affected by the nature of their fate. He was a small, shy man of thirty years, with a gentle voice and manner, in marked contrast with those of some of the companions chance had forced upon him. Curiously enough, his presence among them was due to that very mildness of his character, and to his inability to make immediate decisions for himself. He had sailed in the *Bounty* in the capacity of assistant to Mr. Nelson, the botanist of the expedition, and had spent five happy months on Tahiti, studying the flora of the island and helping to collect and care for the young breadfruit trees. Upon the morning of the mutiny he had been shaken from sleep by Martin, who had thrust a musket into his hands and ordered him on deck. There he had stood with his weapon, during the uproar which followed, completely bewildered by what was taking place, appalled by what he had unwittingly done, and incapable of action until the opportunity for it had been lost. Christian had been as surprised as grieved when, later, he discovered Brown among the members of his own party; and Brown of necessity transferred to Christian his dependence for the protection and guidance furnished up to that time by his chief, Mr. Nelson. He knew nothing of ships or the sea, but he had a profound knowledge of soils and plants, and his love of nature compensated him, in a measure, for hours of desperate homesickness.

He suffered no more from this cause than did many of the women of the *Bounty's* company. They longed for the comfort of numbers; for the gaiety of their communal life at Tahiti; for the quiet lagoons lighted at night by the torches of innumerable fishermen; for the clear, full-running mountain streams where they had bathed at evening. They longed for the friends and kindred whom they knew, now, they could never hope to see again; for the voices of children; for the authority of long-established custom. Conditions on this high, rock-bound island were as strange to them as the ways of their white lords, and the silence, the loneliness, awed and frightened them.

Two only of their numbers escaped, in part, the general feeling of forsakenness: the young girl whom Mills had taken, and whom he had named, with unconscious irony, "Prudence," and Jenny, the consort of Brown. Jenny was a slender, active, courageous woman of Brown's own age, with all the force of character he lacked. She was the oldest of the women, but she was sprung from the lower class of Tahitian society, and, although of resolute character, she maintained toward Maimiti and Taurua, the consorts of Christian and Young, the deference and respect which their birth and blood demanded that she should. To Moetua, as

well, the same deference was extended; for she too was of
the kindred of chiefs, and her husband, Minarii, had been
a man of authority on Tahiti.

Gradually the sense of loneliness, common at first to all,
gave place to more cheerful feelings, and men and women
alike set themselves with a will to the work before them.
A tract of land near the temporary settlement was chosen
for the first garden, and for the period of a week most of
the company was engaged in clearing and planting. This
task finished, the garden was left to the charge of Brown
and some of the women, while the others, under Christian's
direction, were occupied with house-building.

The site chosen for the permanent settlement lay beneath
the mountain which they called the "Goat-House Peak," a
little to the eastward of a narrow valley whose western wall
was formed by the mountain itself. By chance or by mutual
agreement they had divided themselves into households, and
all save Brown and Jenny, who wished to live inland, had
chosen sites for their dwellings on the seaward slope of the
main valley. Christian's house was building below the gigantic banyan tree where he and Maimiti had halted to rest on the
day of their first visit ashore. The second household was that
of Young and Alexander Smith, with their women, Taurua
and Balhadi. Mills, Martin, and Williams formed the third,
with Prudence, Susannah, and Fasto; Quintal and McCoy,
Sarah and Mary, the fourth; and the native men, the fifth.
This latter was the largest household, of nine members:
Minarii, Tetahiti, Tararu, Te Moa, Nihau, and Hu, with the
wives of the three first, Moetua, Nanai, and Hutia. Te Moa,
Nihau, and Hu were the three men unprovided with women.

The white men, with the exception of Brown, were erect-
ing wooden houses made partly of the *Bounty* materials and
partly of island timber, and the roofs were to be of pandanus-
leaf thatch. The dwelling for the native men was situated

in a glade a quarter of a mile inland from Bounty Bay. Quintal and McCoy lived nearest to the landing place. The houses of the other mutineers were closer together, but hidden from one another in the forest that covered the valley.

The native men, helped by the stronger of the women, were allotted the task of carrying the supplies to the settlement while the white men were building a storehouse to contain them. Christian, with the general consent, grudgingly given by some of the men, took the stores into his own charge and kept the keys to the storehouse always on his person.

He ruled the little colony with strict justice, granting white men and brown complete liberty in their personal affairs so long as these did not interfere with the peace of the community. An equitable division of labour was made. Williams was employed at his forge, with the native, Hu, as his helper. Mills and Alexander Smith had charge of the saw pit; Quintal and McCoy looked after the livestock, building enclosures near the settlement for some of the fowls and the brood sows. Brown was relieved of all other employment so that he might give his full time to the gardens. The native men were employed as occasion demanded, and during the early months of the settlement it was they who did the fishing for the community and searched for the wild products of the island — plantains, taro, candlenuts for lighting purposes, and the like. Christian and Young had general supervision of all, and set an example to the others by working, with brief intervals for meals, from dawn until dark. As for the women, they had work and to spare while the houses were building, in collecting and preparing the pandanus leaves for thatch. These had first to be soaked in the sea, then smoothed and straightened and the long, thorn-covered edges removed; after which they were folded over light four-foot segments of split canes and pinned thus with slender midribs from the leaves of palm fronds. Some two thousand canes of these *raufara*, as they were called, each of them holding about forty pandanus leaves, were needed for the thatching of each dwelling.

From the beginning Christian had set aside Sunday as a day of rest, in so far as the community work was concerned. Neither he nor Young was of religious turn of mind, and the other white men even less so; therefore no service was held and each man employed himself as he pleased.

Late on a Sunday afternoon toward the end of February, Christian and Young had climbed to the ridge connecting the two highest peaks of the island. It was an impressive lookout point. To the eastward the main valley lay outspread. On the opposite side the land fell away in gullies and precipitous ravines to the sea. Several small cascades, the result of recent heavy rains, streamed down the rocky walls, arching away from them, in places, as they descended. Small as the island was, its aspect from that height had in it a quality of savage grandeur, and the rich green thickets on the gentler slopes, lying in the full splendour of the westering sun, added to the solemnity of narrow valleys already filling with shadow, and the bare precipices that hung above them. The view would have been an arresting one in the most frequented of oceans; it was infinitely more so here where the vast floor of the sea, which seemed to slope down from the horizons, lay empty to the gaze month after month, year after year.

The ridge at that point was barely two paces in width. Christian seated himself on a rock that overhung the mountain wall; Young reclined in the short fern at his side. Sea birds were beginning to come home from their day's fishing far offshore. As the shadows lengthened over the land their numbers increased to countless thousands, circling high in air, their wings flashing in the golden light. The two friends remained silent for a long time, listening to the faint cries of the birds and the thunder of the surf against the bastions of the cliffs nearly a thousand feet below.

The spirit of solitude had altered both of these men, each in a different way. Brief as their time on the island had been, the sense of their complete and final removal from all they had known in the past had been borne in upon them swiftly, and had now become an accepted and natural condition of their lives.

Christian was the first to speak.

"A lonely sound, Ned," he said at length. "Sometimes I love it, but there are moments when the thought that I can never escape it drives me half frantic."

Young turned his head. "The booming of the surf?" he asked. "I have already ceased to hear it in a conscious way. To me it has become a part of the silence of the place."

"I wish I could say as much. You have a faculty I greatly admire. What shall I call it? Stillness of mind, perhaps. It is not one that you could have acquired. You must have had it always."

Young smiled. "Does it seem to you such a valuable faculty?"

"Beyond price!" Christian replied, earnestly. "I have often observed you without your being aware of the fact. I believe that you could sit for hours on end without forethought or afterthought, enjoying the beauty of each moment as it passes. What would I not give for your quiet spirit!"

"Allow me to say that I have envied you, many 's the time, for having the reverse of my quietness, as you call it. There is all too little of the man of action in my character. When I think what a sorry aide I am to you here . . ."

"A sorry aide? In God's name, Ned, what could I do without you? Supposing . . ." He broke off with a faint smile. "Enough," he added. "The time has not come when we need begin paying one another compliments."

They had no further speech for some time; then Christian

said: "There is something I have long wanted to ask you.
. . . Give me your candid opinion. . . . Is it possible, do
you think, that Bligh and the men with him could have
survived?"

Young gave him a quick glance. "I have waited for that
question," he replied. "The matter is not one I have felt free
to open, but I have been tempted to do so more than once."

"Well, what do you think?"

"That there is reason to believe them safe."

Christian turned to him abruptly. "Say it again, Ned!
Make me believe it! But, no. . . . What do I ask? Could
nineteen men, unarmed, scantly provided with food and
water, crowded to the point of foundering in a ship's boat,
make a voyage of full twelve hundred leagues? Through
archipelagoes peopled with savages who would ask nothing
better than to murder them at sight? Impossible!"

"It is by no means impossible if you consider the character
of the man who leads them," Young replied, quietly. "Remember his uncanny skill as a navigator; his knowledge of
the sea; his prodigious memory. I doubt whether there is
a known island in the Pacific, or the fragment of one, whose
precise latitude and longitude he does not carry in his head.
Above all, Christian, remember his stubborn, unconquerable
will. And whatever we may think of him otherwise, you
will agree that, with a vessel under him, though it be nothing
but a ship's launch, Bligh is beyond praise."

"He is; I grant it freely. By God! You may be right!
Bligh could do it, and only he! What a feat it would be!"

"And it may very well be an accomplished fact by now,"
Young replied. "Nelson, Fryer, Cole, Ledward, and all the
others may be approaching England at this moment, while we
speak of them. They would have had easterly winds all the
way. They may have reached the Dutch East Indies in time
to sail home with the October fleet."

"Yes, that would be possible. . . . If only I could be sure of it!"

"Try to think of them so," Young replied earnestly. "Let me urge you, Christian, to brood no longer over this matter. You are not justified in thinking of them as dead. Believe me, you are not. I say this not merely to comfort you; it is my reasoned opinion. The launch, as you know, was an excellent sea boat. Think of the voyages we ourselves have made in her, in all kinds of weather."

"I know . . ."

"And bear this in mind," Young continued: "there are, as you say, vast archipelagoes known to exist between the Friendly Islands and the Dutch settlements. It is by no means unlikely that Bligh has been able to land safely, at various places, for refreshment. How many small uninhabited islands have we ourselves seen where a ship's boat might lie undiscovered by the savages for days, or weeks?"

He broke off, glancing anxiously at his companion. Christian turned and laid a hand on his shoulder. "Say no more, Ned. It has done me good to speak of this matter, for once. Whatever may have happened, there is nothing to be done about it now."

"And if Bligh reaches home?"

Christian smiled, bitterly. "There will be a hue and cry after us such as England has not known for a century," he replied. "And the old blackguard will be lifted, for a time at least, to a level with Drake. And what will be said of me . . ."

He put the palms of his hands to his eyes in an abrupt gesture and kept them there for a moment; then he turned again to his companion. "It is odd to think, Ned, that you and I may live to be old men here, with our children and grandchildren growing up around us. We will never be found; I am all but certain of that."

Young smiled. "What a strange colony we shall be, fifty years hence! What a mixture of bloods!"

"And of tongues as well. Already we seem to be developing a curious speech of our own, part English, part Indian."

"English, I think, will survive in the end," Young replied. "Men like Mills and Quintal and Williams have a fair smattering of the Indian tongue, but they will never be able to speak it well. It interests me to observe how readily some of the women are acquiring English. Brown's woman and that girl of Mills's are surprisingly fluent in it, even now."

"Do you find that you sometimes think in Tahitian?"

"Frequently. We are being made over here quite as much as the Indians themselves."

"I feel encouraged, Ned, sincerely hopeful," Christian remarked presently. "Concerning the future, I mean. The men are adjusting themselves surprisingly well to the life here. Don't you think so?"

"Yes, they are."

"If we can keep them busy and their minds occupied . . . For the present there is little danger. That will come later when we've finished house-building and are well settled."

"Let's not anticipate."

"No, we shan't borrow our troubles, but we must be prepared for them. Have you noticed any friction between ourselves and the Indian men?"

"I can't say that I have. Nothing serious, at least, since the day when Martin chucked their sacred temple stones into the sea."

Christian's face darkened. "There is a man we must watch," he said. "He is a bully and a coward at heart. The meanest Maori in the South Sea is a better man. Martin will presume as far as he dares on his white skin."

"It is not only Martin who will do so," Young replied; "Mills and Quintal have much the same attitude toward the Indians."

"But there is a decency about those two lacking in Martin. I have explained him to Minarii and Tetahiti. I have told them that Martin belongs to a class, in white society, that is lower than the serfs among the Maoris. They understand. In fact, they had guessed as much before I told them."

Young nodded. "There is little danger of Martin's presuming with either of them," he said. "It is Hu and Tararu and Te Moa whom he will abuse, if he can."

"And his woman, Susannah," Christian added. "I pity that girl from my heart. I 've no doubt that Martin makes her life miserable in countless small ways." He rose. "We 'd best be going down, Ned. It will be dark soon."

They descended the steep ridge to the gentler slopes below and made their way slowly along, skirting the dense thickets of pandanus and rata trees, and crossing glades where the interlaced foliage, high overhead, cut off the faint light of the afterglow, making the darkness below almost that of night.

In one of these glades two others of the *Bounty's* company had passed that afternoon. Scarcely had Christian and Young crossed it when a screen of thick fern at one side parted and Hutia glanced after the retreating figures. She was a handsome girl of nineteen with small, firm breasts and a thick braid of hair reaching to her knees. She stood poised as lightly as a fawn ready for flight, all but invisible in the shadows; then she turned to someone behind her.

"Christian!" she exclaimed in an awed voice. "Christian and Etuati!"

Williams was lying outstretched in the thick fern, his hands clasped behind his head.

"What if it was?" he replied gruffly. "Come, sit ye down here!" Seizing her by the wrist, he drew her to him fiercely. The girl pushed herself back, laughing softly. "*Aué*, Jack! You want too much, too fast. I go now. Tararu say, 'Where Hutia?' And Fasto say, 'Where my man?'"

Williams took her by the shoulders and held her at arm's length.

"Never ye mind about Fasto, ye little minx! Which d' ye like best, Tararu or me?"

The girl gave him a sly smile. "You," she said. Of a sudden she slipped from his grasp, sprang to her feet, and vanished in the darkness.

CHAPTER V

A PATH, growing daily more distinct, and winding picturesquely among the trees, led from Bounty Bay along the
crest of the seaward slopes as far as Christian's house, at the
western extremity of the settlement.   Close to his dwelling a
second path branched inland, along the side of a small valley.
This led to Brown's Well, a tiny, spring-fed stream which
descended in a succession of pools and slender cascades,
shaded by great trees and the fern-covered walls of the ravine
itself.   The uppermost pool had been transformed into a rock
cistern where the drinking water for the settlement was
obtained.   A larger one, below, was used for bathing, and
during the late afternoon was reserved for the exclusive use
of the women.   This was the happiest hour of the day for
them.

At the bathing pool they cast off, with the strange English
names bestowed on some of them by the mutineers, the constraint they felt in the presence of the white men.   But in
the midst of their laughter and cheerful talk there were
moments when a chance remark concerning Tahiti, or a passing reference to something connected with their old life there,
would cast a shadow on their spirits, passing slowly, like the
shadow of a cloud on the high slopes of the valley.

One afternoon several of the women were sunning them-
selves on a great rock which stood at the brink of the pool.
Their bath was over and they were combing and drying their
hair, while some of them twined wreaths of sweet fern.
Moetua had spoken of the *tiare maohi,* the white, fragrant
Tahitian gardenia.

"Say no more!" said Sarah, her eyes glistening with tears, "We know that we shall never see it again. Alas! I can close my eyes and smell its perfume now!"

"Tell me, Moetua, if all were to do again, would you leave Tahiti?" Susannah asked.

"Yes. Minarii is here, and am I not his wife? This is a good land, and it pleases him, so I must be content. Already I think less often than I did of Tahiti. Do not you others find it so?"

"Not I!" exclaimed Susannah bitterly. "I would never come again. Never! Never!"

"But we were told before we left that the ship was not to return," remarked Balhadi quietly. "Christian made that known to all of us."

"Who could have believed it!" said Sarah. "And Mills and the others said it was not so, that we would surely return. . . . Do you remember, you others, the morning after we set sail from Matavai, when the wind changed and the ship was steered to the westward?"

"And we passed so close to the reefs of Eimeo?" Susannah put in. "Do I not remember! Martin stood with me by the rail with his arm tight around me. He knew that I would leap into the sea and swim ashore if given the chance!"

"Quintal held me by the two hands," remarked Sarah, "else I should have done the same."

"Why did the ship leave so quickly?" asked Nanai. "No one in Matavai knew that she was to sail that night."

"They feared that you would change your minds at the last moment," Moetua replied.

"That is how I was caught," said Prudence. "Mills went to my uncle with his pockets filled with nails, the largest kind; he must have had a score of them. My uncle's eyes were hungry when he saw them. 'You shall spend the night on the ship, with the white man,' he told me. So he was

given the nails and I went with Mills.   When I awoke at daybreak, the vessel was at sea."

"And you like him now, your man?" Hutia asked.

Prudence shrugged her shoulders.   "He is well enough."

"He is mad about you," said Susannah.   "That is plain."

"He is like a father and a lover in one," the girl replied.
"I can do as I please with him."

"For my part," observed Moetua, "I would not change
places with any of you.   I prefer a husband of our own race.
These white men are strange; their thoughts are not like ours.
We can never understand them."

"I do not find it so," said Balhadi.   "My man, Smith, might
almost be one of us.   I can read his thoughts even when his
speech is not clear to me.   White men are not very different
from those of our blood."

"It may be so," replied Moetua, doubtfully.   "Maimiti
says the same.   She seems happy with Christian."

"It is different with Maimiti," Sarah put in.   "Christian
speaks our tongue like one of us.   The others learn more
slowly."

Prudence had finished combing her hair and was beginning
to plait it rapidly, with skillful fingers.   She glanced up at
Sarah: "How is it with you and Quintal?" she asked.

"How is he as a lover, you mean?"

"Yes, tell us that."

Sarah glanced at the others with a wry smile.   "Night
comes.   He sits with his chin on his great fists.   What are
his thoughts?   I do not know.   Perhaps he has none.   He
is silent.   How could it be otherwise when he is only beginning to learn our speech?   He pays no heed to me.   I wait,
well knowing what is to come.   At last it comes.   When
he is wearied, he rolls on his back and snores.   *Atira!*   There
is no more to tell."

Prudence threw back her head and burst into laughter.

The others joined in and the glade rang with their mirth. Sarah's smile broadened; a moment later she was laughing no less heartily than the rest.

"What a strange man!" said Nanai, wiping the tears of mirth from her eyes.

Sarah nodded. "He thinks only of himself. I shall never understand his ways."

"What of the men who have no wives?" asked Moetua, presently.

"How miserable they are!" said Hutia, laughing. "Who is to comfort them?"

"Not I," remarked Balhadi. "I am content with my man, and will do nothing to cause him pain or anger."

"Why should he be angry for so small a thing?" asked Nanai.

"You know nothing of white men," said Prudence. "They consider it a shameful thing for the woman of one man to give herself to another. Nevertheless, I will be one of those to be kind to the wifeless men."

"And I!" exclaimed Susannah. "I fear Martin as much as I hate him, but I shall find courage to deceive him. To make a fool of him will comfort me."

"This matter can be kept among ourselves," said Moetua. "The white men need never know of it."

"Christian would be angry, if he knew," remarked Balhadi gravely. "It is as Prudence says: the white men regard their women as theirs alone. Trouble may easily come of this."

"Then Christian should have brought more women, one for each," replied Moetua. "He must know that no man can be deprived of a woman his life long."

"He knows," said Susannah. "He is a chief, like Minarii, and would protect me from Martin, if it came to that."

"And it *will* come to that," observed Prudence.

"Yes," put in Nanai. "You should go to Christian now, and tell him how you are treated. Martin is a *nohu*."

"He is worse than one," Susannah replied gloomily. "I believe that he has not once bathed since we came here. I can endure his cruelty better than his filth. . . . Alas! Let us speak of something more pleasant. I try to forget Martin when here with you."

All of these women were young, with the buoyant and happy dispositions common to their race. A moment later they were chatting and laughing as gaily as though they had not a care in the world.

The garden was now in a flourishing condition. The red, volcanic soil was exceedingly rich, and the beds of yams, sweet potatoes, and the dry-land taro called *tarua* gave promise of an early and abundant harvest. The pale green shoots of the sugar cane were beginning to appear, and young suckers of the banana plants were opening in the sun. An abundance of huge old breadfruit trees had been found in the main valley, but Brown had, nevertheless, carefully planted the young trees brought from Tahiti, clearing a few yards of land here and there in favoured spots.

Like the plants, the livestock loosed on the island throve well. The hogs grew fat on the long tubers of the wild yam, and the place was a paradise for the fowls, with neither bird nor beast of prey to molest them, and food everywhere to be had for the picking. The small, brown, native rat had, as yet, no taste for eggs and did not harm the young chicks. The fowls began to increase rapidly, and the cheerful crowing of the cocks was a welcome sound, relieving the profound silence which had been so oppressive to all during the first days on shore. On the further side of the high peak, to the west of the settlement, a house and a pen had been made for the goats, where they were fed and watered each day.

From the main ridge of the island to the cliffs on the southern side the land sloped gently, forming an outer valley as rich as that on the northern side. This was named the Auté

Valley, from the circumstance that the first gardens of
the *auté*, or cloth-plant, fetched from Tahiti, were set out
here.

Brown had chosen to live on this southern slope, remote
from the others; his little thatched house stood in a sunny
glade, embowered in the foliage of lofty trees and near a
trickle of water sufficient for one family's needs. He and
Jenny had cleared a path through the thickets behind and
above them, over the ridge and down to join another path
which led through the heart of the Main Valley to the settlement.

Jenny, Brown's girl, though small and comely, had all the
resolution the gardener lacked. They had lived together on
shore during the long months at Tahiti while Captain Bligh
was collecting his cargo of breadfruit plants, and the thought
of returning to her had been Brown's only solace after his involuntary part in the mutiny. Her feeling toward him was
that of a mother and protectress, for Jenny was one of those
women of exceptionally strong character who choose as
husbands small, mild men, in need of sterner mates.

Like Brown, Minarii had a deep love of nature and of
growing things. Nearly every evening he came to exchange
a word with Jenny and to mark the growth of the young
plants; little by little, a curious friendship sprang up between
the stern war-chief and the lonely English gardener. A
man of few words in his own tongue, Brown was incapable of
learning any other, but Jenny spoke English by this time,
and with her as interpreter he spent many an evening listening to Minarii's tales of old wars on Tahiti, and of how he had
received this wound or that.

One evening late in February, Minarii and Moetua, his
wife, came to Brown's house. The native set down a heavy
basket, and his grim face relaxed as he took Brown's hand.

"We have been down over the southern cliffs," Moetua told
Jenny. "The birds are beginning to lay. Here are eggs

of the *kaveka* and *oio,* which nest on the face of the cliff. You will find them good. Minarii made a rope fast at the top and we clambered down. Fasto came as well."

"Thank them," Brown put in to Jenny. "I shudder to think of any man, to say nothing of women, taking such risks!"

Minarii turned to his wife. "Go and eat, you two, while I prepare our part."

While Brown went to fetch some wild yams, Minarii kindled a fire, heated several stones, and dropped them into a calabash of water, which began to boil at once. Eggs were then dropped in till the calabash was full, and the yams hastily scraped and roasted on the coals. The two men made a hearty meal.

The moon came up presently and the visitors rose to leave. When they were gone, Jenny spread a mat before the doorstep and sat down to enjoy the beauty of the night. She patted the mat beside her, and Brown stretched himself out, with his head on her knee. The night was windless; the moonlight softened the outlines of the house and lay in pools of silver on the little clearing. Smoothing Brown's hair absently, Jenny recounted the gossip of the settlement.

"I have been talking with Moetua," she said. "There is trouble coming, and Williams is the cause of it. Do you know why he sent Fasto with them to-day?"

"I suppose he wanted some eggs," said the gardener, drowsily.

"Perhaps he likes eggs, but he likes Hutia better. He meets her in the bush each time he can get Fasto out of the way. And Tararu is a jealous husband, though a fool. Jealous! Yet he would like to be the lover of Mills's girl!"

"Of Prudence? That child?"

"Child!" Jenny gazed down at him, shaking her head wonderingly. "You yourself are only a child," she said. "You understand only your plants and trees."

John Williams was working alone on his house, while Martin and Mills carried plank up the path from Bounty Bay. The framing of the two-story dwelling was now finished, and he was sawing and notching the rafters. The three women had worked well in preparing the thatch, and he planned to finish the roof before beginning on the walls and floor. It was close to midday and the sun was hot in the clearing. Williams was naked to the waist; the sweat streamed down his chest, matted with coarse black hair. He put down his saw and dashed the perspiration from his eyes.

"Fasto!" he called.

A short, dark, sturdy woman stepped out of the shed where their cooking was done. She was of humble birth, silent, docile, and industrious. Williams appreciated to the full her devotion to him, as well as her skill in every native pursuit.

"Dinner ready?" he asked. "Fetch me a pail of water."

She dashed the water over his head and shoulders, while he scrubbed the grime from his face. Then she brought his dinner of roasted breadfruit, yams, and a dozen tern's eggs, spreading broad green leaves for a tablecloth beside him on the ground. He squeezed her arm as she leaned over him. "Hard as nails! Sit ye down and eat with me, old girl." She shook her head. "Oh, damn yer heathen notions! . . . Any more eggs? No?"

Ignorant of the native tongue, which he held in contempt, Williams had forced the woman to learn a few words of English. Tears came into her eyes, for she felt that she had been remiss in her wifely duty. Struggling to express herself, she murmured: "Fetch more eggs, supper."

"Aye. There's a good lass. Work hard and eat hearty, that's Jack Williams."

As he rose, he gave her a kiss and a pat on the back. Fasto smiled with pleasure as she went off to the cookhouse with the remnants of the meal.

Toward mid-afternoon, when he paused once more in his

work, the blacksmith had put in nine hours on the house and accomplished much. Fasto had gone off an hour earlier with her basket, toward the cliffs on the south side of the island. Martin and Mills were still engaged in their task at the cove. Scrubbing himself clean, Williams hitched up the kilt of tapa around his waist and glanced quickly up and down the path. Sounds of hammering came from McCoy's house, but no one was in sight. Crossing the path, he disappeared into the bush.

A quarter of a mile south of the settlement, in the midst of the forest, an old pandanus tree spread its thorny leaves to the sun. Its trunk, supported on a pyramid of aerial roots, rose twenty feet without a branch. Hutia was descending cautiously, taking advantage of every roughness of the bark. The ground was littered with the leaves she had plucked for thatch. She sprang down lightly from the tree and began to gather up her leaves in bundles, working mechanically as she glanced this way and that and stopped to listen from time to time. Then suddenly she dropped her work and stepped into the shadow of a thick-spreading *purau* tree close by. Williams appeared, walking softly through the bush. He glanced aloft at the pandanus tree and down at the bundles of leaves on the ground. Peering about uncertainly, he heard the sound of soft laughter. Next moment the girl was in his arms.

"Where is Fasto?" she asked apprehensively.

"Never ye mind about her; she'll not be back till dark."

While Williams lingered in the bush and his mates toiled up from the cove with the day's last load of plank, Prudence sat by the house, stripping thorns from a heap of pandanus leaves beside her. She was scarcely sixteen, small of stature and delicately formed, with a pale golden skin and copper-red hair.

She turned her head as she heard the sound of a footfall on the path. From the corner of her eye she saw Tararu approaching. Bending over her work as if unaware of his coming, she gave a little start when he spoke.

"Where are the others?" he asked.

"*Aué!* You frightened me!"

Tararu smiled, seating himself at her side. "Afraid of me? I must teach you better, some day when Mills is not so close. . . . Where are the other women?"

"Collecting leaves."

"You have worked well. How many reeds of *raufara* are needed?"

"Two thousand," said Prudence. "One thousand eight hundred and seventy are done."

With eyes cast down upon her work, she began to sing softly, a rhythmic and monotonous little melody sung in Tahiti by the strolling players of the *arioi* society. Tararu bent his head to listen, chuckling silently at the broad double-meaning in the first verse. She began the second verse, and as he listened to the soft, childish voice, the man regarded her intently.

> "A bird climbs the cliffs,
>   Robbing the nests of other birds,
>   Seeking eggs to feed her mate.
>   But the mate is not building a nest. No!
>   He is hiding in a thicket with another bird."

Prudence sang on as if unaware that she had a listener, making no further mention of the doings of birds. After a futile attempt to catch her eye, Tararu rose and walked away inland. Like many philanderers, he felt the most tender solicitude concerning the virtue of his own wife.

Hutia was making her way down to the settlement with a heavy bundle of leaves on her back. She moved silently through the bush, with eyes alert, and was aware of her husband a full ten seconds before he knew of her approach. Her gait and posture changed at once, and she looked up wearily as the man drew near.

"Lay down your burden," Tararu ordered.

She dropped the bundle of leaves with a sigh. "It was good of you to come."

Tararu gazed down at her without a smile, but she returned his glance so calmly that his suspicions were shaken. He was deeply enamoured of her, though always ready for a flirtation with another girl, and he desired nothing more than to be convinced of her innocence. No guilty wife, he thought, could meet her husband so fearlessly. He smiled at last, took up the bundle, and led the way to the settlement.

One evening in early March, Hutia was making her way to the bathing pool. She had had words with Tararu, who had knocked her down while two of the native men stood by, and, wishing to nurse her anger alone, she had delayed her bath until an hour when the other women should have returned to the settlement.

She had no eyes for the beauty of the glade. Hedged in by thick bush, which made a green twilight at this hour, the place was deserted save for Prudence at her bath. The girl stood knee-deep in the water, her back to Hutia and enveloped to the waist in her unbound hair. She had a small calabash in her hand and was bending to take up water when Hutia spoke.

"Make haste!" she said harshly. "I wish to bathe by myself."

Prudence glanced coolly at the other girl. "Who are you? Queen of this island? Am I your servant, me, with a white man for husband?"

"Husband!" exclaimed Hutia angrily. "Aye, and you'd like to have mine as well. Take care! I have seen you looking at him with soft eyes!"

"Keep him!" Prudence said jeeringly, turning to face the other. "Keep him if you can!"

"What do you mean?"

"What I say!" Prudence laughed softly. *"You* keep him!
A black-haired loose woman like you!"

She was of the *ehu,* or fair Maoris, and her words stung
Hutia to the quick. "Red dog!"

"Sow!"

Hutia sprang on the smaller girl fiercely, seized her by the
hair, and after a short tussle succeeded in throwing her down
in the pool. There, astride of her enemy's back and with
hands buried in her hair, she held her under water, jerking
at her head savagely till the younger girl was half drowned.
At last she was satisfied. She stood up, turned her back
scornfully, and began to bathe.

Prudence rose from the pool, donned her kilt and mantle
with trembling hands, took up her calabash, and disappeared
into the bush. Stopping to compose herself and to arrange
her hair before she reached the settlement, she went straight
to the cookhouse where she knew that Fasto would be at
work.

"There is something I must tell you," she said to the elder
woman, who sat on a little three-legged stool as she grated
a coconut for her fowls. "You have been kind to me. I am
young and you have been like a mother. Now I must tell
you, before the others begin to mock."

"Aye, child, what is it?" said Fasto.

This simple and industrious woman had a soft heart, and
the girl's youth appealed to the mother in her. She took her
hand and stroked it. "What is it, child?" she repeated.

Prudence hesitated before she spoke. "It is hard to tell,
but will come best from one who loves you. Open your
eyes! Williams is a good man and loves you, but all men
are weak before women's eyes. Hutia has desired him long.
Now they meet each day in the bush, while you and Tararu
are blind. . . . You do not believe me? Then go and see
for yourself. Hide yourself near the great pandanus tree at

the hour when Williams goes inland to bathe. Your man will come, and Hutia will steal through the bush to meet him."

Fasto sat in silence, with bowed head and eyes filling with tears as she continued to stroke the girl's hand.

"I cannot believe it, child, but I will do as you say. Should I find my husband with that woman . . . There will be no sleep for me this night."

When the moon rose on the following evening, Williams was striding along the path that led to McCoy's house. Most of the inmates were already in bed, but Mary sat cross-legged on the floor, plaiting a mat of pandanus by the light of a taper of candlenuts. She was a woman of twenty-five, desperately homesick for Tahiti. Williams called to her softly.

"Mary! Eh, Mary! Is Will asleep?"

McCoy rose from his bed of tapa and crossed the dim-lit room to the door. "Jack? I was only resting. We 're dead beat, Matt and me."

"Come outside. . . . Have 'ee seen Fasto?"

"No. What 's up?"

"She went off to fetch eggs; before I had my bath, that was, and not a sign o' her since. I was cursing her for a lazy slut at supper time, but, by God, I 'm afeared for her now! Her lazy! The best wench on the island, pretty or not!"

"I 've seen naught of her," said McCoy. "Wait, I 'll ask Mary."

He went into the house, and Williams heard them whispering together. Presently he returned. "Aye, Mary 's seen her; she passed this way late in the afternoon. Mary gave her a hail, but she never turned her head. She 'd her egging basket. Like enough she was making for the Rope."

The blacksmith stood irresolute for some time before he

spoke. "Thank 'ee, Will. I'll be getting home. If she's not back by morning, I'll make a search."

His heart was heavy and his thoughts sombre as he trudged home through the moonlit bush. Though he lay down on his sheets of clean tapa, smoothed by Fasto's hands, he could not sleep.

At daybreak he set out with Martin and one of the native men. They launched the smaller canoe and ran her out through the breakers. The morning was calm, with a light air from the west, and as they paddled around Ship-Landing Point, they scanned the declivities above. Beyond the easternmost cape of the island, flanked by jagged rocks offshore, they entered the half-moon cove at the foot of the Rope. As the canoe rose high on a swell, the native gave an exclamation and pointed to the beach of sand at the base of the cliffs, where something lay huddled beneath a small pandanus tree.

"Steer for the shore!" the blacksmith ordered gruffly.

They had a near thing as a feathering sea swept them between two boulders, but Williams paddled mechanically, face set and eyes staring at the beach ahead. He was out of the canoe before it grounded; while the others held it against the backwash, he hastened across the narrow beach to the pandanus tree.

The cove was a lonely, eerie place, hemmed in by precipices many hundreds of feet in height. The western curve of the cliffs lay in full sunlight, which glinted on the plumage of a thousand sea fowl, sailing back and forth at a great height. Williams came trudging back, took from the canoe a mantle of native cloth, and returned to spread it gently over the bruised and bloodstained body of Fasto. He knelt down on the sand beside her. Hearing Martin's step behind him, he motioned him away.

The others stared in silence for a moment, then walked quickly away along the foot of the cliffs. After a long interval, Williams hailed them. He was standing by the canoe with Fasto's body, wrapped in tapa, in his arms. He laid her gently in the bilges; at a word from the native steersman, the little vessel shot out through the surf. Williams dropped his paddle and sat with shoulders bowed, silent and brooding, while the canoe rounded the cape and headed northwest for Bounty Bay.

CHAPTER VI

A few days after the burning of the *Bounty*, Minarii had chosen a site for the temple he and the other Polynesian men were to build. A homeless wanderer might worship kneeling in the wash of the sea, the great purifier and source of all holiness, but settled men must erect a temple of their own. The six native men were worshipers of the same god, Ta'aroa, and their *marae* would be dedicated to him.

Sometimes alone, sometimes in company with Tetahiti, Minarii had made a leisurely exploration of those parts of the island least likely to attract the whites, and at last, on a thickly wooded slope to the west of the ridge connecting the two peaks, he had found the spot he was searching for. He was alone on the afternoon when he began his clearing, and had not long plied his axe when he perceived that other worshipers had assembled here in the past. As he made his way through the dense undergrowth he discovered a platform of moss-grown boulders, set with upright stones before which men had once knelt. Close by, on rising ground, stood two images of gross human form and taller than a man, and before one of them was a slab of rock which he stooped to raise. The task required all of his strength, but he was rewarded by the sight of a skeleton laid out in the hollow beneath, with hands crossed on the ribs and the mouldering skull pillowed on a large mother-of-pearl shell.

"*Ahé!*" he exclaimed under his breath. "A man of my own race, and from a land where the pearl-oyster grows!"

He gazed at it for some time, then replaced the heavy

slab carefully and descended from the *marae*. Religion entered into every act of a Polynesian's life, and save in time
of war they held the dead and the beliefs of others in deep
respect. The bones would lie in peace, and no stone of the
old temple would be employed to build the new.

Minarii chose another site that lay a stone's throw
distant, and measured off a square six fathoms each way.
There was a plentiful supply of boulders in the ravine below. Here the leisurely task began, all six of the natives
working at it whenever they had an hour to spare. Little
by little the temple of Ta'aroa took form — a rocky platform
set with kneeling stones and surrounding a small pyramid
three yards high, made sacred by the two stones brought from
the ancestral temple at Tahiti. The clearing was shaded by
majestic trees, and a neat fence enclosed the whole, bordered
with a hedge of flowering shrubs.

On a morning early in April, Minarii and his companions
were sweeping the pavement and tidying the enclosure in
preparation for the ceremony of awakening the god. The
shoulders of all six were bared in sign of respect. Presently
while the others waited in deep silence, Minarii stepped aside
to put on the sacred garments of his office. The flush of
dawn was in the east when he returned, clad in flowing
lengths of tapa, dyed black. His companions knelt by their
stones, their faces now clearly revealed in the increasing light,
while their priest turned toward the still hidden sun, holding
his hands aloft as he chanted: —

> "The clouds are bordering the sky; the clouds are awake!
> The rising clouds that ascend in the morning,
> Wafted aloft and made perfect by the Lord of the Ocean,
> To form an archway for the sun.
> The clouds rise, part, condense, and reunite
> Into a rosy arch for the sun."

Bowing his head, he awaited in silence until the sun began
to touch the heights with golden light. He then made a

sign to Tetahiti, who stepped behind the little pyramid and returned with a small casket, curiously carved and provided with handles like a litter. This was the dwelling place of the god, now believed to be present. Minarii addressed him solemnly: —

> "Hearken to us, Ta'aroa!
> Grant our petitions.
> Preserve the population of this land.
> Preserve us, and let us live through thee.
> Preserve us! We are men. Thou art our god!"

The chanting ceased, and a moment of profound silence followed; then the priest concluded: "O Ta'aroa, we have awakened thee. Now sleep!"

The ceremony was over. The casket had been conveyed to its niche at the base of the pyramid, and Minarii had returned to the small hut near by to resume his customary garments, when voices were heard from the thicket and a moment later Mills and McCoy appeared at the edge of the clearing. They halted at the sight of the native men and then came forward to the fenced enclosure. McCoy gazed at the stonework admiringly.

"A braw bit o' work," he remarked. "And the six of ye built this, Tetahiti?"

The native regarded him gravely. "This is our *marae*," he explained, "where we come to worship our god."

"What's that he says?" Mills asked, contemptuously. Without waiting for a reply, he passed through the gate and stood surveying the *marae*. He was about to mount the stone platform when Minarii, who had now returned, laid a hand on his arm.

"Your shoulders! Bare your shoulders before you set foot there!"

Knowing scarcely a dozen words of the native tongue, Mills shook him off and was about to proceed when McCoy called out anxiously: "Are ye horn-mad, John? Bare yer shoulders, he says. It's their kirk, mon! Would ye enter a kirk wi' a covered head?"

Mills gave a harsh laugh. "Kirk, ye call it? It's a bloody heathen temple, that's what it is! I'll have a look, and I'll peel my shirt for no Indian!"

Before he had mounted three steps Minarii seized him by the arm and threw him to the ground so fiercely that he lay half stunned.

"Ye fool!" McCoy exclaimed. "Ye've slashed a het haggis now!"

Minarii stood over the prostrate Englishman threateningly, his eyes blazing with anger. The faces of the other native men expressed the horror they felt at this act of desecration. Fortunately for Mills, McCoy, who spoke the native tongue with considerable fluency, was able to smooth matters over.

"Let your anger cool, Minarii," he said, rapidly. "You are in the right, but this man meant no harm. He is ignorant, that is all."

"Take him away!" ordered Minarii. "Come here no more. This is our sacred place."

Mills struggled to his feet, dazed and enraged, and stood with clenched fists, eyeing the native while McCoy spoke.

"Pull yersel' together, John! Say naught and get out o' this afore there's blood shed! Come along, now. They've right on their side, and he's an unchancy loon to meddle with."

Mills was in middle age, and Minarii's stern face and gigantic figure might have intimidated a far younger man. He turned aside and permitted McCoy to lead him away. The natives gazed after them in silence as they climbed the ridge and disappeared on the path leading to the settlement.

"Go you others," said Minarii, "and let no more be thought

of this.   The man was ignorant.   As McCoy said, he meant no desecration."

Tetahiti remained behind and the two men lingered outside the enclosure surveying their handiwork with deep satisfaction.

"The building was auspicious," said Minarii, after a long silence.   "The sacredness is in the stones."

Tetahiti nodded.   "Did you not feel the god lighten the heavy boulders as we worked?" he asked.

"They were as nothing in our hands.   Ta'aroa is well pleased with his dwelling place.   Here we can offer prayers for our crops and for fishing, and dedicate the children who will come.   Now for the first time my heart tells me that this is indeed my land — our land."

Minarii was silent for some time before he asked: "You know these white men better than I; have they no god?"

"Christian has never spoken to me of these things and I do not like to ask; but I would say that they worship none."

"It is strange that they should be godless.   Captain Cook came three times to Matavai; I remember his visits well.   He and his men were of the same race as these, but they worshiped their god every seventh day, in ceremonies not unlike our own.   They bowed their heads; they knelt and listened in silence while one of them chanted.   Our white men do none of these things."

"It must be that they have no god," Tetahiti replied.

Minarii shook his head gravely.   "Little good can come to godless men.   It would be well if we were alone here with our women.   The ways of these whites are as strange to us as our ways to them."

"There are good men among them," said Tetahiti.

"Aye, but not all.   Some yearn for Maori slaves."

"Martin, you mean?   *Tihé!*   He is slave-born!"

"It is not Martin alone," Minarii remarked, gravely. "Humble folk like your man Te Moa and my Hu rely upon us to protect them, and yet already Quintal and Williams and Mills treat them as little better than slaves. We want no bad blood here. We must be patient for the good of all, but the day may come . . ." He broke off, gazing sombrely before him.

"Christian knows nothing of this," said Tetahiti. "Shall I open his eyes?"

"It would be well if he knew, but these things he must learn for himself. We must wait and say nothing."

For a month or more after the burial of Fasto, Williams had seen nothing of Hutia. The girl was fond of him, in her way, and was wise enough to bide her time. Strive as he might, the blacksmith could not rid his mind of the thought that Fasto had learned of the intrigue, and that in her chagrin she had thrown herself from the cliffs. Though rough and forthright, he was by no means an unkindly man. For a time he had gone about his work in silence, without a glance at Hutia when she passed, but little by little his remorse was dulled, and the old desire for the girl overpowered him. Once more their meetings in the bush had begun, conducted, on her part at least, with greater discretion than at first.

But Williams was far from satisfied; he wanted the girl for his own. What had begun as mere philandering gradually became an obsession. On many a night he lay awake far into the morning hours, torturing his brain in attempts to conjure up some means of obtaining Hutia. Now at last he felt that he could endure no more. One afternoon when he was working with Mills at the forge he put down his hammer.

"Stand by for a bit, John," he said.

Mills straightened his back with a grunt. "What's up?" he asked, incuriously.

"I can't go on the like o' this. Every man of ye has his woman. I've none."

"Ye'll not get mine," growled Mills. "Take a girl from one of the Indians."

"Aye, Hutia'd do."

The other gave a dry laugh. "Ye should know! A pretty wench, but an artful one, Prudence reckons."

"I'm thinkin' what Christian would say; and Minarii . . ."

"Damn the Indians! Call for a show of hands. Ye've the right. Where'd we be without Jack Williams and his forge?"

Christian's house was the most westerly in the settlement, and stood on rising ground close to the bluffs, which sloped more gently here than at Bounty Bay. To the west, a deep ravine led the waters of Brown's Well to the shingle, three hundred feet below. A belt of trees and bush along the verge of the bluffs screened the house from the sea.

The dwelling was of two stories, heavily framed and planked with the *Bounty's* oaken strakes; the bright russet of its thatch contrasted pleasantly with the weathered oak. The upper story was a single large, airy room, with windows on all sides, which could be opened or closed against the weather by means of sliding shutters. It was reached by an inside ladder which led through a hatchway in the floor. It was here that Christian and Maimiti slept.

A partition divided the lower floor into two rooms. One was reserved for Christian's use. A roughly fashioned chair stood by a table of oak which held a silver-clasped Bible and a Book of Common Prayer, the *Bounty's* azimuth compass, and a fine timekeeper by Kendall, of London. Christian wound the instrument daily, and checked it from time to time by means of lunar observations, taken with the help of Young.

Christian had finished his noonday meal and was seated with Maimiti on a bench by the door, on the seaward side of the house. The sun was hot, and the sea, visible through a gap in the bush below, stretched away, calm, blue, and lonely, to the north. Looking up, presently, Christian observed Williams approaching.

The blacksmith touched his forelock to Christian, and saluted Maimiti as though she had been an English lady. "Might I speak with ye a moment, sir?" he asked.

"Yes. What is it, Williams? Do you wish to see me alone?"

"Aye."

The blacksmith remained standing, after the girl had gone, and hesitated for some time before he spoke.

"I doubt but ye 'll think the less of me for what I have to say, but I must out with it. Men are fashioned in different ways — some hot, some cold, some wise, some fools. I reckon ye 'll admit I 'm no laggard and know my trade; but I 've a weakness for the women, if weakness that be. . . . It 's this, sir: I 've lost my girl, and must have another."

He waited, clasping and unclasping his hands nervously. Christian reflected for a moment and said, slowly: "I foresaw this. It was bound to come. I don't blame you, Williams; your desire is a reasonable one. But surely you can see that no man is likely to give up his woman to you. What I propose might seem abhorrent at home, but the arrangement was an honourable one in ancient times. Have you no friend who would share his girl with you?"

Williams shook his head. "It won't do, sir; I 'm not that kind. I must have one for myself."

"Which would you have?"

"Hutia."

"Tararu's wife? And what of Tararu?"

"He 's but an Indian, and should give way."

"He 's a man like ourselves. Consider your own feelings, were the situation reversed."

"I know, sir," Williams replied stubbornly, "but I must

have her!" He clenched his fists and looked up suddenly.
"Damn the wench! I believe she's cast a spell on me!"

"Well, it has come, with a vengeance," Christian said, as
though to himself. He raised his head. "Your seizure of
another man's wife might have the gravest consequences for
all of us. My advice is, do nothing of the kind."

"Ye're right, sir; I know that well enough. But I'm past
taking advice."

"You mean that you would seize the woman regardless of
the trouble you may cause the rest of us? Come, Williams!
You're too much of a man for that!"

"I can't help it, Mr. Christian; but I'll do this, if ye'll
agree. Put it to a vote. If there's more say I shan't have
her, I'll abide by that."

"You've no right to ask for a show of hands over such a
matter," Christian replied, sternly; "the less so since you
are not denied the favours of this woman as matters stand."
He paused to reflect. "Nevertheless, this is a question that
does concern us all, and I will do as you ask. We'll have it
out to-night. Fetch the others here when you have supped."

The evening was windless, after the long calm afternoon,
and the stars were bright as the mutineers assembled before
Christian's house. Brown was the last to arrive. When he
had joined the group, Christian rose and the murmur of
conversation ceased.

"Williams, have you told the others why we are gathered
here?"

"No, sir; I reckoned that would come best from ye."

Christian nodded. "A question has arisen that concerns
every man and woman on the island. Williams has lost his
girl. He says that he must have another." He paused, and
a voice in the starlight growled, "He'll have none of ours!"

"He wants Hutia," Christian explained, "Tararu's wife."

"He's had her times enough," Quintal put in.

Williams sprang up, angrily, and was about to speak when Christian checked him.

"That is no business of ours.   He wants her in his house. He wishes her to leave her husband and live openly with him, and has asked me to put the question to a vote.   His desire for a woman is a natural one; under other circumstances it would concern him alone, but not as we are situated.   Differences over women are dangerous at all times, and in a small community like ours they may have fatal consequences.   The girl's husband is a nephew of Minarii, whom you know for a proud man and a chief among his own people.   Is it likely that he would stand by while Tararu's wife was seized?   And what of Tararu himself?   Justice is universal; the Indian resents injustice as the Englishman does.   We are of two races here; so far there has been no bad blood between us.   To stir up racial strife would be the ruin of all."

He paused, and a murmur of assent went up from the men on the grass.   But Mills spoke up for his friend.

"I 'm with Jack.   Ain't we to be considered afore the Indians?"

"Aye, well spoke!" said Martin.

"Well spoke?" said McCoy.   "I winna say that!   I 'm wi' Mr. Christian.   It 's no fault o' Jack's there 's not been trouble afore now.   I 'm nae queasy.   I 'll share my Mary wi' him."

"Keep your Mary!" growled Williams.

"Are you ready for the vote?" Christian said.   "Remember, this is to decide the matter, once and for all.   We are agreed to abide by the result.   Those who would allow Williams to take Tararu's wife, show hands."   He peered into the darkness; the hands of Mills and Martin alone were lifted.

"We 're six to three against you, Williams," said Christian.   "I believe you 'll be glad of this one day."

"I 'll abide by the vote, sir," the blacksmith replied in a gruff voice.

May passed and June ushered in the austral winter, with cold southwest winds and tempestuous seas. The evenings grew so chill that the people were glad to remain indoors after sundown, natives and whites alike.

Those evenings were far from cheerful in the blacksmith's house. Since the night of the meeting he had become more and more gloomy and taciturn. Mills tried in vain to draw him into talk; at last he gave up and turned to Prudence for company. Williams avoided Hutia. He had given his word, and he knew that if he were to keep it their meetings must cease. He found no peace save in the exhaustion of hard work.

In the dusk of a morning late in June, Mills rose to find Williams already up and gone. He felt mildly surprised, for the blacksmith brooded and paced the floor so late that he seldom wakened while it was still dark. Williams had been busy with a pair of the *Bounty's* chain plates, converting them into fish spears for the Indian men, and during the early forenoon, while Mills worked at clearing a bit of land not far off, he was again surprised, as he rested from his labour, to hear no cheerful clink of hammer on anvil. Toward nine o'clock his vague feeling of uneasiness grew so strong that he wiped the sweat from his face and dropped his axe. Martin limped out of the house as he approached. For a moment Mills forgot the blacksmith.

"Damn 'ee!" he exclaimed. "Ye've done naught but lie abed, I'll warrant!"

"It's all I can do to walk, man!" said Martin. "Work? With an old musket ball in me leg, and the nights perishin' cold? Let the Indians work! That's what we fetched 'em for."

"Where's Jack?" Mills asked.

"That's what I want to know."

"Ye've not seen him?"

"No. And the large cutter's gone. Alex Smith came up

from the cove an hour back. He and Christian are on the mountain now. Not a doubt of it: Jack 's took the boat and made off."

Mills turned to take the path that led past Christian's house and on to the Goat-House Peak. Halfway to the ridge he met the others coming down. "Is it true that Jack 's made off with the boat?" Christian nodded, and led the way down the mountainside at a rapid walk.

They halted at Christian's house while he acquainted Maimiti with the situation and sent for some of the Indian men. He then hastened on to the landing place. The little crowd on the beach watched in silence while Christian had the larger of the two canoes dragged to the water's edge. With Minarii in the stern, they shot the breakers and passed the blackened wreck of the ship, wedged between the rocks. Christian waved to the northeast, took up a paddle, and plied it vigorously.

The wind had died away two hours before, and the sun shone dimly through a veil of high cloud. The sea was glassy calm, with a gentle southerly swell. Before an hour had passed, Minarii pointed ahead. The cutter's masthead and the peak of her lugsail were visible on the horizon, though the boat was still hull-down.

Williams sat on the cutter's after-thwart, his chin propped in his hands. From time to time he raised his head to glance back toward the land. He feared pursuit, but hoped the wind might make up before it came. It was useless to row, he had discovered; with only one man at the oars, the heavy boat would scarcely move.

One of the *Bounty's* compasses lay in the stern sheets, with Williams's musket, a small store of provisions, and several calabashes filled with water. The blacksmith had some idea of where Tahiti lay, and knew that he would have a fair wind, once he could work his way into the region of the

trades. But the thought that obsessed him was to get away
from Pitcairn; as a destination, any other island would do.
He might fetch Tahiti, he thought vaguely, or pick up one
of the coral islands which they had passed in the *Bounty*.
He cared little, in fact, where he went, or whether he died
of thirst or was drowned on the way.

Presently he stood on a thwart, peering ahead with nar-
rowed eyes for signs of wind. Then, turning to glance
backward, he perceived the canoe, scarcely a mile away. He
stepped down from the thwart, took up his musket, measured a charge from his powderhorn, and rammed the wad
home. With sombre eyes, he selected a ball from his pouch.

The canoe came on fast. When it was half a cable's length
distant, the blacksmith stood up and leveled his piece. "Stop
where ye are!" he ordered, hoarsely.

Christian rose to his feet, waving the paddlers on. "Williams!" he ordered sternly, "lay down your musket!"

Slowly, as if in a daze, the black-bearded man in the boat
obeyed, slumping down on the thwart with shoulders bowed.
The canoe lost way, riding the swell lightly alongside, and
Christian sprang aboard the cutter.

"Are you mad?" he asked, with the sternness gone from his
voice. "Where could you hope to fetch up?"

"Aye, Jack," put in Mills, "ye must be clean daft!"

"Leave be, Mr. Christian," muttered Williams. "I'll not
go on as I have. Where I fetch up is my own concern."

Christian seated himself beside him. "Think, Williams,"
he said kindly. "This boat is common property. And how
would we fare without a blacksmith? Tahiti lies three hundred leagues from here. You would be going to certain
death. . . . Come, take yourself in hand!"

Williams sat gazing at his bare feet for a long time before
he spoke. "Aye, sir, I'll go back," he said reluctantly, without raising his head. "I've done my best. If trouble comes
o' this, let no man hold me to account."

CHAPTER VII

FROM now on Williams spent most of his time away from the settlement. On a lonely wooded plateau, on the western side of the island, he set to work to clear a plot of land and to build a cabin. Through the cold months of July, August, and September, he left the house each morning before the others were awake, returning at dusk. Mills respected his silence, and Martin, after one or two rebuffs, ceased to question him. In early October he announced that he was leaving for his new home, and, with Mills to help him, he carried his belongings over the ridge and down to the distant clearing where his cabin stood.

Though small, the cabin was strong and neatly built, with walls of split pandanus logs, set side by side. The floor alone was of plank, and the few articles of furniture had been put together with a craftsman's skill. Mills had not seen the place before. He glanced around admiringly.

"Ye 've a snug little harbour here, Jack," he said as he set down his burden. "All Bristol-fashion, too! So ye 're bound to live alone?"

"Aye."

Mills shrugged his shoulders. "I 've no cause to meddle, but if it 's Hutia ye 're still pinin' for, why don't ye take her and be damned to the Indians?"

"I 've no wish to stir up trouble. Christian 's been fair with us. I 'll do what I can to be fair in my turn. I 'll try living alone away from the sight of her, but I 'm not sayin' how this 'll end. Thank 'ee for the lift, John," he added.   "Tell the lads I'll come over when there's work for the forge."

The shadows were long in the clearing, for it was late afternoon.   Grass was already beginning to hide the ashes about the blackened stumps.   As he sat on the doorstep of his house, the slope of the ground to the west gave Williams a view of the sea above the tree-tops.   Snow-white terns, in pairs, sailed back and forth overhead.   It was their mating season and they were pursuing one another, swooping and tumbling in aerial play.   No wind was astir; the air, saturated with moisture, was difficult to breathe.   Williams rose, cursing the heat, went to the small cookhouse behind his cabin, and kindled a fire to prepare his evening meal.   At last the sun set angrily, behind masses of banked-up clouds, dull crimson and violet.   It was not a night for sleep.   The blacksmith was on foot before dawn, and the first grey of morning found him crossing the ridge, on his way to Christian's house.

Alexander Smith wakened at the same hour.   Like Williams, he had tossed and cursed the heat all night, between snatches of fitful sleep.   He opened the door, rubbed his eyes with his knuckles, stretched his arms wide, and yawned.

The moon, nearly at the full, was still up, though veiled by clouds in the west.   The big red rooster in the *purau* tree flapped his wings, crowed, and regarded the ground with down-stretched neck and deep, explosive cackles.   With a prodigious noise of wings, he left his perch and landed with a heavy thump.   One after the other, the hens followed, and each in turn was ravished as she touched the ground.   The last hen shook herself angrily, the cock made a final sidewise step with lowered wing, and glanced up at his master as if to say: "Well, *that's* over with!   Now for breakfast!" Smith grinned.

The fowls followed him in a compact little flock to the cookhouse, where the coconut-grater stood.   Seating himself astride the three-legged stool to which the grater of pearl shell was lashed, he began to scrape out the coconut meat, a crinkled, snowy shower that soon filled his wooden bowl.

He stopped once to fill his own mouth, and chuckled, as he munched, at the impatience of the fowls, standing in a wistful circle about the bowl.   He rose, calling, as the natives did, in a high-pitched, ringing cry, and while the fowls came running with outstretched wings he scattered grated coconut this way and that.

Hearing the familiar call, the pigs in their sty under the banyan tree burst into eager grunts. *"Mai! Mai! Mai!"* responded Smith, gruntingly, and strolled across to empty the half of his coconut into their trough.   He had the seaman's love of rural things.

It was now broad daylight.   Balhadi came to the door, greeted her husband with a smile, and went to the cookhouse to prepare his breakfast.   Smith stripped off his shirt and dipped a large calabashful from the water barrel for his morning wash.   After scrubbing his face vigorously with a bit of tapa, he made the morning round of his plants.   A fenced enclosure, of about half an acre, surrounded his house, and he derived keen pleasure from the garden he had laid out inside, with its stone-bordered paths and beds of flowering shrubs.   Spring was coming on fast.   He walked slowly, stooping often to examine the new growth or to inhale the perfume of some waxen flower.   Now and again, as he straightened his back, he paused to glance at his newly completed house.   Young was not a strong man, nor clever with his hands, and Smith had put up the building almost alone. He still derived from the sight of his handiwork a deep and inarticulate satisfaction.   It was a shipshape job — stoutly built, weatherproof, and sightly, with its bright new thatch. The Indians said that such thatching would last ten years.

Balhadi was calling him to eat.   She was a short, strongly made woman, wholesome and still youthful, with a firm, good-humoured face.   Smith felt a real affection for her, expressed in robust fashion. He pulled her down to his knee, gave her a resounding kiss, and fell to on his breakfast. Ten minutes later he shouldered his axe and strode away to his morning's work in the bush.

"Alex! Alex O!"

Tetahiti was hailing him from the path. He and Smith were good friends, and both loved fishing. "I came to fetch you," said the native. "Can you leave your work till noon? There is wind on the way, but the morning will be calm. I have discovered where the albacore sleep."

Smith nodded, and stood his axe against the fence. He followed Tetahiti down the path that led to Bounty Bay. They passed Mills's house, and McCoy's, and halted at the dwelling of the natives, not far from the landing place. The men had gone to their work in the bush; Smith chaffed with Moetua while his companion fetched the lines. Hutia was nowhere to be seen.

"Look," said Tetahiti, "we 've octopus for bait. I speared two last night."

The sea was fairly calm in the cove, sheltered from the westerly swell. The native selected a dozen longish stones, weighing three or four pounds each, and tossed them into the smaller of the two canoes. They were soon outside the breakers and paddling to the northwest, while Tetahiti glanced back frequently to get his bearings from the land. At a distance of about a mile, he gave the word to cease paddling.

"This is the place," he said, as the canoe lost way and floated idly on the long, glassy swell. "I have been studying the birds for many days; this is where the fish cease to feed on the surface, and go down to sleep in the depths."

Each man had a ball of line two hundred fathoms or more in length. One end was tied to the outrigger boom; to the other, running out from the centre of the ball, the hook was attached. They now baited their hooks and made fast their sinkers, with a hitch that permitted the stones to be released by a sharp jerk.

"Let us try at one hundred fathoms," said Tetahiti.

Smith lowered his sinker over the side and allowed the line to run out for a long time, until a knot appeared. He pulled sharply and felt the hitch unroll and the release of the sinker's weight. Then, moving his line up and down gently, to attract the attention of the fish six hundred feet below, he settled himself to wait.

The sun was well up by now, but the horizon to the north was ominous. There was not the faintest breath of wind; even at this early hour the heat was oppressive.

"We shall have a storm," remarked the native. "The moon will be full to-night."

Smith nodded. "Christian thinks so, too."

"Your ears are opened," said Tetahiti. "You are beginning to speak our tongue like one of us!"

"I have learned much from you. What day is this — what night, I mean?"

"*Maitu.* To-night will be *hotu,* when the moon rises as the sun sets."

Smith shook his head, admiringly. "I can never remember. We whites have only the names of the seven days of our week to learn. Your people must learn the twenty-eight nights of the moon!"

"Yes, and more; I will teach you the sayings concerning *maitu:* 'A night for planting taro and bamboo; an auspicious night for love-making. Crabs and crayfish shed their shells on this night; albacore are the fish at sea. Large-eyed children and children with red hair are born on this night.' . . . *Mau!*"

He shouted the last word suddenly as he struck to set the hook and allowed his line to run hissing over the gunwale. Smith watched eagerly, admiring the skill with which Tetahiti handled the heavy fish. Next moment it was his turn to shout. For a full half-hour the two men sweated in silence as they played their fish. Smith's was the first to weaken. It lay alongside the canoe, half dead from its own exertions — a huge burnished creature of the tunny kind. Holding his tight line with one hand, Tetahiti seized the catch by the tail while Smith clenched his fingers in the gills. A word, a heave in unison, and the albacore lay gasping in the bilges — a magnificent fish of a hundred pounds or more. Smith clubbed it to death before lending Tetahiti a hand.

The sea grew lumpy and confused as they paddled back to the cove. A swell from the north was now rolling into Bounty Bay, making their landing a difficult one. Minarii was awaiting them on the shingle. He helped them pull the canoe up into the shade.

"You come none too soon," he said. "The sea is making up fast. You are weary; let me carry your fish."

He fastened the tails of the albacore together, hoisted the burden of more than two hundredweight to one shoulder, and led the way up the steep path.

It was nearly noon. The workers had returned from the bush, and smoke went up from the cookhouses of the little settlement. Minarii set down his burden at the native house, and made a sign to his man Hu to cut up the fish. The women gathered about, exclaiming at sight of the catch. There was neither buying nor selling among the Polynesians. When fish was caught, it was shared out equally among all members of the community, high and low alike, a custom already firmly rooted on Pitcairn.

"I will carry Brown's share to him," said Minarii. Hu and Te Moa slung the remaining shares between them on a pole, and walked up the path, followed by Smith. McCoy's Mary stood before her house. She was great with child and had trouble in stooping to take up the cut of fish dropped on the grass at her feet.

"Hey, Will!" called Smith. "Here's a bit of fish for 'ee."

McCoy and Quintal appeared in the doorway. "Thank 'ee, Alex, ye're a lucky loon. Albacore!"

"Aye," put in Quintal. "Next best to a collop of beef!"

After a stop at the house of Mills, Smith dismissed the two natives at his own door and went on to Christian's house, Balhadi accompanying him. She carried a gift of a taro pudding, done up in fresh green leaves.

"For Maimiti," she explained. "This may tempt her to eat."

"When does she expect her child?"

"Her time is very close — to-day or to-morrow, I think."

Christian met them at the door and Balhadi carried the fish and her pudding to the cookhouse.

"A fine albacore, Smith!"

"I reckon he'd go a hundredweight, sir!" said Smith with a fisherman's pride. "And Tetahiti got one might have been his twin brother. All hands'll have a feed of 'em."

"Stop to dine with us."

"I hate to bother ye, sir, at a time like this."

Christian shook his head. "No, no! Jenny's here, and Nanai, to lend a hand. They'll make a little feast of it, with your girl. They're funny creatures, brown or white; birth and death are what they love. Come in."

"Thank 'ee, sir. I've a cut of fish for Jack; I'll just hang it up in the shade."

"He left not ten minutes gone. Come in and rest before we dine. They'll be giving us some of your fish. Do you like it raw, in the Indian style?"

"Aye, sir, that I do!"

"And I, when prepared with their sauce of coconut. We think of the Indians as savages, yet we have much to learn from them."

"I don't know what we'd do without 'em, here. We'd

get no fish without the men to teach us how to catch 'em, and as for the girls, I reckon we 'd starve but for them!"

They were sitting by the table in Christian's room, for Maimiti could no longer climb the ladder to the apartment upstairs, and the dining room was set aside for her use. The two men were silent for a time while the chronometer beside them ticked loudly and steadily. Christian glanced at its dial, which registered the hour in Greenwich, and the sight set his thoughts to wandering back through the past — to his boyhood in Cumberland and on the Isle of Man, to his early days at sea.

"Had that old timekeeper a voice," he remarked, "it could tell us a rare tale! It was Captain Cook's shipmate on two voyages, traveling thousands of leagues over seas little known even now. It began life in London; now it will end its days on Pitcairn's Island."

Smith nodded. "Like me, sir!" he said.

"Were you born in London? I took you for a country-man."

"Aye, Mr. Christian; born there and reared in a foundling's home. I 'm under false colors here. My real name is John Adams; the lads used to call me 'Reckless Jack.' I got into a bit of trouble and thought best to sign on as Alexander Smith."

Christian nodded, and asked after a brief pause: "Tell me, Smith, are you contented here?"

"That I am, sir! My folk were countrymen, till my dad was fool enough to try his fortune in London. It 's in my blood. Happy? If ye was all to leave, and give me the chance, I 'd stop here with my old woman to end my days."

Christian smiled. "I am glad, since I fetched you here. It would be curious, were we able to look ahead twenty years. There will be broad plantations, new houses, and children — many of them — I hope."

"And yours 'll be the first-born, sir!"

Jenny appeared in the doorway, carrying a platter of fish. She smiled at the two men, and beckoned Balhadi in to help set the table. An hour later Smith rose to take his leave.

"Ask Williams to come down to the cove this afternoon," said Christian. "We shall need all hands to get the boats up out of reach of the sea."

A heavy swell from the north was bombarding the cliffs as Smith made his way over the ridge. The heat was sultry, though the sky was now completely overcast, and he knew that the wind could not be far off. Williams met him at the cottage door.

"Come in, Alex. Set ye down. What's that — fish? A monster he must have been, eh? Here, let me hang it up; Puss has smelt it already."

The blacksmith's cat, a fine tabby whose sleekness proved her master's care, was mewing eagerly, and Williams paused to cut off a small piece for her.

"She's spoiled," he remarked. "D' ye think she'd look at a rat? But I hate rusty tools and scrawny living things."

As they entered the cottage, Smith observed, on the floor close to the bed, a round comb of bamboo, such as the women used. Next moment, out of the corner of his eye, he saw Williams kick it hastily under the bed. He glanced about the neat little dwelling appreciatively.

"Ye've the best-built house of the lot," he said, "and the prettiest to look at. Aye, it's small, but all the better for that."

"What d' ye think of the weather, Alex?" Williams asked.

"It 'll be blowing a gale by night. I 'd best be getting back. Mr. Christian wants all hands at Bounty Bay. He's afeared for the boats."

The blacksmith nodded. "I 'll come along with ye," he said.

The wind was making up from the northwest, with heavy squalls of rain, and before the two men reached the cove it hauled to the north, blowing with ever-increasing force.

It was late afternoon when the people began to straggle back, up the steep path to the settlement. The boats and the two canoes had been conveyed to the very foot of the bluff, far above where they were usually kept, and it seemed that no wave, no matter how great, could reach them there.

But at nightfall the gale blew at hurricane force. The deep roar of the wind and the thunder of breaking seas increased as the night wore on. The rocky foundations of the island trembled before the onslaught of wind and wave. There was little sleep for anyone, and there were moments when it seemed that only a miracle could preserve the houses from being carried away. Daybreak came at last.

Toward seven o'clock Smith went trudging up the path to Christian's house. The wind was abating, he thought, though the coconut palms along the path still bent low to the gusts, their fronds streaming like banners in the gale. Smith glanced up apprehensively from time to time as a heavy nut came whacking to the ground. Once, in a place where the path was somewhat exposed, he staggered and leaned to windward to keep his feet. Each time a great comber burst at the foot of the cliffs, he felt the ground tremble underfoot. At last he reached Christian's house.

The sliding shutters on the weather side were closed, but the door was open in the lee. Smith found Christian in the room, with Jenny and Taurua.

"Balhadi is with her," Christian said, drawing the newcomer aside and raising his voice to make it heard. "The pains have begun. What of the boats?"

"Gone, sir, all but the large cutter," replied Smith regretfully. "The sea's higher 'n ye'd believe! All was snug

an hour back.   Then a roarin' great sea came in and carried
away both canoes and the small cutter.   And when the wind
had cleared the air of spray, we looked out, sir, and the old
Bounty was gone!"

Christian paced the floor nervously for a minute or two,
stopping once to listen at the door of the other room.
Then, halting suddenly, he addressed Taurua: 'Go in to her,
you and Jenny; say that I am going down to the landing
place and shall not be long."   He turned to Smith.   "Come,
there is nothing I can do here at such a time."

They found Young and a group of men and women at
the verge of the bluffs, crouching to escape the full force of
the wind while they watched with fascinated eyes the tower-
ing seas that ran into Bounty Bay.   Speech was impossible,
but Young took Christian's arm and pointed out to where the
blackened hulk of the ship had lain wedged among the rocks.
No trace of her remained.

The waves were breaking high among the undergrowth at
the foot of the path, and during the brief lulls, when the
spray was blown ashore, Christian saw that the cove was a
mass of floating rubbish and uprooted trees, and that ava-
lanches had left raw streaks of earth where the sea had under-
mined the steep slopes toward Ship-Landing Point.

The gale was abating when at last the three men turned to
make their way back to Christian's house.   At the door they
heard faintly, between gusts of wind, the wail of a newborn
child.   The door of the other room opened, and Jenny and
Taurua came in, with the smiles of women who have assisted
at a happy delivery.   Balhadi appeared behind them.   She
beckoned to Christian.

"*É tamaroa!*" she said.   "A man-child!"

As she closed the door behind him, Christian saw Maimiti
on a couch covered with many folds of tapa; and close beside
her, swathed to the eyes in the same soft native cloth, an
infant who stirred and wailed from time to time.   Maimiti

looked pale and worn, but in her eyes there was an expression of deep happiness. Balhadi pulled back the tapa that muffled the baby's face.

"Look!" she said proudly. "Was ever a handsomer boy? And auspiciously born! You know our proverb: 'Born in the hurricane, the child shall live in peace.'"

Young smiled when Christian came out of the room. "It is fitting that your child should be our first-born," he remarked, as he held out his hand. "What shall you name him?"

"Nothing to remind me of England," replied Christian. "Smith, Balhadi has proven herself a true friend to-day. You shall be the child's godfather. Give him a name."

The seaman grinned and scratched his head. "Ye'll have naught to remind 'ee of England? I have it, sir. Ye might name him for the day, if ye know what day it is."

The father smiled grimly as he consulted his calendar. "It's a good suggestion, Smith. The day is Thursday, and the month October. Thursday October Christian he shall be!" He glanced out through the doorway. "Here come the others; set out the benches."

The other mutineers and their women were approaching the house. One after another, the men shook Christian's hand, while the women filed in to seat themselves on the floor by Maimiti's couch. When the benches were full, Christian raised his voice above the roar of the wind.

"There's a question that calls for a show of hands. Shall we issue an extra grog ration to-day, and drink it here and now?"

Every hand went up, but McCoy asked anxiously: "How much ha' we left, sir?"

Christian drew a small, worn book from his pocket and turned the pages. "Fifty-three gallons."

McCoy shook his head gloomily. "A scant four months' supply!"

When the glasses were full, the men toasted the child in the next room: —

"A long life to him, sir!"

"May he be as good a man as his father!"

McCoy was the last to drink. He watched the filling of his glass with deep interest, and sniffed at the rum luxuriously before he took a sip.

"I 'll nae drink it clean caup out," he said apologetically, and then, as he held the glass aloft, "Tae our first bairn! I 've run 'ee a close race, sir. My Mary 'll hae her babe within the week!"

CHAPTER VIII

WITH the warm spring rains of November, the planting of the cleared lands began. The weather was too sultry for hard work when the sun was overhead; the men went out to their plantations at daybreak, rested through the hot noon hours, and worked once more from mid-afternoon till evening dusk.

Smith, Young, and Christian had joined forces in clearing a considerable field in the Auté Valley. Now the rubbish had been burned and the smaller stumps pulled, and the volcanic soil, rich and red, lay ready to nourish a crop of yams.

On a morning toward the middle of the month, the three men set out well before sunrise, taking the path that led south, up the long slope of the plateau, and over the ridge. No wind was astir, a light mist hung over the tree-tops, and the fresh spring verdure was beaded with dew. A party of women, ahead, took the path that branched off to the east. Presently, with Christian leading the way, the men toiled up the steep trail to the ridge, and came to a halt. Dropping the heavy basket of lunch, Smith was the last to seat himself. The place commanded a wide prospect to the north — over the rich plateau, christened the Main Valley, to the misty greyish-blue of the sea beyond. It was a custom, well established by now, to rest here for a few minutes each morning before descending to work in the Auté Valley.

The upper rim of the sun was touching the horizon, gliding the small, fluffy, fair-weather clouds. The clearings in the Main Valley were not as yet extensive enough to be visible from the ridge. From the sea to the bare summits of the ridges, virgin forest clothed the land. Here and there, the silvery foliage of a clump of candlenut trees contrasted with the dark green of the bush, and scattered coconut palms curved up gracefully to their fronded tops, sixty or seventy feet above the earth.

In the valley below, the women were at work beating out bark cloth. Each tapa-maker had her billet of wood, fashioned from the heart of an ironwood tree, and adzed flat on the upper surface. They varied from a fathom to a fathom and a half in length, and were supported on flat-topped stones set in the earth, so spaced that no two beams gave forth the same note when struck. They were, in fact, rude xylophones; the women derived great pleasure from the musical notes of their mallets, and the measured choruses produced when several of them worked together. "Tonk, tink, tonk, tonk; tinka-tonk, tink!" — the deliberate notes were sweet, measured, and musical. Young loved the sound of them, which expressed to him the very spirit of rustic domesticity, of the dreamy happiness of the islands, of morning in the dewy bush.

Presently the men rose and made their way down the slope of the Auté Valley, to the glade where Brown's cottage stood. The seed yams, fetched from Tahiti, had been planted early in February in a good-sized clearing near by. The gardener and Jenny had tended them till they were ready to be dug, weeding the rows carefully, and watering the young plants in times of drought. They had been left in the ground until October, and stored on platforms in the shade, out of the reach of rats and wandering swine.

A slender column of smoke rose from Jenny's cookhouse. The gardener was on his knees, absorbed in potting a young breadfruit plant which he had just severed from the parent tree. Christian approached so softly that Brown started at the sound of his voice. He rose stiffly, dusting the earth from his hands. "Morning, sir." He smiled at Young and gave Smith a friendly nod. "What's to be planted to-day, Mr. Christian?"

"Have you many more of the long yams? The *tahotaho?*"

"Aye. There's a-plenty. To my way of thinking, they're the best of the lot."

He led the way to a large raised platform, under a spreading tree. It held two or three tons of sprouted yams, all of the same variety, and averaging no less than fifty pounds in weight. While Christian chatted with the gardener, his companions went to the cookhouse and returned with half a dozen bags of coarse netting and three carrying poles. Each bag was now filled with yams, handled gently in order not to injure the sprouts. Young's load was made light, but Smith and Christian balanced a hundredweight at either end of their poles. In a land where wheels and beasts of burden were unknown, no other method of transport was possible.

Christian squatted, settled the stout pole on his shoulder, raised himself upright with a grunt, and led the way to the new clearing. It lay about four hundred yards distant from Brown's cottage, in a westerly direction, and the feet of the three men had already worn a discernible path through the bush. The land sloped gently to the south, hemmed in by high green walls of virgin forest. Christian dashed the sweat from his eyes when he had set down his load.

The hills were to be about a yard apart, and all had been well lined and staked the day before. Young set to work at cutting up the yams, so large that many of them sufficed to plant twenty-five or thirty hills. Side by side on two rows, Christian and Smith began to ply their mattocks, digging a hole at each stake, filling it in with softened earth and decaying vegetation. Their companion was soon planting the sprouted bits of yam, pressing the earth down carefully over each.

The two men worked doggedly till nearly ten o'clock, striving to keep ahead of Young, never halting, save to spit on their hands and take fresh grips on their mattock hafts. They had cast their shirts aside, and the sweat streamed from their shoulders and backs. The sun was high overhead when Christian flung down his mattock and wiped his face with his bare forearm.

"Avast digging!" he said to Smith.

"Aye, sir; I've had enough."

Young followed them to a shady spot where they sluiced their bodies with water from a large calabash. Smith wandered away into the bush and was back before long, with a cluster of drinking coconuts and a broad leaf of the plantain, to serve as a cloth for their rustic meal. He drew the sheath knife at his belt, cut the tops from a pair of nuts, and offered them to his companions.

Christian threw back his head and finished the cool, sweet liquor at a draught. He smiled as he tossed the empty nut away.

"We've a rare island," he remarked, "where grog grows on the trees!"

"What have the girls given us to-day?" inquired Young, glancing at the basket hungrily. Smith spread the plantain leaf on the ground and began to remove the contents of the basket, displaying a large baked fish, the half of a cold roast suckling pig, cooked breadfruit, scraped white and wrapped in leaves, and a small calabash filled with the delicious coconut sauce called *taioro*. The three men seated themselves on the grass and were beginning their meal when Jenny appeared, carrying a large wooden bowl which she set down before them.

"A pudding," she explained. "I made two."

When she was gone, they fell to heartily, dining with the relish only hard work can impart. The fish disappeared, and the crisp, browned suckling pig; the pudding of taro and wild arrowroot, covered with sweet coconut cream, soon went the same way. Smith sighed.

"I 'm for a nap, sir," he said, as he rose to his feet with some difficulty; "I 've stowed away enough for three!"

Five minutes later he was snoring gently in the shade of a *purau* tree, a stone's throw distant. Christian turned to Young.

"There 's a good man, Ned," he remarked.

"Yes. I 've come to know him well. Had he been reared under more fortunate circumstances . . ."

Christian nodded. "He 's a fine type of Englishman, and a born leader, I suspect. Life 's wasteful and damned unjust! What chance has a man in the forecastle? Who can blame him if he diverts himself with trollops or dulls his mind with drink? Not I! Smith deserved a better chance from Life. He has the instincts of a gentleman."

They fell silent. The sun was now directly overhead, and presently they moved to a place of dense shade where they could sit with their backs to the trunk of an ancient candlenut tree. "Seamen are a strange lot," Christian remarked, presently. "You and I have been together since the *Bounty* left Spithead, and now we shall pass the remainder of our lives on this morsel of land. Yet I know nothing of you, nor you of me! Where was your home, Ned? Tell me something of your life before you went to sea."

"I was born in the West Indies, on St. Kitts, and lived there till I was twelve years old."

"I 've been there! It was eight — no, nine years ago. We cast anchor at Basseterre to load sugar, and I had a run ashore. I was only a lad at the time."

"We lived just outside the town, at the foot of Monkey Hill. I loved the island, and was unhappy when sent away to school. Here in the South Sea I feel more at home than in England."

"Odd that we should both be islanders! My own boyhood

was passed on the Isle of Man. My first speech was the
Manx, not unlike the Gaelic of the Highlanders." Christian
smiled, half sadly. "I can still hear the voice of our old
nurse, singing the lament for Illiam Dhone."

"Who was he?"

"William Christian, my ancestor — 'Fair-Haired Illiam' in
our language. He was executed in 1663, for high treason
against the Countess of Derby, then Queen of Man. He was
innocent."

For two hours or more, till Smith wakened, they chatted
idly of the past. Then, as the shadows began to extend
eastward, the three men fell to work once more. It was
dusk when they laid down their mattocks and filed homeward, past Brown's cottage and over the ridge.

The summer proved warm and rainy and the yams grew
well. They were ready for digging when autumn had dried
out the soil and June ushered in the winter of 1791.

Midway of the settlement, near the house of Mills, the
communal storage platforms, called *pafatas*, had been set up.
Supported on stout posts higher than a man's head, and
floored with a grating of saplings laid side by side, the four
large platforms were designed to hold twenty tons or more
of yams. As with the fish, so with the fruits of the earth;
all hands were to share alike.

As the yams were dug, the men fetched them in on their
carrying poles and passed them up to the women, one by one,
to be stowed aloft. The long yams were laid crisscross, to
allow a free circulation of air; day after day the piles grew
higher, till at last, toward the middle of the month, it was
announced that another day's work would see the harvest
home.

Four large hogs were killed that night, scalded, scraped,
and hung from the branches of a banyan tree. There was
a sense of rejoicing in the houses, of deep satisfaction with

a communal task performed, of happy anticipation of well-earned rest.

At daybreak the people began to assemble by the platforms, exchanging good-natured banter as they eyed the preparations for their evening feast. Hu and Te Moa had been appointed cooks, and were already engaged in scraping out pits for two large earth ovens, one for baking the hogs and one for ti roots, yams, taro, and other vegetables. McCoy slapped the smooth white flank of one of the hogs.

"Ye're forbid to Jews, and no true Scot 'll eat 'ee, but bide here till Will McCoy comes back!" He turned to Quintal: "Vivers for all hands, Matt! Gin we'd ilk a tass o' grog!"

Quintal grinned, and at that moment Christian came around the turn of the path. He was carrying his small boy, now eight months old, and Maimiti followed him. McCoy caught his eye.

"Can't 'ee spare a sup o' grog for to-night, sir? Just a wee tassie all round?"

Christian shook his head. "We've but four bottles left. It was agreed to save that for medical stores."

"Aye, sir," replied McCoy regretfully. "So it was, I mind me; I'll say nae mair."

Presently the men took up their poles and bags of netting; several of the women accompanied them to lend a hand as they scattered to the different parts of the island where their plantations were situated. Christian handed young Thursday October to his mother, shouldered his pole, and took the path with Smith and Young to the Auté Valley.

All day long the yams came in and were stowed aloft, without a halt for dinner or a rest at noon. At sunset the *pafatas* were bending under their loads, and every soul on Pitcairn's Island, save Minarii and his wife, was there by the ovens, still covered with heaps of matting and breadfruit leaves.

Minarii had cleared and planted the largest field on the island, and his crop was the heaviest of all. Aided by Moetua, he had toiled like a Titan throughout the day. Now, in the dusk of evening, they were fetching in the last load. A shout went up from the natives as they came in sight. Minarii was in the lead, half running, half walking, with bent knees. His carrying pole was a mighty bludgeon of hardwood, but it curved and swayed with the man's movements, for no less than two hundredweight of yams was suspended from either end. Behind him came Moetua, trotting under a load Young or McCoy could not have lifted from the ground.

As the couple set down their burdens, several of the natives, men and women, sprang forward to lend a hand. Prudence and Nanai swarmed up the posts of the nearest *pafata* and squatted, clapping their hands. Up went the yams, of forty, fifty, and sixty pounds weight, to be stowed amid shouting and much good-natured mirth. Tararu was about to heave up the last of them when Minarii laid a hand on his arm.

"For the god," he said. "Ta'aroa will be content with his first fruits."

Christian nodded to the two cooks. "Open the ovens!" he ordered.

When Minarii and his wife returned, bathed like the others, and the woman with a wreath of flowers on her hair, the feast had been spread on a stretch of level lawn. Christian sat at the head of the rustic table, and below him the men faced each other in two lines. The women had their meal at a little distance, and a bright fire of coconut husks burned between.

Two hours later, when the last of the broken meats had been gathered up and the natives were drumming and dancing in the firelight, Christian took leave of the company. Maimiti followed him, with her sleeping child on her arm.

"A happy day," he said, as they strolled homeward in the starlight. "We have begun well here. Your people and mine were like brothers to-night!"

It was past midnight when the fire was allowed to die out and the people straggled back to their houses to sleep. The new day began to brighten the eastern sky, and one by one the fowls fluttered down from the trees. Still the doors of the houses remained closed, and the people slept. Only Minarii was afoot.

In the first grey of dawn he had taken the path to the *marae*, bearing a little offering of first fruits for his god. Uncovering his shoulders reverently, he had climbed to the rude platform of stone and laid the basket of food on Ta'aroa's altar. Then, after a brief prayer, supplicating the acceptance of the offering and the continued favour of the god, he had set out to return to his house, where he meant to rest throughout the morning.

Upon reaching the summit of the Goat-House Ridge, he seated himself on a flat rock to rest. The sun was above the horizon now; the sky was cloudless, and there was a light, cool breeze from the west. No music of tapa mallets came up from the wooded depths of the Main Valley; all was still save for the occasional long-drawn crowing of the cocks. He drew a deep breath. Life was good, he thought, and this island, to which the white captain had led him, was a good land. The fish from this sea were sweet; pigs throve here without attention; as for yams, who in Tahiti had seen the equal of these? He had had many wives, but Moetua was the best of them, though she had never borne him a child. A fine, strapping girl, a fit mate for a man like himself! And she had no eyes for the other men. He rose, stretching his arms wide as he turned, and glanced casually and half instinctively around the half-circle of horizon to the west. Suddenly his easy pose became rigid. For a full minute or more he gazed westward, hands shading his eyes. Then he turned and plunged down the steep path toward Christian's house.

Christian, clad only in a loin cloth, was scrubbing himself by the water cask at the rear of the house when Minarii arrived. He hailed the native man cheerily, then paused, with the calabash in his hand, to give him a keen glance. "What is it, Minarii?" he asked.

"I have been on the ridge. Chancing to glance westward, I saw that something broke the line where sea and sky meet. It gleamed white when the rising sun shone upon it. Christian, it is a sail!"

Christian's face was impassive. "You are sure?" he asked.

Minarii nodded: "It is a white man's ship. Our sails of matting are brown."

"Is she steering this way?"

"I could not make out."

"Find Smith," said Christian. "Tell him to come to me at once."

Maimiti sat on the doorstep, suckling her eight months' boy. Christian stopped for a moment to caress her hair and to gaze down tenderly at his son. When he came out of the house, spyglass in hand, Alexander Smith was striding up the path. "We are going to the Goat-House," Christian told the girl.

As they walked away briskly, he informed Smith of Minarii's news. "We'll stop on the mountain till we make certain of her course. It is too early for a ship sent out from England to search for us, but a British vessel may have put in at Matavai by chance and learned of the mutiny from the others there. She would be on the lookout for us."

Both men were panting when they reached the summit, and both turned their eyes westward, where a speck of white broke the line of the horizon. Christian rested his glass in the fork of a scrubby tree, focused it, and gazed out to the west. Three or four minutes elapsed before he lowered the glass.

"She's hull and courses down," he said. "I can make out topsails, topgallants, and royals when they catch the sun."

He handed the glass to Smith, who scrutinized the distant vessel long and earnestly. "She's steering this way, sir," he said at last. "Look again. Ye'll see her fore-topmast staysail."

Christian soon convinced himself of the truth of Smith's words, and they turned to go.

"With this westerly wind, she'll come on fast, sir," remarked Smith.

"Aye," replied Christian grimly, as he picked his way down the steep path. "She should be close in by one o'clock."

He said no more till they were approaching the house. Halting at the door, he turned to Smith. "Go at once to Brown and Williams, and tell any others you meet on the way. Every fire must be put out. I want all hands, men and women, to assemble at McCoy's house. Tell them to waste no time."

"A ship is coming," he told Maimiti, when Smith was gone. "Unless they make a landing, we have nothing to fear. I am going to warn the others. Do you stop here and gather together everything we possess from the ship — plates, knives, axes, tools. All must be well hidden. Should they land, we will conceal ourselves in the bush till they are gone."

At Young's house, Christian stopped to explain the situation and to give his orders. Half consciously, he had taken command of the island as if it had been a ship. All fires were extinguished and the mutineers set to work with their women collecting every article of European manufacture, in preparation for flight to the bush. When all were assembled before McCoy's house, Christian revealed his plan.

"She is making direct for the island," he said. "If the wind holds, she will fetch the land within a few hours. From the cut of her sails she is a small English frigate. She cannot have been sent out in search for us, but it is possible that she touched at Tahiti and learned of the mutiny there. Our course is clear in any case. If they pass without making a landing, they must not know that the island is inhabited. Should they land, we must take to the bush and remain hidden there, with everything that might betray us as white men." He paused, and the men spoke rapidly in low voices among themselves. "Williams and Mills," Christian went on, "I leave the smithy to you. See that the bellows, the forge, and the anvil are safely hidden, and every trace of Williams's work removed. Young, the path leading up from Bounty Bay must be wiped out and masked. Take the Indian men. Yours is the most important task of all! Pile stones in a natural manner here and there on the path, and plant young ironwood trees between; their foliage will not wilt for a day or two. McCoy, take charge of the houses, and see that nothing remains to betray us. Smith, you shall be our lookout, and report instantly should the ship change her course. And remember, no fires! If they land, we shall repair at once to the grove of banyan below the Indian temple. They will never find us there."

Mills slapped the stock of the musket in his hand. "Find us or not," he growled, "I don't mean to be taken. Not while I 've powder and lead!"

"Are ye daft?" asked McCoy. "One shot 'd be the ruin of us all!"

"Aye," said Christian sternly, "McCoy is right!"

The people dispersed to their tasks and Christian walked back to set his own house in order. Smith followed and stopped at the door while the spyglass was fetched.

Less than two hours had passed when Smith returned. "She 's an English man-of-war, sir, not a doubt of it! A frigate of thirty-two, I reckon, and coming straight on for the land."

By early afternoon Christian's orders had been carried out, and the people were assembled not far from McCoy's house and a quarter of a mile from the landing place. The path leading up from the cove had been masked so skillfully that no trace of it was visible, and after a final inspection by Christian the workers had made their way separately up the bluff.

The ship was now close in; Smith was stationed on a point that jutted out beyond a small ravine, to hail the others when she rounded the northern cape. Christian was admonishing the group of men and women on the grass.

"She is a man-of-war, and there will be a dozen spyglasses trained on shore. When she comes in sight, the women must remain here. Maimiti, you will see to that! The men shall go with me to the point, but once there, we must take care not to be seen."

There was a rapid murmur of conversation as he ceased to speak, broken by a hail from Smith. The ship had rounded Young's Rock and was now little more than a mile from Bounty Bay, and at a distance of about three cable lengths from shore. Her courses were clewed up; she came on slowly under her topsails, before the fair westerly wind. At a sign from Christian the men followed him down to Smith's lookout point.

The place was well screened by bush and about three hundred feet above the beach; the rise to the plateau was steep enough here to merit the name of cliff. Each man chose for himself a peephole through the foliage, and seated himself to watch the progress of the ship. There were exclamations from the mutineers: —

"She 's English, not a doubt!"

"A smart frigate, eh, lads?"

Nearly an hour passed while the vessel coasted the island

slowly, sounding as she approached the cove. The men peering through the bush could see the red coats of marines, and a stir and bustle amidships as she drew abreast of Bounty Bay. A boat was going over the side; presently, with two officers in the stern and a full crew at the oars, she began to pull toward the cove, while the frigate tacked and stood offshore.

Though the wind was westerly, there was a high swell from the north, and one of the officers astern rose to his feet as the boat drew near the breakers. At a sign from him, the men ceased rowing, and the cutter rose and fell just beyond the first feathering of the seas.

"They'll never chance it!" muttered Young. Christian nodded without taking his eyes from the boat.

"She's been to Tahiti," growled Mills, "ye can lay to that! Thank God for the swell!"

The taller of the officers, a lieutenant from his uniform, was raising his spyglass to scan the rim of the plateau. For a long time the glass moved this way and that while the officer examined the blank green face of the bush. At last he snapped his telescope together and made a sign to the rowers to return to the ship. Hove-to under her topsails, she was a good mile offshore by now, and the cutter was a long time pulling out to her. Through his glass Christian watched the falls made fast, and the sway of the men at the ropes as the boat went on board. Presently the courses were loosed and the frigate slacked away to bear off to the east.

CHAPTER IX

By the end of the year, the swine had multiplied to an extent which made it necessary to fence all the gardens against their depredations. The fowls, wandering off into the bush, had gone wild and regained the power of flight lost in domesticity. The women caught as many as they required in snares, baited with coconut; when a man wished to eat pork, half an hour's tramp with a musket sufficed to bring a fat hog to bag. Sometimes they shot a fierce old sow, ran down the squeaking pigs, and fetched them in to be tamed and fattened in the sties.

During the breadfruit season, from November till May, the trees planted by the ancient inhabitants of the island produced more than enough to feed all hands. The pandanus abounded everywhere; its nuts, though somewhat laborious to extract, were rich, tasty, and nourishing. The long, slender, wild yams grew in all the valleys, and in the natural glades, where the sunlight warmed the fertile soil, were scattered patches of ti — a kind of dracæna, with a large root, very sweet when baked. *Pia maohi,* or wild arrowroot, indigenous to all the volcanic islands of the Pacific, was here, valuable for making the native puddings of which the white men soon grew fond. The coconuts would have been enough for ten times the population of the island. At the proper season, the cliffs provided the eggs and young of sea birds, the latter, when nearly full grown, being fat, tender, and far from ill-flavoured. Shellfish and crustaceans were to be gathered on the rocky shores when the weather was

calm, and fish abounded in the sea. Once their houses were
built, and the land cleared for plantations of yams and cloth-
plant, the mutineers found themselves able to live with little labour.

There were two small Christians now — Thursday October
and the baby, Charles; McCoy was the father of a boy and
a girl, and Sarah had presented Quintal with an infant son.
The adult population numbered twenty-six, now that Fasto
was dead, and their island would have supported in comfort
at least five hundred more. There had been little friction
during the two years past, for the hard work together, the
sense of sharing a common task, had bred good feeling between whites and Polynesians. Now, as the second anni-
versary of their settlement on the island approached, all began to take life more easily. Minarii and Tetahiti spent
much time at sea in the cutter, fishing for albacore; certain
of the white men took to loafing in the shade, while they
forced the humbler natives to perform the daily tasks too
heavy for womenfolk. Williams was seldom seen at the
settlement, and McCoy, once the most sociable of men, was
frequently absent from his house.

No one knew where he spent so many hours each day,
and none cared save Quintal, who grumbled incuriously at
times when he wished to chat with his friend. Mary suspected that her husband was tired of her and had found
consolation elsewhere, but his absence brought her more
relief than jealousy, for he had been a trial to her since the
daily grog ration had ceased; his cuffs were far more fre-
quent than his caresses. With two small children to occupy
her, Mary would have been content had her husband moved
away for good.

With the secretiveness of a Scot, and unknown to all the
others, McCoy was conducting certain experiments in a narrow gorge on the unfrequented western slope of the island.
In his youth he had been apprenticed to a distiller, and, while

acquiring a rough knowledge of the distiller's art, he had also acquired an inveterate love of alcohol. Unlike most British seamen of his day, McCoy cared little for sprees and jovial drinking bouts, and under ordinary circumstances never went to excess. What he loved was the certainty of an unfailing supply of grog, the glow and gentle relaxation of a quiet glass or two by himself. When the last of the *Bounty's* rum was gone, save for the small amount preserved in case someone fell ill, McCoy's moods of gaiety had ceased, and he had grown silent and morose.

The idea had come in a flash, one afternoon when he was alone at Williams's forge. He was searching for a bit of wire, or a nail, to make a fishhook, and as he turned over the odds and ends of metal fetched from the ship he came on a few yards of copper tubing, coiled up and made fast with a bit of marline. A coil! With a coil, cooled in water, it would be no trick at all to set up a small still!

Hiding the tubing carefully, he strolled home deep in thought. The copper pot from the ship would be the very thing, but it was at Christian's house and not to be had without awkward explanations. There were a number of kettles which had been placed on board for trade with the Indians; he had two of his own, but they were too small to make more than a pint a day; yet a pint a day would be ample for one. It would be best to keep the matter to himself. He suspected that Christian would scent danger and put an immediate stop to it. He might let Matt Quintal in. . . . No, Quintal always went mad when enough grog was on hand. What could he use? Sugar cane was not plentiful, and all of the people were fond of chewing it. He could never get enough without exciting suspicion. Why not ti? The roots would have to be baked to make them sweet, then mashed in water and allowed to ferment. There was plenty of ti; nearly everyone was heartily tired of it.

Deliberately, and with the greatest secrecy, McCoy went about his preparations. Musket on his arm, as if pig-hunting, he wandered about the island casually till he found a spot that suited him. Far off from Williams's cottage, and below the upper slopes frequented by the increasing flock of goats, he found a narrow, walled-in gorge, where a trickle of water wandered down from the peak. Little by little, carrying his light loads before sunrise or in the dusk of evening, he accumulated what he needed there — a kettle, the coil, a supply of the roots, a native pestle of stone for mashing them, and a keg in which to ferment the mash afterwards. Then, still without arousing curiosity, he fetched several bags of coconut shells, which burn with an intense and smokeless heat.

The kettle was of cast iron, and held about two gallons. McCoy set it up carefully on three stones, inserted one end of his coil in the spout, and made the joint tight with a plaster of volcanic clay. He bent the flexible coil so that it passed into a large calabash sawed in half, and out, through a watertight joint, after a dozen turns. A dam of stones and mud across the watercourse formed a little pool, from which the cold water could be dipped to fill the calabash. When all was ready, he cooked a large earth oven of the roots, mashed them with his pestle on a flat rock, and stirred up the mash with water in his keg.

The month was January, and the weather so hot that fermentation was not long delayed. When McCoy lifted the lid of his keg, thirty-six hours after the first stirring, a yeasty froth covered the mash. He stirred it once more, replaced the lid, and strolled homeward, killing a fine yearling hog on the way.

He was so obsessed with his plans, so eager to see and to taste the results of the experiment, that he scarcely closed his eyes all through the night. Long before the others were awake, he took up his musket and stole out, past Mary, sleeping peacefully, with her two children at her side. The stars were bright overhead; the day promised well.

Striding along the starlit path, McCoy passed the house of Mills, passed Young's house, and turned inland along the near bank of the ravine that led down from Brown's Well. He halted for a moment to drink, where the rivulet ran into the upper end of the pool. Starlight was giving place to dawn as he climbed to the small plateau above and toiled up to the summit of the Goat-House Ridge.

Lack of breath forced him to rest for a moment here, where another man might have lingered to admire the wide prospect of land and sea. Beyond the sleeping settlement and the jagged peak of Ship-Landing Point, the sea stretched away, misty and indistinct in the morning calm. But in the east the sun announced its approach in a glory of colour among the low scattered clouds — blended gold and rose, shimmering like mother-of-pearl. McCoy shouldered his musket and took a dim goat-path leading down to the west.

He found the mash working powerfully; there was a rim of froth on the ground about the keg. He put a finger into the mess, tasted, and spat it out. Then, after a thorough stirring, he ladled the kettle full with half a coconut shell. Unwrapping his tinder carefully, he ignited the charred end with a stroke of flint on steel and blew up the dried leaves beneath the kettle to a flame. Soon a hot, smokeless fire of coconut shells was burning brightly.

The lid of the kettle was of heavy cast iron, and fitted tightly, but McCoy now plastered it about with clay before he filled his sawn calabash with water and stood a pewter half-pint on a rock, where it would catch the drip from the coil. The kettle sang, and began to boil at last, while he poured more cool water over the coil from time to time. A drop formed at the end of the copper tube, grew visibly, and fell into the half-pint. Another drop formed and fell; another and another, while the man watched with eager eyes.

When there was an inch or more of spirit in the pot, McCoy could wait no longer. He built up his fire, replenished the mash in the kettle, and substituted his half coconut shell for the pewter pot. Then, after ladling more cool water into the calabash, he seated himself with his back to a tree. He passed the half-pint under his nose, sniffing at the contents critically.

"I've smelt waur!" he muttered, and took a preliminary sip.

McCoy made a wry face and swallowed violently. He opened his mouth wide and blew out his breath with all his force.

"Ouf! There's nae whiskey in Scotland can touch her for strength! I've tasted waur — het from the still, that is."

He took a more substantial sip this time, coughed, sputtered, and rose to his feet. "It's water she needs just now. Gie her time! Gie her time! Ouf! A glass o' this'd set old Matty daft!"

Mixed with a small measure of water, the spirit proved more palatable, though McCoy made many a wry face as he sipped. All through the morning he kept his fire going and the kettle full, drinking the raw spirit as fast as it condensed in the coil. The sun was overhead when he allowed the fire to die out and stretched himself to sleep in the shade, with flushed face and laboured and irregular snores.

He awoke late in the afternoon, and, though his head ached unmercifully, he made his way back to the settlement in deep content.

McCoy's supply of ti had been obtained from a natural glade not far inland from the house where Martin lived with Mills. The plant, more or less rare elsewhere on the island, grew in great plenty here, and at the suggestion of the natives the glade had not been set out to yams, though it lay close in and there was no clearing to be done. In the beginning both natives and whites had eaten the sweet baked roots with relish, but the ti proved cloying after a time and the plants were allowed to flourish undisturbed.

Returning to his house in the cool of late afternoon, McCoy glanced through the scattered bush and perceived Martin in the distant glade, plying a mattock side by side with Hu. He left the path abruptly, and was surprised and displeased to see that they were grubbing up the roots of ti and casting them aside.

"What 're ye up to, Isaac?" he asked angrily.

Martin halted in his work, and the native rested on his mattock-haft. "Get on with yer work, ye lazy lout!" exclaimed Martin. "Did I tell 'ee to rest?" He turned to McCoy.

"What 's that to you?"

"Damn yer eyes! Ye 're grubbing up all the ti!"

"It 's no more yours than mine! Who wants it, anyway? I 'm going to make a yam patch here."

"*I* want it! There 's others on the island beside yersel'! Yams? Ye 've the whole place to plant 'em on."

"Aye. And walk half a mile out to work. If ye 'd a musket ball in your leg like me, ye 'd think different."

McCoy controlled his temper with difficulty. "Listen, Isaac," he said, "I 've a tooth for sweets; not a day but I grub up a root or two. There 's nae patch of ti on the island the like o' this. Ye 've scarce made a start; be a good lad and plant the yams elsewhere!"

After considerable persuasion, Martin agreed to leave the glade undisturbed. He summoned the native in a manner brutal and contemptuous, and led the way to the house, mumbling his discontent. McCoy picked up his musket and went home.

Late the same evening he was reclining with Quintal on a mat spread before the doorstep. The women and children had gone into the house to sleep. McCoy had been brooding over his argument with Martin. Sooner or later, he feared, someone more intelligent than Martin might preempt the ti patch, and put him in a position from which he would be unable to extricate himself without disclosing the secret of the still.

"Matt," he said, breaking a long silence, "did 'ee ever think o' dividing the land? We live like Indians here — sharing all hands alike; it ain't in white human natur to keep on so."

Quintal nodded.

"When I clear a bit o' land," McCoy went on, "and put in yams, or plantains, or what not, I'd like to think it's mine for good, and for little Sarah and Dan when I'm underground. Ye've young Matty to think on, and there'll be more bairns coming along."

"Aye," said Quintal, "I'm with 'ee there."

"Let every man gang his ain gait! If ye fancy yams, plant 'em for yersel'. Gin it's taro ye want, though it's nae white man's vivers to my mind, why, plant taro, and damn the rest! That's a Scot's way, and an Englishman's too."

Slow in thought and with no gift of words, Quintal had a high opinion of McCoy's sagacity. "Aye, Will," he said, "the land would divide up well. There's enough and to spare, for the nine of us. We could make a common of the west end, for the goats."

"Nine, ye swad! And the Indian men?"

Quintal grunted contemptuously. "Never mind them! Give 'em land, and they'll not work for us."

McCoy gave his companion a quick glance. "Matt! Ye're nae dowff as ye look! Aye . . . there's summat in that. But we must no put their beards in a blaze!"

One morning, about a fortnight after Quintal's talk with McCoy, Tararu was fishing from the rocks below Christian's house. The sea was calm, for this part of the coast was sheltered from the southerly swell.

Tararu was the nephew of Minarii, and well born in Tahiti, though neither his person nor his character was such as was usual among the native aristocracy. He was of low stature and slight build, and there was more cunning than determination in his face. An idle fellow, who preferred the company of women to that of men, he spent much of his time in solitary fishing excursions, which gave him an excuse to be absent when there was hard work to be done. The tuna-fishing offshore was too strenuous for his taste, and, though the others jeered at him for following a sport usually relegated to women, they were always glad to share his catch.

He squatted on a weed-covered rock, beside a shallow pool left by the receding tide. The water was deep, close inshore, at this place. Tararu's line was made of native flax, twisted on his naked thigh; his barbless hook was of pearl shell, and his sinker a pear-shaped stone, pierced at its small end to allow the line to be made fast. He baited his hook with a bit of white meat from the tail of a crayfish, whirled the sinker about his head, and cast out. The coiled line flew from his left hand, the sinker plunged into the sea twenty yards away. He drew in a fathom or two tentatively, till he felt the line taut from his stone, and squatted once more to wait for a bite.

The birds were beginning to nest, and many hundreds of them came and went about their business over the calm sea. The morning was so still that he could hear, very faintly, the clink of Williams's hammer at the forge, and the bleating of young goats on the ridge to the west. The sun was not yet high enough to be unpleasantly warm. Though his eyes were open, Tararu seemed to doze, as motionless as the black rock beneath his feet, and scarcely more animate.

But he was on the alert when at last a fish seized his bait. He did not strike as a white fisherman would have done; his incurved hook of pearl shell did not permit of that. Tararu kept a taut line, allowing the fish to run this way and that, while the hook turned and worked ever deeper into its jaw. It was a large, blue-spotted fish of the rock-cod kind, called *rod,* and weighing ten pounds or more — a rare prize. Presently, he swung it up out of the sea, disengaged the hook, and slid the fish into the pool beside him, where it sank to the bottom with heaving gills. Slowly and methodically he baited his hook once more.

The sun was high overhead and the pool well stocked with fish when Tararu coiled his line and laid it on a ledge above him to dry. The last wave but one had wet him to the ankles and streamed hissing into the pool. He opened his knife, and began to sharpen it on a flat pebble. The blade was half worn away by long use.

"Tararu! Tararu O!"

One of his countrymen was approaching, clambering down over the rocks. Tararu greeted him with a lift of the eyebrows, and held out his knife.

"Look," he said, pointing to the pool, "I have been lucky! Clean and string them while I rest."

Hu was a small, humble, dark-skinned man, whose ancestors for many generations had been servants to those of Minarii. He grunted with pain and put a hand to his side as he stooped over the pool.

"Are you hurt?" asked Tararu. "Have you had a fall?"

"Not a fall," replied the other, beginning to clean the first fish that came to hand. "Martin again."

"Did he beat you?"

"Aye . . . with a club."

"What had you done?"

Hu shook his head. "Done? How can I say? Nothing I do pleases him. We went together to the yam field. He sat in the shade and directed me at the work. The holes I dug were not deep enough, or too deep. I put in too many dead leaves when I filled them; I cut up the seed yams too fine! I am your man, and your uncle's — not Martin's slave! I told him so; then he beat me."

His hands trembled as he worked, and he caught his breath in a sob of anger. "What can I do? Will you not protect me, you or Minarii?"

Tararu reflected for some time with downcast eyes. "There is only one way," he said at last. "I dare not stir Minarii too deeply, for if trouble comes with the whites, they will take their muskets and shoot us all. Kill Martin! Kill him in a way that none will suspect."

"*Mea au roa!*" exclaimed Hu, looking up from his task with gleaming eyes. "But how is it to be done?"

Tararu leaned over the pool, fumbled among the fish remaining there, and drew forth an odd creature, about a foot long, with a small mouth and a strange square body, checkered in black and white. "With this!" he said.

"A *huéhué*," remarked the other. "I have heard that there is poison in them."

"The flesh is sweet and wholesome if the gall bladder is removed entire. The gall is without colour and has no strong taste, yet four drops of it will kill a man. Squeeze out the bladder on a bit of yam or on a pudding. He will be dead before the setting of the sun."

Hu shook his head. "Leave poisoning to wizards and old women. Not even Martin could I kill in that way!"

Tararu shrugged his shoulders, and the other went on: "But it might be done on the cliffs. He has ordered me to go with him to the Rope this afternoon. The birds are beginning to lay."

When the fish were cleaned and scaled, Hu shouldered the heavy string and followed Tararu in the stiff climb to the plateau.

Toward mid-afternoon, Martin and Smith sauntered down the path to the house of the natives. They carried egging baskets and coils of rope, and found Hu waiting to accompany them. Smith led the way to the ridge, and a short walk brought them to the verge of the cliffs hemming in the little half-moon bay. The Rope was exposed to the full force of the southerly swell, and the thunder of the breakers came up faintly from far below. Sea birds in thousands sailed back and forth along the face of the cliff.

Smith peered over the brink and dropped the coil of two-inch line from his shoulder. Making fast one end to the trunk of a stout pandanus tree, he tossed the coils over the cliff, slung his basket about his neck, and began to reconnoitre the ground. There were many nests in the scrub pandanus bushes that stood out almost horizontally from the wall of rock. Birds sat in some of them; in others, deserted temporarily during the heat of the day, he perceived the clutches of eggs. Martin was making fast his rope at a place about thirty yards away. It was his custom to take one of the natives on these egging excursions, to perform the task he had no stomach for.

Smith gripped the rope with both hands and scrambled over the brink of the cliff, pressing the soles of his bare feet against the rock. Little by little he lowered himself to a jutting rock fifty feet below, where he could rest at ease, and where he had spied two well-filled nests within reach. He had transferred the eggs to his basket when the sounds of a scuffle and angry shouting reached his ears. Smith listened for a moment, set his lips, and began to climb the ropes rapidly, hand over hand, aiding himself with his feet. At the summit, he set down his basket before he rose from his knees. Then, half running through the scrub, he made for the sound of Martin's angry voice.

"Kill me, would 'ee? Take that, ye Indian bastard! And that, God damn 'ee!"

Martin stood over the bloody and prostrate form of Hu, kicking him savagely at each exclamation. He swung about as he felt Smith's hand on his shoulder, and said, still shouting: "The bastard! Tried to rush me over the cliff, he did!" He made as if to kick the native once more, but Smith's powerful grip held him back.

"Avast, Isaac!" ordered Smith, and then, glancing down, he asked: "Is this true?"

"Aye," groaned the prostrate man, who could scarcely speak, "it is true."

Martin wrenched himself free and aimed another kick at Hu. Smith sprang on him and pulled him back roughly. "I 'll not stand by and see the like o' this!" he exclaimed.

"Damn your blood, Alex!" said Martin angrily. "I tell 'ee, he tried to push me over the cliff!"

"D 'ye think I 'm blind, man? Ye 've given him cause, and to spare!"

Anger got the better of Martin's customary caution. Smith had released him, and now stood between him and the native, who was rising painfully to his feet.

Martin clenched his fists. "This is my lay! Stand by! Or d' ye want a clout on the jaw?"

Next moment, with a light of insane rage in his eyes, he sprang forward and struck Smith a heavy blow. The smaller man grunted without flinching, put up his hands, and lowered his head. The fight was over in two minutes; Martin lay on the ground with a bruised jaw and breathing heavily through his nose. When he sat up dazedly at last, Smith spoke.

"We 'll say no more of this. . . . It 's best so. Mind what I say, Isaac, it 'll go hard with ye if I catch ye bullying this man again. And Hu, — though I can't say I blame ye much, — remember, no more such murderin' tricks!" He touched his lips. "*Mamu* 's the word!"

CHAPTER X

IT was a calm night in February 1792; the sky was cloudless and the rising moon low over the sea. The natives had supped and were reclining on the grass before their house, gossiping in subdued voices, broken by the occasional soft laughter of the women. Minarii lay in silence, hands behind his head. Tararu stood alone at some little distance, gazing up the moonlit path. Though they spoke lightly of other things, one thought was in every mind, for Hutia had not returned.

In their love of decorum, the Polynesians resemble the Chinese; to their minds, an action is often less important than the manner in which it is performed, and the appearance of virtue more so than virtue itself. Like the others, Tararu had long known where the girl spent so many hours each day, but hitherto she had conducted her affairs with discretion, taking care to put no affront upon her husband's dignity. Now at last the persuasions of Williams had overcome her fear of a scene. Turning his head slightly Minarii perceived that Tararu was gone. He sat up, seemed to reflect for a moment, and lay down once more, his lips set in a thin, stern line.

The moon was well up when Tararu emerged from a thicket near the lonely cottage of Williams. Stepping lightly and keeping to the shadows, he reached the open door and listened for a moment before he peered into the house. His wife was asleep on a mat just inside, her head pillowed on the blacksmith's brawny arm. For an instant, passion overcame his fear of Williams; had he carried a weapon, he

would have killed the blacksmith as he lay. Hutia's small
naked foot was close to the door, and Tararu stretched out
a shaking hand to rouse her. At first she only murmured
incoherently in her sleep, but when he had nearly pulled
her off the mat, she opened her eyes.

"Come outside!" he whispered fiercely.

Williams sat up. "What do you want?" he growled.

"My woman!" exclaimed Tararu, in a voice that broke
with anger. "My woman, you white dog!"

The blacksmith sprang to his feet. His fists were clenched
and his short black beard bristled within an inch of Tararu's
chin. "She's my woman now! Clear out!"

Williams looked so formidable, so menacing, that the
native cast down his eyes, but his sense of dignity would
not permit him to turn away quickly enough to please the
other man. As he turned slowly, trembling with anger and
humiliation, a kick delivered with all the strength of the
blacksmith's sturdy leg sent him sprawling on all fours. He
rose with some difficulty while Williams stood over him.
"Now will you go?" he asked truculently.

Tararu clenched his teeth and limped away up the moonlit slope.

Though the others had gone into the house to sleep,
Minarii still lay outside, wide awake, when Tararu returned.
He sat up to listen impassively to a torrent of whispered words,
and when the other fell silent his reply was a grunt of contempt.

"You call yourself a man," he remarked after a short
pause, "and come to me with this woman's tale! *Atira!*
If you want the woman, rouse her and fetch her home."

Tararu hesitated. "I did waken her," he admitted. Then
emotion got the better of him, and he went on incoherently:
"My words roused Williams — he kicked me and knocked
me down!"

Minarii's deep voice interrupted him. "Were you not my

sister's son . . ." He rose, with an expression of stern displeasure on his face. "*Tihé!* To think that I should take a hand in such affairs! Wait for me here; perhaps soft words will right the wrong. If not . . . " He shrugged his great shoulders as he turned away.

The night was warm and Alexander Smith was working in the little garden before his house. Young and Taurua had gone early to bed; Balhadi had been helping her man to water some ferns planted the day before, but drowsiness had overcome her, and she too had retired. The moon was so bright that Smith watered and raked and weeded as if it had been day. It was late when he stopped and sat down on the rustic bench by the path. He had been fishing with Tetahiti the day before, and a long siesta in the afternoon had left him with no desire to sleep.

The moon was nearly at the zenith when he raised his head at the sound of a step on the path. It was Minarii, and Hutia walked behind him, bowed and sobbing. He halted at sight of Smith.

"It is fortunate that you are awake, Alex," he said. "There is trouble — trouble that may lead to graver things." He went on to recount the happenings of the night.

"Where is Williams?" Smith asked.

"On the floor of his house," replied Minarii grimly. "He fought like a man. . . . Look!" He pointed to a great black bruise on his jaw.

Smith thought for a moment before he spoke. "We must act quickly. Only Christian can handle this. Stop here while I rouse him."

When he was gone, Minarii seated himself with his back to a hibiscus tree and the girl crouched beside him. Presently his hand fell on her shoulder in a grip that made her wince. Concealed in the deep shadow of the tree, they watched the blacksmith move down the path toward the house of Mills.

Williams was in no mood for half-measures. He limped painfully, and halted from time to time to spit out a mouthful of blood. When he had wakened Mills, they walked side by side to the house of McCoy.

"Damn him, he was too much for me!" said the blacksmith, thickly. "Had you or Matt been there, we'd have murdered him!"

Mills grunted sympathetically. "Here we are," he remarked. "I'll go in and fetch 'em."

A moment later he came out with McCoy and Quintal, rubbing the sleep from their eyes. They listened attentively to what the blacksmith had to say.

"Where are they now?" asked Quintal.

"At the Indian house, I reckon."

McCoy smiled sourly. "This'll mean a fight. Curse ye, Jack! Ye have yer woman week days and Sabbaths to boot; must ye stir up the whole island because ye can nae sleep wi' her nights?"

Williams turned away angrily. "Then stop where ye are. Come along!" he said to Mills. "We'll fetch the muskets."

"Ne'er fash yersel', Jack," put in McCoy. "We'll help ye fast enough, but it's an unchancy business for all that!"

"We'd best get it over with," said Mills. "Teach the bloody Indians their place. . . . Who's this?"

Christian was striding rapidly down the moonlit path, followed by Smith and Minarii. Hutia brought up the rear, half trotting to keep pace with the men. She longed to slip into the bush and escape, but dared not. Williams moved forward truculently when he perceived Minarii, only to fall back at sight of Christian's face.

"What is all this?" Christian asked sternly, coming to a halt.

"I made up my mind last night, sir," Williams replied with a mingling of defiance and respect. "I told my girl to stop

with me and leave her Indian for good. He came to fetch
her when we were asleep. I woke and kicked him out.
Then Minarii came." He drew a deep breath and spat out
a mouthful of blood. "He was too much for me. When I
came round, he was gone and my girl with him. What could
I do but make haste down to the settlement and fetch the
others to lend a hand?"

Minarii stood with head high and arms folded on his bare
chest. His face was impassive and sternly set. Christian
turned to him. "Shall I tell you what Williams says?"

"He has not lied."

Christian glanced down distastefully at Hutia, cowering
on the grass with her head in her arms. "Is the peace of this
land to be broken because of a loose girl and two men who
forget their manhood?"

"Well spoken!" said Minarii. "On that point we see
alike. But I cannot stand by while my sister's son is shamed
before all, and cursed and kicked by a commoner, even
though he be white."

"Then fetch Tararu. He must come at once."

As Minarii walked toward the natives' house, Christian
turned to the four mutineers. "I'm going to settle this
matter here and now!" he said. "We have had more than
enough of it. The woman shall choose the man she wishes
to live with, and there is to be no murmuring afterward.
Let that be understood."

"I'm with ye, Mr. Christian!" exclaimed McCoy.

"Aye," muttered Quintal. "That's the way to settle it."

When Minarii returned, followed by his nephew, Christian
spoke once more. "Tararu," he said, "stand forth! The
woman shall choose between you. And let the man re-
jected keep the peace."

"Stand forth, Williams," he went on. "Minarii, tell her
that she is to make her choice and abide by it."

The girl was still crouched on the grass, face hidden in her

arms.   Minarii spoke to her in a harsh voice before he pulled
her roughly to her feet.   With eyes cast down, but without
a moment of hesitation, she walked to the blacksmith and
linked her arm in his.

Autumn came on with strong winds from the west, and
fine rains that drizzled down for days together.   In early
April the weather turned so cold that the people spent much
of the time in their houses.   Situated more than seven degrees
of latitude to the south of Tahiti, Pitcairn's Island lay in the
region of variable westerly winds, and its climate was far
colder and more invigorating than that of the languorous
isles to the north.

One night in April, the wind shifted from west to southwest and blew the sky clear.   While the stars twinkled
frostily, the sleepers in the house of Mills stirred with the
cold, half wakening to pull additional blankets of tapa up
to their chins.

Mills and Prudence slept in the room upstairs, on a great
standing bed-place filled with sweet fern and covered with
many layers of soft bark cloth.   Prudence lay on her side,
her unbound hair half covering the pillow, and one arm
thrown protectingly over the tiny child who slumbered between her and the wall.

Presently the open window on the east side of the room
became a square of grey in the dawn.   The old red cock from
Tahiti, roosting in the *tapou* tree, wakened, clapped his wings
loudly, and raised his voice in a long-drawn challenging crow.
Prudence stirred and opened her eyes.   The baby was already
awake, staring up gravely at the thatch.   The young mother
roused herself, leaned over to sniff fondly at the child's head,
on which a copper-red down was beginning to appear, and
sat up, shivering.   Taking care not to waken Mills, she
threw a sheet of tapa over her shoulders, picked up the child,
and stepped lightly over the sleeping man.

With her baby on one arm, the girl climbed nimbly down the ladder, crossed the room where Martin snored beside Susannah, opened the door softly, and went out. It was broad daylight now and the glow of sunrise was in the east. Save for mare's-tails of filmy cloud, the sky was clear; the trees swayed as the strong southwest wind hummed through their tops. Prudence drew a long breath and threw back her head to shake the heavy hair over her shoulders.

In the maturity of young motherhood, she was among the handsomest of the women. Her brown eyes were set wide apart under slender, arched brows; though small, her figure was perfectly proportioned; her beautiful hair, of the strange copper color to be found occasionally among Maoris of un-mixed blood, fell rippling to her knees. Her race was the lightest-skinned of all brown folk, and the chill, damp winds of Pitcairn's Isle had brought the glow of young blood to her cheeks.

Mills was deeply attached to her, in his rough way; she had been happy with the dour old seaman since the birth of their child. Eliza raised her voice in a wail and Prudence smiled down at her as she walked to the outdoor kitchen.

"There!" she said, as she deposited the baby in a rude cradle Mills had made, and tucked her in carefully. "Lie still! You shall have your meal presently."

As if she understood, the child ceased to cry and watched her mother gravely as she struck a spark to her tinder and blew up the flame among some chips of wood. When the fire was burning well, Prudence filled the pot from the barrel of rain water and set it on to boil. She took up Eliza, seated herself on the stool used for grating coconuts, and teased the child for a moment with her breast, offered and with-drawn. Soon the baby was suckling greedily; after a time, before the kettle had boiled, her eyelids began to droop, and presently her mother rose to place her in the cradle once more, sound asleep.

Prudence now took some eggs and half a dozen plantains from a basket hanging out of reach of rats, and dropped them into the boiling water. From another basket she took a breadfruit, cooked the day before. She heard Mills at the water barrel, washing his face, and turned to greet him as he appeared at the kitchen door. He stooped over the cradle and touched the sleeping baby's head with a stubby thumb.

"Liza, little lass," he said, "ye 've a soft life, eh? Naught but eat and sleep."

Prudence set food before him, and stood leaning on the table as he fell to heartily. "I am hungry for fresh meat," she said. "See, the weather has changed. Take your musket and kill a hog for us."

Mills swallowed half of an egg and took a sup of water before he replied. "Aye, that I will, lass. Fire up the oven, for I 'll not fail. Ye must eat for two, these days."

When he was gone and she had eaten her light breakfast of fruits, she spread a mat in the shelter of the banyan tree by the forge, and fetched her sleeping child and an uncompleted hat she was weaving for Mills. Susannah was stirring in the kitchen, but Martin would not be on foot for another hour or two.

Prudence glanced up from her work at the sound of a footstep and saw Tararu approaching, an axe on his shoulder. She had scarcely laid eyes on him since the trouble with Williams; he had ceased his former gossiping and flirtatious way with the women, and spent most of his time in the bush. He caught her eye and made an attempt to smile. Polynesian etiquette demanded that some word be spoken, and he asked, in a hoarse voice: "Where is Mills?"

"Gone pig-hunting," she replied.

The *Bounty's* grindstone stood close by, near the forge. Tararu took the calabash from its hook, filled it at the water barrel, and replaced it so that a thin trickle fell on the stone. Picking up his axe, he set to work. Prudence bent over her plaiting, glancing at the man from time to time out of the corner of her eye. He ground on steadily, first one side of the blade and then the other, halting occasionally to test the edge with his thumb. An hour passed.

Something in Tararu's manner, and in the meticulous care with which he worked, struck the girl as out of the ordinary. He was a lazy, shiftless fellow as a rule.

"Never have I seen an axe so sharpened!" she remarked. He grunted, intent on his task, and she went on: "What is your purpose?"

He looked up and hesitated for a moment before he replied. "I have been clearing a field for yams. Yesterday I found a *purau* tree, tall, straight, and thick. To-morrow I shall fell it, and begin to shape a canoe."

As he went to work once more, Prudence's quick mind was busy. Canoe-building was practised in Tahiti only by a guild of carpenters called *tahu'a*, which included men of all classes, even high chiefs. Minarii was an adept, but Tararu knew no more of the art than a child of ten. Yet why should he lie to her?

After a long time the axe was sharpened to Tararu's satisfaction, bright and razor-edged. He shouldered it, gave Prudence a surly nod, and walked away into the bush. The girl took up her child, gathered her work together absently, and went into the house, deep in thought.

When she reappeared, a mantle of tapa was thrown over her shoulders, and she carried her child, warmly wrapped against the wind, on one arm. She had plaited her hair in two long, thick braids, twisted them around her head, and pinned them in place with skewers of bamboo. Walking with the light and resilient step of youth, she took the path that led past Smith's house and Christian's, and up, over the summit of the Goat-House Ridge. Half an hour later, she was approaching Williams's lonely cottage. At some distance from the door she halted and gave the melodious little cry with which a Polynesian visitor announced his presence to the inmates of a house.

Hutia appeared at the door and greeted the other without a smile.

"Where is your man?" asked Prudence.

"At work in the bush."

"Hutia," said the younger girl earnestly, coming close to her old enemy, "you and I have not been friends, but should anything happen to Williams, my man would never cease his mourning, for the two are like brothers."

"Come into the house," Hutia said, her manner changing. "The wind is over cold for *aiu.*"

She took the baby from the younger girl's arms and covered the little face with kisses before she closed the door. "Now tell me what is in your mind," she went on.

Prudence recounted at length how Tararu had sharpened his axe, how he had replied to her question, and her own suspicions. The other girl's expression turned grave.

"Aye," she said at last, "I fear you are right. He is a coward at heart and will come by night if he comes."

"So I think," replied Prudence. "Who knows? I may be wrong, but you will do well to warn your man."

"Guard him, rather; I shall tell him nothing. He would only mock me for a woman's fears. If I convinced him of danger, he would go in search of Tararu, bringing on more trouble with Minarii. No. We have two muskets here. I can shoot as straight as any man!"

Prudence stood up after a time and took her child. "I must return to light the oven," she remarked. "Mills has gone to shoot a pig."

"Let us be friends from now on," said Hutia. "There is no room for bad blood on this little land."

When the young mother was gone, Hutia set about her household tasks, and greeted Williams with her usual cheerful and casual manner at dinner time. But when he had supped that evening, and stretched himself out, dead-tired, she waited only until certain that he was in a sound sleep before making her preparations. In the light of a taper of candlenuts, smoking and sputtering by the wall, she loaded the two muskets, measuring the powder with great care, wadding it with bits of tapa, and ramming the bullets home with patches of the same material, greased with lard. The last skewered nut was ablaze when the task was finished, giving her time to see to the priming and wipe the flints carefully before the light flickered and winked out. With a heavy musket in each hand she stepped softly across the room and out into the starlit night. Like many of the women, Hutia understood firearms thoroughly.

The house had only one door. Shivering a little in the chill breeze, she stationed herself in a clump of bushes, one musket across her knees, the other standing close at hand. Even in the dim starlight, no one would be able to leave or enter the house unperceived, and she knew that two hours from now she could count on the light of the waning moon.

A long time passed while the girl sat alert and motionless. At last the sky above the ridge began to brighten and presently the moon rose, in a cloudless sky, over the wooded mountain. The shadow of the house took form sharply; the clearing was flooded with cold silvery light, bounded by the dark wall of the bush.

It was nearly midnight when Hutia turned her head suddenly. Pale and unsubstantial in the moonlight, the shadowy figure of a man was moving across the cleared land. The girl cocked her musket as she rose. Tararu approached the cottage slowly and softly. When he was within a dozen yards of her, Hutia stepped out into the moonlight.

"*Faaea!*" she ordered firmly, in a low voice. He gave a violent start and endeavoured to conceal his axe behind him. "Come no closer," she went on, "and make no sound. If you waken Williams he will kill you. I know why you are here."

Tararu began to mumble some whispered protestation of innocence, but she cut him short, scornfully. "Waste no words! It is in my mind to shoot you as you stand."

Hutia's hands were shaking a little with anger. Her former husband was only too well aware of her high temper and determined recklessness when roused. With a suddenness that took her aback, he sprang to one side and bounded away across the clearing, axe in hand. She raised the musket and took aim between his shoulders. For five seconds or more she stood thus, her finger on the trigger she could not bring herself to pull. She lowered the weapon, watched the runner disappear into the bush, and turned toward the cottage.

When Williams rose next morning, he found Hutia up before him as usual and his morning meal ready.

"Ye 've a weary look, lass," he remarked. "Sleep badly?"

"Aye — I had bad dreams." She looked up from her work. "The sea is calming down. I shall go fishing this morning, in the lee."

The blacksmith nodded. "Good luck to ye. I could do with a mess of fish!"

Toward noon of the same day, Tararu was at work on a small clearing in the Auté Valley. None of the men, save Martin perhaps, had a deeper dislike of work; his chief object in clearing the little yam field was to be alone. He was beginning to hate the house of the natives, where he now spent as little as possible of his time. Their ideas of courtesy prevented an open display of contempt, but Minarii treated him coldly, and he could not face the disapproval in Tetahiti's eye. The morning was cool, and he plied his axe with more diligence than usual.

Tararu's basket of dinner hung from the low branch of a *purau* tree at the edge of the clearing, and he was working at some distance, unaware that he was not alone. Peeping

through a screen of leaves, Hutia had reconnoitred the cleared
land and was now approaching the basket cautiously, unseen
and making no sound.   She glanced at the man, whose back
was turned to her, reached into the basket, took out a large
baked fish, done up in leaves, and unwrapped it, crouching out
of sight.   Glancing up warily once more, she squeezed something which had the appearance of a few drops of water into
the inside of the fish, holding it carefully to give the liquid
time to soak in.   A moment later the fish was wrapped up
and returned to the basket, and Hutia disappeared, as
quietly as she had come.

Ten minutes had passed when Tararu glanced up at the
sun and dropped his axe.   As he strolled across to where his
basket hung, he heard a cheerful hail and saw Hu.

"You 've not eaten?" asked the newcomer.   "That is well.
I 've brought you some baked plantains; the women said you
had none."

"Fetch a banana leaf to spread the food on, and you shall
share my meal."

The servant was the only one of his countrymen whose
manner toward him had not changed; Tararu was grateful
for the little attention and glad of his company.   They ate
with good appetites, gossiping of island trivialities, and when
the last of the food was gone both men lay down to sleep.

CHAPTER XI

ONE afternoon Christian was trudging up the path that led to the Goat-House Ridge. Toiling to the summit, he left the path and turned north along the ridge, to make his way around to the seaward slope of the peak. His path was the merest cranny in the rock, scarcely affording foothold, but he trod the ledge with scarcely a downward glance. Deeply rooted in the rock ahead of him, two ironwood trees spread gnarled limbs that had withstood the gales of more than a century; a goat would have been baffled to reach them by any way other than Christian's dizzy track.

Reaching the trees, he lowered himself between the roots to a broad ledge below and entered a cave. It was a snug little place, well screened by drooping casuarina boughs — ten or twelve feet in depth, and lofty enough for a tall man to stand upright. Half a dozen muskets, well cleaned and oiled, stood against the further wall; there was a keg of powder, a supply of bullets, and two large calabashes holding several gallons of water.

The cave was a small fortress, where a single resolute man might have held an army at bay so long as he had powder and lead. It was here that Christian spent an hour when he wished to be alone, lost in sombre reflections as he gazed out over the vast panorama of lonely sea and listened to the booming of the surf many hundreds of feet below. For the situation of the mutineers and the native men and women with them he felt a deep and tragic sense of responsibility, and since the passing of the frigate he had realized that sooner

or later their refuge was certain to be discovered. He had
resolved not to be taken alive when that day came.

Christian now took up his muskets, one after the other,
and concealed them with his powder and ball among the
roots of the further ironwood tree. When nothing but the
calabashes of water remained in the cave, he made his way
back to the ridge and took the path to the settlement, walking
rapidly. He found Maimiti with her baby, Charles, seated
on a mat in the shade of a wild hibiscus tree. Nanai, the
wife of Tetahiti, was beside her. Thursday October
Christian, a sturdy boy of two, had trotted down the path
to Young's house, where he spent much of his time with
Balhadi and Taurua, childless women who loved the small
boy dearly.

"Come with me," said Christian to his wife. "There is
something I wish to show you. You'll look after the baby,
eh, Nanai?"

"Shall we be gone long?" Maimiti asked.

"Till sunset, perhaps."

She followed her husband up the trail to the ridge and
along the breakneck path to the ironwood trees. When he
lowered himself to the ledge before the cave and held up his
arms for her, she gave an exclamation of surprise.

"*Ahé!* No one knows of this place!"

"Nor shall they, save you. I want no visitors here!"

He seated himself on the ledge, with his back to the wall
of rock, while Maimiti examined the cave with interest.
Presently she sat down beside him and they were silent for
a time, under a spell of beauty and loneliness. Sea birds
hovered and circled along the face of the cliff below, the
upper surfaces of their wings glinting in the sun and their
cries faintly heard above the breakers. The wind droned
shrilly through the foliage of the ironwood trees, thin, harsh,
and prickly. At length Christian spoke.

"Maimiti, I have brought you here that you may know

where to find me in case of need. I love this place. Sometimes, in its peace and solitude, I seem to be close to those I love in England."

"Where is England?" she asked.

He pointed in a northeasterly direction, out over the sea. "There! Across two great oceans and a vast island peopled by savage men. Such an island as your people never dreamed of, so wide that if you were to walk from morning till night each day it would take three moons to cross!"

"*Mea atea roa!*" she said wonderingly. "And Tahiti — where is my island?"

"Yonder," replied Christian, pointing to the northwest. "Are you no longer homesick? Are you happy here?"

"Where you are, my home is, and I am happy. This is a good land."

"Aye, that it is." He glanced down at her affectionately. "The cool weather is wholesome. Your cheeks grow pink, like an English girl's."

"Never have I seen boys stronger and better grown than ours."

"All the children are the same. And since we came here not a man or a woman has been ill. Were not some of the fish poisonous, our island would be like your *Rohutu Noanoa*, a paradise."

"Do you believe that Hu and Tararu died of eating a fish?"

He turned his head quickly. "What do you mean?" he asked. "Surely they died of poisoning; they were known to have eaten a large fish declared to be poisonous in Tahiti."

"The *faaroa* is harmless here; I have eaten many of them."

"What do you mean?" he repeated, in a puzzled voice.

She hesitated, and then said: "It was whispered to us by one who should know. The others suspect nothing. What if Tararu hated Williams more bitterly than we supposed? What if he sharpened an axe expressly to kill him by night,

and found Hutia waiting with a loaded musket, outside the
door? I think she made it her business to poison Tararu's
dinner, and that Hu partook of the food by chance!"

Christian knew that suspicion was foreign to Maimiti's
nature, and the seriousness of her words made him look
up in astonishment. "But have your people poisons so
subtle and deadly?" he asked.

"Aye, many of them, though they are not known to all.
Hutia's father was a sorcerer in Papara, an evil man, often
employed by the chiefs to do their enemies to death. The
commoners believe that such work is accomplished by incantations; we know that poison is administered before the
incantations begin."

Christian remained silent, and she went on, after a pause:
"The others suspect nothing, as I said."

He sighed and raised his head as if dismissing unpleasant
thoughts from his mind. "It is ended," he said, rising to his
feet. "Let us speak no more of this."

Three years had passed since the arrival of the *Bounty* at
Pitcairn, and the little settlement presented the appearance
of an ordered and permanent community. The dwellings
had lost their look of newness and now harmonized with the
landscape as if they had sprung from the soil. Each house
was surrounded by a neat fence enclosing a small garden of
ferns and shrubbery, and provided with an outdoor kitchen,
a pigsty at a little distance, and an enclosure for fattening
fowls. As in Tahiti, it was the duty of the women to keep
the little gardens free of weeds, and to sweep the paths each
day.

Winding picturesquely among the trees, well-worn trails
led to the Goat-House, to the western slope where Williams
lived, to the Auté Valley where the principal gardens of the
cloth-plant had been laid out, to the yam and sweet-potato
patches and plantain walks, to the rock cisterns Christian had

insisted on building in case of drought, to the Rope, and to the saw pit, still used occasionally when someone was in need of plank.

The smithy, under the banyan tree by the house of Mills, looked as if it had been in use for many years. The vice and anvil bore the marks of long service; the bellows had been mended with goatskin, to which patches of hair still clung; there was a great pile of coconut shells close to the forge, and another of charcoal made from the wood of the *mapé*. The ground underfoot was black with cinders for many yards about.

The life of the mutineers had become easy, too easy for the good of some. Quintal, Martin, and Mills had taken to loafing about their houses, forcing most of their work on Te Moa and Nihau. Happy with the girl who had given him so much trouble in the past, Williams saw little of his friends. Smith and Young worked daily, clearing, planting, or fishing for the mere pleasure of the task.

For more than a year McCoy had kept the secret of the still. Only a Scot could have done it, one gifted with all the caution and canny reserve of his race. Little by little he had exhausted the principal supplies of ti, and for many months now he had been able to obtain no more than enough to operate his still twice or, rarely, three times each week. A small stock of bottles, accumulated one by one, were hidden where he concealed the still when not in use; by stinting himself resolutely, he managed to keep a few quarts of his liquor set aside to age. In this manner, which had required for some time a truly heroic abstinence, McCoy was enabled to enjoy daily a seaman's ration of half a pint of grog.

His temperament was an unusual one, even among alcoholics. When deprived of spirits, he became gloomy, morose, and irritable, but a glass or two of rum was sufficient to make him the most genial of men. Mary had been astonished and delighted at the change in him. He conversed with her for an hour or more each evening, laughing and joking in the manner the Polynesians love. He romped with two-year-old Sarah and took delight in holding on his knees the baby, Dan. With his grog ration assured, there was no better father and husband on the island than McCoy.

He longed to make a plantation of ti, but decided after much thought that the risk was too great. Explanations would be lame at best, and the sharper-witted among his comrades would be certain to suspect the truth. Meanwhile, he realized with a pang that the island produced only a limited supply of the roots, bound to be exhausted in time. Even now, fourteen months of distilling had so diminished the ti that McCoy's cautious search for the roots, scattered here and there in the bush, occupied most of his waking hours. He took the work with intense seriousness, and though by nature a kindly man, not inconsiderate of others, he now joined heartily with Quintal in forcing Te Moa to perform their daily tasks in the plantations and about the house. If the native was remiss in weeding a yam patch or chopping firewood, McCoy joined his curses to Quintal's blows. The unfortunate Te Moa was rapidly sinking to the condition of a slave.

After Hu's death, Martin had similarly enslaved Nihau, and Mills, seeing that his neighbours were comfortable in the possession of a servant who did nearly all their work, soon fell into the same frame of mind. The natives resented their new status deeply, but so far had not broken out in open revolt.

On a morning in late summer, McCoy set out on one of his cautious prowls through the bush. He took care to avoid the clearings where others might be at work, and carried only a bush knife and a bag of netting for the roots. Making for a tract of virgin bush at the western extremity of the Main Valley, where he had formerly spied several plants which should be mature by now, he was surprised and displeased, toward eight o'clock, to hear the strokes of a woodsman's axe not far ahead. He concealed his bag, which contained three or four smallish roots, and moved forward quietly, knife in hand and a frown on his face.

Tetahiti was a skilled axeman who loved the work. He was felling a tall candlenut tree, and each resounding stroke bit deep into the soft wood. Warned by a slight premonitory crackle of rending fibres and the swaying of branches over-head, he stepped back a pace or two. A louder crackling followed; slowly and majestically at first, and then with a rushing progress through the air, the tree which had weathered the gales of many years succumbed to the axe. McCoy had just time to spring aside nimbly as it crashed to earth.

"Who is that?" called Tetahiti, in dismay.

"It is I, McCoy."

"Had I known you were there . . ."

McCoy interrupted him. "*Eita e peapea!* It was my fault for approaching unannounced." He was irritated, but not on account of the tree. "What are you doing here?" he asked.

The native smiled. "You have heard the men of Tahiti call me 'Tupuai taro-eater.' We love it as the others love their breadfruit. I never have enough, so I am clearing this place, where the soil is rich and moist."

"Aye," said McCoy sourly, as he caught sight of several splendid ti plants hitherto concealed by the bush, "the soil is good."

Tetahiti pointed to where he had thrown together several roots larger than any McCoy had seen. "Where the ti flourishes as here, taro will do well." Seeing the other stoop to examine the roots with some show of interest, he went on: "These are the best kinds; the *ti-vai-raau*, largest of all, and the *mateni*, sweetest and easiest to crush."

"Are you fond of it?"

"No, its sweetness sickens me. But I thought I would fetch in a root for Christian's children."

"Then give me the rest."

The native assented willingly, and before long McCoy was trudging over the ridge and down toward his still, bent under a burden far heavier than usual. His thoughts were gloomy and perplexed as he prepared a ground oven to bake the roots.

It was late afternoon when he returned to the house. He found Quintal alone, sitting on the doorstep with his chin in his hands. His expression was morose, and he seemed to be thinking, always a slow and painful process with him.

"What's wrong, Matt?" asked McCoy.

"The Indians, damn their blood!"

"What ha' they done?"

"It's Minarii. . . . I'd a mind to put Te Moa to work on my valley — ye know the place, a likely spot for the cloth-plant. I took a stroll up that way and found Minarii clearing the bush. 'Chop down as many trees as ye like,' said I, 'but mind ye, this valley is mine!' He looked at me cheeky as a sergeant of marines. 'Yours?' he says. 'Yours? The land belongs to all!'"

"Did ye put him in his place?"

Quintal shook his head. "There'd been bloodshed if I had."

"Aye, he's a dour loon."

"We was close enough to a fight! It was the thought of Christian stopped me; I want him on my side when the trouble comes."

McCoy nodded slowly. "Ye did right; it's a fashious business, but we'll ha' peace gin we divide the land."

"How'll we go about it?"

"We've the right to a show of hands. I'll see Jack Williams, and Isaac, and Mills; we'll be five against the other four. Then we'll go to Christian."

Quintal brought his huge hand down resoundingly on his knee. "Ye 've a level head!   Aye, let every Englishman have his farm, and be damned to the rest!"

"Ilka cock fight his ain battle, eh?" said McCoy, with a complacent grin.

Late the next evening Tetahiti was trudging up the path from the cove. He had been fishing offshore since noon, and carried easily, hanging from the stout pole on his shoulder, nearly two hundredweight of albacore. At the summit of the bluff he set down his burden with a grunt and seated himself on a boulder to rest for a moment. He glanced up at the sound of a step on the path, and saw that Te Moa was approaching at a rapid walk.

"I was hastening down to help you," said the man apologetically.

"Let us stop here while I rest," Tetahiti replied; "then you can carry my fish to the house. There is enough for all."

"I must speak!" said Te Moa after a short silence. "I can endure no more!"

"Are the white men mistreating you again?"

"They take me for a dog! Quintal sits in his house all day, like a great chief. McCoy is always away in the hills; I think he has secret meetings with some of the women. In the beginning I did not dislike these men; I shared their food as they shared in the work, and McCoy smiled when he spoke, but they are changed, and little by little I have become a slave. Have you noticed Quintal's eyes? I fear him — I believe he is going mad."

"Aye, I have seen him on his doorstep, talking to himself."

"What can I do? If I displease him, he beats me, both he and McCoy."

Tetahiti flushed. "They are dogs, beneath a chief's contempt! Let them work for themselves. Cease going to their house."

"I fear Quintal.   He will come and fetch me."

"Let him try!"   Tetahiti's deep voice was threatening.
"I will deal with him.   We have been patient, hoping to avoid
bad blood.   Once he affronts you in public, Christian will
put an end to all this."

He rose and helped the other to shoulder the heavy load of
fish.

Half an hour later, stopping at Quintal's house to give
Sarah a cut of albacore, Te Moa found the women alone.
"They are gone to Christian's," Mary explained, "on some
business that concerns them all.   Best wait till morning to
distribute your fish."

The sun had set, and in the twilight, already beginning to
lengthen with the approach of spring, the mutineers were
seated on the plot of grass before Christian's house.   He and
Young sat on a bench facing the men.   Williams was the
last to arrive.   The hum of talk ceased as McCoy rose to his
feet.

"Mr. Christian," he said, "there's a question come up that's
nae to be dismissed lightly.   Ye've bairns, sir, as have I, and
John Mills, and Matt Quintal here.   We've them to think
on, and the days to come.   A man works best on his ain
land.   The time's come, I reckon, to divide up the island,
giving each his share."

Christian nodded.   "Quite right, McCoy!" he said heartily.
"Mr. Young and I were speaking of the same thing only last
week.   As you say, a man works with more pleasure when
the land is his, and the division will leave no grounds for
dispute after we are dead.   The island can be divided so that
each will have a fair share; I have already given the matter
some thought.   A show of hands is scarcely necessary.   Are
there any who disagree?"

"Not I, sir!" said Alexander Smith, and there was a chorus:
"Nor I!   Nor I!"

"Then it only remains to survey the place and see that all

are dealt with fairly.   Mr. Young and I will undertake the
task, and propose boundaries for the approval of all hands.
Let us meet again one evening, say a fortnight from now."

"Ye 've an easy task, sir," remarked McCoy; "John Mills
and I was talking of it an hour back.   The island 'll divide
itself natural into nine shares."

"Nine!" exclaimed Christian.   "Thirteen, you mean."

"Surely ye 're nae counting the Indians, sir?"

"Would you leave them out?"

"There 's nae call to share with 'em."

Christian controlled his temper with an effort.   "Is this
your idea of justice, McCoy?" he asked quietly.   Alexander
Smith spoke up.

"Think of Minarii, Will!   Think of Tetahiti!   How
would they feel if we did as ye propose?   There 's land and
to spare for five times our numbers!   We 'd be fools to stir
up bad blood!"

"We 've oursel's to think on, Alex," replied McCoy stubbornly.   "Oursel's and our bairns.   The Indians can work
our lands and share what they grow."

"That 's my notion!" put in Martin approvingly.

"I 'm with 'ee, lad!" remarked Quintal, and Mills exclaimed: "Aye!   Well spoke!"

"Listen!" ordered Christian quietly.   "Think of the consequences of such a step.   All of you know something of
the Indian tongue.   They have a word, *oere*, which is their
greatest term of contempt.   It means a landless man.   Two
of our four Indian men were chiefs and great landowners on
their own islands.   Would you reduce them to the condition
of *oere* here?   Attempt to make them slaves, or dependents
on our bounty?   We have land and to spare, as Smith says.
To leave the Indians out of the division would be madness!
Their sense of justice is as keen as our own.   Do you wish to
make enemies of them, who will brood over their grievances
and hate us more bitterly each day?   Make no mistake!   I

would feel the same were I treated as you propose to treat these men who have been our friends!"

McCoy shook his head. "I can nae see it that way, sir. We 've oursel's to think on, and we 've the right to call for a show of hands — ye promised that!"

"Mr. Christian is right," said Young. "Such a course would be madness. Bloodshed would come of it — I 'm sure of that!"

Brown ventured to remark, "Well spoken, Mr. Young," but he shrank before the black look Martin turned on him.

"We want a show of hands, sir," growled Mills, "and we want it now!"

"You 're in the right," Christian said sternly. "See that you don't misuse it! McCoy's proposal is folly of the most dangerous kind! So be it. . . . Shall we divide the island into nine shares, leaving the Indians out?"

McCoy raised his hand, as did Quintal, Mills, Williams, and Martin. They were five against the other four.

"One thing I must insist on," said Christian, after a moment's pause. "The decision is so serious, so charged with fatal consequences, that you must give it further thought. We shall meet again, the first of October. I trust that one or more of you will change his ideas on reflection, for the step you propose would be the ruin of our settlement. Yes, the ruin! Think it over carefully, and before you go each man is to give me his promise to say nothing of this to the Indians."

Young and Christian remained seated on the bench after the others were gone. Neither man spoke for some time. The evening was warm and bright with stars.

"They hold the Indians in increasing contempt," said Young, "and would make slaves of them, were it not for you."

Christian smiled grimly. "Make a slave of Minarii? Or of Tetahiti? For their own sakes I hope they attempt nothing so mad!"

"They are no better and no worse than the run of English seamen, but a life like ours seems to bring out all that is bad in them.   They are better under the stern discipline of the sea."

"They 'll get a taste of it if they persist in this folly! McCoy is at the bottom of this!   Unless he has changed his mind when we meet to settle the matter in October I shall be forced to take stern measures, for his own good!"

"Aye, we are facing a crisis.   I fear it was a mistake to give them the vote.   You 'll have to play the captain once more, to save them from their own folly!"

Young rose to take his leave.   When he was gone, Christian entered the house and climbed the ladder to the upper room. The sliding windows were open and the starlight illuminated the apartment dimly.   He crossed the room on tiptoe to the bed-place where Maimiti and her two boys slept under blankets of tapa.   Maimiti lay with her beautiful hair rippling loose over the pillow; the younger boy slept as babies sleep, with small fat arms thrown back on either side of his head.

Presently Christian descended the ladder and lit a taper of candlenuts in the lower room.   The *Bounty's* silver-clasped Bible lay on the table; he took up the book and began to read while the candlenuts sputtered and cracked.   He read at random, here and there, as he turned the pages, for he could not sleep and dreaded to be alone with his thoughts. The Bible, which had brought comfort to so many men, brought none to Christian that night.

"And the Lord passed by before him," he read, "and proclaimed, The Lord, The Lord God, merciful and gracious, long-suffering, and abundant in goodness and truth, keeping mercy for thousands, forgiving iniquity and transgression and sin, and that will by no means clear the guilty; visiting the iniquity of the fathers upon the children, and upon the children's children, unto the third and to the fourth generation."

The man sighed as he turned the pages, and presently he read: "I will punish you seven times more for your sins. . . . I will scatter you among the heathen, and will draw out a sword after you. . . . And upon them that are left alive of you I will send a faintness into their hearts in the lands of their enemies; and the sound of a shaken leaf shall chase them; and they shall flee, as fleeing from a sword; and they shall fall when none pursueth."

Christian closed the book slowly and set it down on the table at his side. He covered his face with his hands, and sat bowed, elbows on his knees. The last of the candlenuts burned down to a red glow and winked out, leaving the room in darkness, save for the faint starlight that found its way through the window.

Though the bearing of the five trouble-makers grew more arrogant with the assurance that the land would soon be theirs and the Maoris their bondsmen, three weeks passed without an open break. Minarii and Moetua were building a house in the small valley Quintal considered his own; the native had disregarded with contempt Quintal's warning that he was a trespasser and only McCoy's dissuasion had prevented a serious quarrel between the two. "Bide yer time, mon," the Scot admonished him more than once. "Ye 've only to do that and we 'll put him off all lawfu' and shipshape." Quintal watched the building with an increasing dull anger. "Bide the devil!" he would growl in reply. "Wait till his house is finished. . . . I 'll show him who owns the land!" McCoy would shrug his shoulders impatiently. "It 's nae beef nor brose o' mine, but ye told Christian ye 'd bide!"

Minarii's house was small, since only he and his wife were to live there, but it was handsomely and strongly built, with a thatch of bright yellow pandanus leaves and a floor of flat stones chinked with sand. It stood in the new clearing, on a slope of Quintal's valley.

Tetahiti had helped the builders with the ornamental lashings of the ridgepole, and on the morning when the house was finished, toward the end of the month, he strolled up to admire the completed work. Minarii was sprinkling sand from the watercourse into the chinks of his stone *paepae*, and straightened his back as he perceived the other approach.

"Come in!" he called.

"It is finished, eh?" remarked Tetahiti, glancing critically about the single lofty room. "You two have worked well. A pretty house! You of Tahiti are more skillful carpenters than the men of my island."

"It is but a bush hut. Nevertheless we shall soon come here to live. It is in my mind to make a large enclosure for the breeding of swine."

Tetahiti nodded. "Aye. Pigs thrive on this island."

"Let us go inland together. I was about to set out when you came. Yesterday, in the Auté Valley, I marked down a sow with eight young pigs of an age to catch."

The other shook his head. "I am going back to the house to sleep. It was dawn when I came in from the night fishing."

The sun was overhead when Tetahiti awoke from his siesta. He lay on a mat in the shade of a *purau* tree near his house, and for a moment, while he collected his thoughts confused by dreams, he stared up wild-eyed at the broad, pale green leaves which made a canopy overhead. Hearing his wife's footstep, he sat up, yawning.

Nanai was approaching with a basket of food. She smiled at her husband as she set down his dinner beside him on the mat.

"Have you slept well?" she asked. "Nihau prepared your meal. There's a joint of cold pig, and baked plantains, and fish of your own catching with coconut sauce."

She retired to a little distance while he ate, and fetched him a calabash of water to rinse his hands when the meal was done.

"Tetahiti," she said earnestly, "there is something I must tell you while we are alone. You must know, though I cannot believe it true." He nodded to her to go on, and she continued: "Susannah told me, swearing me to secrecy. Martin told her, she said. When I tell you, you will understand why I break my word."

"*Faaite mai!*" ordered Tetahiti, a little impatiently.

"Susannah says that the whites have had a meeting, unknown to us, and have decided to portion out the land, setting stones on the boundaries of each man's share."

"You cannot believe it?" he interrupted. "Why not? It is our ancient custom and would avoid dissension here."

"Aye, but let me finish. She says that the Maori men are to be left out of the division, that you will be *oere* from now on, slaves to work the lands of the whites."

Tetahiti laughed scornfully. "A woman's tale!" he exclaimed. "You know little of Christian if you suppose he would allow such a thing!"

"I told you I did not believe it!" said Nanai.

She left him, a little piqued in spite of herself at his reception of the news. The man lay down once more, hands behind his head. Though incredulous of Susannah's tale, he could not dismiss the thought of it, and little by little, as he reflected on certain things that had seemed without significance hitherto, and on the increasingly overbearing attitude of the whites, the seed of suspicion took root in his mind. He rose slowly and took the path to Martin's house.

He found the woman he sought alone. Mills was at work in the bush, and Martin lay snoring in the shade of the banyan tree. Though dark and by no means pretty, Susannah had once been a pleasant, light-hearted girl. Three years of Martin had broken her spirit. She went about her household duties mechanically, and rarely smiled. She gave a start at the sound of Tetahiti's voice. He beckoned her to the doorway, and asked in a low voice: —

"The tale you told Nanai . . . is it true?"

"She told you?" asked Susannah nervously.

"Aye. It was no more than her duty. Did you invent this woman's story?"

"I told her only what Martin told me."

He glanced at her keenly, perceived that she was speaking the truth. "Why should he invent such lies?"

"Lies?" said Susannah, shrugging her shoulders. "Who knows? Perhaps it is the truth!"

Martin awakened suddenly, perceived Tetahiti at the door, and sprang to his feet. He came limping across to the house. "What d' ye want here?" he asked, unpleasantly.

Tetahiti turned slowly and looked at the black-browed seaman with stern disdain. "To learn the truth. I think your words to this woman were lies!"

"*Aué! Aué!*" moaned Susannah, wringing her hands.

"What words?" asked Martin, unable to return the other's glance.

"That you white men have portioned out the land among you, unknown to us, and that we are to be left landless! Did you tell her that?"

Martin stood with downcast eyes. "No," he muttered after a moment's pause; "she must have invented the tale."

The native took one stride, seized him by the neck, and shook him angrily. "You lie! Now speak the truth lest I choke it out of you!" He released Martin, who stood half crouched, his knees trembling visibly. "Have you agreed to portion out the land?"

Reluctantly the seaman met the angry native's eyes. "Aye," he replied, sullenly.

"And *we* are to be left out of the division?"

Martin nodded once more, and Tetahiti went on still more fiercely: "Did Christian consent to this?"

"Aye."

Without further speech Tetahiti turned on his heel and

strode off rapidly in the direction of Christian's house. Pale
and badly shaken, Martin stood watching him till he was
out of earshot, before he entered the house, seized Susannah
by the hair, and began to cuff her brutally.

Christian had taken a brief nap after his dinner, and when
he awakened Maimiti was standing in the doorway, a basket of
tapa mallets in her hand. Balhadi stood outside. Seeing
that he had opened his eyes, Maimiti said: "We are going to
Brown's Well to beat the cloth."

He sat up with a sharp twinge, for he had had a headache
since dawn and felt irritable and out of sorts. "Let Balhadi
go. Don't work to-day. Who knows at what moment the
pains may begin!"

"Our child will not be born before night."

"Then work at something here if you must work. It is
madness to go inland at a time like this."

Usually the most affectionate and docile of wives, Maimiti
was now in one of the perverse humours which accompany
her condition. She shook her head stubbornly. "I desire
to go, and I am going. Men do not understand these things!"

He said no more as the two women turned away and
walked down the path. He was thinking, in a mood of de-
jected irritation, of the gulf which divided Polynesians and
whites. No man respected the good qualities of the natives
more, but they seemed willful as children, believing that the
wish justified the act, and living so much in the present
that they were incapable of worry, of plans for the future,
or of ordered thought. He rose and stood in the doorway,
with a hand on his aching head.

The short, burly figure of Alexander Smith appeared beneath the trees. He was coming down the path from the
Goat-House, and perceiving Christian at the door, he approached, holding up a rusty axe.

"I found it, sir!" he announced.

"Good! Where?"

"On the ridge. Where Tetahiti was felling that *tapon* tree."

Christian sighed as he took the axe and felt its edge absently. "It 's the best I have left. The Indians! When they finish a bit of work, no matter where, they drop their tools and forget where they 've left 'em. . . . They 're all alike!"

Smith grinned. "Ye 're right, sir! D 'ye think I can learn my old woman to put things back where they belong? Not if we was to live in the same house for a hundred years!"

"Aye, there are times when they would try a saint."

Presently Smith took leave of Christian, who went into the house once more and lay down on his settee. The violent throbbing of his headache moderated as he closed his eyes; he was drifting into a troubled sleep when the sound of rapid steps aroused him.

Never in his life had Tetahiti entered any man's house — chief's or commoner's — without the customary hail and pause for the invitation from within; to do so was a most flagrant breach of the first law of Polynesian courtesy. But now he entered Christian's garden, strode up the path without a halt, and in through the open door.

Christian opened his eyes. Before he could speak the man was standing over him with a scowl on his face, blurting out in a voice vibrant with anger: "Is it true? True that you whites have held a secret meeting? That you have dared to divide the land among you, leaving us as *oere*, as slaves?"

Taken completely by surprise, Christian said: "Who told you this?"

"No matter!" replied Tetahiti furiously. "Is it true?"

"Yes . . . no . . . let me explain to you . . ."

"I knew it!" the other cut him short.

Christian controlled his temper with an effort. "Sit down, Tetahiti. I will explain."

"Explain! There is nothing to explain. It is shame I feel that I should have regarded you as my friend! A chief? You are no better than Quintal! Aye, no better than Martin, that base-born hog!"

The white man sprang up and faced the other so sternly that he recoiled a pace. Then, composing himself with a violent effort, he went on: "Sit down! You must know . . ."

The native interrupted him fiercely: "Enough!" He spun on his heel and flung himself out through the door. "Wait!" called Christian in a voice anxious and peremptory. There was no reply.

Tetahiti strode down the path to Bounty Bay, glancing neither right nor left, nor returning the salutations of his countrywomen in the houses of the mutineers. He found his wife awaiting him at the door. She had been watching his approach with anxious eyes.

"Where is Minarii?" he asked gruffly.

"Is it true?"

"Where is Minarii?"

"He has not been here; I think he is at his new house in the bush. Is it true?"

He made no reply; Nanai took his arm and gazed up anxiously at his face. He shook her off without a word and turned away as abruptly as he had come.

It was mid-afternoon; a still, warm day in early spring. The trees shadowing the lower parts of Quintal's valley were beautiful with the pale green of new foliage; a clear, slender brooklet, revived by recent rains, trickled down the watercourse. While still at some distance from the house of Minarii, Tetahiti became aware of a faint scent of burning wood; glancing up, he perceived that a column of smoke rose above the tree-tops ahead. As he reached the edge of the clearing, he gave a deep exclamation of astonishment.

Only a pile of smouldering embers marked the spot where the newly completed house had stood. Close by, with arms folded, and head bent as if deep in brooding thought, he perceived the gigantic figure of the chief. Minarii turned his head as the other approached.

"What is this?"

"I did not see it done. It is Quintal's work!"

They were silent for a time, both staring at the embers with sombre eyes. At last Tetahiti said: "Let us sit down, Minarii. There is something you must know."

CHAPTER XII

THE house of Quintal and McCoy had long been in darkness. Their sleeping rooms were on the upper floor, divided by a partition of matting. The ground floor was used as a common room and was furnished with two tables, some roughly made chairs and benches, and a cupboard used for food and to contain various household utensils. Some time after midnight, Minarii stole silently out of this dwelling and proceeded in the direction of Christian's house. A light was burning there, for Maimiti was in labour with her third child, and a number of the women were gathered to assist Balhadi, who was the most skillful midwife among them. Minarii advanced with the greatest caution and halted at the edge of the clearing, where he crouched for some time, listening and watching. It was a clear, starlit night, and he could make out the forms of Christian and Young walking back and forth across the grassplot on the north side of the house, and those of various women seated on the bench by the open doorway.

Withdrawing as noiselessly as he had come, he crossed the belt of forest land, skirting some of the nearer gardens of the settlement until he came to a footpath leading over the western ridge. Crossing the ridge and descending the slope for some distance, he struck into another path which entered the ravine which the white men called Temple Valley by reason of its having been set aside by Christian for the use of the native men in the practices of their religion. This valley, narrow and rocky, was, in fact, little more than a gorge, and near the head wall, in a cleft not a dozen paces across, the natives had erected the stone platform that served as their *marae*. The path leading to it was steep, winding over the roots of great trees and among rocks that had fallen from the heights above; but Minarii was familiar with every foot of the way, and, dark as it was, he proceeded without hesitation. Mounting steadily, he came at length to a huge boulder that all but blocked further passageway. Here he halted.

"Tetahiti?" he called, in a low voice.

"*È, teié,*" came the reply, almost at his side.

The darkness was intense; scarcely a gleam of starlight penetrated the foliage of the great trees overarching the ravine. Minarii seated himself with his back to the rock. "The others have come?" he asked.

"We are here," a voice replied.

"Listen well," said Minarii. "In the house of Quintal and McCoy there were, as you know, two muskets. I have taken these, and the powder and ball kept by them. You have done what was agreed, Tetahiti?"

"I have the muskets from Young's house, and Nihau has those of Mills and Martin. We have powder and ball for twenty charges."

"Will not the weapons be missed?" Nihau asked.

"That is a chance that must be taken," said Minarii.

"I have my ironwood club," said Nihau. "I care not whether I carry a musket."

"You speak foolishly," Minarii replied. "We have not to do with men of our own race, here. Our purpose is to kill them, and quickly. I have my club, but I shall carry a musket as well, and you shall do the same."

"It must now be decided whether any are to be spared," said Tetahiti. "I am thinking of Christian."

"Wait," said Minarii. "Let us first consider the others. Five I can kill with joy in my heart — Quintal, Williams, Martin, Mills, and McCoy."

"We waste words in speaking of these," Tetahiti replied.
"I long to see them dead," Nihau added, fiercely, "and
their bodies trampled in the mud!"

"Good. Four remain. We must be of one mind about
them. Tetahiti, speak now of Christian."

"You ask a hard thing, Minarii. He is a brave and good
man, and our friend."

"Our friend?" There was scorn in Minarii's voice.
"Does a friend insult his friends? He is a chief in his
own land. He knows you and me to be chiefs in ours.
And he has agreed to divide the land among his own
men, leaving us with nothing, as though we were slaves!
Had he spit in our faces, the shame could not have been
greater."

"Your anger is just," Tetahiti replied, "but what he has
done was not meant to shame us, this I know."

"And how do you know?"

"This is what he once told me: his men must have a
voice here, equal with his own. Those who are strongest
in numbers have their will, even against the desire of their
chief."

"That is a lie!" Minarii replied. "One of two things
must be true: either he is no chief, as we have believed, or
he wishes to shame us. The first cannot be so. Would he be
ruled, then, by pigs of men such as Quintal and Mills and
Martin? Would he bow to them in a thing so important as
the division of our lands if he did not wish us ill?"

"I have nothing to reply," said Tetahiti. "My mind is
as dark as your own; yet I cannot believe that Christian
wishes to shame us."

"Why, then, should he do so?" Minarii asked. "A chief
does what he wills. Christian and Young shall both be
killed," he continued, quietly. "Let their deaths be at my
hands. Even though it were as you have said, do you not
see that they must die? The blood of their countrymen

would cry out for ours. Christian and Young are men. They would take their just revenge upon us."

Tetahiti was long in replying. "It is true," he said at length. "There is no other way. But understand this, Minarii: he who kills Christian shall call me friend no longer."

"Let that be as it will," Minarii replied, grimly. "The island is large enough. You can go with your women to one side. I will go with mine to the other."

"Minarii," said Tetahiti, "Brown is your friend. Is he to be spared?"

"He is like my brother, a younger brother. He has nothing but good in his heart. He will see us coming and suspect nothing. Who could strike him down?"

"It can be done," said Te Moa. "Let him be among the last when our blood is hot and the lust for killing upon us all. I could do it then."

"If Christian is not to be spared, Brown shall die," said Tetahiti.

"I see that it must be so," Minarii replied; "but you shall not touch him, Te Moa! Tetahiti shall kill my friend, since I am to kill his. But see that you do it swiftly, you man from Tupuai!"

"My hand shall be as steady as your own. His death shall be as swift as you make that of Christian."

"It remains to be seen whether this land will seem as large as I thought, with the white men dead," said Minarii. "It may be too small to hold us two."

When Tetahiti replied, the anger was gone from his voice. "Enough, Minarii. Let there be no hot words between us. I see that my friend must die. Can you be blind to the need of death for your own? His life, alone, among the slayers of his countrymen would seem to him worse than death. Do you not see this?"

"I see it," Minarii replied, coldly. "Let no more be said of him."

"One remains to be spoken of. What of Smith?"

"A brave and good man who has done none of us harm," said Nihau. "Evil is the need that calls for his death."

"There is no other way," said Minarii. "It must be as Nihau says."

They were silent for some time; then Minarii again spoke. "I say this for you, Nihau, and Te Moa. We four have nine to kill. There must be no blundering, and you must do exactly as we say."

"So it shall be," Nihau replied.

"The plan shall be in your hands, Minarii," said Tetahiti. "It falls to you of right as the older man."

"I am content," Minarii replied, "and I must be obeyed as you would obey a chief in war."

"It is agreed," said Tetahiti.

"This is not war, and it will be a shame to us forever that we must kill men as hogs are killed for the oven; yet it must be done."

"If we used no secrecy in this affair, Minarii, but challenged those five to fight us four?" asked Tetahiti.

"That is spoken like a chief," said Minarii. "It is what I, myself, would most desire, but Christian would never allow them to accept such a challenge; then our purpose would be known and our chance for killing them gone."

"We could wait," said Nihau, "making a pretence of friendship until their minds were again at rest. When they believed we had forgotten we could fall upon them as we plan to do now."

"Speak no more of this," said Minarii, sternly. "Could you wait in patience for such a time? If I have my way they shall all be dead before another sun has set."

"If it is willed," said Tetahiti. "That must first be known."

"It is willed that they shall die; that is certain," said Minarii. "Whether or not it shall be in the coming day we shall soon know."

The strip of sky above them was now suffused with a faint ashy light, sifting like impalpable dust into the gloom of the ravine. Soon the dim outlines of trees and rocks and the crags above them could be discerned, and the forms of the men, who had long been only voices in the darkness, were revealed to each other. Minarii sat by the boulder where he had first halted. He was a man of commanding presence. Naked, save for the strip of bark cloth about his loins, he seemed equally unconscious of the chill dampness of the night air and of the long fatigue of his motionless position. Tetahiti sat near him, his back to a tree and his legs outstretched. The thick mantle of tapa around his shoulders was wet and limp with the heavy night dews. Nihau and Te Moa were seated on the lowest of the roughly laid stone steps that led to the *marae*. The ravine was extremely narrow at this point, and beyond the stone platform the fern and moss-covered head wall rose toward the ribbon of sky in a series of giant steps of basaltic rock.

Presently Minarii rose. Nihau and Te Moa made way for him as he mounted the stone staircase to the platform of the *marae*. Tetahiti removed his mantle and followed, the other two bringing up the rear. They waited in silence at the summit of the staircase while Minarii retired to a small thatched house at one side of the *marae*. He appeared a moment later in his ceremonial robes, whereupon Tetahiti proceeded to the rocky recess where the casket containing the god was kept. This was brought to the altar stone in the centre of the platform. All four now took their places at the kneeling stones and the ceremony of awakening the god was carried out. A moment of deep silence followed; then Minarii made his prayer: —

"Our God, who listens: hear us!
Judge, Thou, if we have summoned Thee amiss.

Judge, Thou, if our wrongs are great and our cause just.
Known to Thee is the cause before tongue can speak;
Therefore it is told.
If our anger is Thy anger, let it be known!
If the time favours, speak!"

A few moments later the four men filed down from the *marae*, and as soon as they were beyond sacred ground Minarii halted and turned to face his companions.

"Our success is sure," he said, "and now we must not rest until they are all dead."

"What is first to be done?" asked Tetahiti.

"You and I should return to the village," said Minarii. "Our absence may be wondered at, but if we two go down they will suspect nothing."

"I have promised to obey you," said Tetahiti, "but this thing I cannot do. Maimiti's child must now have come. I cannot face her and Christian, knowing what we have to do."

"That was to be expected, and we shall not go down," Minarii replied. "Nihau alone shall go."

"What shall I do there?" Nihau asked.

"Tell the first woman you meet that I am hunting pig, with Williams, and that you three will be fishing until evening from the rocks below the western valley. Go now and return quickly."

The path from the settlement to the western valley crossed the high lands a little below the Goat-House Peak. Here it branched, a second trail leading southward along the ridge to the partially clear lands of the Auté Valley. The ridge was bare at the junction of the two paths, and at this point was a rustic bench used as a resting place on journeys across the island. Not far to the right rose a small heavily wooded spur which commanded a view of the ridge and of the valleys on either side. Here Minarii, Tetahiti, and Te Moa now lay concealed, awaiting the return of Nihau.

The sun had not yet risen, but a few ribbed clouds, high in air, glowed with saffron-coloured light. A faint easterly breeze was blowing, fragrant with the breath of sea and land. The summit of the spur was only a few yards in extent. Tetahiti and Te Moa, their muskets beside them, lay at a point directly above the junction of the two paths. Minarii watched the steep approach from the settlement. That people were astir there was evident from the thread-like columns of wood smoke that rose straight into the air above the forests until caught by the breeze, which spread them out in gossamer-like canopies above the dwelling houses. The houses themselves were hidden from view; not even the clearings, some of them of considerable extent, could be seen from above. Save for the smoke, the island, in whatever direction, presented the appearance of a solitude that had never been disturbed by the presence of man.

Half an hour passed. Minarii crept back to where the others were lying. A moment later Nihau appeared; he crossed the open space by the rustic bench and plunged into the thicket to the right. When he had joined them the four men crouched close, talking in low voices.

"They suspect nothing," said Nihau. "I met Nanai, Moetua, and Susannah on their way to the rock cistern. They will be making tapa to-day."

"You saw Christian?" asked Tetahiti.

"No. He and Young are still at Christian's house. Maimiti's child was born just before the dawn."

"Is the child a boy or a girl?"

"A girl."

"What men have you seen?" asked Minarii.

"Only Smith, carrying water down from the spring to Christian's house."

"Minarii, it is a hard thing to kill Christian on this day when his child is born," said Tetahiti.

"It is a hard thing," Minarii replied, "nevertheless we shall do as we have planned, and now two of us shall go quickly to Williams's house and not return to this place until he is dead."

"Then he shall fall at my hands," said Tetahiti. "Christian may work in his yam garden to-day. He may be the first to come this way and I would not be the one left to meet him here."

"That is as it should be," said Minarii. "Te Moa shall go with you. See that Williams's woman is not allowed to escape. Take her and bind her. Carry her to the lower end of the small valley behind Williams's house. She must be left there until we come to release her."

"It shall be done," said Tetahiti.

He grasped his musket and was about to rise when Minarii laid a hand on his arm. A moment later Hutia appeared on the path leading from Williams's house. She carried a basket with a tapa mallet projecting from it, and was humming softly to herself as she sauntered along the path. Upon reaching the bench she seated herself there for a moment to examine a scratch on her leg. She wet a finger and rubbed the place; then she held her small pretty hands out before her, regarding them approvingly as she turned them this way and that. The valley was all golden now in the light of the just-risen sun. The girl rose and stood for a moment looking down over the forests. Still singing, she went lightly down the path and disappeared among the trees.

"It is plain from this that our god was not awakened unwisely," said Minarii. "He is ordering events to suit our purposes and now none of you can doubt that this is the day appointed for what we must do."

"I see it," said Tetahiti. "Wait here. We shall soon return."

Followed by Te Moa, he made his way through the thick bush below the spur, and was soon lost to view.

"It will be well if Christian comes now," said Nihau.
"Nothing shall be done here," said Minarii. "If any
turn into the path for the Auté Valley, we will follow. If
they go down into the western valley, we will wait here
until Tetahiti returns. Now watch and speak no more."

Christian and Young were seated in a small open pavilion
on the seaward side of Christian's house. Christian held his
eldest child, now a sturdy lad of three years, on his lap.

"You must make haste, Ned," he was saying, "else I shall
have such a start as you will never be able to overcome."

Young smiled. "Taurua and I are both envious of you
and Maimiti," he replied. "The poor girl is beginning to
fear that we are to have no children."

"Taurua? Nonsense! She'll bear you a dozen before
she's through. What a difference children will make, here,
in a few years' time! What a change they have brought
already!"

"What are we to do in the matter of their education?
Have you considered the matter at all?"

"Mine shall have none, in our sense of the word," Christian replied.

"You shan't teach them to read and write?"

"What end would it serve? Consider the difficulty we
should have in trying to give children, who will know life
only as they see it here, a conception of our world, our
religion. Let their mothers' religion be theirs as well. Save
for the cult of Oro, the war god, the Indian beliefs are as
beautiful as our own, and in many respects less stern and
savage. We believe in God, Ned; so do they. It would
be a mistake, I think, to mingle the two conceptions."

"You may be right," Young replied, doubtfully; "and
yet, when I think of the future . . ."

"When our children are grown, you mean?"

"Yes. What would our parents think, could they see

their grandchildren, brought up as heathens, worshiping in the Indian fashion?"

Christian smiled, bleakly. "There's small chance of their ever knowing of these grandchildren."

They were silent for some time. Christian sat stroking the thick black hair of the solemn little lad on his lap. "If the chance were offered, Ned, of looking into the future, would you accept it?"

"I should want time to consider the matter," Young replied.

"I would; whatever it might reveal, I should like to know. What would I not give to see this boy, twenty years hence, and the second lad, and the little daughter born this morning! God grant that their lives may be happier than mine has been! It is strange to think that they will never know any land but this!"

"We can't be certain of that."

"Not completely certain, but chances are strongly against any other possibility. We must make it a happy place for them. We can and we shall," he added, earnestly. "But get you home, Ned, and sleep. Your eyes look heavy enough after this all-night vigil."

"They are, I admit. And what of yourself? Why not come to my house for a little rest? We shan't be disturbed there."

"No, I feel thoroughly refreshed, now that Maimiti's ordeal is over. This evening I shall call the men together. Whether they will or no, the division of land shall be altered to include the Indians and on equal terms with ourselves."

"It is a wise decision, Christian; one we shall never regret, I am certain of that."

Christian accompanied his friend a little distance along the path. Returning to the house, he tiptoed to the door of Maimiti's chamber and opened it gently. Balhadi sat cross-legged on the floor by the side of the bed. The newly born infant lay asleep in a cradle made of one of Christian's sea chests. He crossed the room softly and stood for a moment looking down at Maimiti. She opened her eyes and smiled wanly up at him. "I knew you had come," she said. "I heard you in my sleep."

He knelt down beside the bed, stroking her hair tenderly. She took his other hand in both of hers.

"*Aué*, Christian! Such a time this little fledgling gave me! Her brothers came so easily, but I thought she would never come."

"I know, dear. Are you comfortable now?"

"Yes; how good it is to rest! Does she please you, this little daughter?"

"She will be like you, Maimiti. Balhadi and Taurua both say so. Already I love her."

"There — I am content. Balhadi, let me have her. . . . Oh, the darling! How pretty she is!"

Balhadi laid the sleeping child in the mother's arms, and a moment later Maimiti herself had fallen into a profound slumber.

On the spur overlooking the ridge, Minarii and Nihau were still waiting, so well concealed that no scrutiny from below could have revealed their hiding place; nevertheless, they had a clear view of the ridge and of the bench there which faced eastward, a little to the left of the path. The sun was well above the horizon when the sound of voices was heard from below, and shortly afterwards Mills appeared, followed by Martin. The men were bare to the waist and wore well-patched seamen's trousers chopped off at the knee. Their heads were protected by handkerchiefs knotted at the four corners. Upon reaching the summit of the ridge they halted. Martin walked to the bench and sat down.

"Do as ye like, John," he said, "I'll have a blow."

"Aye," said Mills, "ye'd set the day long if ye could have yer way."

"Where's the call for haste? Come, set ye down, man, and cool off. There'll be time enough to sweat afore the day's done."

Mills joined his companion, and for a time the two men had no further speech.

"Have ye seen Christian this morning?" Martin asked, presently. Mills shook his head. "My woman was over half the night. This bairn's a girl, she says."

"Aye; that makes seven, all told, for the lot of us, and three of 'em Christian's."

"And where's yours?" Mills asked. "What's wrong with ye, Marty, that your woman's not thrown a foal in three years?"

"Ye've no great call to boast, with the one," Martin replied. "The fault's Susannah's — that I'll warrant."

"Aye, lay it to the woman," Mills replied scornfully.

"And why not? I board her times enough. If she was a wench from home, now, she'd be droppin' her young 'un a year, reg'lar as clockwork. She's bloody stubborn, is Susannah."

"Is she takin' to ye better now?"

"She's not whimperin' for Tahiti all the while, the way she was. I've beat that out of her. . . . What's that? A shot, wasn't it?"

"Aye. That'll be Williams. Huntin' pig, I reckon."

"I've a mind to go myself this afternoon; there's a fine lot o' pig runnin' wild in the gullies yonder. What do ye say we invite ourselves to dinner with Jack? I've not seen him this week past."

"I'm willin'; but come along now. We've work and to spare, to get through afore dinner time."

"Damn yer eyes, John! Can't ye set for half an hour? The day's young yet."

"Dawdle if ye like, ye lazy hound!   I'm goin'."

"Fetch my axe from the tool-house; I'll be along directly," Martin called after him.   Mills went on without replying and was lost to view below the crest of the ridge.

Nihau turned slightly and slipped his musket forward, glancing at Minarii as he did so.   The chief, without turning his head, stretched out a hand to stay him.   In the stillness of the early morning the crowing of the cocks could be heard and the rhythmical sound of tapa mallets in the valley below.   Martin sat leaning forward, his elbows on his knees, his hands clasped loosely, gazing vacantly at the ground between his bare feet.   Presently he turned to look down the path along the ridge to his right.   Tetahiti and Te Moa were approaching, their bodies half hidden by the fern on either side of the path.   After a casual glance, Martin turned away again.   At sight of him, Tetahiti stopped short, then came quickly on, changing his musket from his right hand to his left.   As they neared, Martin again turned his head slightly to give them a contemptuous glance.

"So ye're pig-hunters, are ye?" he said, derisively.   "And where's the bloody pig?   Safe enough, I'll warrant!   Which of ye missed fire?   I heard but the one shot."

The two natives stood before him without speaking.

Martin rose, lazily.   "Give me yer piece," he said, to Te Moa.   "I'll learn ye how to put in a charge, and much good may it do ye."

He stepped forward, holding out his hand for the musket. With the quickness of a cat, Tetahiti seized him by the wrist. At the same moment Minarii and Nihau appeared from the bush at the side of the ridge.   Passing his musket to Te Moa, Nihau stepped forward and seized Martin by the other arm, and before the white man could again speak he was half pushed, half dragged along the path leading to the Auté Valley.   For a few seconds he was too astonished to offer resistance; then he held back, making violent efforts to wrench himself free.

"What's the game?" he cried, hoarsely. "Let me go, ye brown bastards! Let me go, I say! . . . John! John!"

"Loose him," said Minarii.

Tetahiti and Nihau released their holds. Minarii reached forward and grasped him by the back of the neck. Martin howled with pain in the powerful grasp of the chief, who held him at arm's length, with one hand. "Don't 'ee, Minarii!" he cried, in an anguished voice. "Don't 'ee, now!" The chief dropped his hand. "Walk," he said.

About one hundred yards beyond there was a broad slope of partially clear land. They turned off here. They had gone but a little way when Martin again halted and turned toward Minarii. His eyes were dilated with terror. He glanced quickly from one to another of the four men. "What do ye want?" he cried in a trembling voice. "Te Moa! . . . Nihau! . . . For God's sake, can't ye speak?"

Minarii again reached forward to grasp him. Of a sudden Martin's legs went limp and he fell to his knees. They lifted him up and he fell again. "Carry him," said Tetahiti. Nihau and Te Moa grasped his arms, lifting him, and carried him along with his legs dragging on the ground. At a sign from Minarii they dropped him at a spot where a great pile of brush had been heaped up for burning. Martin fell prone. He turned his head, his eyes glaring wildly. Minarii motioned to Te Moa, who stepped back, unloosing the long bush knife fastened by a thong to his belt. Martin struggled to his knees. "Oh, my God! Don't 'ee, lads! Don't 'ee kill me!" With an awful cry he sprang to his feet, but Nihau was upon him at once, and, throwing out his leg, tripped him and sent him sprawling. "Be quick," said Minarii in a contemptuous voice. As Martin again rose to his knees, Te Moa swung the long, keen blade with all his force, taking off his head at a blow.

The air seemed to be ringing still with the last despairing cry of the murdered man. The head, which appeared to leap from the body, had rolled a little way down the slope. Te Moa ran after it and held it aloft with an exultant shout, letting the blood stream down his arm. Scarcely had he done so when Mills appeared, axe in hand, at the edge of the clearing. At sight of Te Moa, whose back was toward him, he stopped short; then with a bellow of fury he rushed upon him. Te Moa turned and leaped aside just in time to save himself.

The impetus carried the white man past him, and before he could again turn and raise his axe, Minarii, concealed from his view by the brush pile, sprang out, and with a quick blow of his club broke Mills's arm and sent the axe flying from his hand. The boatswain lurched to one side, and Nihau, swinging his club at arm's length, brought it down with crushing force on the man's head.

They dragged the two bodies into the thicket beyond the clearing, where Nihau, with a clean stroke of his knife, severed the head of Mills from the trunk. Te Moa cut a small straight branch from an ironwood tree, shaving it down and rounding it, sharpening it to a needle's point at one end. Laying Martin's head on the ground, he drove the ironwood splinter through it, from ear to ear. A thong of bark was pulled through with it, and he then fastened the head at his hip, to his belt of sharkskin. Nihau did the like with Mills's head. Minarii and Tetahiti squatted near by, watching.

Minarii rose. "Come," he said. He grasped his club and his musket and made his way noiselessly through the bush toward the ridge. The others followed. They came to a little hollow under the western side of the ridge, well screened by fern and not more than a dozen paces below the junction of the paths. Here Minarii halted, and the others crouched beside him. Minarii turned to Nihau. "Watch there," he said, pointing to the spur above them. "If any come, throw a handful of earth here where we wait."

Nihau took his musket and disappeared in the fern.

"This plan was well made," said Tetahiti.

"There is no honour in killing men so; yet it must be done," said Minarii. They spoke no more after that.

Presently there was a light patter of earth and small pebbles among the fern that sheltered them. Minarii lay on his belly, and drew himself forward a little way. Several minutes passed; then they heard the light tread of bare feet along the path in front of them, and a slight rustling and rasping of the bushes on either side. Minarii pushed himself back to where Tetahiti lay. He waited for a few seconds, then rose to his knees and glanced to left and right over the top of the fern.

"Who passed?" Tetahiti asked.

Minarii avoided his glance. "You have agreed to obey me this day as you would obey a chief in war. Wait here, then — you and Te Moa."

Tetahiti rose to his knees and looked down over the thickly wooded land below them, but there was no one to be seen. Stooping, he seized Minarii's musket and thrust it into his hand. "Your club shall be left here," he said. "Go quickly."

Two hundred yards from their hiding place, on a shaded knoll, a combined tool- and store-house had been erected for the common use. Minarii crept forward until he could command a view of this house. He saw Christian appear with an axe in his hand and go on down the path. Minarii then examined carefully the charge in his musket. He waited where he was until he heard the clear steady sound of axe strokes in the forest beyond. Taking up his musket, he proceeded in that direction.

Several small clearings had been made on these upland slopes. Minarii halted opposite the second one. Christian was at work a short distance from the path, hewing down a large *purua* tree. He swung his axe steadily, with the deliberate measured strokes of a skilled woodsman. His back was toward Minarii, who approached stealthily, his musket held in one hand, until he was not ten paces distant.

"Christian," he called, quietly.

Christian turned his head. Seeing who it was, he leaned his axe against the tree. "Oh, Minarii." He straightened his back and flexed the muscles of his shoulders, turning toward the native as he did so. Of a sudden the faint smile on his face vanished. "What is it?" he asked.

For a second or two they stood regarding each other, Minarii grasping his musket in both hands. An expression of amazement, of incredulity, came into Christian's eyes, then one of sombre recognition of his danger. He stepped back quickly, reaching behind him as he did so toward his axe. With a swift movement, the chief raised his musket to his shoulder and fired. Christian staggered back against the tree; then sank to his knees, his head down, swaying slightly. Of a sudden he fell forward and lay still.

CHAPTER XIII

ALEXANDER SMITH's taro garden lay in swampy ground within a five-minute walk of the settlement. He had been at work there for some time, knee-deep in mud, clearing the weeds and water grass from around the young plants. Having reached the end of a row, he waded to firm ground, cleaned his muddy hands on the grass, and sat down to rest. Rising presently to resume his work, he stopped short, hearing his name called. For a moment he saw no one; then Jenny appeared from behind a covert and ran headlong toward him.

"What is it, Jenny?"

"Come quickly!" she said, in an agonized voice. She ran ahead of him into the forest beyond the clearing. Halting there, she was unable to speak for a moment, holding out her hands, which were smeared with blood. Then she burst into a torrent of words. "It is Brown's blood, not mine, that you see! Tetahiti has killed him! Have you heard no shots?"

"Yes, but . . ."

"Tetahiti has killed him, I tell you! They are all together — Tetahiti, Minarii, Nihau, and Te Moa. They have muskets, clubs, and knives. Three are already dead. Where is Christian?"

"He has gone to the Auté Valley."

"Then he too must be dead! Come quickly! Arm yourself!"

"Wait, Jenny! You say . . ."

"Will you come?" she cried, wringing her hands. "Mills's head I have seen! It is hanging at Nihau's belt! They are seeking you now!"

Faintly, from far to the eastward, the sound of a shot was heard.

"There! Will you believe me? It is not pig they are shooting, but men!"

She turned and sped down the slope toward the settlement. Smith ran after her and seized her hand.

"Maimiti must know nothing of this, Jenny! You understand? Now do as I tell you! Young is asleep in his house. Go and warn him. Tell him I will meet him there. I must fetch Christian's musket."

The woman nodded and sped on down the path.

All was silent in Christian's house. The door stood open. Smith entered softly. Balhadi lay asleep on the floor by the door leading to Maimiti's chamber. Smith shook her gently by the shoulder. She sat up quickly, rubbing her eyes. "*Aué!* Oh, it is you, Alex. Shh! We must not disturb Maimiti. She is having a good sleep. She needs it, poor child!"

"Where is Christian's musket, Balhadi?"

"His musket? Let me see. Yes, it is hanging on the wall in the other room."

"Fetch it, with the powder flask and the bullet pouch."

Smith returned to the door and looked out. The little glade lay peaceful and deserted. Balhadi returned with the musket. "What is it, Alex?" she asked, in a low voice. Motioning her to follow him, Smith went around the dwelling to a small outbuilding used as a storehouse.

"Listen, Balhadi, what you feared has happened. The Maoris are killing the white men . . ."

"*Aué!*"

"I have met Jenny. Three are already dead, she says. She has seen Nihau with Mills's head at his belt. Te Moa has

Martin's. Brown is dead. Christian may be, but that is
not known. Where is Young?"

"At his house, I think. Go quickly, Alex!"

"You must stay with Maimiti. Say nothing to her . . ."

"No, no! Do you think you need to tell me that? Go!
Make haste!"

Save for the clearings made for the houses and the path
to the cove, the forests of the island had been little disturbed
along the seaward slope of the plateau. Smith ran across
the path into the heavily wooded land, making his way with
great caution toward Young's house. Jenny, Prudence, and
Taurua were standing in the dooryard. Smith revealed himself at the edge of the clearing. Taurua ran toward him at
once.

"Ned is not here, Alex," she said, in a trembling voice.
"He came home to sleep — that I know. I left Maimiti
only a little time ago. Ned was not in the house when I came,
and we can't find him."

"You *must* find him!"

"We shall if he is alive, but we are afraid to call out. Two
shots have been fired in the direction of Quintal's plantation."

"I heard them. Fetch my musket, and the powder and
ball. Run!"

Taurua returned, bringing only a cutlass. Jenny followed her.

"The muskets are gone, both yours and Ned's," she said.
"They must have taken them in the night."

"Then you must keep this one for Young," he said, handing
her the weapon. "Give me the cutlass."

"What shall you do?"

"I must find Christian, if he is alive. Now go, all three
of you, and search for Young. I shall make my way to the
Auté Valley. If I find that the others are dead, I shall hide
near the Goat-House. Tell Young to come there."

He then reëntered the forest and was lost to view.

The three women separated and continued their search. Taurua, having hidden the musket, went along the seaward slope, examining every hollow among the rocks, every clump of bushes. Presently she found Young, stretched out on a grassy slope, asleep. She roused him and clung to him a moment, unable to speak; then she quickly informed him of what had happened. He gazed at her in silence for a moment.

"Ned! Are you awake?" she cried. "Do you understand what I say?"

"Only too well. Christian is dead, I fear. You say Alex left his musket for me? Why did you let him, Taurua?"

"Why? Because he is stronger than you! He can defend himself well with a cutlass."

Young rose. "I must find him at once," he said. "Where is the musket?"

Taurua went ahead. A moment later she beckoned Young to follow. Prudence and Jenny had returned to the house. There was a window at the eastern end of the dwelling overlooking the path in the direction of the cove. Prudence, her child in her arms, kept watch there. Jenny watched from the window at the opposite end of the house. Taurua brought the musket from the bushes where she had hidden it. The powder flask was half filled, and there were only four balls in the bullet pouch. Young had just seated himself to charge the musket when Prudence called softly from the window: "Hide, Ned! . . . Minarii!"

Taurua seized him by the arm and pulled him into the room adjoining. Two large chests stood there, near the bed. Young crouched between them and Taurua threw over him a large piece of tapa. Jenny concealed herself behind the curtains of the bed-place. Prudence remained at the window, crooning softly to her child. Taurua reëntered the common room and quickly seated herself on a stool in

one corner, resuming a task, interrupted some time before,
of grating coconut meat into a bowl. She had herself well
in hand. A moment later Minarii appeared in the doorway.
He now carried only his musket. He greeted them casually.
Taurua looked up, smiling. She did not trust herself to
speak at first.

"Where are you going, Minarii?" Prudence asked. "Is it
you who has been shooting pig this morning?"

"*É*," he replied, "Williams and I. We wounded a large
boar on the ridge. He ran down into the Main Valley. We
have not yet found him. Where is Young, Taurua?"

"Fishing, at the cove. He went early this morning."

Minarii glanced around the room.

"If you pass Brown's house," said Prudence, "will you
tell Jenny that I have the bundle of reeds for her? I 'll
carry it up this afternoon."

"I 'll tell her if I see her." He took up his musket, nod-
ding to the two women as he turned away.

"*A noho, orua.*"

"*Haere oé*," they replied.

He turned and went back the way he had come. Prudence
remained at the window. "We have fooled him, Taurua.
He thinks we know nothing."

"Is he keeping to the path?"

"Yes. . . . He is out of sight now."

Taurua rose and went quickly into the other room. A
moment later Young, waiting his chance, ran out of the
house and disappeared into the forest.

It was getting on toward mid-morning. Young had been
gone for some time. The three women sat on the bench
by the doorstep, talking in low voices.

"Minarii would have saved Brown?" Taurua was saying.

"He could easily have killed him had he meant to do so,"
Jenny replied. "This happened: We were weeding the yam

garden near the house. Minarii found us there. 'There is little time for words,' he said. 'Three of the white men are dead. Tetahiti, Nihau, Te Moa, and I have killed them. They shall all die except Brown. Him I will save if I can. When I shoot my musket over his head he must fall to the ground and lie as dead. He must not move till the others have passed; then let him hide in the woods. It is his only chance.' Then he fired into the air and pushed Brown and sent him sprawling. 'Go into the house!' he said to me. 'Go at once and stay there! The others are close behind.' He went on into the forest. Soon came the other three. I watched from a tiny hole in the thatch. They halted when they saw Brown lying on his face. They walked toward him and stopped again. Brown could not have heard them. He moved, turning his head a little. Tetahiti was not ten paces from him. He raised his musket and shot him through the head. When I saw what he would do, I ran from the house and sprang on him from behind, but it was too late. Then the three of them bound my hands and feet and carried me into the house. As soon as I could free myself I ran to warn Alex."

"I see how it was," said Taurua. "Minarii must have killed Christian. They must have quarreled over who should die, and . . ."

"The beast! The vile dog!" Jenny exclaimed, her eyes blazing. "Tetahiti shot my man as he lay on the ground! Aué! Aué!"

She put her head in her arms, rocking back and forth on the bench; but she made no further outcry. The time for weeping had not come. All three women were too stunned for tears.

"Nanai must have known of this," said Prudence, fiercely. "Both Nanai and Moetua must have known of what was to happen to-day, and they gave us no warning."

"You are wrong, Prudence," Taurua replied. "Minarii

and Tetahiti would never have told their wives of such a plan."

"I shall hate them forever!"

"That can be understood," said Taurua, "but they are not to be blamed. I saw them both early this morning. Had they known, I could have guessed it at once. No, they are as innocent as ourselves."

They talked in low voices, waiting, listening, hearing nothing save the crowing of cocks in the forest and the soughing of the wind through the trees. Prudence's child awoke and began to cry. She reëntered the house and took it up, nursing it in her arms as she walked the room. Taurua laid a hand on Jenny's arm. "Listen!" The two women turned their heads at the same moment. At the turn of the path below the house Mary and Sarah appeared, half running, half walking, carrying their children in their arms. Taurua and Jenny ran forward to meet them. Mary was weeping hysterically. "You know, Taurua? They have been here?" she cried.

"Tell us quickly — are your men dead?"

"They must be! Minarii . . ."

"Hush, Mary," said Sarah. "We don't know that they are dead."

"They must be! McCoy has only his bush knife. Quintal has nothing to defend himself with. How can they escape? *Aué*, Prudence! Are you here? Do you know that your man is dead? Ours will be next!"

The moment they had entered the house, Mary sank to the floor and lay there, her head buried in her arms. Taurua took up her child. "What has happened, Sarah?" she asked.

"You heard the shots?"

"Yes."

"They were fired at Quintal. He and McCoy were to make a fence to-day, and Quintal had gone up the valley to carry down some posts he had cut. He left me to sharpen his axe. I was carrying it up to him when Minarii and Te Moa stepped out from behind some bushes. Te Moa was covered with blood and he had Martin's head hanging at his belt. Minarii took the axe from me and told me to go back to the house. Just then I saw my man come out of the bush with a bundle of poles on his shoulder. I shouted to him. Minarii and Te Moa ran toward him. Both fired, but they must have missed, for Quintal ran back into the forest.

"What of McCoy?"

"He was still at the house. I ran down to warn him, and before any of them came to look for him he had time to escape."

"Had the muskets at your house been taken?" Jenny asked.

"Yes. I must have looked at the very hooks where they hung, early this morning, without wondering why they were not there."

"Who came to search the house?"

"Tetahiti and Nihau. McCoy had just gone. I asked Tetahiti if they had killed Quintal. He would say nothing, but as they went out again Nihau stopped at the door. 'You want to know if your man is dead?' he asked. 'Yes,' I replied. 'I will tell you this,' he said; 'you will be one of my women to-morrow, and Te Moa shall have Mary.' Then he ran on after Tetahiti."

"Which way did they go?"

"Inland, up the valley. What of Ned, Taurua? And Christian and Alex?"

"They are dead! They must be by this time!" Mary cried in a terrified voice. Again she broke out in hysterical weeping. She clutched and held fast to Taurua's legs. Jenny took her roughly by the shoulders. "Hush, Mary!" she said. "What a coward you are! Stop, I say! Have you no spirit?"

"Could there be a more worthless woman?" said Prudence, in her soft voice. "Leave her, Jenny; there is nothing to be done with such a thing as she is."

They tried in vain to quiet her. She became more and more hysterical, clinging to Taurua with all her strength. Sarah was, herself, on the verge of panic, but controlled herself. Of a sudden, Mary raised her head. Her eyes were dilated with terror.

"Come," she said, in a low gasping voice. "We must hide! They will kill us, too! Yes . . . they will kill us all! Shhh! Do you hear anything?"

She sprang to her feet, gazing wildly toward the door; Taurua spoke to her soothingly. "Be silent, Mary. You are in no danger. None of the women will be killed."

"Yes! Yes! You have not seen them! They are like sharks maddened with blood!"

Prudence stepped forward and struck her across the face with her open hand. "Will you be silent?" she said. The sharp blow, better than words could have done, quieted the terrified woman. She sank down again, whimpering in a low voice. Taurua lifted her up. "Come, Mary; lie you down in the other room. We will watch. No one shall harm you." The others waited in silence. Presently Taurua returned. "The poor thing has worn herself out," she said. "She will sleep, I think."

"May she sleep well," said Jenny. She held Mary's two-year-old boy on her lap. "What will this son be like," she added, "if he has his mother's nature?"

Taurua went to the door and stood for a moment looking into the forest beyond the path. "I must return to Maimiti," she said. "Balhadi is alone there. Stay here, you three."

"And wait, doing nothing, while all our men are killed?" Jenny asked. "Not I!"

"What would you do?" Sarah asked.

"One thing at least I can do. My man lies on the ground

before our house, a prey to the ants. His body shall be left
there no longer. Prudence, will you come with me?"

"No, no, Prudence! Stay!" Sarah begged. "Don't leave
me alone with Mary!"

"Sarah, no possible harm can come to you here," Taurua
said. "If they had meant to kill us, do you not think that
they would have done so before now? Jenny is right. Something may be done to help our men. Listen, Jenny, this
you shall do: Find Hutia; she may be at the rock cistern.
She will go with you. When you have cared for your man's
body, then learn if you can what ones are dead; if you can
find Alex and Young, let them know that we think McCoy
and Quintal are still living. Or, if you will, stay with
Maimiti and I will go in your place. Prudence has her
child; she must remain here with Sarah and Mary."

"Stay you with Maimiti," Jenny replied. "I will go."

So it was decided, and the two women set out on the path
to Christian's house.

It was late afternoon. Prudence sat alone on the bench
before Young's house. Sarah and Mary remained within
doors, their children around them, talking in whispers.
Mary was quiet now. Three hours had passed and nothing
had been heard, nothing seen. Prudence turned her head.
"Taurua is returning," she said. The other two women rose
and came to the door, waiting anxiously. Taurua was alone.

"Jenny has not come?" she asked.

Prudence shook her head. "We have seen no one since
you left," she replied. "Who are at Christian's house?"

"A little time after I went there, Susannah came. She was
at the rock cistern with Hutia. They knew nothing until
Jenny brought them word. Both have gone with Jenny.
We must wait."

Taurua went to the outdoor kitchen, returning with some
cold baked yams and plantains, which she placed on the table,

"Here is food," she said, "for those who need it.   Prudence, you and Mary should eat for the sake of your babies."   She prepared some food for the two older children, who seized it greedily, but the women themselves ate nothing.

Now that Taurua had come, Mary and Sarah ventured to the bench by the doorstep, and the four women sat there, talking little, peering into the forest beyond the path, streaked through with shafts of golden light.

"Maimiti has not been told?" Prudence asked.

"She had just wakened when I went back," Taurua replied. "She is so happy with her little daughter.   She said to me: 'Now, Taurua, I have nothing more to wish for.'   Every little while she would send Balhadi or me to the door to look for Christian.   How could we tell her?   How?   Who could do it?"   Her eyes filled with tears.   "*Aué*, Maimiti '*ti é!*'"   In a moment all the women except Prudence, who sat dry-eyed, forgetting themselves and their own sorrows, were weeping together for the mother of the newly born child.   "What will she do, Taurua?" Sarah asked, at length.

"We must not think of it now," Taurua replied, drying her eyes.   "And we do not yet know that he is dead.   Let us hope while we can."

The sun had disappeared behind the western ridge before Jenny returned.   Hutia and Susannah were with her.   Their kirtles of tapa were torn and soiled and their arms and legs covered with cuts and bruises.   As soon as they had entered the house, Taurua closed the doors and the wooden shutters to the windows.   "Now, Jenny?" she asked.

The women were breathing hard.   "Give us some water," Jenny said.   "Our throats are dry with dust."   They drank greedily.   "We have seen Minarii and Nihau, but no one else," Jenny began.   "They passed almost within arm's length of where we lay hidden in the fern."

"If we had had muskets we could have killed them both," Hutia added.

"They must have gone again to the Auté Valley, for they were coming down from the ridge. As soon as they had passed we went on. We went first to Hutia's house. Williams's body was lying in the doorway. He had been shot through the head. We carried him inside. Then we went to Christian's new clearing just below the ridge. We found an axe leaning against a tree half cut through. There was blood on the ground close by, but what happened there we do not know. We searched everywhere, but could not find his body.

"You saw Mills's body?" Prudence asked.

Jenny hesitated, glancing quickly at Hutia. "No," she said, "it must have been hidden."

"And you saw none of our men, Jenny? No one at all?" Sarah asked, in a trembling voice.

Jenny shook her head.

"That is not strange," Taurua said, quietly. "They lie concealed."

"They are dead!" Mary cried, burying her face in her hands.

"Hush, Mary! What a foolish woman you are! They may be together now, all of them. It must be so."

"But if they are, Taurua, what can they do without weapons?"

"Ned has a musket. Alex Smith has a cutlass. Quintal is a man as strong of body as Minarii. He will cut him a club in the bush. We have reason to hope, I tell you!"

"Do you think that Minarii will rest until they are all dead? Never! He well knows that his own life will not be safe until all the white men have been killed."

"It is true," Sarah said, wretchedly. "We shall never know peace now until one party or the other are all dead."

"And who wishes for peace until those four are killed?" Jenny exclaimed. "I saw Tetahiti shoot my man as he lay helpless on the ground. Do you think I shall rest until he himself is dead?"

"Let us speak no more of this," said Taurua. "There has been bloodshed enough . . ."

She broke off. The report of a musket shot was heard close by. Mary ran into the house, her hands pressed to her ears. The other women rose quickly and looked at one another.

"Let us go in," said Taurua, "and make ready the house. Some of our men may have to come here to defend themselves."

"And one of them may be lying dead within sound of our voices," said Jenny. "I must know what has happened. You others prepare the house." Without waiting for a reply, she ran across the path and plunged into the forest.

She quickly crossed the wooded land bordering the path. Beyond this, and not more than one hundred and fifty yards from Young's house, there was half an acre of cleared ground planted to sweet potatoes and yams. The report of the musket shot had come from this direction. Jenny halted within the border of the woodland and looked out across these gardens. She saw no one. She skirted the plantations and was about to proceed farther into the valley, when she came upon a cutlass lying half hidden by a clump of plantains. There was fresh blood on the dead leaves near by and she discovered naked footprints in the moist earth of the plantain walk a little way beyond. She had proceeded but a short distance farther, when she came upon Alexander Smith lying face down, groaning feebly. She knelt beside him, and, putting her arms around him, lifted him to a sitting position with his head resting against her shoulder. He opened his eyes drowsily. "Jenny?" he said. She examined him swiftly. The ball had entered at his shoulder and had come out at the neck. "Alex, could you walk with me to help?" He nodded. With one arm around her shoulders, he struggled to his feet, but they had gone only a few steps when his body went limp. With both arms around him, she held him for a moment and then let him sink gently down. She ran back to Young's house and returned with Taurua and Hutia. Smith was a solidly built man and it was all the three women could do to lift and carry him, but a quarter of an hour later they had him in Young's bed. He was breathing heavily and had lost much blood.

"It is a clean wound; the ball has passed through," said Taurua. "The great artery has not been touched — that is certain. Otherwise he would be dead."

The women worked quickly and in silence. Susannah carried water while Taurua and Jenny staunched the flow of blood from Smith's wound and bound it well. He was now unconscious and his face ghastly pale. Hutia kept watch by the door and Prudence by the window. The sun had set and the shadows began to deepen in the room.

"They left him for dead — that is clear," said Jenny. "Did Minarii know that he still lives, mad with killing, as he now is, he would come and club him as he lies."

"Yes," said Taurua, "and we must be prepared if they come here. I shall go now for Balhadi. Keep watch, you two. If you see any of them coming, cover Alex at once with the tapa mantle as though he were dead and kneel all of you by the bed, wailing and crying. They will believe and not molest you. When Balhadi comes she can be prepared to gash herself with a *paohino*. Seeing her face streaming with blood, they will be sure to think her man dead."

"The plan could not be better," said Jenny. "Make haste, Taurua; we shall do as you say. Balhadi must lose no time in coming."

Taurua set out for Christian's house. It was a lonely way between the two dwellings, with ancient forest trees overarching the path. She had gone about half the distance when she heard her name called, and halted. Nanai came out from behind a screen of bushes and beckoned to her, earnestly. Taurua went to where she stood and regarded her coldly, waiting for her to speak. Nanai was deeply agitated, but controlled herself.

"Hate me if you will, Taurua, for what my man has done this day," she said, "but believe, if you can, what I say: I knew nothing of their plans, and Moetua is as innocent as myself."

"I am willing to believe it," Taurua replied, "but this will not give life to murdered men. Speak quickly if you have more to say, for I have little time to spend here."

"Your man lives . . ."

Taurua grasped her by the arm. "You know this? Where is he?"

"On the Goat-House Peak, hidden in a spot where they will never be able to find him. It was I, Taurua, who told him of the place and led him there."

Taurua gazed at her searchingly. "We have long been friends," she said. "You would not deceive me — that I could never believe."

Nanai's eyes filled with tears. "You are like my own sister, Taurua, and Ned has been as a brother. Ask your heart if I could act basely toward you. But this I ask in my turn. If Ned is spared, he must put thoughts of revenge from his heart. Tetahiti is my husband."

"Though he and those with him were killed, the dead cannot breathe again. I cannot promise that his word will be given, but I shall do what I can to bring this about."

"It is enough, Taurua. Minarii is terrible in anger, but the desire for killing is short-lived. Ned has only to remain hidden. His life will be spared. Tetahiti will wish it — of that I am sure. Moetua and I will stand with you all in this."

"Alex is badly hurt. We have carried him to our house. We know nothing of Christian."

"Listen, Taurua. Moetua is close by. We shall go together in search of him. Perhaps we can help him if he still lives. Whatever has happened, I will bring you word when we know. Do what can be done to soften the hearts of the others toward us two. What our men have done is done. That cannot be forgiven, but let them know that Moetua and I are blameless."

"That I shall do," Taurua replied, "but keep well aloof from them until a later time, and most of all from these three — Jenny, Hutia, and Prudence. Their men have been murdered by your husbands. Their anger toward you can be understood."

"They shall not see us," Nanai replied.

"Now I must hasten to Maimiti," said Taurua. "Go, and good go with you for your kindness to me."

Nanai clung to her for a moment; then she turned and disappeared in the shadows of the forest.

Balhadi had seen Taurua approaching. She came quickly to the door and the two women spoke in whispers. "He will live, Balhadi, this I believe," Taurua was saying. "I would not tell you so if I thought there was no hope. But do as I have said if Minarii or the others come. Cover Alex as you would cover a corpse, and all of you wail over him as for one dead. They will believe and not molest him."

A moment later she was alone in the room. She went to the door of Maimiti's bedroom and halted there, listening; then she returned to a bench near the table, and seated herself, her chin in her hands, staring unseeingly out of the window. Her eyes brimmed with tears, and for a time she wept silently.

Presently she heard Maimiti's voice calling Balhadi. Drying her eyes quickly, she entered the room where the mother was lying.

"Balhadi has gone to her house, Maimiti."

"Oh, is it you, Taurua? Christian has not come?"

"Not yet.   Shall I light a taper?"

"There is no need.   I love this dim light of evening.   Such a good sleep I have had!   Look, Taurua, how she sucks!   She is like a little pig.   Where can Christian be?   He told me he would come early in the afternoon, and here it is past sundown!"

"He will come soon."

"Go up the path to meet him, dear.   He must surely be coming now.   What a strange father he is!   You would think he had a little daughter born to him every day!   Go quickly, Taurua.   Tell him to hasten."

Taurua nodded and turned hastily away.   She stood for a moment outside the door gazing up the path now barely discernible in the dim light of evening.   A moment later she seated herself on a bench there and buried her head in her arms.

CHAPTER XIV

In the rich little valley between Ship-Landing Point and the easternmost cape of the island, Tetahiti and Nihau lay in the fern where they had slept, conversing in voices inaudible a few yards away. The moon had set long since, but the first faint grey of dawn was in the east. Nihau sat up, shrugged his shoulders, and spat.

He began to count on his fingers. "Nine muskets we have; fourteen were landed from the ship. Five are missing, though Young may have taken that which always stood in Christian's house."

Both men started and seized their weapons at the sound of a footfall close by, but relaxed at a low hail from Minarii. He was followed by Te Moa, who carried a bunch of ripe plantains on his back. He set down the fruit, as well as four drinking nuts fastened together with strips of their own fibrous husk, and Tetahiti reached into the fern behind him for a basket of baked yams.

They ate quickly and in silence. When the meal was over, Tetahiti remained for some time deep in thought. "Minarii," he asked, "will you not consent to spare Young? Quintal and McCoy must be hunted down, but Young . . ."

"He too must die! Speak no more of this! They must all be killed, and quickly!"

"Where can the others be?" said Nihau.

"Wherever they are, they shall not live to see the end of this day."

Minarii rose, taking up his musket as he spoke. "Go with

Nihau and search the western slopes," he went on. "Waste
no more powder at long range. With Te Moa, I shall comb
this end of the island, so that a rat could not escape our eyes.
Let us meet a little after nightfall in the thicket close to
Quintal's house."

Minarii beckoned to his follower, and led the way up to
the head of the valley and across the ridge. It was a stiff
climb and both men were panting as they skulked along
the ridge to the brink of the curving cliffs called "the Rope."
Their feet made no sound on the rocky path, and, though the
stars were only beginning to pale, Minarii moved with the
alert caution born of years of bush warfare. He halted in
a clump of pandanus at the very edge of the cliff.

"I had not thought of this place," he said to Te Moa in a
low voice. "Keep watch while I scan the beach below. It
will soon be day."

He set down his musket and stretched himself out at full
length to peer down the dizzy face of the precipice at the
narrow strip of beach many hundreds of feet below. Though
the morning was windless, a southerly swell had made up
during the night, and great seas came feathering and smoking
into the shallow bay, to burst with long-drawn roars that
seemed to shake the solid rock. The spray of the breakers
hung in the air, oftentimes veiling cove and beach from the
eyes of the watcher above. Sea fowl wheeled and soared
before their nesting places.

The light grew stronger. Presently the sun's disc broke
the horizon to the east. Peering down through a tangle
of thorny pandanus, Minarii gave a sudden low exclamation.
He beckoned over his shoulder to the other man.

"I see him!" exclaimed Te Moa in a whisper. "There by
the big rock! Ah, he is gone!"

"Who is it?"

"I could not tell for the drifting spray."

Minarii reached for his musket, measured the distance

with his eye, and shook his head. Some time passed before
Te Moa whispered rapidly: "Look! At the eastern end of
the sands!"

"McCoy or Young," said Minarii. "Quintal is a span
wider in the shoulders."

The fog of salt spray closed in again; when it dispersed, the
man or men on the beach had disappeared. Minarii backed
away from the verge of the cliff and crouched in the
pandanus thicket. "What think you?" he asked. "Your
eyes are younger than mine. Are there two, or one?"

"Two, I think. Quintal and McCoy."

"Perhaps. Yet one man might have walked the distance
in the shelter of the scrub."

"Whether one or two, they are trapped," said Te Moa.
"No man could climb the cliffs nor enter those breakers and
live."

"And safe from us," remarked Minarii, musingly. "This
sea is a *miti vavau*, sprung from a distant storm. It made
up quickly and will calm down as fast. I will keep watch
here. Go you to the landing place and lash the outrigger on
our canoe. Go softly. When the work is done, hide yourself near the path at the top of the bluff. If the swell goes
down, I will hasten across to you. If not, we shall meet
as appointed, near Quintal's house."

When Te Moa was gone, Minarii settled himself to watch.
He lay as immobile as the basalt crags of the ridge. Twice
during the hours of the morning he had glimpses of a figure
below, but the swell grew heavier as a south wind made up;
the cove was now one smother of foam, half invisible under
the wind-driven spray. The sun reached its zenith and
began to decline. In spite of the south wind, it was warm
in the shelter of the scrub. Minarii grew drowsy as the
afternoon advanced. He was stifling a yawn when his quick
ear caught the sound of a footstep not far off. He took up

his musket, cocked it noiselessly, and turned his head to peer out through the matted leaves.

Twenty yards to the west, the low scrub parted and Matthew Quintal stepped out into the open, glancing this way and that. He wore a knotted handkerchief on his head, and a pair of trousers cut off roughly at the knee. His eyes were bloodshot and his great arms crisscrossed with scratches beneath the growth of coarse red hair. He came to a halt, crouching to avoid showing himself against the sky line, and began to gaze intently at the ridges and hillsides to the westward, one hand shielding his eyes from the sun.

Firearms — even bows and arrows — were regarded as cowards' weapons by the men of the island race, and Minarii hated Quintal so fiercely that he yearned to kill him with his bare hands. He set down the musket softly beside his club, and stepped out of the thicket, a look of sombre rejoicing in his eyes. Flexing the huge biceps of his left arm, he smote the muscle a resounding blow with his right hand; the native challenge to combat. The blow rang out like a pistol shot. Quintal spun on his heel; then he rushed toward Minarii.

They came together crouching, with their hands low. Minarii feinted and lashed out with his right fist, a mighty blow that drove home smacking on the other's jaw. Only Quintal's great bull neck saved him; he blinked, staggered, and rushed in under the native's guard, seizing him beneath the arms in a hug that might have cracked the ribs of an ox. Minarii grunted as he was lifted off his feet; next moment he drove his thumbs deep into his enemy's throat. With eyes starting from his head, Quintal brought his knee up sharply, and as the other released his grip and staggered back, grunting with pain, the white man sprang on him and brought him to the ground. They grappled, twisting fiercely as each strove for a throttling hold on the other's neck. Then suddenly, as they had fallen, they were up again, but this time

Quintal had his left arm braced on the native's chest, and a grip on Minarii's great sinewy right wrist. A breath too late, the warrior realized his danger. As they turned in a half-circle, his battering fist rained blows on Quintal's head, but the Englishman held on doggedly, exerting all of his enormous strength.

Next moment, with a loud snap, the bone broke. Grunting with pain and anger, Minarii wrenched himself free and got in a blow that caught Quintal unaware. His head flew back; as he stood swaying with vacant eyes, the native's uninjured hand shot up under his chin and closed on his throat. Both men were bleeding from a score of deep scratches, for they were fighting in the thorny pandanus scrub on the very brink of the cliff.

With huge fingers sunk in his enemy's neck, Minarii dragged him toward the precipice. Dazed, throttled, and in great pain, Quintal reached up feebly, felt for a finger, and bent it back with all the strength that remained to him. As the clutching hand at his throat let go, he struggled to his feet. At that moment Minarii aimed a mighty kick at his chin. Had the toughened ball of the warrior's foot found its mark, the fight would have been over; but, as it chanced, the crumbling rock on which he stood gave way. He staggered, waving his left arm in an effort to regain his balance. The white man sprang forward, seized the upraised foot of his enemy, and hurled him backward.

Quintal craned his neck and saw the warrior's body rebound from a crag a hundred feet down, crash through a thicket of dwarf pandanus standing out horizontally from the cliff, and plunge on and down, to fetch up against a stout palm-bole, five hundred feet below.

The Englishman was scarcely able to stand. One eye was swelling fast, he was scratched and bruised from head to foot, and his throat bore the red imprints of the dead man's fingers. He swallowed with difficulty, coughed, spat out a mouthful of blood, and felt his neck tenderly. Then, after a long rest with head in his arms, he set out at a limping shuffle, across the ridge and down into the valley to the west.

Only the bent and torn pandanus leaves and a sprinkle of blood here and there on the rocky ground bore witness to the combat. The sea fowl still soared before their eyries on the Rope, with the afternoon sun glinting on their wings. The sun went down at last behind the western ridge, and the bowl of the Main Valley began to fill with shadows.

In the thick bush, well back from the settlement, Tetahiti and Nihau were making their way cautiously toward the place of rendezvous. All through the day they had searched the western half of the island, without a glimpse of the men they sought. Tetahiti was in the lead. He halted as they came to one of the paths that led inland; then he seized Nihau's arm and pulled him back into the bush. Next moment Moetua came into view. She was unaccompanied.

Tetahiti called to her in a low voice: "Moetua O!"

As she turned, he beckoned her to follow him into the bush. "Where is Minarii?" she asked.

"With Te Moa, searching for the white men."

She was nearly of his own stature, and now she looked him squarely in the eyes, without a smile. "Tetahiti," she said earnestly, "have you not had enough of killing? Will you spare none?"

"All must die. Those are your husband's words. Have you seen Quintal or McCoy?"

"No. As for Young, if I knew where he was concealed I would not tell you!"

Tetahiti shrugged his shoulders. "I am of the same mind, yet Minarii is right; it is the white men or ourselves. None shall be left alive."

"Blood! Blood!" she said in a low voice as she turned away. "Men are wild beasts. To-day I hate them all!"

Te Moa was awaiting them at the rendezvous, an area of unfelled bush not far from Quintal's house. He told Tetahiti of what they had seen at the Rope, and of the chief's instructions to him.

"Here is food," he said. "You two are weary and I have done nothing all day. Sleep when you have eaten. Minarii will soon be here. I will keep watch and arouse Nihau when I can stay awake no longer."

Prudence and Hutia sat close together on the floor of Mills's house. The smaller girl caressed, from time to time, the head of the sleeping baby on her knees. The door opened softly. Hutia called in a low voice not without a slight quaver: *"Ovai tera?"*

"It is I, Jenny!"

She closed the door and felt her way across the darkened room. "Listen!" she whispered rapidly. "Our chance has come! Have you courage to seize it?"

"Courage for what?" asked Prudence coolly.

"To kill the slayers of our men!"

Prudence rose, set down her child on a bed, and came back to Jenny's side. "Now tell us what is in your mind."

"I have found Tetahiti and Nihau and Te Moa asleep. Te Moa lies with his back to a tree at some little distance from the others. His musket is between his knees. They must have posted him as a sentinel, but sleep has overcome him. We have an axe and two cutlasses. Are your hearts strong? Will your arms not falter?"

"Not mine!" said Hutia grimly.

"I claim Nihau," remarked Prudence, in her soft voice.

"Aye," said Jenny, "and Tetahiti is mine!"

Hutia slapped her knee softly. *"Eita e peapea!* I will bear my part, so that the three die. . . . But Minarii, where is he?"

"He may come soon," said Jenny. "We must make haste.

The moon will set before long. Take the cutlasses and let me have the axe."

They rose and took up their weapons. Prudence bent over her sleeping child for a moment before she left the house.

An hour passed and the moon hung low over the western ridge. Quintal was making his way down toward the settlement. He walked with a limp, slowly and cautiously, keeping in the shadows of the bush. Passing the blackened platform of stones where Minarii's house had stood, he began to reconnoitre the thicket which separated him from the cleared land surrounding his own deserted house. He was about to emerge into the moonlight when he caught his breath suddenly, halted, and whispered: "Christ!" Next moment he stooped to take up the severed head of Te Moa, and turned the face to the moon. McCoy's old cat, fetched from Tahiti, was a great night wanderer in the bush. He rubbed his back against Quintal's leg, turned away, and began to lap at something on the ground. Fiercely and noiselessly, with his bare foot, Quintal kicked him away.

He glanced this way and that, walked to a tree that stood at a few yards' distance, and came to a halt before the bodies of Tetahiti and Nihau. "All dead!" he muttered. "And a good job, too! Who could ha' done this?"

With three muskets under his arm, Quintal now took the path to the settlement.

The candlenuts were alight in the house of Mills, but the windows and doors were barred. Quintal whistled softly outside, and after a moment's pause Jenny called, "Who is it?" in an uncertain voice. He made himself known. Presently the door was unbarred and he entered the house. Prudence was on the floor, suckling her child; Hutia started to her feet nervously at sight of him.

"Where is Minarii?" asked Jenny, closing and fastening the door.

"Dead. I killed him. What Englishmen are dead? I found Jack killed by a musket ball, and the headless bodies of Martin and Mills."

Jenny told him briefly all that she knew, and he asked: "Where is Will McCoy?"

She shook her head. "Who killed the men I found yonder in the bush?" he went on.

The three women exchanged glances, and at last Jenny spoke: "If I tell you, will you keep the secret? *Parau mau?*"

"Aye!"

"They were the murderers of our husbands," said Jenny slowly. "We killed them as they slept."

Quintal blinked bloodshot eyes as his slow mind considered this information. "Damn my eyes!" he exclaimed. "Women's work, eh?"

"Listen," Jenny said. "It was our right and duty to kill these men. But their wives may have other thoughts. They must not know the truth. There has been trouble enough on this unhappy land. Will you tell the others that you killed those three?"

"Aye, if you wish it; why not?"

"You will tell no one, not even Sarah?"

"No. Where is she?"

"At Young's house."

Prudence covered her breast and laid the sleeping child on Mills's bed. "We are glad to have you here," she remarked. "We feared Minarii, and the spectres of the newly dead!"

Quintal limped across to Mills's bed-place and lay down. Hour followed hour while the three women whispered nervously and lit fresh tapers of candlenuts. At last the stars paled before the light of dawn. When the last of the fowls had fluttered down from the trees, Hutia slipped out of the house. Jenny was moving about in the outdoor kitchen, and Prudence sat astride a rude little three-legged stool by the door, grating coconuts. Presently the basket was full and she stood up.

"*Pé! Pé! Pé!*" she called, ringingly, while the fowls began to run with outstretched wings, increasing their speed as the girl flung out handful after handful of the crinkled snow-white flakes. She upturned the basket, dusted her hands, and entered the house. Quintal still slept heavily, face turned to the wall. Prudence bent over her child, her lips caressing the cool little forehead. She took a comb of bamboo from the shelf above the bed, seated herself on the doorstep, and began to undo the long and heavy plait of her hair. Shaking her head impatiently, she raised a hand to dash the tears from her eyes.

Mary and Sarah were approaching the house, leading McCoy's children and Quintal's boy. As Prudence glanced up, Sarah asked, "Where is he?"

"He still sleeps."

Without rising, she moved a little to let the older girl pass into the house. Mary stood before her, her eyes red with weeping. McCoy's two children clung to the folds of her kirtle.

"Has Matt seen my man?"

Prudence shrugged her shoulders. She felt only contempt for this soft, unready woman who became hysterical when it was time to act.

Sarah was kneeling at Quintal's side. He turned uneasily and opened his eyes. His two-year-old son was trying to climb on to the bed. The father's eye brightened and he smiled.

"Up, Matty!" He lifted the child to his side. "There's a stout lad! Eh, Sarah, old wench!"

"Where is McCoy?" she asked.

"Dead, like enough. We must search for him."

He rose, stretching his muscles gingerly, limped out through the back door to the water barrel, and dashed a calabash of water over his head. His injured leg had stiffened during the night, and he found it next to impossible to walk. Sarah spread a mat for him close to the door and fetched him a breakfast of half a dozen ripe plantains. He ate half-heartedly, for he was only beginning to realize the full extent of the catastrophe. Will McCoy dead, no doubt, and Christian, too. And Jack Williams . . . old John Mills. Murdering bastards, those Indian men. Damn their blood, why couldn't they have kept the peace? Alex Smith would probably die, from what the women said. Quintal drew a deep breath and raised his head. The woman beside him leaned forward at sight of his gloomy face.

"Ye must help me," he said, "I can scarce walk. There's naught to hurt ye in the bush; take Mary and make a search for Will. The children can stop with me."

"Where shall we search?"

"Try the eastern cape. Let Mary follow the ridge west above Tahutuma. If ye don't find him, there, work down the Main Valley. He may be living; hail him, from time to time, on the chance."

Sarah nodded as she rose, but Mary would not go until Jenny agreed to accompany her. Sarah set out to the east, while the other two crossed the Main Valley to the ridge.

The sea had calmed during the night. The sun was about an hour up and the morning cool and cloudless. Sarah glanced fearfully this way and that as she walked. Now and then she stopped and hailed: "Will! Will O! Will McCoy!" but for some time her clear hails died away without a response in the morning calm.

When she had turned inland and was gazing down over the broad wooded bowl of the plateau, she heard a faint rustle in the bushes and a hoarse voice.

"Sarah? Are ye alone?"

"Yes."

"Duck down off the sky line! Where's Matt?"

McCoy was close to her now, and she started as the leaves were pushed aside and his haggard face appeared, ugly with a three days' growth of red stubble. He stared wildly at her, as though doubting her word.

"Where's Matt?" he asked again, in a low voice.

"At the house. Come back with me. They are all dead."

"Who are dead?"

"All of the Maori men."

"And the Englishmen?"

"Come back with me. Quintal will tell you."

"Are ye speaking truth?"

"Yes!" replied Sarah impatiently.

Some rat or lizard made a slight rustling sound among the dead leaves a few yards off. McCoy gave a violent start and peered about him in terror. The shirt and ragged trousers he wore were wet with salt water. He scrutinized the woman suspiciously.

"Fetch Matt. I'll believe it when he tells me."

Sarah shrugged her shoulders wearily. "There is nothing to fear. Yet I will fetch him if you wait."

"Be off!"

When she was gone, he moved cautiously through the bush to higher ground, where he could overlook the rendezvous without being seen.

While McCoy awaited the coming of his friend, Taurua was walking rapidly along the western side of the plateau, toward Christian's yam plot. From time to time she called softly: "Moetua! Nanai!" At last, in a thicket near the steep path leading to the ridge, she found those she sought.

The two girls sat by a litter of *purau* saplings lashed with bark. Christian lay on this rude couch, ghastly pale and with a stubble of black beard on his chin. His eyes were closed; only his rapid, shallow, and laboured breathing showed that he lived. Moetua and Nanai sat cross-legged by the stretcher, moistening bits of tapa with cool water from a calabash and laying them on the wounded man's forehead. His fever, perilously high, dried the cloths fast.

Moetua looked up at the newcomer with the slight smile courtesy demands of her race, but the sight of Taurua caused her to rise instantly.

"What is it, Taurua?" she asked, with a tremor in her voice.

Nanai stood up, twisting her hair hastily into a knot and scanning Taurua's face anxiously. "Aye, speak out!" she said.

The other girl cast down her eyes and drew a long breath. "I would that another might have told you," she said slowly. "I am the bearer of ill tidings. . . ."

"Speak!" commanded Moetua.

"Your husbands . . . both are dead, and Te Moa and Nihau."

Moetua's face turned pale. After a long time she said, "The gods have forgotten. There is a curse on this unhappy land." Nanai stood with bowed head. The taller girl put a hand on her shoulder, and turned to Taurua once more. "Who killed Minarii?"

"Quintal has killed them all."

"Young had no hand in it?"

"No."

Moetua's eyes were full of tears as she looked Taurua straight in the face. "You are sure?"

"Sure! I swear it!"

Taurua turned away and sank down on her knees beside Christian. "The fever consumes him," she said to Moetua. "We must carry him to Young's house."

"Go back to Maimiti. We will fetch him down," said Moetua.

When she was gone, the two girls sat for some time in silence, with bowed heads and stony eyes. At last Moetua rose and made a sign to Nanai to take up one end of the litter.

Carrying their burden easily, and still in silence, they took the path to Young's house.

They found Young with Balhadi in the room. Alexander Smith lay in the bed on the seaward side, unconscious and with closed eyes. Though he had lost much blood, his face was flushed with fever. Balhadi sat beside him on a stool. She looked up at the sound of footsteps outside the door.

Without a glance or a word of greeting, the two girls carried the litter into the room, set it down by the bed opposite Smith's, and lifted Christian's unconscious body on to the fresh spread of tapa. Young rose as they entered and was about to speak when he caught sight of Moetua's face. Still without a word, she turned and beckoned Nanai to follow her out through the door.

Young crossed the room hastily to Christian's side. He listened to the wounded man's breathing, opened his shirt with gentle fingers, removed the dressing of native cloth, and examined the wound. As he rose from his knees his eyes met Balhadi's anxious glance.

"Can he live?" she asked.

"He must!" he replied, in a low voice. "He must and he shall!"

CHAPTER XV

THE American sealing vessel *Topaz* was steering west-by-south with all sail set, before a light air at east. The month was February and the year 1808. Her captain, Mayhew Folger, was one of the first Yankee skippers who were beginning to round the Horn, venture into the Spanish waters off the American coast, and steer west into the vast and little-known South Sea, in search of sealskins, whale oil, or trade.

The *Topaz* was ship-rigged, and, although small, she had the sturdy weather-beaten look of a vessel many months outbound and well able to find her way home. The coast of Peru was now more than a thousand leagues behind her and she sailed a sea untracked by any ship since 1767, when Captain Carteret's *Swallow* had passed that way.

When Folger had taken the sun's altitude, at noon, he went below to make his calculations and to dine. Turning to go down the companionway, he caught the mate's eye.

"Keep her as she is, Mr. Webber," he said.

The mate was an Englishman of thirty, or thereabout, with a clear, ruddy complexion and an expression firm, reserved, and somewhat serious. He stood with arms folded, not far from the helmsman, glancing aloft from time to time to see that the sails were drawing well. It was midsummer in the Southern Hemisphere; the sky was cloudless, and the sun, tempered by the east wind, pleasantly warm. The ship rolled lazily to an easy swell from the northeast.

Two bells sounded, and shortly afterward the man in the

crow's nest hailed the deck. He had sighted land, distant thirty-five miles or more. A moment later the captain appeared, wiping his lips with the back of his hand and holding an old-fashioned spyglass which he extended to the mate.

"Get aloft, Mr. Webber, and see what you make of it."

Folger strode the deck until the other returned and handed him the telescope.

"A high, rocky island, sir, from the look of it. The bulk of the land is still hull-down. It bears sou'west-by-west."

"Hmm! A likely place for seals, I should think. You can alter the course to steer for it."

When Webber had given the necessary orders, the captain addressed him once more. "A discovery, sure as I'm a Yankee! There's nothing charted hereabouts save Pitcairn's Island, and Carteret laid that down a good hundred and fifty miles to the west."

The *Topaz* approached the land slowly, for the wind was dying to the lightest of light airs. At sundown the land was still far distant; it was not until past midnight that the ship was put about to stand off and on. Shortly after daybreak the land bore south — a small island, high and wooded to the water's edge, with a heavy surf breaking all along shore.

Captain Folger came on deck in the grey of dawn. As he was focusing his leveled telescope, the mate, standing at his side, gave an exclamation of astonishment.

"Smoke, sir! Yonder, above the bluffs!"

The captain peered through his glass for a moment before he replied. "Aye, so it is. The place is inhabited, without a doubt. I can see the smoke of four different fires." He sighed as he lowered his glass. "Well, there go our hopes of seals — and half our water casks empty. They'll be Indians, of course, apt to be hostile in this sea."

"Inhabited or not," remarked the mate, "no boat could land on this side. She would be dashed to pieces."

"And all hands drowned," Folger added, once more peering through his glass. "There's not a sign of a beach, and the coast is studded with rocks, offshore. . . . Bless me! Here's some of 'em now! Three, in a canoe!"

Webber's unassisted eye soon made out the tiny craft, appearing and disappearing as it approached over the long swell. The ship was allowed to lose what little headway she had, and within a quarter of an hour the canoe was close by — a long, sharp, narrow craft, with an outrigger on the larboard side. Her crew backed water at a distance of about thirty yards from the *Topaz,* and sat, paddle in hand, as though prepared to flee back to the land as swiftly as they had come. They regarded the ship with looks of wonder and awe, not unmingled with apprehension. In spite of repeated hails to come on board, they neither spoke nor came closer for some time. The mate gazed at these strange visitors with the keenest interest, observing that they were lads, the eldest no more than eighteen or nineteen. If Indians, they were, certainly, lighter in complexion than any he had seen. Their faces were bronzed by a life in the open air, but scarcely darker than those of white seafaring men. The stern paddler, who wore a straw hat of a curious shape, ornamented with feathers, seemed somewhat reassured by his scrutiny.

"You are an English ship?" he called, in a strong, manly voice.

"What in tarnation!" Folger exclaimed under his breath. And then: "No. This is an American vessel."

The three youths looked at one another and spoke together briefly in low voices.

"Who are you?" Folger called.

"We are Englishmen."

"Where were you born?"

"On the island yonder."

"How can you be English?" asked the captain.

"Because our father is an Englishman," came the quiet reply.

"Who is your father?"

"Alex."

"Who is Alex?"

"Don't you know Alex?"

"Know him? God bless me! How should I know him?"

The lad in the canoe regarded the captain earnestly, then turned to his companions again for another low colloquy in an unintelligible dialect. At length he said, "Our father would make you welcome on shore, sir."

"Come aboard first, my lads. You've nothing to fear from us," Folger replied in a kindly voice.

The steersman glanced at his companions, and, after a moment of hesitation, they dashed their paddles into the water and drew alongside. A line was dropped to them and made fast, and the three young islanders swarmed on deck with rare agility. The captain stepped forward to greet them, a smile on his kindly, weather-beaten face.

"I am Captain Folger," he said, extending his hand to the tallest lad, "and this is Mr. Webber, the mate."

"My name is Thursday October, sir. This is my brother, Charles, and this is James."

The spokesman, for all his youthful appearance, was a full six feet in height, and magnificently proportioned, with a handsome, manly countenance and a ready smile. All were barefoot, bare-chested, and bare-legged, and dressed in kilts of some strange cloth which reached to their knees. Their manner was easy and they showed no further signs of timidity, though they stared about them in round-eyed wonder at what they saw.

"What a huge, great ship, sir!" remarked Thursday October in a voice of awe. "We've heard of them from our father, but have never seen one before."

The people of the *Topaz* were crowded as far aft as convention allowed, regarding their visitors with glances as interested as those the three lads bestowed on the ship.

"You shall be shown over her, presently," said the captain, "but I want to ask you about your island, first. Is there a landing place on the other side?"

"Only one, and that dangerous. We land and embark in the cove yonder."

Folger glanced toward the land and shook his head. "Our boats could never risk it. You have plenty of fresh water here?"

"Yes, sir."

The captain pointed to the scuttle-butt, outside the galley door. "We've a score of casks like that one. Could they be landed in your bay?"

"That would be easy, sir," Thursday October replied, quickly. "If you would tow them to the edge of the breakers, we could swim them in, one by one."

"And you could fill them, once on shore?"

"Yes, sir; though we would have to fetch the water down in calabashes."

"How long would it take?"

"Brown's Well is the nearest water." The lad thought for a moment, measuring with his eye the cask by the galley. "With all of us at work, I'll warrant we could do it in two or three days."

"And you'd be willing to lend us a hand?"

The lad's face lighted up. "To be sure we would, sir! There's a plenty of us ashore to help."

"Good! Never mind the work, young man. You shall be well rewarded. Now the boatswain will show you over the ship, above decks and below. Keep your eyes open and choose what will be most useful to you. Within reason, it shall be yours for filling my casks."

As the three lads followed the boatswain forward, Captain

Folger turned to the mate. "The weather has a settled look, Mr. Webber; yet I don't feel free to leave the ship. Will you go ashore and see that no time is wasted in filling the casks?" Webber's expression of pleasure was so transparent that Folger went on without waiting for a reply. "I envy you! Who can they be? There's a mystery here; you must solve it."

"I'm to go in the canoe, sir?"

"Yes, and you'd best stay ashore until the work's done. We'll tow the casks in with the longboat. Tell Mr. Alex, or whoever he is, that we'll be off the cove, ready to work, by noon."

When the young islanders had finished their tour of the ship, they proved reluctant to make known their wants. Being urged, they at length informed the captain that a couple of knives, an axe, and a copper kettle would be more than ample compensation for watering the ship. Folger, who had taken a great fancy to the lads, gave them the kettle at once, and then forced upon them half a dozen each of large clasp knives and axes.

"And what style of man is Mr. Alex?" he asked, as they were handing down their things into the canoe. "Is he tall or short?"

"Like yourself, sir," Thursday October replied. "Short and strong-made."

Folger went below and returned with a new suit of stout blue broadcloth on his arm.

"Take this to Mr. Alex with my compliments."

Thursday October's eye lit up with pleasure. "God will reward you for your kindness, Captain! We have no such warm clothes as these. Our father is no longer young and often feels the cold in the wintertime."

The three then shook hands warmly with Folger and the boatswain, waved to the others, and sprang down into the canoe, followed by the mate. A moment later they had cast off and were paddling swiftly toward the cove, now about three miles distant.

Webber was seated amidships, and as they drew near to the land he forgot his curiosity in admiration of the sixteen-year-old lad who sat on the forward thwart. Never, he thought, as he watched the play of muscles on the paddler's back and shoulders, had he seen a nobler-looking boy. His countenance, when he turned his head, had the open, fearless look of a young Englishman, yet there was something at once pleasing and un-English in his swarthy complexion, his black eyes, and the thick black hair falling in curls to his shoulders.

They were close in with the land now, to the east of the little cove, where a huge rock, rising high above the waves, stood sentinel offshore. A bold and lofty promontory, falling away in precipices to the sea, gave the cove some shelter from the southeast winds; the swell, rising as it approached the land, rushed, feathering and thundering, into the caverns at the base of the cliffs, each wave sending sheets of spray to a great height. The cove itself was studded with jagged rocks, black and menacing against their setting of foam. It seemed incredible, at first glance, that even skilled surfmen could effect a landing at such a place. The cove was iron-bound, save at one spot where Webber now saw a tiny stretch of shingly beach, at the foot of a steep, wooded slope. A score or more of people were gathered there, staring at the approaching canoe. To reach the shingle, Webber perceived, the little craft would have to be steered with the greatest nicety, through a maze of rocks that threatened instant destruction. Yet the young paddlers seemed wholly unconcerned and approached with an air of complete confidence.

They halted briefly on the verge of the breaking seas, and then, at a word of command from Thursday October, all three dashed their paddles into the water at once. A great feathering sea lifted the canoe and bore her forward as swiftly as a flying fish on the wing. She turned, flashed between two boulders, and was swept high on to the little beach. Half a dozen sturdy lads rushed into the surf to hold her against the backwash; the paddlers sprang over the side to seize the gunwales, and with the next comber they carried her high up on the shingly sand.

The little crowd on the beach, Webber observed with some surprise, was made up of boys and girls who might range from ten to eighteen years of age. Not a grown man or woman awaited the canoe. Where were the parents of all these youngsters? Thursday October had said that they had never before seen a ship. It seemed remarkable indeed to the mate of the *Topaz*, if Alex, the father, were truly an Englishman, so long cut off from humankind, that he and the other adults should show so little interest in visitors from the outside world.

The young people seemed shy, almost apprehensive. None stepped forward to greet the stranger; they seemed rather to shrink from him, whispering together in little groups and regarding him with bright eyes which expressed curiosity and wonder. The boys, like the three who had come out to the vessel, all wore kilts of figured cloth; the girls were neatly clad in the same materials, and most of them wore chaplets of sweet-scented flowers. Some of the girls would have attracted attention anywhere, though their beauty was more of the Spanish than of the English kind. When they whispered together, they spoke in some jargon unknown to the visitor.

The three paddlers now returned from a long thatched shed, well above high-water mark, where they had carried their canoe. The youngest, known as James, carried the suit of clothes, and now the boys and girls clustered around him, feeling of the cloth and exclaiming softly in wonder and admiration. Thursday October touched Webber's arm.

"Come this way, sir," he said.

The land rose steeply from the beach to the sloping plateau above, in a wooded bluff perhaps two hundred feet in height. A zigzag path led to the summit, and the lads and lasses were already trooping upward and were soon lost to view. Webber followed his guide, envying the agility of the lad, who strode along freely and without a halt, while he himself panted with his exertions and was obliged from time to time to cling to the roots of trees, bushes, or tufts of grass. At length they reached the summit, where the mate halted to regain his breath. The young islander then led the way along a well-footed path that followed the seaward bluffs, winding this way and that among great trees whose deep shade felt deliciously cool. After crossing two small valleys, or ravines, they reached a kind of village, consisting of five houses scattered far apart along a stretch of partially cleared land which sloped gently toward the sea.

The houses were of two stories and thatched with leaves of the pandanus. They looked old and weather-beaten, but were strongly timbered, and three of them were planked with oak which Webber recognized as the strakes of a shipwrecked vessel. As they passed the first house he saw a dark, gypsy-looking woman peering out at him, and, at another open window-place, a second, somewhat younger, with a handsome face and thick rippling hair of a copper-red color the Englishman had never seen before. He caught glimpses of several other women at the farther dwellings, but they were no more than glimpses. Faces vanished from view the moment he looked toward them.

Presently they came to an ancient banyan tree on the seaward side of the path. Its huge limbs, from which innumerable aerial roots depended, like hawsers anchoring the tree still more firmly to the earth, seemed to cover half an acre or more. Directly opposite, on the inland side of the path at a distance of about thirty yards, stood a dwelling, delightfully pleasant and neat like all of the others, with a greensward dappled with sunlight and shadow and bordered with flowers and flowering shrubs.

A man of about fifty stood in the doorway. He was short and powerfully built, clad in the same strange cloth the others wore, but neatly cut and sewed into the form of frock and trousers, after the fashion of the old-time British tar. His grey hair fell upon his shoulders, and his features and the glance of his eye expressed strength tempered with benevolence.

"Welcome, sir," he said, stepping forward and extending his hand.

"My name is Webber. I am mate of the ship yonder."

With a word of apology to the visitor, Thursday October now stepped forward and spoke rapidly and briefly to the old man, in the same curious jargon the mate had heard on the beach — a language in which certain words of English were discernible, but whose sense was unintelligible to him. Presently the old man dismissed the lad with a nod and ushered the Englishman into the house.

"Dinah!" he called. "Rachel! Where are ye, lasses?"

Two little girls not yet in their teens appeared at the door, regarding the stranger with bright-eyed timidity.

"Fetch some coconuts for the gentleman," their father went on, "and what fruit ye can find."

The children dashed away without replying, while their father brought forward a chair. "Sit ye down, sir, and rest, and taste of what our island affords. Ye 've been long at sea, I take it?"

"Three months and more," the mate replied. "Little we thought there was land anywhere hereabout. What is the name of your island?"

"It 's Pitcairn's Island, sir. No doubt ye 've been misled by the chart. Captain Carteret laid it down a hundred and fifty miles west of its true position."

"But he called it uninhabited."

"Aye, so it was in his day. . . . Ye need water, the lad says. We 've plenty here, but it 'll be a three-day task at best to get it down to the beach. Can ye bide the time?"

"We 've no choice. Scarcely a spit of rain have we had since we left the coast of Peru. Most of our casks are empty."

"And what might your errand be in these parts?"

"We 're a sealing ship," Webber replied. "We were bound to the westward when we raised your island. Are there seals hereabout? In that case we 'd like well to fish here, if you 've no objection."

The islander shook his head. "Ye 'd have no luck, Mr. Webber. I 've seen a few of the animals on the rocks at rare times. The last was all of ten years back."

The old man fell silent, elbows on the rude table and chin in his hands. Webber had a slightly uncomfortable feeling that he was being studied and appraised. His curiosity concerning the inhabitants of this seagirt rock was so intense that once or twice he drew breath to put the direct question, but he thought better of it each time. His host was, plainly, a man of intelligence, who would realize how strange this little community must appear to a man from the outside world. If he had reasons for keeping silent, they should be respected. If willing to satisfy a stranger's curiosity, he would do so in his own good time.

"Ye 're an Englishman, I take it?" said the islander at last.

"Yes. But the ship is American. She hails from Boston, in New England."

The old man gave him a keen glance. "Say ye so!" he replied. "Then there 's still peace between us and the Colonies?"

"Aye, and a brisk trade, too."

The old man sighed and paused for a moment before he spoke. "Close on to twenty years I 've been here, Mr. Webber. Ye 're the first man to set foot on shore in all that time."

Webber looked up in astonishment. "Twenty years!" he exclaimed. "Then you 've heard nothing of what 's happened in the world — of the revolution in France; of old Boney, of Trafalgar, and all the rest!"

The children now returned, bringing drinking nuts and a dozen great yellow plantains in a wooden bowl, together with other fruits which were strange to the mate. He partook of them with the relish of a sailor long at sea, and, while he ate, narrated briefly the events of the stormy years at the end of the eighteenth century and the beginning of the nineteenth. The old man displayed little interest in political happenings and battles on land, but the account of England's naval victories brought a flush to his cheek and a sparkle to his eye. Yet all the while he seemed to labour under a baffling and unnatural reserve, maintaining a silence concerning himself out of keeping with a countenance as frank and open as that of John Bull himself.

The sun was high when Thursday October returned to escort the visitor down to the beach. "I 'd take it kindly, sir," said the old man as he rose to his feet, "if ye 'd stop with me whilst the watering is done. Or will your captain come ashore?"

"He 'll want to stretch his legs before we leave," the mate replied, "but he will remain on board till the work is finished. I shan't put you out if I accept?"

The islander laid a hand on his arm. "Put me out, Mr. Webber? God bless ye, sir, never in the least! Ye 'll be welcomed, and hearty, by one and all — that I promise ye!"

The longboat was towing the first of the barrels into the cove when the mate arrived at the beach. All the young people engaged in the task of swimming them in through the surf, shouting and sporting in the breakers, where they seemed as much at home as on land. Webber had never seen such swimmers; they appeared and disappeared in the swirling white water among the rocks, guiding the great clumsy casks to the landing place, where they were beached without the slightest mishap. Soon all the first lot were ashore and rolled to a piece of level land that had been dug out of the hillside, while the longboat pulled back to the ship, now two miles distant.

Toward the close of the afternoon, Webber went for a ramble about the plateau, with some of the younger children as his guides. They led him first to a rock cistern in the depths of the valley and retired while he refreshed himself with a bath. No man could have asked for merrier companions, once their shyness had worn off. They brought him fruits and flowers, and spoke freely, even eagerly, of the trees and plants of the island, of the wild swine, the goats and fowls; but, for all their childlike faith and trust in him, Webber was aware of the same reserve so noticeable in the man they called father. They seemed to be partakers in a conspiracy of silence concerning their history; and it was silence the guest respected, however much his curiosity was aroused.

Toward sunset he returned to the house where he had been bidden to sup and spend the night. He found his host seated on a bench outside the door with half a dozen of the smaller children seated on the grass around him. He was giving them an exercise in dictation, and the mate observed that he read from the Bible — a copy so worn and well thumbed that it was falling to pieces. He read slowly, a phrase at a time, while the children, with lips pursed and chubby fingers clasped round their pencils, — the blunt spines of a kind of sea-urchin, — set down the words as he pronounced them. For slates they used thin slabs of rock ground smooth on both sides.

"Avast!" said the old man as he perceived his guest. "That 'll do for to-day, children. Rachel, run and tell Mother we 're ready to sup. Come in, Mr. Webber. Ye 've an appetite, I hope? I must tell ye, sir, ye 've filled my old

head so full of republics, and battles, and what not, I 've
been woolgathering all the afternoon!"

As they were about to seat themselves at the table, a woman
of forty or forty-five came in through the back door, bearing
a large platter containing baked pig and heaped up with
sweet potatoes, yams, and plantains, all smoking hot. She
had a pleasant homely face and the mate perceived at once
that she was not of white blood.

"This is Balhadi, Mr. Webber, the mother of the little girls
yonder." The mate stepped forward to greet her, and as
he did so, his host spoke to her in the curious speech the islanders used among themselves. As soon as he had finished,
she stepped forward and took the stranger's hand in both of
hers, caressing it as a mother might do, her eyes glistening
with tears as she peered up at him; then she turned and with-
drew.

The two men seated themselves, and when the old man
had heaped their plates he bowed his head, and, quietly and
reverently, asked God's blessing on the food of which they
were about to partake. Webber was a religious man in the
fine sense of the word; cant and snuffling were hateful to
him, and he felt his heart touched and uplifted by the sim-
plicity and the deep sincerity of the brief prayer.

Twilight was fading to dusk by the time they had finished
the meal. While they were still at the table the mate had
observed, through the open doorway, small groups of people
turning in at the gateway and gathering on the grassplot
before the dwelling. His host now led the way outside and
for a few moments they remained seated on the bench by the
door, looking on in silence at the scene before them. All
the inhabitants of the island seemed to have assembled there.
They sat in groups on the grass, speaking in soft voices
among themselves. They were clothed in fresh garments
and the younger women wore newly made wreaths of fern and
flowers pressed lightly down over their loose dark hair. The

visitor gazed about him with the keenest interest, thinking that he had never seen a group of healthier, happier-looking children. Counting them idly, he found that the young people numbered four-and-twenty, and seated among them were eight or nine women of middle age, the mothers, evidently, of this little flock. It was clear that they were all of Indian blood. But where were the fathers? With the exception of his host and himself, not a man of mature age was present.

Presently the old man rose to his feet, and at a sign from him the older women came forward to greet the visitor. The first to take his hand was a tall and slender woman of forty; the Englishman thought he had never seen a face at once so sad and so maturely beautiful.

"Mr. Webber," said his host, "let me make ye known to Maimiti, Thursday October's mother."

She greeted him in a soft, low voice, making him welcome in a few words of English spoken with a strange accent, very pleasant to hear. Following her came a woman of commanding presence, a head taller than the mate himself, whom his host introduced as Moetua. In her fine carriage, the poise of her head, most of all in the proud spirit that looked out of the dark eyes, Webber was reminded of some mother of the heroic stage, or of some queen of the Amazons capable of performing deeds worthy to be handed down in the legends of primitive races.

Next came four women with English names, — Mary, Susannah, Jenny, and Prudence, — although they were evidently of the same race as the others. It was Prudence whose handsome face and copper-red hair he had admired at the window of the house he had passed on the way from the cove. These were followed by three more with strange Indian names which he found it impossible to keep in mind. Some greeted him in silence, merely shaking his hand; others spoke to him in the English tongue, though in a manner which revealed that they were little accustomed to the common use of it; but, whether silent or not, all made him feel, by the simple sincerity and kindliness of their manner, that he was indeed a welcome guest.

Meanwhile, some of the younger people had brought a small table and two chairs from the house which they placed on the greensward, and a moment later Dinah appeared carrying her father's Bible, and Rachel with a kind of taper made of a dozen or more oily nuts threaded like beads on the midrib of a coconut leaflet which was stuck upright in a bowl of sand. The topmost nut was burning brightly, with hissings and sputterings, while a slender column of smoke rose from it, ascending vertically in the still air. The little company now seated themselves on the grass before the table, and the murmuring of voices ceased. The old man turned to his guest.

"This is the hour for our evening worship, sir," he said. "We should be pleased to have ye join with us."

A chair was placed for the visitor at one side of the group, whereupon his host seated himself at the table and opened his silver-clasped Bible, holding the volume close to the flickering light. He turned the pages slowly with his large, rough fingers. Presently, clearing his throat, he began to read.

"I say then, Hath God cast away his people? God forbid."

Webber felt himself carried back to his boyhood, twenty years before. His grandfather, a white-bearded yeoman farmer, had read a chapter from the Bible each evening, in just such a quiet, earnest voice, after the same admonitory clearing of the throat; but how different a scene was this to the one he so well remembered in the north-country farmhouse of his childhood! The old man read on, his finger slowly following the lines, while the members of his little congregation listened with an air of the deepest interest and

respect. When the lesson was at an end, all knelt and repeated the Lord's Prayer in unison, and as the guest listened
to the voices of youths and maidens mingling with the clear,
childish accents of the little children, he felt that here indeed
was worship in purity of heart, in simple unquestioning trust
in God's loving-kindness toward His children. It was as
though all felt His presence there among them.

The service over, old and young came forward to bid the
stranger good-night before dispersing to their various homes.
When the last of them had gone, it seemed to Webber that
his host looked at him with even more kindness and with less
reserve than hitherto.

"It's plain that ye've a great love of children, Mr. Webber," he said. "Ye've some of your own, I take it?"

"That I have; three of them, the oldest about the age of
the lad I had on my knee a moment ago. Whose child
is he?"

"My own, though he's living with his foster mother just
now. . . . It's over early for bed, sir. Would ye relish a
bit of a walk? I've a bench not far off, overlooking the sea.
It's a pretty spot and the moon will be up directly."

He led the way along the path toward the cove, but turned
off in a moment on another leading through the groves to a
rustic seat placed at the very brink of the cliff which fell
steeply to the sea.

"Many's the time I come here of an evening, Mr. Webber,"
he explained, as they seated themselves. "Ye may think me
fanciful, but there's times when the breakers seem the very
voice of God — comforting at a time like this, wrathful on
a night of storm. . . . Look! Yon she comes!"

The moon, a little past the full, was rising above the lonely
horizon, flashing along the white crests of the breakers far
below and glinting along the motionless fronds of the coconut
palms.

The islander turned to his guest, hesitated, and said at last:

"No doubt ye 've wondered at my not naming myself. Smith 's my name — Alexander Smith."

He watched his companion's face closely, as though to divine what effect the mention of the name might produce. As there seemed nothing to say, Webber remained silent.

"And ye must have wondered about other things," the old fellow went on, after a long pause. "Who we are, set down on this bit of land so far from any other."

The mate smiled. "I should have been more or less than human had my curiosity not been aroused."

His companion sat leaning forward, elbows on his knees, his hands clasped loosely, as he gazed out over the moonlit sea.

"Ye 're an honest man, that 's sure," he said, at length, "and a kind-hearted man. . . . I 'd never believe ye could wish harm to me and mine?"

"Harm you? God forbid!" the mate replied, earnestly. "Set your mind at rest there, my friend. I would as soon harm my own little family as this flock of yours."

"What happened, Mr. Webber, was long ago — more than twenty years back. . . ." Of a sudden he turned his head. "Did ye ever hear of a ship called the *Bounty?*"

The words came to Webber like a thunderclap — like a blaze of lightning where deep darkness had reigned a moment before. In common with most seamen of his day, he had heard of the notorious mutiny on board the small armed transport sent out from England to fetch breadfruit plants from the island of Tahiti to the West Indies. He remembered clearly the principal events in that affair. The fate of the *Bounty* and those who had been aboard her constituted one of the mysteries of the sea.

The mate turned to his companion and said, with emotion in his voice, "Then you 're . . ."

"Aye," Smith interrupted quietly, "one of Fletcher Christian's men, Mr. Webber. It was here we came."

A hundred questions crowded into Webber's mind, but his companion was now more eager still.

"What can ye tell me of Captain Bligh?" he asked, anxiously. "Was he ever heard of again?"

"Indeed he was! He got home, at last, with most of his men, after the greatest open-boat voyage in the history of the sea."

Smith brought his hand down resoundingly on his knee. "Thank God for that!" he exclaimed, reverently. "Ye've done me a great service, sir. Now I'll sleep better of a night. And the men we left on Tahiti? What became of them?"

"I've read a book or two on the subject," Webber replied; "and the tale is well known. A ship-of-war was sent out to search for the *Bounty.* Let me see . . . *Pandora,* I think she was called. They found a dozen or fifteen of the *Bounty's* company on Tahiti. The *Pandora* seized them and they were being taken home in irons when the vessel was wrecked off the coast of New Holland. A number of her company and several of the prisoners were lost, and the rest of her people were forced to take to the boats. They reached England nearly a year later, as I remember it, when the prisoners were tried by court-martial. Three or four, I believe, were hung."

Smith had been listening with an air of almost painful eagerness. "Ye don't recollect the names of the lads was hung?" he asked.

Webber shook his head, as he was forced to do when his companion asked after numerous men by name.

"I'm sorry; I can tell you the fate of none of them," he replied. "Of the *Bounty's* company I remember only Captain Bligh, and Christian, the officer said to have led the mutiny."

"It was Mr. Christian's son, Thursday October, that brought ye ashore."

"And where is Christian, and the others who came with

you?   As I remember it, there were a dozen or more in all."

"Nine," said Smith.   "That is, nine of us white men.
Besides, there was six Indian men and twelve women that
came with us from Tahiti.   The women ye met this evening
are the mothers of these lads and lasses."

"But where are the fathers?"

"There's none left, save me."

"You mean they've gone elsewhere?"

Smith shook his head.   "No.   They're dead, sir."

The mate waited for him to proceed.   The old fellow sat
staring before him.   At length he said: "Are ye a patient
man, Mr. Webber?   Could ye listen to a story 't would take
me a couple of evenings to tell?"

"An account, you mean, of what has happened here?"

"Aye."

"I should like nothing better!   Why, man, there are
scores in England would travel a hundred leagues to hear
the tale from your lips!   Have no fear!   You'll find me
a patient listener, I promise you!"

"I've no wish to tell it, God knows," Smith continued,
earnestly.   "And yet, if so be as I could . . . it would ease
my heart more than I could well say.   I've little
learning — that ye can see for yourself; but I've forgot
nothing that's happened here.   Ye shall have the truth,
Mr. Webber.   I'll keep nothing back, but I'll ask ye to bear
in mind that the Alex Smith who speaks is not the Smith
of the *Bounty* days.

"Well, sir, to begin at the beginning . . ."

As he listened, the mate of the *Topaz* was lost to the
present moment.   He felt himself carried, in an all but
physical sense, into the past.   In place of Alexander Smith —
stout, middle-aged, and fatherly — he saw a rough young
seaman in the midst of as strange a company as ever sailed
an English ship.   He was conscious of the heave of the

Bounty's deck beneath his feet, of the hot suns, the wind and weather of bygone days. He found himself looking on at old unhappy scenes, sharing the emotions and hearing the voices of men long since dead — voices that had broken the silence of this lonely sea and still lonelier island, nearly twenty years before.

CHAPTER XVI

WHERE was I, sir? (Smith proceeded, on the following evening). Aye, if ye recollect, Mr. Christian and me was lying wounded in the house. Save for what I learned afterwards, I can tell ye nothing of the time that followed. Ye can fancy the state the women was in. Moetua and Nanai went off into the bush by themselves after they'd fetched Mr. Christian. Jenny and Taurua stopped with Mrs. Christian, who kept asking for her husband and wondering why he did n't come back. Ye'll recollect that she'd been brought to bed of a daughter on the morning the killing began.

Hutia stopped with Balhadi to care for us. Mr. Christian had lost so much blood, he lay quiet as a dead man. I'd a high fever; for three days without a let-up, they told me, I babbled, and cursed and raved. The rest of the women, with McCoy's children and little Matt Quintal and Eliza Mills, gathered in one house. They was that dazed and listless they might have starved, I reckon, if they'd not had the little 'uns to think on. They sat huddled on the floor the day long, with scarce a word exchanged, some of 'em crying softly with heads covered, as Indians do. The days was bad enough; it was the nights they dreaded most. They've strange notions, not like ours. They reckon that the spirits of the new dead, no matter if dear friends or husbands in life, are fierce, ravening things, hating the living. Of a night, the women in Mills's house would bar every door and window, and huddle with the children by their candlenut torch, quaking at every little sound outside.

Quintal stopped alone at his place, sitting on the doorstep most of the time, with his chin in his hands, and he'd speak to no one. I've no notion what was going on in his mind. It may be he felt the loss of Mills and Jack Williams, or was thinkin' of the fix Mr. Christian was in, and how he'd brought the trouble on by burning Minarii's house.

The killing started at dawn, as ye know. September twenty-second, it was, 1793, a date I'll not forget. The last of the Indians was killed on the night of the twenty-third. Next morning, when Moetua and Nanai was gone, Taurua came across from Mr. Christian's house to speak to my old woman. She told her Mrs. Christian was in such a state it was all they could do to keep her in bed. It was agreed by all she'd have to be told.

Mr. Young said, long afterwards, he'd as soon face the hangman as live through that morning again. They tried to soften the news to Mrs. Christian, but she guessed what they held back.

Up she got, in her kirtle, threw a mantle over her shoulders, took up her newborn babe, and went out the door without a word. When they reached our house, she went straight to the bed-place, motioning Hutia away.

Mr. Christian's eyes was closed and his fever was high. Hutia took the child, and his wife settled herself at the head of the bed-place to keep the cloths on his forehead wrung out cool and fresh. Ye know what a shock the like of that will do to a woman. Mrs. Christian's milk had begun to flow strong and good that morning; by nightfall her breasts was dried up. When the baby cried, Balhadi fed it on what the Indians call *ouo*, the sweet jelly they scrape out of young coconuts. Aye, and she throve on it; for the next year she'd naught else.

All that night, through the next day and the night following, Mr. Christian and I lay there, tended by the women and Mr. Young. He'd told Mrs. Christian what had happened;

after that she scarce spoke a word. It must have been the
morning of the third day when the fever left me and I
opened my eyes.

Here I was in my own house, weak as a cat and bad
wounded. My left shoulder and my neck was all stiff and
sore. When I tried to move, it pained me cruel. My head
was light from the fever and it was a good bit afore I could
set my thoughts in order. It came back slow — how Jenny 'd
come to my taro patch, how I 'd climbed the Goat-House,
hoping to meet up with Mr. Young, and hid myself alongside the path in the Main Valley, on the chance of cutting
down one of the Indians and getting his musket. Towards
sunset I 'd crept down to Mr. Young's plantain walk, for
I 'd had naught to eat all day. Then I recollected Te Moa,
and Nihau, with Mills's head at his belt, stepping out sudden
as I was reaching up for some ripe fruit, and the shot that
knocked me down; how I 'd scrambled up and made a run
for it; then something to do with Jenny, and no more. Three
was killed, she 'd told me at the taro patch. That was all
I knew.

My bed-place was on the north side of the room, by an
open window. It was a calm, sunny morning, with scarce
enough breeze to move the tree-tops. Here and there, where
the screen of bush was thin, the sea showed blue through
the trees. Beautiful, it was, and peaceful; ye 'd never have
thought men could plot murder in such a place. I set my
teeth and turned my head the other way.

I saw someone on the other bed, across the room, but
could n't make out who it was. Mrs. Christian sat on the
floor beside him with her back to me, and I could see neither
her face nor his. He never moved, and I took a notion he
was dead. Taurua and my old woman was feeding a tiny
baby on a mat, and Mr. Young stood near by. I called out to
him.

Balhadi sprang up, baby and all; and Mr. Young came

across to me. "Hush, Alex!" said he. "Thank God ye 're better, now the fever 's down!" My old woman tried to smile at me, and nodded with a hand on my head.

"Who 's that yonder?" said I.

"Mr. Christian."

"Is he living?"

"Aye."

Mrs. Christian came over and spoke to me kindly. When she 'd gone back to sit by Mr. Christian, I had a glimpse of his face. One look was enough. There 's no mistaking a dying man. Mr. Young signed to Balhadi to take the baby away, and sat on a stool close by.

"Ned," I whispered, "tell me what 's happened, else ye 'll have me in a fever again."

When he had, I lay there thinking on it and wondering what the outcome 'd be. It was a black business. Ye won't wonder I felt bitter toward Quintal and McCoy. They'd done more 'n anyone else to bring on trouble with the Indians, and come through scot-free. God meant this island to be a little Garden of Eden, and we 'd made a hell of it. Mr. Christian had done all a man could. Now he lay dying for his pains. Knowing him as I did, I reckoned he 'd be glad to go. We 'd had our chance, and we 'd failed. Why? It was n't the Indians' fault; they 'd had cause enough for what they 'd done. I thought of Tetahiti, who 'd been my friend; and of Minarii — both high chiefs on their own islands. Because their skins was n't white, McCoy and Quintal and Martin and Mills reckoned they was n't fit to own land. I went back to the beginning, to the day we landed here, trying to make out how we 'd got on the wrong course. No, it was no fault of the Indians. All the men asked was to be treated like men; they 'd have been our best friends had we met 'em halfway. As for the girls, ye 'd travel far to find a better lot. Real helpmates, they was, ready to take their share in all that was going. And none

o' your sour, scolding kind.   *We* was to blame, and no one
else.   In the first place, we should have seen to it, afore ever
we left Tahiti, that each man had his girl, with some to spare.
That might have kept Williams out o' mischief.   *Might,* I
say, for ye could never tell with a man like Jack.   He and
his precious Hutia was the start o' the trouble.   But it was
bound to come, girls or no girls.   There was them amongst
us reckoned the Indians was made to be used like dogs.
That's the first and last of it, sir, in few words.

I slept most of the morning.   I felt a deal better when I
woke up again, and grateful just to be alive.   Maimiti was still
at the foot of Mr. Christian's bed, watching him with a look
on her face would have melted a heart of stone.   All at once
I saw her eyes light up; she came quickly and softly to the
head of the bed and knelt down beside him, taking his hand.
The fever had left him and he was conscious.

He looked at her in a puzzled way at first.   "What's this,
Maimiti?" said he.   "Where are we?"

"In Ned's house."

She fetched him some water, and I could see by the look
in her eyes that hope was springing up in her.   He drank a
little and said no more for a bit; then he asked, "Is Ned
here?"

Mr. Young was at the door.   He came in and stood at the
foot of the bed.   He did n't trust himself to speak.

"What is it, Ned?   What has happened?"

"Don't worry or try to talk just now," said Mr. Young.

"Where is Minarii?"

"He is dead."

"And the other Indian men?"

"All dead."

Mr. Christian turned his head slow on the pillow and saw
me.   "Are ye hurt, Smith?"

"Aye, sir, but not bad," said I.

His voice was stronger when he spoke next.

"Ye must tell me the whole of it, Ned.   I want to know."
There was no getting out of it. Mr. Young told him,
quick and short.   However he felt, he gave no sign; just
lay there, a-starin' up at the ceiling; then his eyes closed,
and Mr. Young tiptoed out o' the room.

Mrs. Christian never moved from her place at the foot
of the bed, where she could watch his face. She was blind
to what I could see. Trust a good woman to hope. It
was afternoon when he came round again and drank a little
of the water she offered him.   Then a long time passed without a word said. It was well on toward eight bells when
young Thursday October came to the door.   He was three
at the time, and ye never saw a handsomer little lad.   He'd
a finger in his mouth as he stood in the doorway, looking into
the room with his round eyes.   At last he came in on tiptoe,
half afraid, even after he'd made his father out. Mr.
Christian turned his head and saw the little fellow.   Deso-
late, his face was; such a look as I hope never to see another
man wear.

"Take the child out," said he.

His wife took up the lad and set him down outside the
door.   She was gone for a minute or two; I think it took
her that long to get herself in hand.

The afternoon wore through. Balhadi fed me a bit of
sweet coconut water now and again.   I could look out the
window, as I told ye. A fine breeze had made up; the trees
was swaying, and there was whitecaps out at sea. All the
womenfolk was gathered outside, waiting. Mr. Christian
was conscious this while, but he spoke no more than a word
or two.   He knew he was dying, most like, and felt glad to
go. All he'd touched was ruined, he'd be thinking: the
Bounty's voyage, the men set adrift with Captain Bligh in
the launch, those who'd stopped on Tahiti, and now our
little settlement, where he'd hoped for so much. Aye . . .
I'll warrant there was never a man waited his end with

greyer thoughts than Mr. Christian.   My heart bled for him.
The breeze died away after sundown, as it often does here.
I don't recollect a stiller, more beautiful evening.   It was
spring in these parts, as ye 'll remember, and the twilight
came on slow.   Mrs. Christian gave her husband a sip of
water, set down the cup, and stopped where she was, seated
on the bed beside him.   He put a hand on hers and looked
up with a faint smile.   Then he turned his head, slow.

"Alex," he said.

"Sir?"

When he spoke again it took me by surprise, and I 'm not
certain of the words to this day.   He said, "There 's a chance,
now," or "There 's still a chance" — one or the other.

He seemed to expect no reply, so I made none, but lay there
trying to make out just what he meant.   If he 'd said,
"There 's a chance, now," the words was the bitterest ever
spoke, for he must have meant that with him dead and out
of the way there might be hope for us.   I can scarce believe
he spoke so, but it may have been.

After a long time I heard his voice again: "Never let the
children know!" and those was the last words I heard him
say.

I must have dozed off then, and when I opened my eyes it
was dark in the room.

It was Mrs. Christian's low, hopeless cry that woke me.   I
could n't see her, or Mr. Christian, but I knew the end had
come.

CHAPTER XVII

THE month that followed was a sorry time, with the silence of death over all. I was afeared, at first, that Mrs. Christian might lose her reason. She was n't one to weep, and that stony kind of grief ain't natural in a woman. Tears would have helped but none came. It made my heart sore to see her going about the house with that dazed, dead look on her face, like as if the truth had n't come home to her yet. And there was nothing ye could do to help. She had to fight it through alone. Sometimes a whole day 'd pass without her speaking a word.

Aye, it was a numb, hopeless time for all, and I 'll never forget how lonesome it seemed with so many gone. There was one, Martin, I 'd have had no wish to see back. We was all of a mind about him: he was better dead; but the others, whites and Indians alike, was sore missed, and most of all, of course, Mr. Christian. We could see better, now, the man he 'd been, and the deep need we had for him. There was no one could take his place. We was like sheep without a shepherd.

Mr. Young was the hardest hit of any of the men, I reckon; ye 'd scarce believe the change that came over him. He 'd sit on the bluffs for hours at a time, lookin' out over the sea, or wander about the settlement like a man walkin' in his sleep. There 'd been no one fonder of a joke in the old days, but after Mr. Christian's death I never again heard him laugh. My bein' hurt and needin' a bit of care was a help to him. When Maimiti or Balhadi was n't settin' by me, he was, and

I'd try to get his mind on other things: plans for the future — how we'd divide ourselves up, now, amongst the houses, the new gardens we'd make, and the like. He'd try to show interest, but it was plain he had no heart for anything.

But Mrs. Christian wouldn't give in, and having the children to see to and the other women to comfort was a godsend to her. Little by little she became more like her old self, and she'd hearten the others with her quiet ways. I don't know what some would have done without Maimiti.

One day when she and Mr. Young was by me in the house, she spoke of Moetua and Nanai. Ye'll mind that they was the wives of Minarii and Tetahiti. They'd not been near the settlement since the day they brought Mr. Christian down, but lived by themselves in Jack Williams's old house on the other side of the island. Some believed they must have known their men meant to kill all the whites, and there might have been a war and a massacre amongst the women-folk if it hadn't been for Maimiti and Taurua; they knew well enough that Moetua and Nanai had naught to do with it and was as innocent as themselves.

Well, Mrs. Christian asked Mr. Young to go across and coax 'em down, if he could. "Tell 'em to come for my sake, Ned," said she.

All the women liked Mr. Young; they'd do anything he said. Inside of an hour he was back, and they with him. He came in first and they stood at the door. Ye've seen Moetua, sir; ye can picture what she was in her young womanhood. I've seen thousands of Indian women, whilst on the *Bounty*, on islands scattered all over this ocean, but none to match Moetua for strength and beauty. She was like a young oak tree. I can't say better than that she was a fit wife for Minarii. It'd done my heart good just to see them two going about together.

It wasn't fear of Prudence and Hutia or all the women-folk together that kept her away from the settlement at this time. She'd have been more than a match for the lot of 'em. But she knew Quintal had killed her husband, and she was afeared she might take her revenge on him. She'd not his great brute strength, but, with the fire of hate in her heart, I'll not say she couldn't have mastered him and put him to death.

Nanai had a softer nature. She was of the best Indian blood: ye could tell at a glance the difference there was between her and women the like o' Jenny or Hutia. She was gentle. She needed someone to cling to, and it was a blessing she had Moetua, after Tetahiti was killed. Half crazed as some o' the women was, after the killing, I reckon they might have found a way to murder Nanai if she hadn't been with Moetua.

As I've said, they stood at the door, waiting. The minute she saw 'em, Maimiti came across and took 'em by the hands and brought 'em in. "Moetua," said she, "what our men have done is done. It may be that your husband killed mine; now both lie dead. Nanai, Christian and Tetahiti were friends. We have been like sisters in the past. I have nothing but love in my heart for ye two. Will ye come here and live with me?"

I can tell ye what was said, but not how it was said. Never a woman lived with a more kind, gentle nature than Mrs. Christian. Moetua took her in her arms and held her close. She had a beautiful husky voice, near as deep as a man's. "Aye, that we will!" said she. Then the three of them wept together, with their arms round each other. Glad I was to see that meeting. It was the first time Mrs. Christian had shed tears.

As soon as I was able to walk, she asked me if I'd let her have my house and move over to hers. I knew how it was with her: she'd a terror of setting foot in the house where she and Mr. Christian had lived. So we moved down there — my old woman, and Hutia, and Prudence, who was to live

with us. Mr. Young took Mills's house, with Taurua and
Jenny. Quintal and McCoy stopped where they always
had, with their own two girls and Susannah.

My wound healed slow. I was able to walk by the end of
October. But it was close to Christmas before I had any
use of my left arm. I was good for little this while and
had to stop indoors. It was a quiet time, but desperate
lonesome, as I 've said. Quintal and McCoy kept clear o'
me, and I was glad they did, for my heart was bitter towards
both. I knew we 'd mostly them to thank for bringin'
trouble to a head with the Indians. I would n't have cared
if I 'd never set eyes on either of 'em again.

Ye 'd have said, sir, that God had give us that time to mind
us of the past and the mistakes we 'd made, and to make sure
of our ways for the days to come; but some of us was too
ignorant to profit by it, and the rest too weak or stubborn.
I 'm speakin' of the men. What followed was no fault o'
the women. Them that went our ways did it because we
led 'em or forced 'em to it.

I 've spoke of McCoy's still. He had it going long afore
the killing started, but he was that close about it not even
his crony, Matt Quintal, knew what he was up to. There 's
no better way to show ye what a sly clever man Will McCoy
could be. On this mite of an island, where there was so
few of us, he 'd been able to make spirits, enough for his
own use, and none of us knew.

It was n't till later I learned all that went on. McCoy had
been shook bad by the days he was in the bush with the
Indians after him. A time or two they all but had him;
they 'd passed within a few feet of where he lay hid, and he 'd
seen Mills's bloody head, and Martin's, hangin' at their belts.
Aye, he 'd been near daft with fear, and, when all was over,
the women who went in search of him could n't coax him
back to the settlement. He 'd not even believe Mary, his
own girl, and it was n't till Quintal came and showed him

the Indians' dead bodies that his mind was set at rest. Then off he went again, no one knew where.

Quintal was crazed himself, in a different way. There 'd always been something a little queer about Matt; I 'd noticed it in the old days on the *Bounty*. It was n't often, but now and again something he 'd say or do would show ye the man was n't quite right in his head. The trouble got worse, after the killing. He 'd set on his doorstep muttering to himself, the women said, and act so queer, most of the time, they was afeared of him. For all that, he began to work about his place again, chopping wood, doing a bit o' weedin' in the gardens, and the like. Then it came over him, of a sudden, that McCoy had quit the house. Slow and dogged, Quintal began to search for him, and found him at last in one of the gullies on the west side of the island. McCoy had made him a hut, close by his still, a dry, cozy little place with a soft bed of fern inside.

"So this is where ye hide out!" said Matt. "What 's come over ye, Will, and what 's all this gear ye 've got?"

McCoy saw he 'd have to tell, and he was glad, in a way, that Quintal 'd found him. "Set ye down, Matt," said he. He pulled a bottle out of the fern, and a pewter half-pint he had by him.

"Taste that," said he, and he poured him out a big dollop of spirits.

Quintal took a sniff and then poured it down. "It ain't bad, not by a long way," said he; "but what is it? Where 'd ye get it from?"

"I made it," said McCoy, "out o' ti roots."

Then he told Quintal how it was done. They got the *Bounty's* big copper kettle. The other McCoy had was too small to make spirits for more than one; with the big one they could brew any amount and set some of it aside to age. A new still was set up, and so new trouble started.

In the beginning they went at their drinking quiet-like.

It was noticed, of course, that they'd be off together some-wheres, but the womenfolk was glad to have 'em gone, and took no thought of what they might be up to. After a few weeks they'd bring their grog to the house, and they teached their girls and Susannah to drink with 'em. It was n't long till Prudence and Hutia took to goin' there of an evening, and sometimes even Jenny would go. That's how I first got wind of it.

I'll say this for myself, sir, and it's the one right thing I did in all that time: I tried to hold Hutia and Prudence back, at first. But they'd found that grog could make 'em forget the troubles we'd had. Once they knew that, there was no keepin' 'em away from McCoy's house; but the women I've spoke of was the only ones that ever touched the stuff. The others would have naught to do with it.

One evening before I was able to get about much, Mr. Young came in to see me. He was like a new man, and it was easy to guess where he'd been.

"Alex," said he, "I've brought ye what will do ye a world of good."

"What's that?" said I, knowing well enough what it was.

He'd a bottle under his arm, which he set on the table.

"Will McCoy's sent this along to ye, with his hearty good wishes," said he; "and it's grand stuff, Alex. Ye'd scarce know it from the best London gin."

"Ye've had a good sup already, Ned," said I. "That's plain to be seen."

"I have so," said he. "Where's the sense of our holding out against a tot o' good grog now and again? It's a sad lonesome life we lead here. God knows a little good cheer won't harm us."

"Ned," said I, "I'll not say I don't wish I had a cag o' the same, but have ye reckoned what this might lead to? Ye've never seen Quintal in his cups. I have. He's the devil himself!"

"He was quiet and pleasant as ye please to-night," said Mr. Young.

"That may be," said I. "There's times when he's harmless enough; but ye never know when he'll be the other way."

"Quintal or no Quintal," said he, speakin' a little thick, "I'm for the grog! I've not felt like this in months, lad. My idea is that a little o' this — seamen's rations, mind ye, like we had in the old days — will harm none of us."

I said naught for a bit. Of a sudden he looked at me in a sober way, and got up from his chair.

"God forgive me, Alex!" said he. "If ye wish to abstain, I'd cut off my right hand before I'd be the one to urge ye!" He grabbed up the bottle and was about to go, and, fool that I was, I begged him to set down again. I'd been away from spirits for so long, I could just as well have kept off it; and I knew how it would be once I started again. No seaman ever loved his rum more than myself. I'd been used to it from the time I was a mere lad, and words can't say how I coveted a share o' that bottle.

Well, sir, the long and the short of it was that I fetched a couple of half-pints and a calabash of water, and between us we finished the whole bottle. And Mr. Young was right: it did me a world of good. I'd been low-spirited enough, but after a few drinks everything was bright and sunny. Balhadi looked on at the two of us, pleased as anything to see us so cheerful again. At this time none of the womenfolk knew the harm there was in drink. In years past there'd been a spree or two in the bush, but these they'd not seen, and for the most part we'd drunk our grog rations from the old *Bounty's* supply quiet and peaceable till all was gone. So the womenfolk, bein' ignorant, made no fuss at all, at first, about the still. Most wouldn't drink because they couldn't abide the taste o' spirits, but they didn't mind us doing it.

As soon as I was able to get about, I took to joinin' the
others at McCoy's house.   At first there was no harm in any
of us.   We 'd agreed each man was to have his half-pint a
day and no more.   It was even less at the start, because we
had n't enough to make up a half-pint around, but that was
soon mended.   We 'd never worked harder in the old days
than we did now at clearing land for ti-planting.   Quintal
and me took charge o' that, and Mr. Young and McCoy
minded the still.   They soon had a cag o' spirits set by to
age and started filling another.   We hunted the island over
for wild ti roots whilst them we 'd planted was coming along.
The food gardens was left to the womenfolk.

Ye can guess what followed, sir.   We was young seamen,
save Mr. Young, and the eldest of us scarce five-and-twenty.
As soon as there was a good store of spirits set by, no more
was said about half a pint a day, though Mr. Young held fast
to that at first.   The rest of us drank as much as we 'd a mind
to, and the five girls with us.   There was Sarah Quintal, and
McCoy's Mary, and the three others I 've spoke of — Susannah, Hutia, and Prudence.   These last had no men o' their
own, and the grog made 'em as wild and hot-blooded as ourselves.   Ye 'll not need to be told how it was with us.   We
took no thought o' wives or anything else.

There was trouble a-plenty afore many weeks.   Mrs. Christian was n't long in seein' the truth o' things.   She 'd come
to Mr. Young and me and beg us to leave off for the children's sakes if for naught else.   And we 'd be shamed to the
heart and promise to do better; but, a few days after, back
we 'd go and all would be as before.   It got so as Mrs. Christian and the other decent women would have naught to do
with us.   She gathered the children away from McCoy's
house, and she fitted bolts and bars to her house, well knowing what a dangerous man Quintal was, at times, when he
was drunk.   One night, when the rest of us was too far
gone to stop him, he near killed Sarah.   She and Mary both

had more than enough bad treatment. They'd have been only too glad to leave the house, but didn't dare to, for fear o' what their men might do.

So it went with us for another three months; then a thing happened that brought even such brutes as we'd become to our senses.

The four of us men was at McCoy's house, drunk as usual, with Prudence and Hutia and Susannah. Mary and Sarah had got to the place where they was more afraid to stay than to go, and Mrs. Christian had taken 'em in at her house. Quintal had been of a mind to fetch 'em back, but the rest of us had talked him out o' that and got him quieted down. McCoy didn't mind Mary going, for he still had some decency in him and he knew she'd be best away with the children.

I came stumbling back to my own house about midnight and Balhadi got me into bed. She'd stayed by me all this while, and Taurua had done the like by Mr. Young, which only goes to show how patient and long-suffering good women can be. But they was near to the end of their patience, as I'm about to tell ye.

It seemed to me I'd scarce closed my eyes when I was shook awake by Balhadi. "Quick, Alex!" said she. "Rouse the others and come! Quintal's just gone by toward Maimiti's house! He means mischief!"

I set out at a run for McCoy's house and roused him and Mr. Young, who was sleeping there. Before we'd come halfway back, we heard Quintal batterin' at the door of Mrs. Christian's house. The sound of it sobered us, I can promise ye!

The moon was about an hour up. Quintal was at the door with a fence post he'd picked up, and all but had it battered down by the time we got there. McCoy yelled at him, but he gave no heed. We could hear the children crying indoors, and then Mrs. Christian's voice, cool and quiet. "I 've a musket here," said she. "I 'll shoot him if he sets foot inside. Stand away, ye others!"

McCoy was the only one of us who could ever manage Quintal with words. He ran up now and took hold of his arm. "Matt, are ye mad?" said he. Quintal turned and gave him a shove that threw him clear across the dooryard. "I want Moetua," said he.

I dragged him back, and Will was at his legs and Mr. Young tried to hold one of his arms. The three of us was no match for him, and that 's the truth. Then the women took a hand.

Balhadi pitched in with us; then what was left of the door was broke down and out came Moetua. Hating Quintal as she did, she was better than two men. She got her fingers round his throat and would have killed him if it had n't been for Maimiti. We tied him up and carried him, half dead, back to McCoy's house.

That was the last straw for the women. Even Prudence and Hutia left us, wild young things that they was in those days, and they took Susannah with 'em. They joined the others at Mrs. Christian's house. We 'd bound Quintal hand and foot, so he could n't move, and had to keep him so all the next day, for he was like a wild animal. Nothing we could say would quiet him.

That same morning, Balhadi went down to Mrs. Christian's and was gone till afternoon. There was a scared, sober look on her face when she came back. I noticed it, though I was still muddled and sleepy with the drink I 'd had. She 'd a mind to tell me something, — I could see that, — but she held off, and I did n't coax her to come out with it, whatever it was. The fact is, I was ashamed and disgusted with myself, thinking how I 'd used Balhadi all these months, and I was short and surly with her to hide how I felt. Around the middle of the afternoon I told her to fetch me a bite to eat, which she did. When I 'd finished I lay down for a nap, and having had no sleep the night before, I did n't wake till daylight the next morning.

Balhadi was nowhere about. It was a day of black squalls, makin' up out of the southeast, with hot calm spells betwixt 'em. I went to the edge of the bluffs, as I always did of a morning, for a look at the sea and sky. While I was there, a squall came down so sudden I 'd no time to run to the house, and squatted in the lee of a clump o' plantains, takin' what shelter I could. It was over in ten minutes, and I was looking out to the eastward when I saw something afloat about a mile offshore. For all my bleary eyes, it looked like a capsized boat. I rubbed and looked again and made out what I thought was people in the water alongside, and some up on the keel.

I 'd no notion of the truth, but ye 'll know the start it gave me to see a capsized boat, with men clinging to it, in this lonely ocean. In all the years we 'd been here we 'd sighted but the one ship I 've told ye of. I scanned the horizon all round, as far as I could see, for the ship this boat belonged to, but there was none in view; then I ran to McCoy's house to get the spyglass.

Him and Mr. Young was there, still asleep. I shook 'em out of it and the three of us hurried down to the lookout point above the cove. Ye know how it is when ye get a glass on something far off — it jumps right up to your eye. What I saw was our cutter, upside down, and all our women-folk around it, some swimming, some clinging to the boat as best they could, while they held their little ones up on the keel.

Ye 'll know the shock it gave us — such a sight as that. Even with it there before our eyes, we was hard put to believe it was real. We ran back to McCoy's house to fetch Quintal. He was snoring fit to shake the place down. We pulled him out of the bed-place tryin' to waken him. "Rouse him out of it," said I to Will. "Kick him awake somehow!

Let him know young Matt's out there like to drown!"
Then Mr. Young and me ran to the cove.

We dragged the biggest of the canoes down into the water.
By good luck there was no great amount of surf and we was
soon beyond it. We made the hafts o' them paddles bend,
I promise ye!

Afore we was half a mile out, another black squall bore
down on us — solid sheets of water, and wind fit to blow the
hair off your head. It passed, quick as it had made up, and
there was the cutter, not a cable's length off.

Had the girls been women from home, more than one of
the children would ha' been drowned that day; but these
knew how to handle themselves in the sea. Prudence and
Mary came swimmin' to meet us, and passed up their babes
afore they clambered aboard. Next minute we was alongside, and took little Mary from Mrs. Christian. Then the
older ones they had on the keel was passed over to us.

McCoy and Quintal was on the way by this time in the
other canoe. Quintal was in the stern. He made the water
boil and no mistake!

"Is Matt safe?" he yelled when he was still a quarter of a
mile off.

"Aye, safe!" I hailed back. "And all hands!"

Mary was in our canoe, with their two little ones, half
drowned, in her lap, and I'll not forget the look on Will's
face when he saw 'em. We was takin' the other women on
board, Mrs. Christian the last. The two canoes held the lot
of us. We took the cutter in tow and made for the cove.

Some of the women was weeping, but not a word was spoke
all the way. Mrs. Christian sat on a thwart with little Mary
in her arms. She'd a look of hopelessness and despair that'll
haunt me to my last day.

We ran the breakers and got the women safe ashore, and
them with the children hurried on to the settlement. The
others helped us get the cutter righted and bailed out and

back in the shed. We had no words with 'em or they with us. We was too shocked and sobered by what they'd tried to do to have a harsh word for any of 'em.

Will ye believe it, sir? They'd meant to sail off with the young 'uns in that bit of a cutter! Mrs. Christian understood the compass, and they minded some low islands we'd passed in the *Bounty* on the way from Tahiti. That's where they was bound, if so be as they could find 'em. Unbeknownst to us, Mrs. Christian had got 'em together, provisioned the cutter, and set sail to the north. Had they not made the sheet fast and capsized in a squall, they'd all ha' been lost, as certain as sunrise!

But this'll show ye how desperate they was. They was sickened to the heart's core of men, and they'd come to hate the island where there'd been so much bloodshed and misery. We'd drove 'em to the point where they'd sooner chance death by drowning, or thirst and starvation, than live with us and have their children brought up by such fathers as we'd become.

That evening the four of us got together, but not to drink. It was McCoy himself that spoke first. "Mr. Young," said he, "I'm done with it! I know how much blame falls to my share in all that's passed. I'll be the cause o' no more trouble. We've children and good women here. I'm for a decent life from now on."

"I'm with ye, Will!" said I, standin' up, "and there's my hand on it!"

We was all of a mind, Quintal as hearty and earnest as the rest. There was to be no more distilling, that was agreed on and swore to, and we went to our beds sober and peaceable for the first time in many a day. Aye, we thought we was turning a new leaf that evening. There was to be naught but peace and quiet in the days to come.

CHAPTER XVIII

Now, sir, I 'll pass over three years. It was a time I don't like to think about. I said I 'd tell ye the truth of what 's happened here, and so I will, but ye 'd not want to hear the whole of it. There 's little to be said about those years save that we went from bad to worse. Not all at once. For two or three months after the womenfolk tried to leave the island we kept our word, and not a drop of spirits was touched. We did try, the four of us, to make a new start; then it was the old story over again: our solemn promises was broke, and the end of it was that Maimiti left the settlement with her three children and went over to the Auté Valley to live, and Moetua and Nanai went with her. They built a house with no help from any of us, and not long after, Jenny and Taurua, Mr. Young's wife, joined 'em, and they gathered all the children up there, away from us. I was glad they did. The settlement was no place for children, that 's the truth of it.

Balhadi had stayed by me all this while, hoping I 'd come to my senses, and Mary had done the like by McCoy, but little heed we gave to either of 'em. Four of the women — Hutia, Susannah, Prudence, and Sarah, Quintal's girl — stayed on with us, for the most part, and we lived together in a way it shames me to think of.

Mr. Young made one with us in this. Ye 'll wonder he could have done it. He was a gentleman born. How did it come he could join with men the like of Quintal, McCoy, and myself? My belief is he 'd lost all heart and hope, seein' how things went. He was never a man to lead. He must have thought we could never be made to go his way, so he went ours. But it was plain he hated himself for doing it. Never have I seen a sadder face than Mr. Young's at this time. It was a blow to him when Taurua left to join Maimiti, but he did n't change his ways. He took to drinking harder than ever, like as if he wanted to kill himself. For all that, he was a gentleman in whatever he did. I knew well enough it was only the grog that made him able to abide the rest of us.

So things went till the end of 1797. I mind me well of a spree we had in the fall of that year. We 'd started by killing a pig and making a feast. There was the four of us and the women I 've spoke of. It happened that Jenny and Moetua had come down to the settlement that day. They found us in a carouse that was the worst, I reckon, we 'd ever had up to that time. McCoy recollected that it was four years to the very week from the time when the last of the Indian men was killed. He was so drunk he cared for naught, and he told the women we 'd made the feast to mind us o' that. Then Quintal made him brag before Moetua, who 'd been Minarii's wife, about how he 'd thrown her husband over the cliff at the top of the Rope. I was far gone in drink myself, then, and I 've no doubt I did my part to make the women hate us the more.

I 've little recollection of what happened after, but I know the women was horror-struck at our brute ways. There was fighting 'twixt Quintal and McCoy and some o' them, but I was too drunk to take part in it. I was awake early next morning and found I 'd climbed to the loft, somehow. Mr. Young was asleep on a bed on the other side of the room. I went down the ladder and found Quintal and McCoy sprawled out on the floor, and a precious-looking pair they was! McCoy was scratched and bruised all over his body, and he had every stitch of clothing torn off him. Quintal's

face and beard was smeared and caked with blood from a
deep gash on his head; one of the women must have given him
an awful knock. The benches and tables was upset, and
glass from broken bottles was scattered all over the floor.

I went along home for a bit, but there was no one about,
or in any of the other houses. I went on to Mr. Christian's
old place where Prudence and Susannah lived at this time.
Maimiti had never set foot there — or in the settlement, for
the matter of that — since the day she'd moved to the Auté
Valley.

The *Bounty's* chronometer was at Mr. Christian's house.
He'd kept it going from the time the ship was seized from
Captain Bligh to the day he was killed. Mr. Young minded
it after that, till he took to drinking so hard; then I'd
looked after it, and if I did nothing else I saw that it was
never allowed to run down. I don't know why I did it,
for time meant nothing to us and we'd the sun to go by.
Likely it was because the clock was a link with home and
minded me of the days before we'd brought so much
misery on ourselves. Anyway, I never missed a day in winding it, and I took charge of Mr. Christian's calendar. He'd
said to me once: "Alex, if anything happens to Mr. Young
or me, see that ye keep my calendar going; else ye won't know
where ye are."

Ye might have thought the four of us would sober up
now, after such a spree as we'd had, but it wasn't the way
with us then. We was at it again all that day, and the next,
but on the third morning I'd had enough. It was then I
began to suspicion something was amiss with the womenfolk. Not one had come near us, and we'd nothing left
to eat in the house save a bunch of plantains. Quintal and
McCoy and me made out a meal with 'em, and I carried
some up to Mr. Young, who was lying down in the loft.
He always kept to himself as much as he could. He'd come
down now and again, but he said not a word more than was

needed to any of us. I told him about the women, but he was in a black mood and begged me to go away and leave him alone.

McCoy and Quintal had lost track of the days; they did n't know how long we 'd been drinking steady and they did n't care. The two of them was in a stupor again when I left the house about the middle of the morning.

The settlement was empty, just as it had been the past two days. I went along to the pool below Brown's Well; there was hardly an hour of the day but ye 'd find some of the women at the spring, but there was none that morning, so I went along the trail that goes along the western ridge and into the Auté Valley from that side.

When we first came here, all that high land was covered with forest, but we 'd cleared bits of it here and there. It was as pretty a place as ye could wish to see, high and cool, with rich little valleys running down to the north, and paths amongst the trees, and open places where we 'd made gardens. We 'd left the forest standing round about.

For three months past none of us men had set foot in the Auté Valley. As I 've said, we 'd hardly drawn sober breath in all that time; the work was left to the womenfolk. Balhadi and Taurua had kept Mr. Young and me supplied with food, and Mary and Sarah had done the like for the other two. Hutia and Prudence and Susannah would come to McCoy's house now and again, but we 'd seen little enough of the others. They kept away, and we 'd not lay eyes on 'em for weeks together.

I went along the old trail, amongst the woods and fields, till I came to open sunny land that stretched south to the cliffs above the sea. And there I stopped.

All the land here was cleared and laid out in gardens, and the women was at work amongst them, and they 'd made pens for fowls and pigs to one side. But what made me stand and stare was a kind of stockade, beyond, and close against the cliffs to the south'ard. It was made of the trunks of trees set close together deep in the ground and all of a dozen feet high. I judged it to be about twenty yards square. I could see it was new built, and it was as strong a little fort as men could have made.

I was so took aback that I stood stock-still for a bit; then I went on, slow, till some of the women spied me, and four of 'em came up to meet me.

Mrs. Christian was in front. Moetua and Prudence and Hutia came with her, and each one carried a musket. They halted and waited for me, and when I was about a dozen yards off Maimiti said, "Stand where ye are, Alex! What is it ye want?"

I did n't know what to say, I was that surprised, and I was ashamed to meet Maimiti face to face, knowing what she must think of such a drunken useless thing as I 'd become. The last time I 'd seen her was a day long before, at Brown's Well. She spoke about Mr. Christian, and how well he 'd thought o' me. She begged me to take hold of myself, and I 'd give my solemn promise I would. Three days after I was back at McCoy's house, and things went on just as they had before.

A man who 's lost his self-respect will try, like as not, to brazen it out, if he can, and so I did.

"Where 's Balhadi?" said I. "I want her to come home."

Mrs. Christian looked me straight in the eyes; then she said, very quiet: "Go back where ye 've come from. Balhadi wants nothing more to do with ye."

"Let her tell me that herself," said I. I knew well enough it was so. For three years Balhadi and me had lived together as happy as heart could wish, and I knew she 'd been as fond of me as I was of her. But after the still was started everything fell to pieces. At last she let me go my own way.

Maimiti beckoned to the others, who 'd gathered in the gardens below and stood looking toward us. They came to where we stood. Balhadi was amongst them, and when Maimiti asked if she wanted to go back with me she said, "No."

Then Maimiti said, "Now go ye back, Alex, and mind ye this: Ye 're to stay on the other side of the island. Ye may do as you please there; but from this day, if any of ye set foot in the Auté Valley, it will be at your peril. We have all the muskets here, and the powder and ball, and the lead for making more. Ye know that the half of us can shoot as well as any of ye men, so get ye gone to your friends and let them know what I 've said."

"Do ye think, Maimiti," said I, "that we 'll rest with matters in this state? Our wives had best come back if they know what 's good for 'em."

Then Taurua spoke up. "Say ye so, Alex? We 've give ye chances enough, and ye 're worse than pigs, the lot of ye. Not one of us shall go, and ye 'd best let us alone."

They was in dead earnest; I could see that. In my heart, I was proud of their spirit and well knew they had all the right on their side; but the badness in me came to the front, and I said things I was ashamed of even as I said 'em. I began to threaten and bluster and talk big, and I was mean enough to tell Sarah that Quintal would half kill her as soon as he could lay hands on her. She had a deathly fear of Quintal, and with reason. Many 's the time he 'd beat her in the past.

The old scared look I 'd seen so often came into her face; it was like as if she saw Quintal behind me. Mrs. Christian put an arm around her shoulders as a mother might have done. She had a gentle, womanly nature, but no man could better Maimiti in courage. There, before the others, she told me what miserable things the four of us was. She did n't raise her voice, but what she said struck home. "And let Quintal know this," she went on in her quiet way. "We keep watch here day and night. If he or any of ye try to

molest us, I promise it shall be for the last time. Now be
off, for we 've no more to say to ye."

I went back the way I 'd come, and the women stood
watching until I was out of sight in the forest. When I 'd
reached the ridge below the Goat-House Mountain I sat down
on a bench we had there and looked out over the land, all
so peaceful and quiet and sunny. I thought of the times
I 'd rested in the place with Mr. Christian as we 'd go back
and forth from the settlement. He 'd tell me about his
hopes and plans, and ask my advice about this and that. He
was always thinking of ways to do us good and make us more
happy and contented as time went on. I never heard him
speak of the mutiny, but I knew he thought he 'd ruined
the lives of all of us, and felt bound to do what he could to
make up for it. He planned and worked with that in mind,
and if we 'd backed him up the way we should have, not a
drop of blood would ever have been spilt here.

Little comfort I had from my thoughts that morning.
I saw no light ahead, and I did n't care what happened.
I 've no mind to defend myself. I knew right from wrong,
but I 'd a reckless streak in me that made me take to the
bad at this time as though to spite myself.

I went down to the village and searched through the
houses. The women had took every musket and pistol, as
Mrs. Christian said, and all the powder and ball and lead
was gone from the storehouse. They 'd carried away their
own things as well, but none of ours was touched save the
weapons. Mr. Young and me had some fowls penned up
near the house. I 'd clean forgot 'em and the poor things
was half dead. I fed and watered them and went along to
join the others.

Quintal and McCoy was still dead drunk; I could n't have
roused 'em if I 'd wanted to. Mr. Young was n't in the
house, but I found him on the slope to seaward. I could
see from the look he gave me that he 'd no wish for com-

pany, but I thought I'd best tell him what had happened. When I had, he smiled in a bitter way. "It's what we might have expected," he said. "The wonder is they have n't all left us long since."

"What 's to be done now?" said I. I could see how little heart he had for anything.

"What 's to be done? Nothing, Alex. I mean to leave 'em alone. The rest of ye can do as ye 've mind to," and with that he got up and went off amongst the trees, home. I would have liked well to go with him, but I knew he wanted to be alone, so I stayed where I was.

Before I go on, I 'd best tell ye something more about Quintal and McCoy. McCoy was a good neighbor when he was sober. He was quiet and hard-working and fond of his wife and children, but there was an ugly streak in him that showed now and again. It was n't often ye 'd see it, and then it was best to leave him alone. I 've known him to beat Mary black and blue, and be so sorry for it, after, there was nothing he would n't do to make it up to her. He 'd more brains than the rest of us seamen together, but spirits was a thing he could n't resist. Once the still was set going, he thought of naught but that. He would drink more than any two of us, and I often wondered how long he could keep it up at that rate.

Quintal was a big man — not tall, but thick through and strong as a bull, and slow-witted as he was strong. He 'd sit for hours at a time, saying nothing, and ye 'd wonder if he ever had a thought in his head. There was little harm in him, sober, but all the women except Moetua had a mortal fear of him, drunk. Maimiti he 'd never laid hands on, but the others whose men had been killed he thought of as his own property to do as he liked with. Moetua was near as strong as Quintal himself. He 'd tried to handle her, but she taught him a lesson or two he did n't forget. All the womenfolk hated him except his Sarah. They 'd come to think of him as worse than a wild beast, which was n't far from the truth.

In the afternoon, when McCoy and Quintal woke up, I told 'em what the women had told me.

"It could n't have happened better," said McCoy. "Let 'em go their way and we 'll go ours."

"What!" said Matt. "And have naught to do with 'em for the rest of our lives?"

"Rest ye patient," said McCoy. "D 'ye think they 'll stop as they are for long? They 'll come to heel soon enough if we take 'em at their word. It 's Maimiti and Taurua 's put 'em up to this, with two or three more to back 'em. Leave 'em alone. We 'll have our cronies back soon enough."

Quintal was in one of his ugly spells. "I 'll not leave 'em alone," said he. "They 'll play none o' their games with me. I 'll fetch a pair of 'em down."

"Ye 'll do naught o' the kind, Matt," said McCoy. "Don't be a fool. They 've all the muskets, and there 's a good half-dozen can shoot as well as any of us. They 're in no way to be trifled with now, that 's plain; but if we set quiet here we 'll have 'em back of their own wish."

"Set quiet if ye like," said Quintal. "I 'm going." Up he got and off he went, out of the house and across the valley, without another word.

"What d' ye think, Alex?" said McCoy. "Will they try to harm him?"

For all Maimiti had said, I did n't believe they would. We 'd had our way so long, doing as we pleased and giving no heed to any of 'em, that we 'd come to fancy we could keep on using 'em as we 'd a mind to.

"They 'll not shoot," said I, "unless he tries to climb their stockade, and he 'll not do that, for it 's all of a dozen feet high."

"We 'd best go and see what happens," said McCoy. "I 'd like well to have a look at the fort they 've made."

So we followed across the valley to the southern ridge. We did n't catch sight of Quintal till we 'd reached the upper side of the Auté Valley. He was standing at the edge of a thicket, staring down at the fort. "God bless me!" said McCoy when he saw the place. The three of us stood for a bit, looking out across the valley. Some of the women was at work in the gardens about a hundred yards away, and others farther on. They did n't see us, for we kept hid amongst the trees.

"When could they ha' done all this?" said Quintal. The pair of 'em was surprised as I 'd been at sight of the fort; for all I 'd told them, they was n't expecting to see such a strong-made place.

"There 's no matter o' that now," said McCoy. "Ye see it, Matt, and if ye 're not daft ye 'll come back with Alex and me. Ye 'll only make things worse if ye try any hard usage with 'em. Come along down, man, and leave 'em alone."

But there was no talking Quintal over, once he got a notion into his head. He 'd a great conceit of his strength, and was too thick-witted to believe the women would dare to hold out against him, even with muskets in their hands.

"Stand ye here and watch," said he. "I want none o' yer help, if that 's what ye 're afeared of."

Quintal had n't washed himself for days, and he had a great bushy beard that half covered his chest. He 'd no clothes on save a bit of dirty bark cloth about his middle, and with his club in his hand he looked worse than any naked savage I 've ever laid eyes on.

All that piece of land down from the ridge had been cleared; the women had seen to that, so as they could have a view of anyone coming. The minute Quintal showed himself out of the forest there was a conch shell blown by someone on watch on a platform inside the stockade. Those at work in the gardens had spied him at the same time. There

was half a dozen outside, and instead of running back to the
fort, as we 'd expected, they spread out in a line and waited
for Quintal to come on. I saw Moetua and Prudence in the
centre. Moetua carried a cudgel and Prudence had a musket. Mrs. Christian was off to one side, with Hutia; and
Balhadi and Taurua stood on the other side.

Moetua got down on her knees, and Prudence, who was a
little thing, but as good a shot as any man, stood behind with
the musket resting on Moetua's shoulder. Mrs. Christian
knelt down behind a boulder and rested her piece on that.
They 'd not been twenty seconds in getting ready for Quintal.
He was a good sixty yards off when he halted; then he went
on, slow and steady, like the thick-skulled simpleton he was.
Afore he 'd gone three steps farther, Maimiti blazed away
at him, and we saw Quintal half swing round and go down.
He gave a bellow and leaped up again, and at that, Prudence
fired. Quintal waited for no more. He ran back up the
slope as fast as he could go, with the women after him,
Moetua in the lead. He came crashing into the thickets and
on he went down into the Main Valley. McCoy and I
did n't wait to see what the women meant to do. We followed Quintal.

He was on a bench by the door, holding his hand over
his left shoulder, and with blood streaming down one side
of his face. Maimiti's shot had torn through the muscles
of his shoulder, but Prudence had meant to kill, and a near
thing it was for Quintal. The ball had all but took off one
of his ears. McCoy and I was busy for the next hour
getting him bandaged.

We 'd no more doubt that the women was in earnest.
Quintal had learned the only way he could — by being hurt;
he had to lay up for near two months while his wounds was
healing. He was in an ugly temper all this while, and it was
as much as we could do to get a word out of him. Whether
it was drink, or lonesomeness, or both together, I don't know,

but McCoy and I could see he was getting more queer in his head every day. He'd talk to himself, even with us in the room, and half the time ye could make naught of what he'd say.

Things went on quiet enough for a while. Quintal and McCoy worked on at making spirits, and before they was through they filled up every bottle we had, with a cag or two beside. I kept clear of 'em as near as I could. I did some gardening again, and with that and fishing I was busy most hours of the day. But when night came I'd set me down to drink with 'em, hating myself all the while for doing it.

McCoy was sure some of the women would come back. "Rest easy, Matt," he'd say to Quintal. "There'll be no need to chase after 'em. We'll have a two-three of 'em down here before the week's out." But two months went by and not one came near us.

We saw little of Mr. Young. As I've said, he went off home the day I told him about the women leaving, and he came no more to McCoy's house. And never again, to his last day, did he touch a drop of spirits. I was worried about his health. The year before, he was took with what looked like asthma trouble, and it was getting worse. He needed someone to look after him, but he was bound to do for himself, and he wouldn't hear to my letting the women know he was sick. He was always friendly when I went along to see him, but I knew he wanted to be alone and that made me slow to bother him. Not a word did he say about my keeping on with Quintal and McCoy, but I was sure how he felt.

By the time Quintal's wounds was healed, him and McCoy decided they'd had enough of waiting. They'd come to think the right of things was on our side now. I was strong against makin' any move, but they was bound to stir up more trouble.

"What 'll ye do?" said I to Will. "Fetch Mary back, willing or not?"

"Mary?" said he. "I 'd not have her now if she was to crawl on her knees, beggin' me. There 's a-plenty besides her, and one of 'em I 'll take!"

Quintal was gettin' more ugly every day, and he was of the same mind. I knew I could n't keep 'em quiet for long, and I had the notion to go across and warn Mrs. Christian. I should have done it, but, as I 've said, I had a stubborn streak in me. I 'd been told to keep away from the Auté Valley, and so I did.

One day Quintal was bound to go. There was no use arguing with either of 'em, so I tried another plan. I fetched out a bottle of spirits, hopin' to get 'em so dazed with grog they 'd not be able to move.

"There 'll be the devil to pay now," said I, "so we may as well have a good spree afore trouble starts." They was agreeable, and did n't go that day, but early next morning, when I was away, they set out across the island. They was still drunk, but able to take care of themselves, and they 'd sense enough left to recollect the women could shoot. They 'd no mind to go marchin' down amongst 'em the way Quintal had.

I was told what happened, afterward. When they got to the top of the ridge they hid themselves so as they could look across the gardens to the stockade. Some of the women was at work outside and they still carried muskets. They 'd waited a good two hours when they saw Nanai and Jenny come out of the fort. They 'd baskets on their arms, but no weapons, and they went off to the westward.

There 's a steep little valley runs down to the sea below the mountain on the southern side. They waited till they was sure that was where Nanai and Jenny was bound; then they back-tracked and came round to the west side of the Auté Valley, and hid themselves close to the path that goes down this ravine. They'd only to wait to catch the women as they came up.

"I'll take Jenny and you can have Nanai," said McCoy. Jenny was Mrs. Christian's right hand. McCoy believed we had her to thank for coaxin' Prudence and Hutia away from us. He was glad to have this chance to get back at her.

Presently they spied Nanai comin' up amongst the trees, below. It was a stiff climb and she had a carrying pole, with a bunch of plantains at one end and a basket of shell-fish on the other. Nanai was about twenty-three at this time. She'd been Tetahiti's wife, if ye remember. There was none had a greater fear of Quintal.

When she reached level ground she set down her load to rest not three steps from where they was hid. Out Quintal jumped and grabbed her. She was so terrified she made no struggle at all, and they had her tied hand and foot in a minute. They stuffed leaves in her mouth with a strip of bark tied across it, to make sure she wouldn't cry out.

Jenny wasn't far behind, and they had her before she knew where she was. She was small, but wiry as a cat, and she fought like one, tooth and nail. It was as much as Quintal could do to hold her while McCoy put a gag over her mouth. He got the palm of his hand bit through doing it. When they had her tied he took her over his shoulder, and Quintal came after, with Nanai.

I'd come back to the house, in the meantime, and found no one there. I guessed what Quintal and McCoy was up to, but I didn't believe they'd be able to get at the women. In case they had, I didn't want to be mixed up in it. So I went along to Mr. Young's house and spent the night there. I said naught to him about the others.

They brought the girls to the house and Nanai was loosed, but Jenny was kept tied at first. Then McCoy began to crow over Jenny, but she had a fiery spirit and gave him as good as he sent. "Lay hands on me, Will McCoy, and I won't rest till I 've killed ye," said she. "Where 's Alex and Ned Young?"

"Leave Ned out o' this," said McCoy. "He has naught to do with us. He 's been a sick man this long while; yet, betwixt ye, ye 've kept Taurua away from him."

Then he told her I was off on a woman hunt of my own and would be along with another of 'em directly.

Nanai was crouched in a corner, with Quintal on a bench in front of her. All at once she made a spring for the door, but Quintal grabbed her by the hair and dragged her back. Ye 'll not wish to hear what went on after this. First they tried to force the girls to drink with 'em, and in the end they abused both in a shameful way. In the night, when Quintal and McCoy was asleep, they got away. When I came down from Mr. Young's next morning I could see there 'd been a fight in the house. McCoy was nursing his bit hand with a rag tied round it. But not a word was said of what had happened. They was a glum surly pair, and no mistake!

CHAPTER XIX

THE next day Mr. Young came along to see us. He was having one of his bad attacks of asthma and it was all he could do to speak. When we'd set a chair for him he broke in a fit of coughing was pitiful to see. It was n't till that morning that it came in to me what a state Mr. Young was in. He'd wasted down to little more than skin and bone. When his coughing spell was over he told us what he'd come for.

"I've been asked to bring ye a message from the women," said he. "Maimiti says the three of ye must leave the island. They're all agreed on this. Ye can take the cutter and what ye need in the way of supplies, but ye must clear out."

"Clear out!" said I. "Where to?"

"I don't know. Tahiti, I suppose. Where ye like, so long as it's away from here. They'll give ye three days to make plans."

"And do they think we'll be fools enough to go?" said McCoy.

"Maimiti says ye must," he replied, almost in a whisper. He had to fight for breath every few words he spoke. "Ye'd best do it. I'll go with ye."

"Go with us?" said I. "That ye won't, Ned. D' ye think we'd allow it, sick as ye are?"

He held up his hand. "Wait, Alex. . . . It's no matter what happens to me. I want to go. . . . Get away from here. . . . We could fetch some island to the westward; one o' them we passed on the way from Tahiti. Try it, anyway."

"And if we won't go, what then?" said McCoy.

"Maimiti means what she says. They'll take action."

Quintal laughed. "Let 'em try!" said he.

My heart went out to Mr. Young. He'd no wish to go,
I knew that well enough; but he was the only one could
use a sextant, and he knew we could never fetch up any place
without him. Even with him our chances would be poor
enough. But he was thinkin' of the women and children
more than us. He wanted them to have a chance to live
quiet decent lives.

"What are ye for, Alex?" said Quintal. "Ye'll wish to
give in to the bitches, I'll warrant — let 'em drive us out.
Damn yer eyes! If it'd not been for yerself and Will, we'd
ha' learned 'em who's masters here long afore this."

"Aye, ye made a brave show, Matt, a while back," said
I, "runnin' up the hill with the lot of 'em at yer heels.
They've had right enough on their side, the womenfolk,
and well ye know it! It'll be yerself and Will has drove
'em to this."

"Drove 'em, did we?" said McCoy. "We've not been near
'em till yesterday, and much good it's done us to keep clear.
But there'll be some drivin' now, I promise ye!"

Mr. Young shook his head. "Take care!" said he. "They
mean what they say."

"Sit ye down, Will," said I. "Let's talk this over quiet,
and see what's best to be done."

But neither of 'em would listen to reason and was all for
doin' something straight off. Mr. Young could have been
no more sick of 'em than I was.

Presently he got up, shaky and weak, and made ready to
go. "I've done all I can," said he. "Now look out for
yourselves!"

"Never ye mind about us," said Quintal. "We'll do
that and more!" I wanted to help Mr. Young along the
path, home, but he wouldn't hear to it and went off alone.

McCoy was uneasy about the still, and nothing would do but it must be hid away. Quintal helped him carry it to a place in the valley where they'd never be able to find it. As I've said, we'd spirits enough on hand to last us for months, and that was stowed away as well, in a safe place.

I didn't know just what to do. Ye may think it strange, but I still had a soft spot in my heart for Will and Matt. We'd been shipmates so long, and I'd the wish to stand by 'em, come what might. And wasn't I as much to blame, or near as much, as themselves? For all that, I wanted bad to follow after Mr. Young and talk things over with him. I'd the notion the pair of us should see Mrs. Christian and try to patch things up; join with the women, mebbe, if they'd have us, and leave McCoy and Quintal to go their own way. But, when I thought it over, that seemed to me a dangerous thing for all. It would oppose us men, two and two, and might lead to the killing of one side or the other. What I wanted above all was for us to keep clear of any more bloodshed. And there was another thing. It shames me to say it, but I couldn't abide the thought of bein' without drink. So the end of it was I did naught, but waited to see what would come.

That day McCoy and Quintal got as drunk as I'd ever seen 'em, and stayed so, and lucky it was that Matt was in none of his ugly spells. He drank himself to sleep with scarce a word said. I had my share, but not so much but I was up and about, doin' my chores. But I mind how low-spirited I was, thinkin' of the lonesome unnatural life we had, when there was no need for it. And all this time I missed the children and craved to see 'em. What fools we was to think more of our grog than we did of them!

The three days went by, but there was no sign of the women. That didn't surprise us, for we'd no idea they'd do anything. After we'd et, at midday, we had our sleep, as usual. It was towards the middle of the afternoon when

I woke up; I could see the streaks of sunlight slanting down through the chinks in the windows. The house had four shutters, two on each side. I got up to open 'em. As I was sliding the first one back, a musket was fired from the edge of the forest, and the ball sang past within an inch or two of my head. I ducked down and slammed the window shut. McCoy was asleep on the floor by the table. He raised up his head. "What's that?" said he, and he'd no more than spoke when another ball splintered through the boards of the shutter I'd just closed. That roused Quintal; he sat up and glared at the two of us. I motioned 'em to keep quiet, and crawled to a knothole in one of the planks that gave me a view across the strip of cleared land, which was about twenty yards wide.

At first I saw naught but a bit of the forest; then I made out the barrel of a musket was pushed through the bushes and pointing at the door, and another farther along. A minute later I had a glimpse of Hutia behind a tree. We'd been caught, right enough, and was still so muddled with sleep, it took us a quarter of an hour to get our wits together. While I was spying out the valley side of the house, Quintal opened the door a wee crack on the other side. Two shots was fired the minute he did it. One grazed his hipbone, breaking the skin. We knew, then, the place was surrounded, and the women meant to kill us if they could. McCoy called out for Mrs. Christian, but there was no answer save another shot through the wall.

For all their warnings, we'd not believed they'd take any such action as this. We'd no mind to give in, now, but all we could do was to keep well hid. Every little while shots would be fired through the windows or doors; we had to lay flat on the floor. There was fourteen muskets amongst 'em, and half a dozen pistols, and the women who couldn't shoot kept the extra ones loaded for the others. Quintal and I was for making a rush out, but McCoy was against this. "Don't be fools," said he. "That's what they hope we'll do, and it's little chance we'd have to get clear by daylight. We'd best wait till dark, unless they take it into their heads to rush us before." So we stayed as we was, with the doors blocked with the benches and tables and some bags of yams and sweet potatoes. We didn't speak above a whisper all this time.

We'd little fear they would try to come to grips with us in the house. They'd keep well off and trust to the musket; but they was bound to get us into the open afore dark, and so they did. Some of 'em slipped up to the ends of the house with torches of dry palm fronds and set fire to the thatch.

In a couple of minutes the whole place was in a blaze. There was no time for anything except to get out as quick as ever we could, and a chancy thing it was. Quintal was so thick-headed as to clear away the benches we'd piled in front of the door. I heard the women on that side shooting at him as I went out one of the windows on the seaward side. I dodged around the cookhouse as one of them fired at me. She was hid behind a rock, and before any of the others could shoot I was across the bit of open ground and amongst the trees.

As soon as I was well out of view I slowed down to a walk, for I was sure they'd not scatter and try to follow us. I went up the western ridge and on to the Goat-House Peak. It was near dark by that time; the house was still in a full blaze, but it soon burnt itself out. I heard no more shots; all was as quiet as though there was no one but me on the island. I knew the women would do no more prowling round at night; they'd keep together and go back to the fort, so I waited till moonrise and then went down to Mr. Young's house.

I made certain there was no one about, and slipped inside. Mr. Young was gone. Afterward I learned that some of the women had come down the day before, with a litter they'd made, and carried him up to their place so's they could look after him. I got a scare and jumped halfway across the room when something brushed against my leg, but it was only one of the *Bounty's* cats was born on the ship on the way out from England. He was a great pet of mine. I went out to the cook-shed to scratch up a coconut for him, and whilst I was at it I heard McCoy's voice calling out for Ned.

He was hid under the banyan tree below the house. He'd been shot through the fleshy part of the leg and had lost a good deal of blood. Moetua had chased him, he said, but he'd managed to get clear of her in the forest. Quintal he'd not seen.

It was a painful wound he had. I cleaned the place and bound it up. As soon as that was done he was all for moving on. He was scared bad. "They mean to kill us, Alex; I take that as certain," said he. "Like enough they've done for Quintal."

"That may be," said I, "but they'll not come in the night. We can rest here till daylight, and then hide out till we know what they're up to."

We went off next morning while it was still dark. McCoy was too lame to go far, but I hid him in a thicket where they could never have found him. I kept watch on the settlement and no one came near it. Not a sign of Quintal did we see in all that time, though I searched far and wide for him. We was both sure he was dead.

We kept away from the settlement for ten days; then we moved into Mr. Young's house. We felt none too easy at first, not knowing but the women might be spying on us and making ready for another attack; but after three weeks we felt certain they meant to leave us alone as long as we did n't molest them. McCoy was laid up this while; I spent a good piece of my time getting food and searching for Quintal's body. It was a lonesome life. I can't say we relished it.

It was in March 1797 that the women burned the house. After that McCoy and I let up on the drinking. We'd have a sup together now and again, but there was no swilling it down the way we'd done before.

One day McCoy was away from sunup, and when he came back he told me he'd seen his girl, Mary. He'd met her in the forest, without the others knowing.

"What did she say of Quintal?" I asked him.

"They thought they'd hit him," said he, "but they could n't be sure what happened."

"Did ye tell Mary we'd not seen him?"

"Aye. He's dead, Alex, for certain. Who knows but he may have lingered on for days, past helping himself, and us knowing nothing about it?"

"What else did Mary tell ye?" I asked. "How did they know but what we'd been killed as well? And yet none of 'em came near to see."

"They've known. They kept watch of us for a fortnight, Mary says. They reckoned Quintal had been bad hurt and we was nursing him."

"There's a thing I'd like well to know," said I. "Did Mary and Balhadi come down with the rest the day they burned the house?"

"They did not; and I'll tell ye more, Alex. They was against the others coming, and Sarah Quintal with 'em. Bad as we'd used 'em, they had no wish to see us dead."

"And what's the mind of the rest about us now?"

"We'll not be troubled, Mary says, as long as we let 'em alone."

"It's a wonder to me, Will, ye did n't try to coax Mary back," said I.

"So I did, but she'll not come. They've had enough of us, Alex. That's the truth of it."

"Will," said I, "could we break up the cursed still and be

sober again? It would be desperate hard at first, but like enough we could do it."

Many 's the time I 've thought, since, of what might have happened if he 'd said, "So we can, Alex! We 'll not rest till it 's done!" I was in the mind, and if I 'd made an honest try I might have coaxed McCoy. But the truth is I was half afraid he 'd agree.

"I could n't, Alex," said he. "God forgive me, I could n't! Where 'd we be, in such a lonesome shut-off place, without a drop to cheer us up now and again?"

"It 's right ye are," said I. "I was daft to think of it," and there was an end o' that.

"How is it with Ned Young?" I asked him.

"He 's been desperate sick, Mary says, and he 's still in his bed."

"It 's little we 'll see of Ned from now on," said I. "He 'll never come back to us, and it 'll be better so for all hands. And now I 'll tell ye, Will, what I mean to do. Ye can go as you 've a mind to, but I 'll keep clear of the women if so be as I can. There 's been trouble enough here. I 'll be the cause of no more."

"There 'll be no need o' that," said he. "I 'll be seeing Mary again, and I 'll have a word with her whenever ye say. I 'll warrant there 's a two-three of the women will be willing enough to come down and pass the time o' day with ye."

But I told him I 'd go it alone for the present.

The next day we roamed the Main Valley over on a last hunt for Quintal's body. There was n't a place he might have crawled into that we had n't searched, but we tried once more. By the middle of the afternoon we was ready to give up. We 'd come out on the western ridge, and McCoy thought we ought to hunt through the gullies on that side, but I was sure no man as bad hurt as Quintal must have been would crawl that far to die. There 'd be no sense in it.

"But it 's what Quintal might do, for all that," said

McCoy. "There was no sense in *him*, poor loon! We'd best look, anyway. I'll feel better when it's done."

I was willing, for I hated to think of poor Matt's body lying unburied; but before we went down on that side we climbed the Goat-House Peak for a look around. And there, close to the top, where the cliffs made a straight drop to the sea, we found an axe handle leaned up against a rock. It was one of them had been in McCoy's house the day it was burned. It gave us a shock to see it, for we knew that Matt himself had carried it there. It was stained with dried blood, and we saw what we thought was blood on the rock itself. It's a chancy place, the Goat-House Peak; the footing is none too sure for a well man; and the axe handle was resting not three feet from the edge of the seaward cliffs. McCoy crawled to the edge and looked over, but there was nothing to see save the surf beating up against the rocks. We looked no farther. We couldn't guess why Matt had come there, but we knew he had, and there'd be no body to find. He might have lost his balance, but, knowing Matt, we thought he must have been so bad hurt he'd thrown himself off to make an end.

We went down without a word. He was a rough, hard man, was Quintal. Ye'll think, sir, from what I've said of him, that he was naught but a great brute we might be glad to think was dead. A brute he was, in his strength, — I've never seen his equal there, save Minarii, — and dangerous bad, times, when drunk. But there'd been a side to him I've not brought out the way I should have. There was none but liked the old Matt Quintal that first came to Pitcairn, and it was that one I was thinking about as we went back to the settlement.

It hit McCoy harder than it did me, for they'd been cronies ever since the *Bounty* left England, and they'd lived together here. Quintal thought the world and all of McCoy, and when he was sober would do whatever he said; but these last years, when he was growing so queer, not even McCoy could manage him.

That night it set in to raining and blowing hard from the east, and it kept on for three days. There was nothing we could do but stay in the house. We started drinking again, McCoy on one side of the table and me on the other. Before half the night was over he'd finished two quarts of spirits, but for all that he'd no mind to leave off. He'd took it into his head he was to blame for all the misery there'd been on the island, and he'd talk of naught but that.

"It's the truth I'm speaking, Alex," he'd say. "I was the first to want the land divided, and talked it up and egged the others on to stand out against Christian. That's what started the killing. There's not a murdered man, Indian or white, but that has me to thank for his death."

And so he went on, the night through, till I was half crazed with hearing the same thing over and over again. Finally I could stand it no more.

"Ye'd best go to bed, Will," I said, and with that I went out of the house. The night could n't have been wilder or blacker. I lost my way and fell down a dozen times before I reached Mr. Christian's house. All wet and slathered in mud, I rolled into his old bed-place and went to sleep.

It was past midday when I woke up, and raining harder than ever. I went out in it for a bath and to feed my pigs and fowls. When I'd cleaned up the muddy mess I'd made in Mr. Christian's house, I went to the out-kitchen and boiled me some yams and cooked some eggs; had my own breakfast and carried some up to McCoy. He was settin' at the table, wide awake, just as I'd left him. He'd finished what was left in the bottle I'd been at the night before, but he spoke to me as sober as though he'd been drinking nothing stronger than water. There was no more weeping talk. I tried to coax him to eat a bite, but he wouldn't touch what I'd brought him.

"Leave me alone," said he. "Go back to Christian's house, or wherever ye 've been. I 'm wanting no company."

"I can manage without yours," said I, and left him there. It rubbed me the wrong way to have him speak like that when I 'd taken the trouble to cook his breakfast and bring it to him.

The wind shifted to the north and blew a gale; low grey clouds was scudding past not much over the trees. I went down the cove to see if the *Bounty's* old cutter was safe. We had it in a shed above the landing place. Not that we ever used it much. I don't think it had been out of the shed since the time the womenfolk tried to go off in it. We might as well have broken it up, for any good it was to us, but we 'd patch and caulk it, none of us knew why, exactly.

I 've never but once seen a heavier surf in the cove than there was that day. It was an awesome sight to watch the great seas piling in, throwing spray and solid water halfway up to the lookout point. The shed was gone and the cutter with it, and the wreckage was scattered far out across the cove. We had two Indian canoes, but they was safe. We 'd lost canoes before, and when we made the last ones we took care to dig out a place for 'em well above the reach of any sea that might make up.

I went back to Mr. Christian's house, and for two days I kept away from McCoy. Then I got a bit worried about him, and after I 'd had my supper I went along to see him whether he wanted me to or not.

The wind had gone down, but it was still cloudy, unsettled weather. McCoy had all the doors and the windows shut. I called out to him, but there was no answer, so I pushed open the door and went in.

It was so dark inside that I could see naught at first. "Will! Where 've ye got to?" said I. Then I heard his voice from the corner of the room. "Is it yourself, Alex? Quick, man! Shut the door!"

I slammed it to in spite of myself, he spoke in such a terror-struck voice. "What is it, lad?" I said. I did n't know but what the women might have changed their minds about leaving us alone; but when he begged me to make a light I knew it could n't be that.

We kept a supply of candlenut tapers ready for lighting on a shelf, along with a flint and steel and a box of tinder. The tinder had got damp with the rainy weather and I was a quarter of an hour getting a taper alight. I found McCoy huddled down in a corner with the table upset and pulled up close, to hide behind. The minute I saw him I knew what was wrong. He had the horrors coming on, for the first time since I 'd known him.

"Alex!" said he, "Alex!" — and that was as much as he could get out at first. He was a pitiful sight, shakin' and shiverin', with his knees under his chin and his eyes staring up at me like a wild man's.

"What 's all this, Will?" said I, in as easy a voice as I could manage. "What 's this game ye 're playin' on me?" And whilst I spoke I righted the table and pulled it back into the middle of the room. "Come aboard, lad! D' ye still hate the sight of an old shipmate?"

He kept his eyes on the door, with a look on his face I 'll not forget. Then up he sprung, and in three steps he was beside me on the bench, and gripped my arm with both his hands, so tight that the marks of his finger nails was there for days.

"Don't let him touch me!" said he, in a voice it sickened me to hear. Then he slid down to the floor under the table and held me fast by the legs.

"What ails ye?" said I. "What are ye afeared of?"

"Minarii," said he, in a whisper. "There by the door!"

"Will, ye daft loon! There 's no Minarii here. Don't ye think I could see him if there was? Come, have a look for yourself."

He got up slow to his knees and turned himself till he could look toward the door.

"Are ye satisfied now?" said I. "There's none here but ourselves."

"Aye, he's gone," said he, in a weak, shaky voice. "Ye've scared him off."

"He's never been here," said I. "It's naught but your fancy. I'll show ye."

I tried to get up, but he held me fast and would n't let go. "Don't leave me, Alex! Stay close here!"

I got him up on the bench again, but he kept tight hold of my arm. I'd seen a man or two with the horrors before. McCoy's was just coming on and I knew what I was in for. I coaxed him to loose me, after a bit, and I got a carrying pole was standing in a corner, and laid it on the table.

"I'll let no one touch ye, Will; ye can lay to that!" said I. "I'll knock 'em silly with this afore they know where they are."

That quieted him some, but try as I would I could n't get him to bed. He was afeared to lie down. There was eight empty bottles scattered about the room. One I'd about finished the last night we was together. The rest McCoy had emptied alone, and I would n't have believed it unless I'd seen it.

He got worse as the night went on. He babbled wild and I could n't make sense of it; but what he'd see was Minarii, with the heads of the murdered white men, and he was possessed with the notion that he'd come for ours. Time and again he'd be certain Minarii had opened the door, and I'd grab up the carrying pole and rush at naught, making out I'd drove him off. McCoy would think I had, and rest quiet for half an hour, maybe; then it would be the same thing over again.

So it went till long past midnight. I kept a light going until I'd burned all the tapers we had in the house. It had been bad enough before; ye can fancy what it was when the light was gone. I was twice McCoy's heft, and three times as strong, or so I 'd believed; but it was all I could do to hold him when the terror was on him, and the screams he let out was like nothing human. Once he got loose and dashed his head so hard against the wall that it knocked him out for a bit. That gave me a chance to get him on to the bed and there I held him to daylight. He was in convulsions at the last, and if ever ye 've held a man in that state, ye 'll know what I went through.

It was just beginning to get light in the room when his body went limp under me and I saw he 'd dozed off. I was done up and no mistake. It was as much as I could do to walk to the table and set down. Every muscle of me was tired and I was famished for sleep. I put my head on my arms and knew no more till I was roused by another yell, and before I could get my wits together McCoy was out of the door and running down the path toward Mr. Christian's house.

I followed, but the path 's no easy one to race over, especially after such rains as we 'd had. I slid and fell and got up again, and stumbled over the roots of trees, and by the time I got to Mr. Christian's house McCoy was making straight for the bluffs above the sea. I yelled, "Will! Come back!" But he never turned his head, and down he went, out of sight.

The sea was higher if anything than it had been the day before. When I reached the edge of the bluffs where I could look over, McCoy was halfway down. Whether he jumped or fell I don't know, but all at once he made a fearsome drop and struck amongst the rocks far below, just as a great sea came roaring in and took him, throwing up spray as high as where I stood. Another came directly after, and I caught a glimpse of his body being washed down and under it. I stood there for a half an hour, but I saw him no more.

CHAPTER XX

I FOUND his body the next afternoon. It had been washed to the mouth of the little valley west of Mr. Christian's house, and it was so battered and crushed 'twixt the rocks and the sea, ye 'd scarce have thought it was anything human. Ye 'll know how I felt when I had to take it up, but take it up I did, and buried it.

Then, sir, I went straight to the place where we 'd hid our store of spirits. It was in a hole amongst the rocks on the seaward side of McCoy's old house. And I bashed in the two small cags and emptied 'em, and I took the rest, bottle by bottle, and broke every one into a thousand pieces against the rocks. Then I went to the place where we 'd hid the still, and I took the copper coil and ran back to the bluffs, and I threw it as far as ever I could; and when I saw it splash in the sea I said, "God be thanked, there 's an end of it!"

What with watching over McCoy and searching for his body all the next day, I was knocked up. I felt I could sleep for a week, but I could n't bring myself, then, to go back to Mr. Christian's house, or to any of ours. I went to the place where the Indians had lived. It was in a pretty glade not far from where the path goes down to the cove. Many an evening I 'd spent in that house afore there was any trouble amongst us. I 'd a great liking for the Indians, and for Minarii and Tetahiti in particular. You 'd go far to find two better men, brown or white. I 'd been with 'em, day after day, and to say the truth, I 'd found more pleasure with them than with my own mates. I 'd puzzled now and again to think why they 'd wanted to kill the lot of us. I knew they hated some, but I would n't have believed they 'd have wanted all of us dead. But when ye come to think of it, they would n't dare leave any of us alive, once they 'd started killing. There could be no friendship after that. It would have been us or them till one side or the other was wiped out.

I 'd not been near their house in months, and it was a sorry-looking place now. The trail was grown over with bushes and the house going to rack and ruin. It gave me a lone-some feeling to see it, but I went in, and laid me down, and was asleep in five minutes.

I slept till daylight, and the first thing I thought about when I woke up was how bad I wanted a good stiff tot o' grog. I tried hard to put the notion out o' my head, but the more I tried the worse it got, and the end of it was I hurried along to the place where we 'd kept the spirits to see if I might n't have missed a bottle the day before. I found I had n't, and I rested there, looking down at all them bits of broken glass shining on the rocks below, and cursing my-self for the fool I 'd been. There was no shame in me for being such a weak thing. I could think of naught but that I must get me a drink, somehow. Then I was minded of the bottles McCoy had emptied, and I thought I might find a drop left in one of 'em. A drop was all there was. I sup-pose I drained out a couple of spoonfuls from the lot, and then I washed out each bottle with a sup o' water so 's to have it all. But that was only a torment, and I did n't rest till I 'd searched all the houses in hopes of finding a bottle put by somewhere. I found one that had about a half-pint in it, in the tool-shed, and went near daft with joy at the sight of it.

Ye 'll understand, sir, if ye 've been a toper and left off sudden, the state I was in. There 'd not been a day in four years I had n't had my two or three tots o' grog, and most days there 'd been a sight more taken. I 'd got so as I needed spirits more than food or sleep or anything else, and if there was ever a sorry man it was me, that day, thinking how I 'd thrown the copper coil into the sea. We 'd nothing else would serve to distill spirits with. Then I minded how McCoy had made some beer, once, with ti roots. He 'd made a mash and let it ferment. It was bitter stuff, and fair gagged ye to get it down, but it was strong.

I 'd no sooner thought of it than I set off with a mattock over my shoulders for McCoy's ti plantation. I wanted to get a mess of roots to baking straight off; but before I got to the place I stopped. I could take ye to the very spot, sir, and show ye the rock I set on whilst I fought the thing out with myself. I thought of all the misery we 'd brought on the womenfolk and ourselves those last years. I thought of the children. I knew that if I digged up them ti roots I was lost; I 'd finish the way McCoy had. "Never!" said I. "Back with ye, Alex Smith, and make an end, once and for all!"

And so I did, though I went through torments for a fortnight. I could n't sleep, I could n't eat, and I was n't sure but I 'd have the horrors myself afore I was done. But I held fast.

Little by little things got easier for me. I could have my rest at night; there was no more walking up and down till I was so beat I could scarce stand. At times when it was hardest, I set my mind on Mr. Christian, and it would strengthen me to think how pleased and comforted he 'd be if he could know the fight I was makin'. I 'd never forgot the hopeless look on his face the day he died. It was when his lad, Thursday October, had walked into the room. I remembered him saying, "Take the child out," to Mrs. Christian. There 's no father could have loved children more. He could n't bear to see the lad, that was it, thinking what might happen once he was gone. A blessing it was he could n't see what did happen.

It was a rare thing to get back my self-respect. I 'd wake

of a morning with a feeling of peace in my heart, and there was n't a day long enough for the work I had in hand. I cut off the beard I 'd let grow, and shaved regular, like I used to, and kept myself clean and tidy. I moved back into my old house where I 'd lived with Mr. Young, and made everything shipshape there; then I went through the other houses and set them to rights as well as I could, working alone, though why I did it I could n't say. I might have had the notion in the back of my head that the women would want to come back some day.

I was bound not to go too near 'em, for I had my pride. If they wanted to keep clear, they could for all of me, and Mr. Young with 'em. I 'd not be the one to make the first move.

I had work and to spare, days, but night was a lonesome time. There was little I could do after dark but set and think. When I was redding up the houses, I found the *Bounty's* old Bible and Prayer Book. They 'd been Mr. Christian's, before. After his death Mr. Young took charge of 'em, and I 'd often see him reading in one or the other, though he was n't what ye 'd call a religious man. But these was all we had in the way of books, and I reckon they helped him pass the time. I found a couple of the *Bounty's* spare logbooks that he 'd filled with writin', but what it was I could n't make out. Little schooling I 'd ever had in my young days. It was as much as I could do to write my name, but I 'd got far enough along to spell out words of print. I thought, maybe, with the Bible to help, I could bring back what I 'd been teached as a lad, but I had to give up. It was all gone clean out o' my head.

One day — it was around a month after I 'd buried McCoy — I was weeding a bit of garden I 'd made near the house. I 'd set me down to rest when I heard a rustlin' in the bushes behind me. I looked round, and there was my old woman.

Not a word was spoke. In three steps she was down on her knees beside me. She put her arms around me and her head on my shoulder, and began to weep in the soft quiet way the Indian women do. I was touched deep, but I sat lookin' straight in front of me. After a bit, when I was sure I had myself in hand, I said: "Where 's your musket, Balhadi? Ain't ye afeared to go roamin' without it? I might do ye a mischief."

She said naught, but only held on to me the tighter. I reached up and took hold of her hand, and we rested so for a good ten minutes. I 'll not go into all that was said. It was like the old days afore any trouble was started. I told her about McCoy and she had her cry over that, not being a woman to nurse hard feelings towards anyone, and Will was a good man, well liked by all when he 'd been sober. She cried more, for joy, when I told her I 'd destroyed the still and the spirits. I felt paid a hundred times over for the misery I 'd suffered in getting myself in hand. I 'd been hurt that Mr. Young had n't come near me, but Balhadi said it was because he was too sick to come. He'd been in his bed all this while.

"I 'd like well to see him," said I.

"Then come, Alex," said she, taking hold of my hand. "There 's not been a day but he 's spoke of ye, and what ye 've told me will do him more good than any of us women can. Ye 'll be welcomed hearty, that I promise, and there 'll be none gladder to see ye than Maimiti."

So I started along with her, but afore we 'd gone a dozen yards I stopped.

"No, Balhadi," said I. "I 'll rest here in the settlement. Ye can tell Maimiti and the others how it is with me now. If they want to see me, they know where they can find me, and they can do as they 've a mind about coming back. I 'll not be the one to coax 'em."

So off she went, alone. That was the middle of the morn-

ing, and three hours later here they came, all the womenfolk, some carrying children or leading 'em, some with
baskets and bundles, — all they could manage at one time, —
Maimiti in the lead, and Moetua with Ned Young pickaback,
as though he 'd been a child.   Some of the young ones I 'd
never seen; others I 'd hardly laid eyes on for three years.
Thursday October was a fine lad, now, past eight years, and
his brother Charles was six, and little Mary Christian five,
who was born the very day the killing began.   There was
eighteen children, all told, two of 'em mine, and it shames
me to say that neither of these was Balhadi's.   When I saw
that little flock, as pretty, healthy children as a man could
wish to look on, I was grieved past words, thinking of the
fathers of so many dead and buried, never to have the joy of
their own.   It was hard to believe that the four of us that
was left after the massacre had been such crazed brutes when
we 'd all these little ones to cherish and care for.   Whatever
had come over us?   There 's no way to explain or reason it
out.   We was stark, staring mad, that 's all there is to say.

   The women came along one by one to greet me kindly.
Not a word was said of what was past.   I could see Mrs.
Christian's hand there.   Better women never breathed than
herself and Taurua, Mr. Young's girl.   Both had courage
would have done credit to any man, but they 'd no malice in
their hearts.   I began to see from that morning the change
that had come over all the women.   The time that had gone
by had something to do with it, but what they 'd been
through was the main reason.   It aged their hearts and
sobered 'em beyond their years.   Prudence and Hutia, in
particular, had been wild young things when the *Bounty*
came to the island, up to any kind of mischief, and enough
they 'd made, one way and another.   But they 'd grown to
be fine women, and good steady mothers to their children.

   We divided ourselves up into households like we had before.   Mrs. Christian with her children, and Sarah and Mary

with theirs, moved into the house where Mr. Young and me
had lived before. Moetua, Nanai, Susannah, and Jenny
went to the Christians' house; Mr. Young, with Taurua and
Prudence and their children, lived where Mills and Martin
had; Balhadi, Hutia, and me took ours to the Indians' old
place.

In a few days all their things was moved down from the
Auté Valley. It did my heart good to see the houses that
had stood empty so long filled with women and children, and
the paths and dooryards cleared, and the gardens new made.
Mr. Young was like a different man. I never heard him
laugh or joke the way he had in the days afore trouble came,
but he'd found peace again. The old hopeless look was
gone out of his face. His strength was slow in coming back,
and he'd set in his dooryard, watching the children come and
go, and taking deep comfort, as I did, in the sight of 'em.

Thursday October was a son any father might have been
proud to own — as handy a lad as I've ever seen, and bright
and active beyond his years. He'd a deal of his father's nature in him and his mother's as well. There could n't have
been a finer cross in blood than theirs. Next to him was
Sarah McCoy, only a few months younger; then came her
brother, Dan, who was seven, and after him a pair of stout
lads, young Matt Quintal and Mr. Christian's second boy,
Charles. These five followed me about as close as my
shadow, and words could n't tell how I joyed to have 'em
with me. None of the children knew what had happened
here in the past, whilst they was little, and we was all of a
mind they should never know.

One morning I set off with the five I've spoke of for a day
of roaming on the west side of the island. That part, as
you've seen, sir, is all steep gullies and ravines, with bits of
open land between, good for nothing in the way of gardens.
Even if it had been good land we'd not have bothered with

it, having enough and to spare in the Main Valley. I had n't
been down there in months, nor any of the womenfolk, and
the children had never set foot in it.

It was a bright cool morning, quiet and peaceful; we
could hear the cocks crowing far and wide through the
forests. I mind how it came to me, as we was climbing the
western ridge, that this place was home to me at last. Ye
may wonder I 'd not thought of it so long since, seeing we 'd
no means of leaving it. I liked the island fine in the beginning, but after a year or so I always had the notion in the back
of my head that some day a ship would come — not an English ship, in search of us, but a Spanish one, likely, or a ship
from the American colonies. It was in my mind to change
my name and go off in her, and make my way back to England in the end. But now I was thinking of Pitcairn's
Island as home. There 's no better way to show ye the
change that come over me, and it was the children that
brought it to pass.

When we got on the ridge to the south of the Goat-House
Mountain, I set me down to rest, and little Sarah McCoy
with me. The lads was eager to go on, and down they ran
into the western valleys, as sure of foot as the goats that
roamed wild there. I let 'em go, knowing they could n't
lose themselves. Sarah and I followed, after a bit. She was
a quiet little mite, as pretty as a picture, with dark curly
hair like her mother's. It made my heart sore to think her
father could n't have lived to see her as she was then.

There had been a path down to the western shore, but it
was all grown over now, it had been so long since any of us
had gone that way. We came out on an open spot overlooking the sea and waited there. The lads had gone roaming
off in every direction, into the little valleys and down the
rocks to the bit of beach on that side. I 'd no mind to follow, knowing they was well able to take care of themselves.
The fowls had increased wonderful the years we 'd been on

the island; hundreds ran wild through the bush. The boys loved to hunt for their eggs; they 'd find enough in half an hour for all the settlement, and there was even more to be had in this wild part of the island. We 'd not waited long before Thursday October and the two youngest lads came back with a basket full of 'em, and some fine shellfish they 'd found amongst the rocks. Little Matt Quintal had gone off by himself, and, after waiting half an hour or thereabouts, I went in search.

I 'd not gone a quarter of a mile when I spied him below me, scrambling through the thickets as fast as he could go. I thought he was chasing one of the wild roosters, but when I called out he came runnin' towards me, so terrified he could n't speak. I grabbed him up and he held fast around my neck with his face pressed tight against my shoulder.

I set him down on my knee. "What 's this, Matty?" said I. "Was ye tryin' to run away from yer shadow?"

He held on to me like he 'd never let go. I talked quiet and easy to him, and finally he got so 's he could speak. He told me he 'd seen a *varua ino*. That 's what the Indians call an evil spirit. There 's not one of the women but believes to this day in ghosts and spirits of all kinds, good and bad. Many 's the time they claim to see or hear 'em. It 's always tried my patience the way they talk o' such things at night, and tell the young 'uns tales about 'em. I 've wished often enough to put a stop to such foolishness, but ye might as well try to change the colour o' their skins. I would n't mind if it was only to do with the mothers, but the children listen with all their ears and believe every word they 're told.

The lad was half crazed with fear, and shivering all over, but at last I got him to say what he thought he 'd seen. It was a huge great man, he said, a-settin' on a rock.

"Did he see ye?" I asked.

"No; he had his back towards me," said he.

"I 'll tell ye what ye saw, lad," said I.   "There 's some old stone images yonder where ye 've been.   They was made by folk that lived here long ago.   They 're ugly things, bigger 'n a man and made to look like men, but they 're naught but stone, and there 's no more harm in 'em than there is in this rock we 're a-settin' on."

"I saw it move," said he.

"Ye saw naught o' the sort, Matt," said I.   "Ye fancied ye did, I don't doubt . . . "

"No, no!   I did!   I saw it move!" said he, and he stuck to that.   I could n't coax him out o' the notion, so I took him on my shoulder and carried him back to where the other children was.

Brought up as they 'd been, they was all sure that little Matt must have seen an evil spirit.   But they was n't afeared of it with me there.   So I told 'em to wait where they was while I chased that ghost clean off the island.   "If there is one yonder," said I, "as soon as he sees me he 'll go flyin' off beyond the cliffs, and that 'll be the last o' *him*.   He 'll never come back again."

They set there as quiet as mice and made no fuss whatever.   They all believed Father Alex could do anything he was a mind to, and that even *varua inos* was afeared o' him.

What I reckoned to do was go off a piece, out of sight of the children, and then come back and tell 'em the spirit was gone, for good and all.   But when I 'd gone about as far as I thought was needed, I spied something that gave me a shock.   In a bit of soft ground I saw the tracks of bare feet, half again as big as my own.

I 'd seen them tracks before, many 's the time, but I could n't believe these was real, even as I looked at 'em.   I crossed over the place and went along a dry gully for about fifty yards, makin' no noise, till I came to a wall of rock that slanted under, where I 'd sheltered from the rain more than once in the old days.   The Indians had used it for a

camp when they fished on that side of the island; half a
dozen could sleep dry there, and well sheltered from the
wind. I pushed by the bushes and peered through. There
set Matt Quintal with his back to me, just as his own lad
had seen him.

He'd nothing on save what was left of a pair of seaman's trousers; it was the same pair he'd worn the day the
women burned us out of the house. Under the rock was a
bed he'd made of fern and dry grass, and he was squatting
in the Indian fashion, close by, cracking fowl's eggs and
drinking 'em down. There was the carcass of a wild pig
to one side, all torn apart, and the bones of others was scattered around where he'd thrown 'em. The smell of the
place was enough to sicken a dog.

If I'd had my wits about me, I'd have backed off without a word, but I called out, "Matt!" afore I could stop myself. He turned his head slow, looking this way and that,
and then he spied me. When I saw his face I felt the chills
go up and down my back. Ye never saw such a pair of eyes
outside of a madhouse; and he'd a great beard, now, that
reached to his waist, and bushed out the width of his chest.

I tried to be easy and natural. "Matt, ye rogue," said I.
"Where have ye hid yourself this long while? God's truth!
We thought ye was dead!"

I'd no more than got this out when he grabbed up a club
thick as my arm and made a rush at me with a bellow that
was like nothing in nature, brute or human. I ran for my
life, jumping over rocks and dodging amongst the trees;
then I caught my foot in some vines and pitched for'ard.
I turned my head as I fell, thinkin' he was right at my heels,
but he'd stopped thirty or forty yards back; and there he
stood, with his great club in one hand, looking around in a
puzzled way, like as if he wasn't sure I'd been there. I lay
flat amongst the bushes, and I didn't move till he'd gone
back the way he'd come.

When I'd shook myself together I hurried along to the children, and glad they was to see me again. They'd heard the roar Quintal let out, but they'd not seen us, and I thought best to say it was me that made the noise to scare off the evil spirit.

"Did ye see it, Alex?" Dan'l McCoy asked.

"Nay, lads," said I; "but if there was one, I reckon I scared him so he'll bother us no more. But I want none of ye to come down to this side of the island till I've had a good hunt through it, for I saw a great wild boar in the gully yonder. He might do one of ye a mischief."

We went home, then, and Sarah McCoy and little Matt kept tight hold of my hands all the way.

I told Mr. Young what I'd found. The only way we could reason it out was that Quintal had got so crazed he'd clean forgot there was anyone on the island save himself. He couldn't have been roaming the Main Valley or he'd have been seen.

"It's not likely he's ever been across the island since he went down there," said Mr. Young; "but now that he's seen ye, Alex, there's no telling what he may do." He shook his head in a mournful way. "I thought we'd got to the end of our troubles at last," said he, "and here's another sprung up. We must be under a curse."

I was anxious enough, myself, and it was hard to say what was best to be done. One thing was certain: the women would have to be told; so we called 'em together, and I gave 'em the full truth of what I'd seen. They was horror-struck, especially Sarah, who'd been Quintal's woman. For all that, she wouldn't hear to a hand being lifted against him. Jenny wanted us to shoot him and be done with it, and Prudence and Hutia backed her up, but Mrs. Christian and the rest was against this.

"Haven't we had trouble enough here, Jenny," said I

"without hunting down a poor crazed man to shoot him in cold blood?"

"Better that," said she, "than leave him free to harm us and the children. And that he 'll do, sooner or later. The time will come, Alex, when ye 'll wish ye 'd done as I say."

It came sooner than we feared it would. Two days later I was giving some of the women a hand at mending fence at Mr. Christian's house. There was Jenny and Susannah and Moetua, and, natural enough, we had Quintal on our minds. I 'd seen to the loading of all the muskets, and there was two or three in every house, ready for use in case of need. Jenny had a sharp, bitter tongue when she 'd a mind to use it, and she was trying to make out to the others I was afeared of Quintal. I let her run on, paying no heed to her woman's talk, and whilst she was in the midst of it we heard screams from the direction of the Christians' house. Directly after there was shots fired. I ran there as fast as I could and found the women in a terrible state. Little Sarah McCoy had gone to Brown's Well for water, and whilst she was dipping it up she saw Quintal coming down the path from the ridge. The minute he spied her he chased after her. Mrs. Christian heard the screams and rushed out with a musket. Quintal had all but caught the lass when Mrs. Christian fired over his head. At the sound of the shot he stopped short and ran off into the bush.

Sarah was old enough to remember Quintal, but she thought it was his ghost she saw. It made my heart sick to see her shivering and shaking in her mother's arms. She did n't get over the shock for days after.

We didn't dare rest, any longer, scattered as we 'd been. Half of the women and children moved into Mr. Young's house, and the rest came with me. Mr. Young was too poorly to leave the village, but that same afternoon I took a musket to protect myself and went into the valley to spy out Quintal, if I could, but not a sign of him did I see.

Then I climbed the mountain, where I could overlook the island. I had the *Bounty's* spyglass with me and I searched the western valleys bit by bit. There was little ye could see, below, because of the trees and thickets, but at last I spied him as he was climbing down amongst the rocks to go to the beach. I felt easier after that, and ye can imagine the relief it was to the womenfolk to know that he'd gone to his old place. They scarce left the houses after that, not knowing how soon he might take it into his head to come back.

Every day I'd go to the ridge with a musket and the spyglass to keep watch, and most times I'd have a glimpse of him. Once I saw him with the carcass of a wild pig acrost his shoulder, and it sickened me to think of him eating the raw flesh. He'd no way of making fire, but he seemed to care naught about that. Another time I'd a good view of him for near a half-hour. He was stark naked, settin' on a rock. The spyglass brought him as close as though he was within speakin' distance. He was talkin' to himself, and going through queer motions as a crazed man will.

One afternoon I'd no sight of him. It was getting on towards sundown and I was ready to come away when I spied Hutia and Prudence running along the ridge towards where I was. When they saw me they beckoned in a desperate way, but they didn't call out. It didn't take me long to reach 'em.

Quintal was in the Main Valley, but that wasn't the worst of it. He'd come all the way round, by the Auté Valley, more than likely, and he'd rushed out of the forest on Sarah, his own woman, and Mary McCoy. They was not over a hundred yards from the house. Mary told what happened. Quintal had passed her by and chased after Sarah. The poor woman was so terrified she'd run away from the house instead of towards it. Then she saw she was trapped, and the only way she could go was towards the crag we call

Ship-Landing Point, that shuts in the east side of the cove. Quintal was close behind. Sarah went on to the very top of the crag, and when she could go no further she threw herself off, sooner than let him catch her.

Mr. Young had gathered all the women and children at my house by the time I got there. Three had gone down to the cove to search for Sarah's body. No one knew where Quintal had got to. Mary was the only one had spied him and she'd run to the house without waiting to see what he'd do next. I was on my way to the landing place when I met the women coming up. Moetua had Sarah in her arms. She was still breathing, but she died within the half-hour.

It was dark by that time. The women laid Sarah's body out and covered it with a cloth, and some of 'em was crouched down beside it, wailing and crying as the Indians do when there's death in the house. Mr. Young and me tried to quiet 'em, but they was past listening to reason. The children took fright from the mothers, and most of them was crying as well. Mrs. Christian and Taurua was the only ones kept themselves in hand. Mr. Young stood guard on one side of the house and me on the other, and it was as much as we could do to stop there with the women carrying on as they did.

About an hour after Sarah's body was brought up, Susannah was found missing. There was only one candlenut taper burning in the house, and with the light so dim, and so many there, none had noticed that Susannah wasn't amongst 'em. I couldn't believe, at first, that anything had happened to her, for I'd seen her with the others just before I'd gone down to the cove to help bring Sarah's body up. We knew she'd not go roaming off alone, after what had happened. Then one of the children said he'd seen someone going to the out-kitchen, which was about twenty yards from the house. It was getting dark and he couldn't be sure who it was. We'd no doubt, then, that Quintal had been hiding near by, waiting for such a chance, and that he'd grabbed Susannah.

Some thought he might have carried her to one of the other houses; so, dark as it was, I made a search, and glad I was when I'd finished. Wherever Quintal had gone, there was nothing more we could do till daylight. Ye can fancy the night we put in; never was there a longer one. Jenny came out to where I stood guard to tell me it was my fault Sarah was lying dead. "And Susannah will be dead by this time," said she. "If ye'd been half a man, Alex Smith, ye'd have killed the brute the day ye found him." The poor woman was half crazed herself, after all that had happened. I couldn't blame her for letting out at me.

Mr. Young and me set out in search at the crack o' dawn. He was in no fit state to come, but he was bound to do it. We each had a musket and I carried a hand axe in my belt in case of need. We knew we'd got to kill Quintal, and ye can fancy how we felt. We took the path through the settlement and past Brown's Well, and when we got up on the ridge Mr. Young was so tired he had to rest. I've never felt more sorry for anyone than I did for him that morning. It was only his spirit gave him the strength to go on.

We both thought Quintal would go back to his old place in the gully, and it was there we meant to look first. "Alex," said he, "if we see him alone, no matter if his back is turned, we must both shoot, and shoot to kill." That was all the speech we had.

I led the way when we got down into the western valley. We went slow, stopping every few yards to listen. When we got close I whispered to Mr. Young to watch that side whilst I went forward to look.

I crawled through the bushes without making the least noise; then I came to the place. Susannah was lying on her back, without a rag to her body, with her feet tied together and her arms bound to her side with long strips of bark that went round and round her. Quintal was nowheres in sight. I made sure of that, then came out quick as ever I could, and I had her free in five seconds. She was in a terrible state, all covered with scratches and bruises, and one of her ears had been bit clean through, but I thanked God she was alive. She made no sound as I cut her loose. I whispered, "Get ye back yonder, Susannah. Ned's there. Where's he gone?" She motioned that he was somewhere on the far side of the place. I lifted her up; she was scarce able to stand, but she managed to do as I told her.

I looked to the priming of my musket and went for'ard. Quintal was asleep behind some bushes not a dozen steps farther on. As soon as I saw him I backed off to the far side of the gully and raised my piece; but I couldn't pull the trigger. I've never felt worse in my life than I did that minute. I stood lookin' at him, thinking of the Matt Quintal I'd known on the *Bounty*. Then I minded me of the women and children and of Sarah lying dead, and I knew I had to go through with it.

I picked up a handful of pebbles and tossed it on him. He was lying on his back and saw me the minute he raised his head. His club was there beside him. He grabbed it and up he sprang, and as he came for me I pulled the trigger, but the musket missed fire. I'd only time to dodge to one side and grab my hand axe. He made such a rush that he went past me. I ducked under the blow he aimed at me and threw out my leg, and he went sprawling his full length. Then, sir, as he got to his knees, I brought the axe down on his head with all my strength.

CHAPTER XXI

IT was a merciful quick death, sir. He was killed on the instant, without a cry from his lips. I set me down for a bit, shook to the heart; then I put by the axe and went back to where Mr. Young was waiting. Maimiti had give us a tapa mantle to fetch for Susannah, fearin' the state she might be in, dead or alive. She 'd put this over her and was crouched there beside him.

"Go ye back with her, Ned," said I. "The women will be half crazed till they know she 's safe. Ye can tell 'em it 's done. He 'll trouble us no more."

I did n't know my own voice as I spoke, and Mr. Young said never a word. He was not a man of strong nature, even in health, and there 's none hated strife and bloodshed more than him who 'd had to share in so much. I knew the horror he 'd have of seein' Quintal's body. I was bound to spare him that.

Bruised and hurt as she 'd been, Susannah had more strength left than him, and it was her took his arm and helped him up the steep rocky way. Slow they went, and I watched till they was out of sight amongst the trees and appeared again, high above, and crossed over the ridge to the Main Valley. Then I went back to where Quintal lay, and digged his grave with the axe I 'd killed him with. It was hard, slow work, but I did it, and laid him in the place and smoothed over the ground, and covered it with leaves and moss so that none could tell where it was. Then I went down to the sea and threw the axe far out, and washed myself, and walked back across the island.

We buried Sarah the same day. She'd no kin amongst the women, and three was chosen to act as such and mourn her in their fashion, weeping and wailing, gashing their faces and breasts cruel with little sticks they called *paohinos*, set with sharks' teeth. Ye wouldn't have known 'em in that state; it was like as if they was out of their senses. Such things brought home to me how little we understood our womenfolk for all the years we'd lived with 'em. Sometimes they'd seem no different from women at home; then of a sudden ye'd see the gap there was between our ways and theirs. As I've said, they had a mortal terror of the new dead, especially them they'd been afeared of in life. For a week they was all huddled into my house at night, women and children together, with tapers burnin' from sundown to sunup. Not even Moetua would set foot outside the door after dark. But that passed. In the end Mr. Young and me coaxed 'em back to their own houses, and we lived as we had before.

And now, at last, sir, I've reached the end of the evil times. From that day we've had peace here, and, with God's help, so it shall be through all the years to come. Quintal had to be put to death — that I believe. The lives of none would have been safe with him roamin' the island, crazed brute he'd become, ready to spring out on women and children. But it was little comfort I took from thinkin' so as I stood, that day, over his grave. Ye'll know how I felt, after all the blood had been spilt here. I wished I was dead and buried with him.

Aye, peace followed, but there was none in my heart for many a long day.

Mr. Young had used up what little strength he had and was in his bed for a fortnight. Then he began to mend, and I thought he was on the way to full health again. He saw how it was with me, though I never spoke Quintal's name, and made out as well as I could to seem easy in mind. But

he knew, and it was thanks to him and the children that I
got through the worst of that time.

No words could tell the blessing the children was to all.
They made a new life for us, as different from the old as day
from night.   There was twenty-one at this time, all the way
from nine years to a pair of newborn babes.   Three was
Christians, seven Youngs, three McCoys, two Mills, four
Quintals, and there was two of my own.   None, so far as
I know, belonged to the Indian men; they was all ours of
the *Bounty*.   So the women said, but the truth is we did n't
know for certain who was the fathers of some.   There was
no doubt about Mrs. Christian's, but the others of one name
was not always by the same mothers.   Ye 'll bear in mind
the rough, wild way we lived; and the past six years there 'd
been more than twice the number of women there was men.
Some without men of their own wanted children as bad as
the rest.   Aye, for all their hate of us at that time, they still
had the great wish for children.   It gave 'em something to
live for.   If they 'd not cleared out of the settlement,
sickened of our drunken ways, I 'll warrant there 'd have
been half again as many.   Ye may think it strange, but,
now that all was peace, it was the wish of Balhadi and Taurua,
our own two girls, that Mr. Young and me should be fathers
of babes to any that wanted 'em.   And when I recollect
the need there was for children, and the blessings they 've
brought, and the way we 've lived these last years, like one
big family of kind and loving hearts, I can't feel it was
a wrong way of life.   It seems to me it was the right way,
and the only way for that time.

None of the children, God be thanked, was old enough
to recollect the time of the murders.   Four or five remembered McCoy and Quintal, but they soon forgot, as
children do, and we never spoke the names of any that was
dead.   We was bound that no memory of that time should
be carried on to them.

And they healed our hearts, sir, and in the end made this small island like a heaven on earth. That's a strong way to put it, but so it was. There was scarce an acre of ground but had some sad or shameful thing joined with it, and at first they'd come to mind as I'd go from place to place. I'd have a horror of walking about. But the children mended that. They made the earth sweet and clean once more. Before another year was gone they overlaid the whole island with so many new and happy memories that had to do with them alone, the old ones all but faded out beneath 'em.

They took after the Indian ways and spoke their mothers' tongue, as it was natural they should. A happier set of children never grew up together. There was no strife amongst 'em, and that seemed strange to me when I'd recollect the fightin', wranglin' 'uns I'd been brought up with in London, and the bloody noses I got and give from the time I was five years old. I thought it must be so with all children, but amongst these there was never a blow struck or a harsh word spoke. Aye, it was a joy to see 'em.

Ye'll know the comfort Mr. Young and me took to be with 'em from day to day, watchin' 'em grow and blossom out in new ways. If I was partial towards any of the lads, it was to Thursday October and little Matt Quintal, but the truth is I loved every one as though they was my own flesh and blood. I'd take a walk of an evening, after supper, which we always had afore sundown. The mothers would be in the dooryards with the little ones on their laps and the older lads and lasses playin' their games close by; and I'd be struck to the heart with pity that Mr. Christian could n't have lived to see 'em as they was then.

Now I must tell ye of a thing happened close after Quintal's death, for it's the greatest blessing has come to me all the years of my life, though I did n't know it at the time. As a usual thing I'd go along to Mr. Young's house of an

evening, for I could n't abide to be alone with my thoughts.
One evening I 'd gone late. The women and children was
already abed, and Mr. Young was at his table, writin' in one
of the old *Bounty's* logbooks. I 'd often seen him at that.
He gave me a nod and went on with it, and I set me down
to wait till he was through.

"What is it ye write there so often, Ned?" I asked him.
"Is it a journal ye 're keepin'?"

"Aye," said he. "I 've a record here of births and the
like, but that 's not the whole of it." Then he told me
he 'd write down whatever he could recollect out of books
he 'd read in past years. It was Mr. Christian had first
put him in the way of it. About a year after we 'd come
here they begun doing it in their spare time, and they 'd
filled pages and pages. After Mr. Christian's death, Mr.
Young had left off, but now he 'd took it up again in earnest.
He 'd been a great reader from the time he was a lad, and
there could have been little he had n't mastered and kept in
mind.

He read me a bit from a story called *The Pilgrim's Progress*,
as he 'd recollected and set it down. I was taken clean out
of myself and begged him to go on, which he did, from one
piece to another he had there. Mind ye, sir, I was naught
but an ignorant seaman, with no more knowledge of the
joy to be had from books than the pigs that run wild here.
I did n't even know the names of our English writers, not a
blessed one! Mr. Young told me about 'em. I could have
listened the night through.

"Was ye never teached to read and write, Alex?" said
he.

"A little, when I was a mite of a lad," said I, "but it 's all
gone from me now."

"How would ye like to take it up again?" said he. "I 'll
help. Ye 've a taste for it, that 's plain."

"I 'd like it well enough," said I, "but ye 'd soon sicken of the bargain, Ned, for I'm dismal ignorant. Hard work ye'd have tryin' to pound learnin' into my head."

"I'll chance that," said he, "and if ye're willin' we'll begin afore we're a day older."

Little I thought anything would come of it, but I was only too pleased to say aye to that. I was in desperate need of something to keep my mind off Quintal. Whether I could be teached or not didn't matter so much. I could try, anyway, and pass the evenings, which was the worst time of day for me then.

That was the start of it. The next day Mr. Young took me in hand, and slow work he had at first. But he was that patient he could have teached a stone image, and I'll say this for myself: I was bound to learn. And once I had a thing, it was mine. I never forgot.

He began to read to me out of the Bible. In the foundling home where I was raised, I'd heard bits from the Bible, but I was a wild young lad and gave no heed. It was different, now. I listened with all my ears, careful and patient, and Mr. Young was a master reader. We started with the Book of Genesis. Every evening when my lesson was over he'd go through half a dozen chapters, and I'd have that to think over till the next evening.

Our life went on as peaceful as heart could wish. Mornings, as a usual thing, we was all at work in the gardens. Two or three times a week, afternoons, the women would be at their tapa-making below the rock cistern. There was a pretty sight to see, sir. Many's the time I'd go up to look on. There'd be four or five beatin' out the bark at once — they took turns at it — whilst the others looked after the babes and the little ones. They'd be scattered amongst the rocks with the sunlight flickerin' down on 'em through the trees, the mothers combing the children's hair after their baths, and makin' wreaths of ferns for their heads and garlands of flowers to hang around their necks. They could do wonders with blossoms; they 'd spend hours stringin' 'em together in different ways, and whilst they was at it they 'd sing their Indian songs. There 'd been no laughter or singin' for years till after Quintal's death, and it warmed my heart to see such a blessed change in the womenfolk. Their homesickness for Tahiti was gone at last. They 'd talk of it, of course, but not in the old heartsick way, with tears in their eyes. Pitcairn's Island was home, now, to all.

Midday, after we 'd had our dinners, was a time of rest, the Indian fashion. For two hours, or thereabouts, ye 'd hear no sound; then all would be astir again to do as they 'd a mind to. That was the time I 'd take the older lads and lasses to roam the hills and valleys; or we 'd go offshore, when the season was right, in the canoes, to fish. The Indians had showed me how and when to fish in these waters. There 's a skill to it I would n't have believed in the old days; and some of the *Bounty* men was that stubborn they 'd never acknowledge that the Indians knew better about such matters than themselves. But I learned by goin' out with 'em, and I 've passed on all I 've learned to the children. But it 's little they 've got from me compared to what their mothers has teached 'em, or what they 've picked up, natural. They know the use of every plant and tree and flower on the island. They know the winds and the seasons and the nesting times of the birds. If there 's anything they don't know about this island I 'd be pleased to hear what it is. They learned to swim near as soon as they learned to walk. I used to be afeared to let the little ones go into the water, but bless ye, I soon got over that! Birds ain't more at home in the air than these lads and lasses are in the sea. In these days the older ones swim all the way around the island for the fun of it. To see 'em sport in the breakers ye 'd think they was born amongst 'em.

But there 's no need to tell ye all this, sir, for ye can see for yourself how it is with us. It 's the same now as it was then, save that the little tots has grown up more. But I like to mind me of the days when it was all new and we could scarce believe in the peace that had come at last.

I had my lessons with Mr. Young late of an afternoon, and evenings as well. Some of the children took to comin' in to watch, and it was n't long till I found they was gettin' the hang o' things just from listenin' to what Mr. Young would tell me. Not their letters, of course, but the way of speakin' English. They 'd carry away any amount of it in their heads. One day I spoke to Mr. Young about this.

"They 're as bright as new buttons, Ned," said I. "If ye was to teach them along with me, I 'll warrant they 'd soon catch the meaning and go on full sail, leagues ahead of the place I 've reached."

"Aye," said he, "I 've thought o' that." He got out of his chair and walked up and down the room for a bit, turning the thing over in his mind.

"But where 'd be the good of it, Alex? We want to do what 's best for them. I 've come to think Mr. Christian was right. It was his wish they should have their mothers' ways and their mothers' beliefs. No, let 's keep 'em as they are. If I was to teach 'em to read, they 'd have naught but the Bible for their lesson book, and what they 'd find there would only puzzle and upset their minds."

I believed then he had the right of it, and no more was said. Mr. Young had brought me along as far as the Book of Leviticus, and I did n't know what to make of a good part of what I 'd listened to, myself. I could fancy how it would have puzzled the children. There was the story of the children of Israel, and God favouring them and hardening Pharaoh's heart so Moses could bring plagues on the Egyptians: rivers of blood, and swarms of vermin and frogs, and diseases for their cattle, and the like. If it was God had hardened Pharaoh's heart, I could n't see that Pharaoh was to blame; and I wondered about the innocent people amongst the Egyptians, for there's always good as well as bad in any land. Why should they be made to suffer for the evil ones amongst 'em? Mr. Young told me it was a story the Israelites had wrote for themselves, to show their side of things. That's how it looked to me, but I took a powerful interest in the Bible for all that. Many's the night we sat over it till the small hours, for Mr. Young was as pleased to read as I was to listen.

We went on so for nine months, and slow but sure I learned to read. I could n't well say how pleased and proud I was when I found I'd got the way of it; and I worked at writin' as well. What I'd lost as a lad came back, but it was hard work that brought it. Not a day passed without my lesson, and I'd study by myself for hours together.

Then Mr. Young's health give way again. He'd never got back his strength, and the old asthma trouble came on worse than ever. We had a long spell of cold rainy weather, and that may have brought it. The women tried all their Indian medicines of herbs and poultices and the like, but this was a thing they'd never seen before, and they could n't find a cure for it. If ye've ever watched a man drown, sir, powerless to help him, ye'll know how it was with us. He'd be took bad four or five days together and fight for his breath in a way was pitiful to see. And all that time he was getting weaker. So it went for three long months, but we never give up hope.

We tried all ways we could think of to give him a little ease. One afternoon we had him propped up with pillows in a chair I'd made for him. He'd been better that day, but I saw a look in his face that told me he knew he was dying. He did n't talk much — just sat with his hands in his lap, lookin' through the trees to seaward. We was alone in the room.

Presently he turned his head.

"Alex," said he, "there's a thing or two I want to speak of, while I can."

My heart smote me, the way he said it. He wanted so bad to live. There was a time, after Mr. Christian's death, when he'd no wish to go on, but the children had changed that. He wanted to grow old amongst 'em, along with me, and see 'em reared to manhood and womanhood.

"If ever a ship should come," said he, "and it's likely there will, soon or late, ye'd best tell who ye are. If there's a good man aboard of her — one ye can trust — I'd make a clean breast to him, Alex, of what's happened here. Let him know the truth."

"I will so, Ned," said I.

"It's yourself has been spared of all of us to bring up the children. It's a great trust and a sacred one. Guard it well. Be faithful to it. I know ye will."

He took my hand and held it. "That's all," said he. "I'd have liked well to stay on with ye, lad. But it's not to be."

I couldn't speak, sir. All I could do was to hold his hand in both of mine, with the tears streamin' down my face. Then Mrs. Christian and Taurua came in. I couldn't bear to set with him longer. I had to leave the room.

He died that same night, the three of us by him, and we laid him to rest the following day. Words can't say how we missed him. For all he was so far above me in blood and rearing, I loved him as if he'd been my own brother. He had the most kind and gentle nature. If ever ye could have laid eyes on him, ye'd have known at first sight he was a good man, one ye could love and trust. When we lost him we was that stunned and grief-stricken there was naught we could take up with the least relish or pleasure. It seemed as if we couldn't go on without Mr. Young.

Aye, it was a dark, lonesome time that followed. But lonesome's not the word. It was worse than that for me.

It was as if I'd been told that of all the *Bounty* men that
sailed from England together there was none left save myself. I walked the island with a heart heavy as lead. I
thought of the mutiny and the part I'd played in it, and
how I'd helped to set Captain Bligh and eighteen innocent
men adrift in a little boat, in the middle of the ocean. As
I lay in bed at night I'd see the launch riding the waves,
and them in it dead of thirst or starvation; or a picture
would come to mind of the lot of 'em bein' murdered by
savages on some island where they'd landed. I'd think
of the blood spilt here, and Quintal's face would come before
me; night and day I'd see it, until I was near desperate, not
knowing how I was to live with such memories behind me.

The children was no help to me, then. I was struck with
fear at the very sight of 'em, thinking of what might happen when they was grown men and women. I minded what
Mr. Young had read to me once: that the sins of the fathers
would be visited on the children for generations. I'd come
to believe that. I believed it was God's law them innocent
babes should be punished for our sins, and us through them.
I tried to pray to Him, but I did n't know how, and ye'll
mind I thought of Him, then, as a God of wrath and vengeance. I'd heard naught and read naught of a God of for-
giveness and love. But that was to come. I was to be led
into the way of peace at last; but it was a long way, sir,
and I can't tell ye the torment I suffered through afore I
found it.

Aye, if ever a man felt lost and desperate, it was Alex
Smith, sir. I could n't believe there was any hope for me.
It may have been because I was alone, with no other man
I could open my heart to. However it was, I believed the
blood of all the innocent men that had died since the mutiny
was on my head. I believed it was meant I should be made
the scapegoat for the guilty ones and be punished for 'em.
By thinkin' so much over the past, I'd come to believe it was

God's will I should be destroyed, by my own hand. One day — it was around two months after Mr. Young's death — I went to the great cliff on the south side of the island with the intent to throw myself off. I was out of my mind, sir — that 's the truth of it.

Ye 've been to the top of the Rope. Ye know what a fearsome place it is, with a straight drop to the sea, hundreds of feet below. It was there Quintal and Minarii had battled with their bare hands, when Minarii was pushed to his death over the cliff. I reached the place not knowing how I got there, stumbling along like a blind man, with my heart bitter as gall. It was midday when I crossed the island. I thought all the women and children was in the settlement having their usual rest, but I was n't more than half a dozen steps from the brink of the cliff when I spied three of the children curled up there, asleep, like kittens in the sunshine. There was little Matt Quintal, and Eliza Mills, and Mary, Mrs. Christian's youngest, who was seven years old at that time. Matt had a little pole beside him he 'd cut from the bush, with a basket of yams on one end and a small bunch of plantains on the other. The lasses had their eggin' baskets filled and put away in the shade close by; and afore they 'd gone to sleep they 'd made garlands of blossoms to hang around their necks.

I stepped back and stared at 'em like a man has been waked out of a horrible dream, and all at once there flowed into my heart a flood of hope and joy and love I could never explain. It must have been God's mercy that showed me that pretty innocent sight, for as sure as ye hear me, sir, if they had n't been there I 'd have flung myself off the cliff. I sank down on my knees beside 'em. The tears ran down my cheeks, and a voice inside me spoke as plain as words, tellin' me I was to live for them children, and love and cherish 'em, and think no more of evil times past and done with.

Ye 'd have said Mary heard that voice. She opened her

eyes and looked at me in a puzzled way. The next minute she jumped up and had her little arms around my neck.

"Alex! What is it?" says she, but my heart was so full I could n't speak. All I could do was hold her close. Presently I said, "Never mind, darlin'. I'm weepin' for joy, if ye wish to know, and the love I have for ye lads and lasses."

Our voices roused up the other two, and they did n't know what to make of seein' me in such a state. Eliza came on the other side and I gathered her in with Mary and held the two of 'em so; and Matty stood on his knees in front of me with a look of wonder on his face. He had n't a trace of his father in him. He 'd gone all to the mother's side, as handsome a lad as ye could hope to see, with dark curly hair and great brown eyes, true and trustful like them of a dog.

"Alex, are ye hurted?" says he.

"Nay, lad," says I, "but ye 've give me a turn, the three of ye, lyin' asleep so close to the edge of the cliff. You might have rolled off it."

Then Eliza's face brightened up and she laughed at me, and the others with her. "Was ye weepin' for *that*, Alex?" says she. "Why, we 've climbed down there many 's the time."

"What!" says I. "Not over the Rope?"

"Aye," says she; and afore I could think, the lad jumped to his feet. "I 'll show ye, Alex," said he, and over he went. I was scared out of my wits. The cliff is all but sheer, and a missed handhold or foothold would send ye to your death, hundreds of feet below; and there went Matt, like a crab down a wall of reef! I called and begged him to come back, scarce darin' to breathe, and when he 'd gone down, twenty-five feet or so, to show how easy he could do it, up he climbed again, as cool as ye please. In my heart I was proud of his pluck, but I did n't let on. Many a fright the children has

give me since, the lot of 'em, the way they clamber down
cliffs and along ridges that would scare a goat, but they
never come to grief, and I 've got used to seein' 'em now, in
a way.   They 're as much at home on the rocks and ledges
as they are in the sea.

I like to mind me of that day.   I was n't a Christian
man, Mr. Webber, I don't know if I 'll ever merit to be called
one, but if it was n't God's love that saved me, what could
it have been?   It must have been that!   He must have seen
and took pity on me for the children's sakes.   He had work
for me to do.   There 's no explainin' it, else.   And somehow
the load of misery was lifted from my heart so that I never
felt it again so sore and heavy as at that time.

I 'd left off my study at readin' and writin' when Mr.
Young was took sick.   Now I went at it again, though why
I did I could n't have said for certain.   I think I had the
notion to go on so as I could read the bits Mr. Christian and
Mr. Young had wrote down in the old *Bounty's* logbooks.
I took more interest in them than I did in the Bible, and
I got to the place where I could read and understand the most
part.   But all this while, sir, I was bein' led.   I know that,
now.   God was bringin' me to a knowledge of His love in
His own way.

I went back to the Bible, takin' it up where Mr. Young
had left off readin' to me.   If I 'd known what I know now,
I 'd have gone straight to the New Testament, but like enough
it was best I should have burrowed along, slow and patient,
like a mole in the dark.   I did that for three years.   I did n't
read all.   There was parts too knotty for me and I 'd have
to pass them by; but others, like the Psalms and the Proverbs,
I 'd come back to again and again till I got so I knew most
of 'em by heart.

I 've heard tell of men bein' led all of a sudden, in a day or
a week, to the knowledge of God.   It was n't so with me.
I was brought to it little by little, but when I came to the

Life of Jesus, my heart began to open like doors swingin'
apart. Once I was sure God was a loving and merciful
Father to them that repent, it seemed to me I could feel His
very presence, sir, and I grew more sure every day of His
guiding hand. And I knew, in the end, that I 'd come to
the way of Life — the only way. I 'll say no more of this,
for it 's a sacred, holy thing, but I was certain I 'd found it
because of the peace that came to me and has never left me
since.

But I was troubled about the children. Not as they was
then, but over what might happen when they was grown
men and women. They had their fathers' blood in their
veins. How could I know something would n't happen
to lead 'em into our old ways? For all Mr. Young had said,
I could n't believe it was God's wish they should be kept in
ignorance of His Holy Word. The more I thought about it,
the more strong it came in to me that I 'd been led so as I
could lead them. It seemed to me I could hear the very
voice of Jesus: "Suffer little children to come unto me, and
forbid them not, for of such is the kingdom of Heaven."
And I did, sir. I brought 'em to Him, and their mothers
with 'em.

Ye 'll wonder an ignorant seaman could have done it.
I could n't have, alone. It was God showed me the way.
I began with the mothers. I 'd gather them together of an
evening and tell them the story of the Bible. Not the whole
of it, of course. There was a deal I did n't know, but I had
the main parts well in mind. It was a joy to see the interest
they took. It was the story they fancied in the beginning,
but they soon got to see there was more to it than that.
What made it easier for me was that they was all young
women at the time we left Tahiti and their minds was not
hardened into the Indian beliefs; and I teached 'em in a way
that surprised me. I 'd never have thought I could do it so
well. It seemed as if I was told what to say, and I 'd have

an answer ready for every question they'd ask. It was God's doing, the whole of it.

If it was a joy to teach the mothers, ye'll know what it was when I started with the children. Their little hearts was so eager and open and ready to receive there was times I was afeared to speak, lest I'd have God's teaching wrong. They'd believe without the least question of doubt. That made me slow and careful. I said naught about sin, for they didn't know what it was, and I saw no need to put any idea of it into their hearts. I teached 'em what I believed Jesus would wish 'em to be teached: to love one another, to speak truth and act it, to honour their mothers and do as they'd be done by.

All this was in the Indian language, which I'd learned to speak near as well as themselves. But as I went on I saw I'd got to do more. I looked to the years to come, when I'd be gone and they left without the skill to read God's Word for themselves. They might forget what they'd heard from me and drift into evil ways as we had. I saw I had to teach 'em their letters. Aye, it was a sacred duty. Once I was sure of that, I didn't rest till I'd started a school for the older ones.

As ye know, likely, the Indians has no letters of their own. Theirs is naught but a spoken tongue, and it would have puzzled a better head than mine to know how to go about such a task. Mr. Young would have known, and sorry I was I hadn't pleaded with him till he'd agreed to teach the children along with me. There was times I thought I'd have to give up. It wasn't the children's fault. They was bright and quick. Often they'd see what I was drivin' at afore I was sure of it myself. All I had on my side was the deep wish to teach 'em and a stubborn streak in me that wouldn't let me give in till I'd showed 'em what letters meant, and how they was put together to make words. Their knowin' bits of English was a great help, but if ever a man sweat blood over a thing was past his skill, that man was myself.

But they got the notion of it at last, and, once they had, it would have amazed ye to see how fast they went on. Thursday and Charles Christian and Mary McCoy was the best, but there was little to choose amongst the five I took into the first school. I'll not forget how proud they was when they got so as they could read a few lines and write little messages to one another. Their mothers thought it was the wonder of the world, and when ye come to look at it, there's few things to equal the wonder of writin'. I'm blessed if I can see how men ever came to the knowledge of it in the first place.

There was a writin' chest had belonged to Captain Bligh, with a good store of paper in it, and ink, and pens. I cherished them sheets of paper as if every one was beat out of gold. When the ink was gone I made some that did famous out of candlenut ash, and pens we had a-plenty, with all the fowls there is on the island. When the last of the paper was gone, I made slates for the children out of slabs o' rock. There's a kind of rock here ye can chip off in thin layers. They's what we used for slates, and we still do; but it's hard to grind it down and make it smooth.

The school was a pride to the children as much as it was to me. I didn't have to coax 'em into it. Bless ye, no! They all wanted to learn their letters. I took the young ones in as fast as they came to an age, and the older ones was a great help with them. And the questions they'd ask, once they learned to read a bit! They'd make my old head swim! I didn't let 'em read the Bible for themselves. There was parts would only have puzzled 'em, as Mr. Young said. I picked out the chapters, and the most of it was Christ's teaching to His disciples. And they'd take it to their hearts, sir, and keep it there — aye, and live by it.

And now I'm near to the end of the story. I might go

on for another night, or a week of nights, for the matter of that, tellin' ye what 's happened these past five years; but I 've no wish to try ye past the limit of patience. Ye can see how it 's been. Our life has gone by as quiet as a summer's day. There 's never been the least strife amongst us since the day Quintal was killed. We 've lived for the children. Their mothers and me has never had a thought save how we can make their lives as happy as ours was miserable in the old days. They 're good mothers, for all they was heathens before, and still are, in some of their ways. But there 's heathen ways, sir, us white men could study to our profit. I have. There 's been time for it here. I 've learned more from these Indian women than ever I 've been able to teach them.

Aye, it 's a quiet life and a good life we 've had here these nine years. I doubt if ye could find anywhere a family of human beings that lives together with more kindness and good will. We 're at peace, in our lives and in our hearts. There 's the sum of it, in few words.

Now and again, when I go out to fish, I pass over the place where the hulk of the *Bounty* lies. I look down at her and mind me of the times I trod her decks. I mind me of the day we put out from Portsmouth, all of us so eager for the voyage ahead, and thinkin' what we 'd see amongst the islands we was bound for. Little we knew what was to come! Little we guessed how soon we was to be scattered far and wide, and the ends some of us was to meet!

We did a cruel wrong when we set Captain Bligh adrift with all them innocent men. He was a hard man and an unjust man. But, no matter how sore we was tried, we should never have seized the ship, and none knew it better than Mr. Christian when it was too late. Ye 'll know from what I said that he never had a moment's pleasure or peace of heart from that time to the day of his death. Aye, it was a cruel, lawless deed, and all that can be said for us is that the mutiny was n't a cold-blooded, planned-out thing. It was the matter of half an hour and was over with afore it came in to us what we 'd done. Then it was past mending. We was punished for it as we deserved, but I 'll say no more o' this, for it 's over and ended.

Ye 'll never know the joy it 's give me to hear that Captain Bligh and his men won through to safety. I can be truly at peace from this time on. That knowledge was the one thing needful, and I never thought to have it.

Now I 've done what Mr. Young wished I should do: told ye the story from start to finish, and kept nothing back. I 'd have told ye, regardless, Mr. Webber, for it 's been a burden on my heart all these years. I thank ye kindly that ye 've let me ease the weight of it.

It 's a late hour. Ye 'll be ready for bed, and we 'll go along to the house.

The last of the casks is filled, Thursday says, and ready to be towed out. It 's been a rare treat to the children to be of service to ye. They 've a sea stock on the beach will last ye halfway home, I should n't wonder — pigs and fowls and fruits and vegetables. We 've food and to spare here. Bless ye! We could fill a score of ships like the *Topaz* and never miss it in the least.

There 's one thing more I 'd like to speak of. It 's about the children. If only I could keep 'em as they are, Mr. Webber — ignorant of the world, and the world ignorant of them! That would be my heart's wish! Maybe ye 'll say it 's a foolish wish; but if ye could be in my place, see and be with 'em from day to day, ye 'd feel as I do. Aye, ye would so — I 'm certain of it. They 've missed so much that children outside is laid open to, almost from babyhood. I 'd not have ye think they 're perfect, without flaw or blemish. They 're human. But I do believe ye might search the world around without finding children more truly innocent and pure-minded than these.

When I think they was sprung from rough, hard seamen, for the most part, mutineers and pirates, I can scarce believe they 're our own flesh and blood. It 's a miracle! There 's no other name for such a thing! Never a night passes that I don't thank God that He 's let these Indian mothers and me live to see it.

Aye, if only we could keep 'em so! I 'll not forget the morning the *Topaz* was sighted. It was Robert Young spied ye first. We was in the school when he came runnin' up from the bluffs. "Alex," said he, "there 's a great canoe comin' over the sea!"

There was an end of lessons. The lads had never seen a ship, though I 'd told 'em there was such things. I had to, for they 'd seen what 's left of the old *Bounty*. We rushed to the bluffs, and when I saw the vessel, Mr. Webber, my heart sank. Shall I tell ye what I wished to do? Ye was still miles off and could n't have seen the smoke of our fires. I wanted to put 'em out, gather the womenfolk and the lads and lasses — every chick and child — and hide with 'em in the forest, in the deepest part of the valley. It was n't that I was afeared for myself. I was thinkin' of the children. I wanted to keep 'em clear of all knowledge of the world their fathers was raised in. I wished sore to do it! But they was so stirred up and eager, it would have broke their hearts if I 'd not let 'em go off to ye and ask ye ashore.

And now ye 've found us, it 'll soon be known we 're here. I 've no doubt it 'll cause a bit of a stir, outside, when Captain Folger tells that he 's found the hiding-place of the old *Bounty's* men. I would n't try to coax him or yerself to keep silent about us, Mr. Webber. It 's your duty to report us — that I know. And other ships will come, once it 's known that Pitcairn's Island is summat more than a lonely rock for sea birds. . . . Aye. Soon or late they 'll come, as Mr. Young said. . . . Well . . .

But God bless me! I must n't keep ye up longer. Ye 'll

be perished for sleep. I'll warrant I could talk the night through, it's been so long since I've had a seaman to yarn with. Good night, sir, and rest well. I'll be astir bright and early to meet Captain Folger.

EPILOGUE

At sunset on the following day, Alexander Smith was seated with half a dozen of the children on the highest pinnacle of the crag, Ship-Landing Point, overlooking Bounty Bay. Below them, at various places along the seaward cliffs, were the other members of the Pitcairn colony, all steadfastly gazing eastward. The *Topaz*, with all sail set, under a fresh westerly breeze, had drawn rapidly away from the land and was now far out, looking smaller than a child's toy vessel against the lonely expanse of blue water.

The hush of early evening was over land and sea. The ravines and valleys were filled with purple shadow, deepening momentarily, and, in the last level rays of the sun, crags, ridges, mountain peaks, and the lofty cliffs that bounded the island on the west stood out in clear relief, bathed in mellow golden light.

The old seaman turned to a little girl at his side, who was weeping softly, her head in her arms.

"There, lass! Comfort ye now. Bless me! Ye 'll have the lot of us weepin' with ye directly."

The girl raised her head, making an attempt to smile through her tears.

"It 's sad to have them go so soon," she replied. "Will they never come back?"

"That I could n't tell ye, darlin'. But who knows? They might."

"But where is it they 're going, Alex?" one of the boys asked.

"Home . . . a long way . . . thousands of leagues from where we are."

"What is a league?"

"A league? Well, let me think. . . . If the land here was half again as big as it is, ye 'd have just about a league from one end to the other."

"And they have thousands of leagues to sail before they reach their home?"

"Aye — thousands, the way they 'll go."

"Then we 'll never see them again!"

"Now, Mary, lass! Don't ye start weepin' along of Rachel! Would n't ye have Captain Folger see his dear ones? And there 's Mr. Webber with three children, the oldest the age of yourself, waitin' for him in his own land. Think of the joy there 'll be the day he comes home!"

"I want them to go home; it is n't that. But I want them to come back. And if it 's so far . . . they do hope to come again, don't they?"

"Aye; and mebbe they will. But ye can't never tell about ships — where they 'll be off to next."

"Where is their home?"

"Off yonder."

"Is it like ours?"

"Aye, in a way, but in some ways it 's nothing like. It 's a great country they live in. Ye could put together hundreds of lands the size of ours — thousands of 'em — and it would n't make one as big as theirs. And it 's cold in the winters. It 's that cold the water freezes in the brooks and streams."

"What does that mean — freezes?"

"Well, I don't know as I can tell ye, exactly. It gets colder and colder, and the end of it is the water in all the streams is froze till it 's hard like rock, and ye can walk on it."

"Alex! It could n't be so! You can walk on the water as Jesus did?"

"Nay, Robbie, it 's not the same. Jesus walked on water

like we have here.   But in them perishin' cold places . . .
well, it freezes and gets hard, like I said.   Anybody can walk
on the froze water.   I 've done it myself."
   Another of the lads turned to him eagerly.
   "I 'd like to see it!   Alex, if they come again, could n't i
go with them to their land?"
   "Would ye wish to go?"
   "Aye."
   A girl of twelve years seized the boy's arm.
   "You would n't go, Dan!   We 'd never let you go!"
   "I 'd come back."
   "I 've no doubt ye 'd wish to come back," said Smith; "but
ye might be away years and years.   Ye might never have
the chance to come home again.   Think how lonesome ye 'd
be, Dan, and all of us, without ye.   Nay, lad, bide here,
whatever comes.   Never any of ye leave home.   Ye don't
know how it is out yonder."
   "But we want to know!   All of us do!   Why have you
never told us of the other lands?"
   "It 's been so long since I 've seen 'em I 'd most forgot
there was such places."
   "But you 'll tell us about them now?"
   "Aye, Alex, do!"
   "Will you tell us to-night?"
   Taking their eyes, for a moment, from the distant ship,
all turned to him eagerly.
   "There, now.   We 'll see. . . ."
   "No, Alex!   Promise you will!"
   "Not to-night, children.   But like enough I will, one of
these days, if ye 've still the wish to hear.   There 's Thurs-
day and Matt comin' in.   Run down and help 'em up with
the canoe, Dan — ye and John and Robbie. . . .   Rachel,
ye lasses had best go home, now, afore it 's dark.   Tell Mother
I 'll be along directly."
   The sun had set and the last light faded swiftly from the

sky. In the east the first stars appeared. The ship was now but a mere speck almost on the verge of the horizon. Motionless, his chin in his hands, elbows on his knees, the old seaman gazed after her till she was lost to view in the gathering darkness. At length he rose and turned away, slowly descending the steep northern slope of the crag to the path which led to the settlement.

THE TRILOGY OF THE "BOUNTY"

CHARLES NORDHOFF and James Norman Hall began in 1929 their preliminary work upon an historical novel dealing with the mutiny on board *H.M.S. Bounty.* It was at first anticipated that one or both of the authors would have to journey to England and elsewhere to collect the necessary source material, but, upon the advice of their publishers, this research was delegated to competent English assistants. With their painstaking help, the archives of the British Museum were searched through, as well as the rare-book shops and the collections of prints and engravings in London, for all procurable material dealing not only with the history of the *Bounty,* but also with life and discipline in the British Navy during the late eighteenth and early nineteenth centuries. With the generous permission of the British Admiralty, photostat copies were made of Bligh's correspondence and of the Admiralty records of the court-martial proceedings. Copies of the *Bounty's* deck and rigging plans were also secured, with special reference to the alterations made for her breadfruit-tree voyage; and a British naval officer, whose interest in these matters had been aroused, then proceeded to build an exact model of the vessel.

Books, engravings, blueprints, photostats, and photographs were finally assembled and sent to the publishers' office, where the shipment was checked, supplemented with material collected from American sources, and forwarded to its final destination, Tahiti, the home of Nordhoff and Hall.

The *Bounty* history divides itself naturally into three parts, and it was the plan of the authors, from the beginning, to deal with each of these in a separate volume, in case sufficient public interest was shown in the first to justify the preparation of the trilogy.

Mutiny on the Bounty, which opens the story, is concerned with the voyage of the vessel from England, the long Tahiti sojourn while the cargo of young breadfruit trees was being assembled, the departure of the homeward-bound ship, the mutiny, and the fate of those of her company who later returned to Tahiti, where they were eventually seized by *H.M.S. Pandora* and taken back to England for trial.

The authors chose as the narrator of this story a fictitious character, Roger Byam, who tells it as an old man, after his retirement from the Navy. Byam had his actual counterpart in the person of Peter Heywood, whose name was, for this reason, omitted from the roster of the *Bounty's* company. Midshipman Byam's experience follows closely that of Midshipman Heywood. With the license of historical novelists, the authors based the career of Byam upon that of Heywood, but in depicting it they did not, of course, follow the latter in every detail. In the essentials relating to the mutiny and its aftermath, they have adhered to the facts long preserved in the records of the British Admiralty.

Men against the Sea, the second narrative, is the story of Captain Bligh and the eighteen loyal men who, on the morning of the mutiny, were set adrift by the mutineers in the *Bounty's* launch, an open boat but twenty-three feet long, in which they made a 3600-mile voyage from the scene of the mutiny to Timor, in the Dutch East Indies. Captain Bligh's log of this remarkable voyage, a series of brief daily notes, was, of course, the chief literary source of this second novel. The voyage is described in the words of one of those who survived it — Thomas Ledward, acting surgeon of the *Bounty,* whose medical knowledge and whose experience in reading men's sufferings would qualify him as a sensitive and reliable observer.

Pitcairn's Island, the concluding story, is, perhaps, the strangest and most romantic. After two unsuccessful attempts to settle on the island of Tupuai (or Tubuai, as it is more commonly spelled in these days), the mutineers returned to Tahiti, where they parted company. Fletcher Christian, acting lieutenant of the *Bounty* and instigator of the mutiny, once more embarked in the ship for an unknown destination. With him were eight of his own men and eighteen Polynesians (twelve women and six men). They sailed from Tahiti in September 1789, and for a period of eighteen years nothing more was heard of them. In February 1808, the American sealing vessel *Topaz,* calling at Pitcairn, discovered on this supposedly uninhabited crumb of land a thriving community of mixed blood: a number of middle-aged Polynesian women and more than a score of children, ruled by a white-haired English seaman, Alexander Smith, the only survivor of the fifteen men who had landed there so long before.

The story of what befell the refugees during the eighteen years before the arrival of the *Topaz* offers a fitting conclusion to the tale of the *Bounty* mutiny. As the authors have said, in their Note to *Pitcairn's Island,* the only source of information we now have concerning the events of those years is the account — or, more accurately, the several discrepant accounts — handed on to us by the sea captains who visited Pitcairn during Smith's latter years. It is upon these accounts that their story is based.

Those who are interested in the source material concerning the *Bounty* mutiny will find an exhaustive bibliography of books, articles, and unpublished manuscripts in the Appendix to Mr. George Mackaness's splendid *Life of Vice-Admiral William Bligh,* published by Messrs. Angus and Robertson, of Sydney, Australia. Among the sources consulted by

THE TRILOGY OF THE "BOUNTY"

Nordhoff and Hall were the following: "Minutes of the Proceedings of a Court-Martial on Lieutenant William Bligh and certain members of his crew, to investigate the cause of the loss of *H.M.S. Bounty*"; *A Narrative of the Mutiny on Board His Majesty's Ship "Bounty,"* by William Bligh; *A Voyage to the South Sea,* by William Bligh; *The Life of Vice-Admiral William Bligh,* by George Mackaness; *Mutineers of the "Bounty" and Their Descendants in Pitcairn and Norfolk Islands,* by Lady Belcher; *The Mutiny and Piratical Seizure of H.M.S. "Bounty,"* by Sir John Barrow; *Bligh of the "Bounty,"* by Geoffrey Rawson; *Voyage of H.M.S. "Pandora,"* by E. Edwards and G. Hamilton; *Cook's Voyages;* Hawkesworth's *Voyages;* Beechey's *Voyages;* Bougainville's *Voyages;* Ellis's *Polynesian Researches; Pitcairn Island and the Islanders,* by Walter Brodie; *The Story of Pitcairn Island,* by Rosalind Young; *Descendants of the Bounty Mutineers,* by Harry Shapira; *Captain Bligh's Second Voyage to the South Seas,* by I. Lee; *Sea Life in Nelson's Time,* by John Masefield; *Life of a Sea Officer,* by Raigersfield; *New South Wales Historical Records; Pitcairn Island Register Book;* Memoir of Peter Heywood; *Adventures of Johnny Newcome,* by Mainwaring.

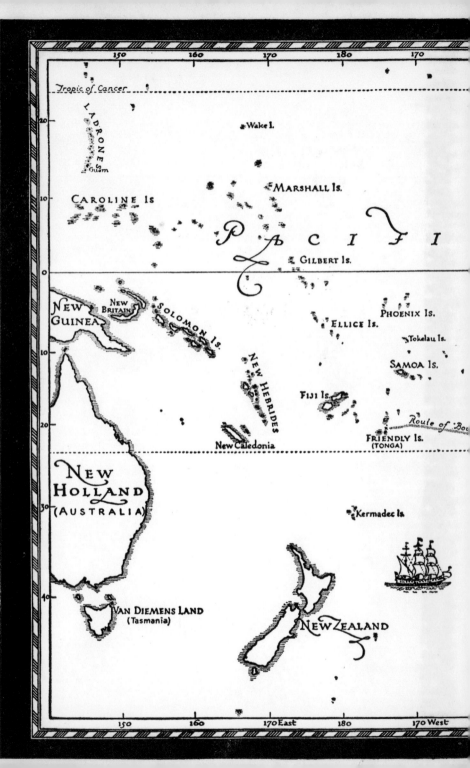